FISHING!

Also by Sarah Stonich

Published by the University of Minnesota Press

Vacationland

Laurentian Divide

These Granite Islands

Shelter

FISHING!

A NOVEL

SARAH STONICH

University of Minnesota Press

Minneapolis • London

First published in 2015 by Lake Union Publishing
as *Fishing with RayAnne,* by Ava Finch

First University of Minnesota Press edition, 2020

Published by the University of Minnesota Press
111 Third Avenue South, Suite 290
Minneapolis, MN 55401-2520
http://www.upress.umn.edu

Library of Congress Cataloging-in-Publication Data
Stonich, Sarah, author.
Fishing! : a novel / Sarah Stonich.
Identifiers: LCCN 2019027081 (print) | ISBN 978-1-5179-0898-0 (paperback)
Subjects: LCSH: Minneapolis (Minn.)—Fiction.
Classification: LCC PS3569.T6455 F57 2020 (print) | LCC PS3569.T6455
    (ebook) | DDC 813/.54—dc23
LC record available at https://lccn.loc.gov/2019027081

Printed in the United States of America on acid-free paper

The University of Minnesota is an equal-opportunity educator
and employer.

25 24 23 22 21 20   10 9 8 7 6 5 4 3 2 1

For the women

1

. . . .

When the conference room lights dim unexpectedly, RayAnne blinks in mild alarm, thinking of the scene in *Dark Victory* when Bette Davis goes so enchantingly blind. But it's only someone fiddling with the dimmer—she's forgotten the meeting agenda includes a screening of the new intro for the show. The rear screen projector descends and strains of accordion and steel guitar swell from nowhere. Under the table, she dribbles an orange Croc back and forth between bare feet until Cassi's studded leather boot gently pins her instep. Of course she's nervous—who wants to watch their own flawed self fumble around on-screen in high-def digital?

The opening scroll of credits has been cleverly redesigned for the second season, the words appearing as monofilament cast from a fishing rod onto the surface of watery ripples. The station's call letters, WYOY, land then dissolve. Then, serenaded by the soundtrack of ironic punk-polka, the name *RayAnne Dahl* is cast, making her grateful for the darkness of the conference room that hides the sudden blush toasting across her face. Her name floats for what feels like eternity before the camera lens slowly lifts its gaze from the water and a speeding boat shimmers in the distance. The POV zooms along the bow of a vintage AquaCraft, the *Penelope*. One of her conditions for agreeing to fill in as host was that the show be taped in her own comfort zone, in RayAnne's boat. Built for speed and flash, *Penelope* looks much younger than her fifty years and has charted many waters in her day. RayAnne can only muse over what stories her boat would tell if she could talk. She's well aware that her attachment verges on irrational, because her entire family and her assistant, Cassi, often remind her, pointing out that *Penelope* is after all only a speedboat. When guests or camera crew are aboard, RayAnne simply does not speak aloud to *Penelope*, only pats her gunnels and caresses her chrome with a chamois as if casually polishing. Besides being almost completely rebuilt from the carburetor up, *Penelope*'s cosmetic work included new teak decking, shining cleats, and jewel-like ruby and amber running lights. Her fish-scale patterned fiberglass has been restored to its original silky pale salmon—a vadge color if ever there was one, claims Cassi.

Afloat somewhere in RayAnne's subconscious is the notion that she and her boat share equal billing on the show, half-supposing viewers might tune in just to see *Penelope* because she would. The camera certainly loves *Penelope*—its point of view now above the speedboat with the *Masterpiece Theatre* pace of a bloated mosquito. It skims her bowsprit, a six-inch stainless steel mermaid with little jutting breasts digitally edited to Barbie smoothness for the public television–viewing audience. RayAnne imagines miniscule chrome nipples on some virtual cutting room floor.

The mosquito cam passes magically through the windshield and over the birchwood steering console to trawl over the contents of RayAnne's open tackle box, where compartments separate spoon lures from Rapalas and spinners from rubbery, rainbow-colored worms that look disturbingly edible despite the hooks. Jointed lures with names like Red Leopards, Jiggle-Jims, and Little Toadies are laid end to end. In another compartment, bottles of nail polish gleam and catch the light. RayAnne occasionally does her toenails during the boring waits between takes.

Cassi whispers in the dark, "Maybe MAC could be an underwriter?"

"The ratings aren't *that* good." RayAnne frowns. "Are they?"

The camera pans across spare leaders and spools of fifty-pound test, then swoops up from the tackle box to skim the depth-finder display with the station's logo moving across the screen like a stoned Pac-Man. Action nearly stops over an open cooler with product-placement items nestled on plastic ice cubes misted to look real: Estra-Boost smoothies, YoGirl acai yogurt cups, and sweating bottles of IceCap designer water siphoned from an actual glacier that the underwriter insists is melting anyway. Diet soda cans are partially obscured. Pepsi is an underwriter, but Cassi wagers that if ratings continue to climb, they could totally be a Coke show. There's a bag of dark chocolate Promises, half-hidden by the ice cubes, though marketing reports their targeted demographic can identify even a partial Dove logo upside down or even backwards. RayAnne cringes at the product peddling, but National Public Television is just doing what it must to stay afloat. Funding is always a battle, but right now the sort of politicians her father votes for would love nothing more than to see Big Bird plucked and roasted in the smoldering ruins of *Downton Abbey*.

Moving on, the view hovers above the hand-embroidered bench cushions, one posing the question *Got Fish?* Another features *His* and *Hers* rulers—*His* short by six inches. RayAnne's favorite cushion has a cross-stitched portrait of Mae West wearing an orange Mae West.

The boat rocks lightly as a pair of canvas Keds step into frame, introducing RayAnne's bare ankles, one sporting the thinnest of silver chains, the other covered with enough makeup to obscure a regrettable tattoo from spring break in the midnineties—a gecko circling to bite its own tail. The camera climbs RayAnne's pedal pushers to pause at belt level to show her elbow poking from its rolled sleeve, then across her tanned forearm to her wrist. Despite pressure from producers, she refuses to wear a product-placement watch, because not wearing a watch is half the point of fishing, isn't it? A pan to her hand and ringless fingers turning the ignition announces *Single!* The POV climbs her shirt buttons and the engine engages to add its low rumble to the soundtrack, taunting, *Wait for it . . . wait for it.*

Come on already. RayAnne sinks a bit in the conference room chair.

And there, finally, she is, turning to the camera, almost convincingly surprised.

"Hey, there. Welcome aboard!"

Like the boat, RayAnne is professionally lit, which she has learned is no easy task outdoors. On cue, she winds her hair—whole wheat, if a color must be named—into a twist and cocks her head into a tartan golf tam, her lucky fishing hat, a souvenir from her first big trout derby in New Brunswick. The original pom-pom is long gone, replaced with a tiny red-and-white bobber. The sequence required ten choreographed takes.

Tam secured, she faces the camera. "I'm RayAnne Dahl." With a slight shrug she invites the viewer along as if it's just occurred to her: "Let's go fishing!" Before donning cat-eye sunglasses, she nods once with a look that says, *Well, are you coming or aren't you?*

Given the choice, you would go—even RayAnne has to admit the scene is that inviting: the sleek boat, the soft (filtered) sun, the waves lapping, and the breeze lifting stray tendrils of hair from the nape of her neck. Set dressers and lighting techs have imbued *Penelope* with the ambiance of a boudoir, as if more than fish might be landed here, as if personal contentment itself might be schooling in the waters just below. And everyone knows there's chocolate on board.

As the soundtrack swells, RayAnne gets down to business and expertly backs the boat away from the dock. She turns back to wave to viewers before taking off, and once up to speed she steers a sway so that *Penelope*'s back end jauntily skirts her own wake. Together they zoom off into the endless expanse of a lake that glints like shattered windshield glass.

The scene and music fade to nothingness—to the black pocket where the show is to be inserted—then the pocket re-opens to the scroll of postshow credits. This is the *until next week* visual, the boat continuing its course into the horizon until it is the size of a water beetle, a final note on the accordion.

The screen goes black a final time as the two new staffers clap until the lights come up and they see the director has caught them in the crosshairs of her gaze.

"Those were the best takes we got."

RayAnne lets out the breath she's been holding. It wasn't bad, actually. Cassi's bicolored eyebrows hitch in silent agreement.

Someone says, "It'll do. Let's move on to issues."

They have three weeks to deal with "issues" before taping commences for the second season. Laptops yawn and iPads blink to life. RayAnne opens her own laptop, more as a shield than anything. She's the only person with an actual notebook, with pen hand poised over it, ready to scribble in the event anything notable gets said. After a ten-minute report from marketing about thirty-day ratings and encore and multiplatform viewer-ship, RayAnne's inner clock is growling, the doodle on her page beginning to resemble lasagna.

"It's not *Antiques Roadshow*," says one of the producers.

A coproducer chimes in, "But with decent ratings to usher in season two . . ."

The producers have high hopes. A few could even kick them-selves for not thinking of it sooner, because in hindsight an all-women fishing talk show is a no-brainer. According to Nielsen, increasing numbers of females between thirty and eighty are tuning in to see guests squirm like the leeches on their lines and cringe as they hook a chub through its eye. Perhaps viewers enjoy the quiet transitions between the action and the interview segments, when *Penelope's* bow quietly hammocks in the waves or a line is cast from RayAnne's reel like a thread of spun sugar. She wonders if viewers are simply lulled by the hypnotic cadence of other women's voices, or the purr of her 2.5 horsepower trolling motor—no louder than a vibrator.

In any case, they aren't changing channels. When ratings or demographics data crop up on RayAnne's screen, she herds them directly into the recycle bin, borrowing Gran Dot's gravelly voice: "Numbers, schmumbers." In her mind's eye, the audience is the size of a large book club or a small studio audience, not a sea of faces but a pond—a smiling, indulgent pond bobbing with women like her mother, her gran, her sister-in-law Ingrid, or the sort of women in her yoga-sculpt class she might ask to coffee if she weren't so shy. If she paid any attention to how many women (and men) were actually watching, she would likely pee her capris. RayAnne assumes that her pond tunes in for the more interesting guests, the ones they must fight for, and for the conversation, because it is a talk show after all. And don't women crave the voices of their own tribe? Whether laughing or crying, rejoicing or lamenting—even shrieking.

Women want to know they're not in it alone.

Truth be told, it hadn't started well. Everyone would like to forget the scrapped pilot of *Fishin' Chicks* with its original host, Mandy Cox. As for the guest roster, producers had insisted on featuring women successful in male-dominated fields, making selections that were admittedly not brilliant—or even vetted. Like the director of environmental films who hurled a wet blanket over the front third of the pilot by pulling a dead, oil-soaked seagull from her bag while predicting another BP-sized spill, citing a certain oil company that happens to be a major underwriter of the station's parent network. The next guest, a physicist from a particle accelerator lab, was pink and perspiring and unintentionally hilarious while singsonging facts about quarks and gluons forming protons and neutrons like some menopausal rapper. A final pall was cast during a diatribe complete with pixeled-out photos by the organizer of a campaign to abolish Third World clitoridectomies.

To understate, Mandy had not handled any of these guests with much aplomb and, after stomping off the set, went straight to legal, citing hazardous working conditions—forget that she never once actually drove the boat; that was RayAnne wearing a wig and Mandy's jacket zipped over two warm bags of microwaved popcorn. The tension around the pilot episode had been palpable to begin with, but then came the call announcing Mandy had indeed wormed out of her contract. Ironically, she was injured on her next gig—a film in which she clung to Matthew McConaughey in a glacial cleft for the duration of the two-star bomb *ClingHorn* after she'd slipped on a mustard packet on the catering yurt floor. Once the pins were removed, Mandy went right back to where she'd been discovered, hosting the cable reality show *Tomboy Trucker Wives*.

The pilot of *Fishin' Chicks* was dashed, and the decision to lighten up on topics had been swift. There are days RayAnne cannot believe that she's on television, although the chain of events landing her there was rather mundane. She'd only been contracted as the pro fishing consultant. Winding up in the host's seat was sheer happenstance. She is the temp, the stunt double, the bridesmaid, the buddy in the romantic comedy—the *sub,* which is what producers call her still.

The morning Mandy jumped ship, reactions around the conference table had been varied. RayAnne's had been to softly bang her forehead on the mahogany, moaning, "I just bought a house!"

Cassi, who had been Mandy's assistant then, had only grinned. "So, no more *Fishin' Chicks?*"

"Oh," sighed the producer. "If only it were that simple."

"We'll get a new Mandy?" RayAnne brightened. Having coached Mandy for eight weeks, she had opinions. "How about somebody less . . . enhanced?" Mandy's double-D implants had proven not only a distraction to the crew but a physical hindrance when casting a line or even climbing in and out of the boat. She was forever mislaying the custom life vest fitted specially for her.

Yes, there would be a new Mandy. Yes, less bombshell. An unknown this time.

Auditions were scheduled. RayAnne took a dozen hopefuls out onto the lake and coached them through the fishing-while-talking bits of their audition tapes. Half of them couldn't remember the plot with their arms akimbo let alone while casting a lure. One had blinked at the reel in her hand and asked RayAnne how to turn it on.

In private, she and Cassi grumbled that the producers must be idiots not to realize the hour could be entertaining *and* politically correct, though the quota for either seemed to change weekly at WYOY. Why not book guests with compelling stories, not just unusual careers—women who with luck might have some personality. Not quite misfits, but near-fits, like RayAnne. And wouldn't it be nice if they found a host older than twenty-five, because really, who wants to go face to face with some pore-less anchor-bot younger by a decade or three? Cassi, with her Svengali-like gift of persuasion, had slyly planted seeds, dropped suggestions, elbowed in with subliminal nudges until producers and the director convinced themselves the idea to change the entire premise had been their own. While she was doing that, RayAnne was more vocal and blunt about how absurd the name *Fishin' Chicks* was, but since she hadn't thought much about alternatives, she'd only shrugged when asked and said, "*Fishing?*" which was thought brilliant for its simplicity.

But RayAnne knew a few hints and a name change alone

weren't going to cut it. To raise the show from the ashes, they needed a host who would be a diamond-in-the-rough discovery. She scheduled another meeting to run tapes, and while producers and staff were all on the edges of their seats, she already knew, having been in the boat with the "talent," that they hadn't even come close to finding a viable replacement for Mandy. RayAnne's mind had been elsewhere, thinking ahead to job possibilities. Settled for the first time in a dozen years, living in one place and finally always knowing where her favorite bra was, the last thing she wanted was to go back out on the pro fishing circuit. While the others watched the auditions, she was concentrating on her résumé, knitting together a mental list of accomplishments that might impress somebody at sporting goods giants like Cabela's or LunkerLand, hoping at best to land some spokespersonship or PR gig, maybe a sales rep position, or, scraping bottom, demo work at the expos and shows.

She barely looked at the screen as her on-camera-self prompted yet another Nordic delight, "Okay, Kelsey, that was a little better, but try speaking *to* the camera, like this." RayAnne squared herself to improvise, recalling shards of sound bites heard on the radio during her drive in. "Today we have a North Dakota grandmother of three on board. Ida Lott survived four days in a prairie blizzard while buried in her Camry, keeping a journal on grocery bags and drinking melted snow. You might know of those scribblings on Roundy's bags as the runaway bestseller *Five Days on a Chiclet,* soon to be a film starring Dame Judi Dench."

One of the staffers had looked curiously from the screen to RayAnne.

Sighing, RayAnne had leaned to Cassi. "They say they don't want another Mandy, yet look who they send me."

In the next screen test, RayAnne coached a gormless blond indistinguishable from any of the Megans on Fox, pleading, "Try more *voice*." Physically turning the young woman to the lens and speaking over her shoulder, RayAnne sounded chipper and engaging: "On board with us this morning is Italian meter maid Parmesana Cannelloni. You may remember her from the recent YouTube viral video wherein Prime Minister Silvio Berlusconi took time out from his busy schedule of *presidente*-ing to dry-hump Ms. Cannelloni near his motorcade in Bologna. *Mamma mia!*"

Staffers made curious harrumphings, a few chuckled. RayAnne looked up from scrolling through her résumé to apologize. "Sorry, I was a little punchy by then. She was like number eight or something."

They watched a few more, then the whole series of a dozen demos was run again from the beginning. Glances were exchanged over RayAnne's head. Halfway through the second run-through, the executive producer hit pause and cleared her throat. "Roxanne?"

Cassi stage-whispered, "*Ray*Anne."

"Right." The producer smiled tightly. "Of course. RayAnne?"

"Here." She looked around to see all eyes on her.

"Didn't you guest-host for a season on *Cat Fishing*?"

"Yesss." RayAnne sat up, immediately wary. "But only for three episodes, when Cat went to Argentina to get a new liver. Why?"

"Well, until we can find a suitable replacement . . ."

"Well, a *replacement* I might be able to get . . ." RayAnne's voice trailed off as she looked from face to face, understanding slowly dawning.

"What? No. *Me*? No-no-no. No *way*."

· · ·

And now the first season is over and, twelve episodes later, she is still the sub. The race to find a replacement has slowed to a stroll as positive viewer responses and ratings pile up. *Something* has been working, but no sooner than the show has begun wriggling nicely into shape, producers are keen to ratchet up the numbers by devoting the top third of the hour to celebrity guests—

ingenues plugging films, chick-lit writers with hit books, singers and musicians flogging CDs and concert tours. B-list, but celebs nonetheless. The rest of the hour they will grudgingly leave to RayAnne and her kooks.

She prefers to think of herself as a moderator. The word *host* only cues up biology-fraught images of tapeworms or roadkill doilied with maggots. RayAnne merely facilitates the interviews that begin as chats and polite palavers that often evolve—some might say devolve—into something more. Aboard the *Penelope,* guests tend to be either exhilarated or unnerved by the speed at which RayAnne pilots her boat (there have been memos). But even when just afloat, guests can feel more or less out of their element because they are—there is something about being on the water that distracts and disarms. Water lapping at the bow seems to wash away trifling thoughts so that guests sometimes nearly forget what they'd intended to say on camera. Like a clapping kindergarten teacher, it is RayAnne's job to keep them focused, though she will as often follow their tangents off topic when they are being funny or revealing. Many are won over by RayAnne's frankness with such questions as "Are you happy?" She is truly curious about her guests and about how the circumstances that have landed them on television have affected their real lives. They tend to answer honestly when asked how, for instance, they felt at the beach when their dog brought them the tennis shoe with the foot still in it. How they felt during the escape from the bunker, or after discovering their husband had three other wives. *How* indeed.

Guests can end up spilling, sometimes a little, sometimes buckets. Cassi, now the show's production coordinator, rates these disclosures on a scale from sniffle to hurl in nasal Red Owl–clerk imitations only RayAnne can hear via the audio feed curling into her ear: *Spill in aisle two. Leaker in dairy. Thaw in frozen fish case.* Sometimes RayAnne must tune Cassi out, switch off the feed while pretending to scratch behind her ear as if at some bug bite. With Cassi cut off, the danger of RayAnne inexplicably snorting on camera lessens, but no Cassi also means no directives such as "Zip it!" when she chews her lip, or "Camera left!" should her gaze wander, or "Posture!" to snap her upright from her habitual slouching—all delivered in a tone one might reserve for obedience class. "Down," in fact, is a frequent imperative: RayAnne is a toucher, a pawer, always has been and cannot help it. Guests from the Midwest often find it too intimate when RayAnne grasps their forearm like an oar or kneads a shoulder in sympathy, though most from coastal regions lean in as if they need the physical contact as much as they need to talk. Some by the end of twenty minutes of revelations are on RayAnne like burrs.

And while most have compelling stories or are sincere or amusing, the occasional objectionable guests will let loose words RayAnne wants to mop up and cram back in their mouths. She's been tempted more than once to tip a woman overboard. The previous week it had been the mediocre writer who'd sold her chick-lit novel to Hollywood for an outrageous sum, then had the nerve to enviously complain about her struggling writer friends, precisely because they were struggling—cutting coupons, shopping thrift stores, and buying lentils in bulk. "Because," Chick-Lit had pouted, "that is the trend now, right? It's hot to be poor." She'd been a typical producer's choice, someone in the throes of their fifteen minutes of fame but not necessarily deserving of them.

From the beginning, RayAnne had set only two conditions: that the show take place on *Penelope* and that she get input regarding guests. Still, she's had to wheedle to get her own discoveries greenlighted, like the soft-porn puppeteer, the former lumberjack now lumberjill, or the nun who raises money for Haitian orphans by bungee jumping into gorges—as Sister pointed out herself, who wouldn't pay to see a nun in a habit go off a bridge?

RayAnne's notebook is full of lists of maybe-probables and sort-of hopefuls she has discovered via blogs, Twitter, Boing Boing, Reddit, obscure cable programs, and numerous news-of-the-weird print sources. At the moment she's optimistic about booking a racehorse masseuse, an ark-building climatologist, and a relationship coach whose seminars on harmonious partnerings are based on methods used by dolphin trainers. These are the sorts of women who provoke RayAnne's curiosity, and she thinks—hopes—those watching might be provoked as well.

She looks around the conference room and stirs real sugar into her cup, stashing another packet to add later when no one is looking. The producer ahems and utilizes the majestic plural. "We are ready to talk about the guest lineup for season two."

Cassi, never one to waste time, clears her throat and stands to present her PowerPoint, going a little too quickly over the list she and RayAnne have painstakingly compiled. After giving everyone a moment for the information to sink in, Cassi repeats the status of each. "We've got Marla from Tweakables, and—"

"Tweakables, that's . . . what, again?" The producer is squinting.

Cassi inhales through pierced nostrils. "Links to this PowerPoint are in your inboxes and printed in the materials in your folders. Tweakables is a tattoo parlor that inks photo-realistic nipples onto the reconstructed breasts of cancer patients. Oprah has called Marla's nipples 'works of art.'" She back-browses until an image crops up on-screen, which prompts muttering and nodding and a debate over whether or not a tattoo of a nipple is allowable on camera since an actual woman's nipple would not be. One staffer mildly objects, "I mean, this is Minnesota, not Denmark."

Cassi manages to not roll her eyes. "It's a *tat*."

RayAnne lets them duke it out while pretending to pay attention, scribbling *tat for tit* on her notepad, double-dotting the *i*. Having actually read all the notes and Cassi's thorough research on National Public Television policies, she knows how the argument will end. Once she stops listening to the individual words, such discussions are easy to tune out, just honks in the background like the adults on *Peanuts*.

The two new staffers have been staring unabashedly at Cassi. RayAnne is used to her appearance and barely registers the clanging bits of chain, the riveted strapping, and the boots that look like they might require tools to take off. Today she's wearing a torn suede tube skirt over laddered tights as if to evoke a recent assault. The fishnet wrist-warmers seem a rather oxymoronic accessory in RayAnne's view, though she can hardly claim to be any judge of fashion, as evidenced by her own ensemble of cargo skirt, T-shirt, and her wardrobe staple for such work meetings, the dress hoodie. Fashion is a realm other people inhabit—she has enough to worry over without adding her own lack of flair, agreeing with her grandmother Dot's assessment—that she doesn't so much dress in the morning as get clad ("I *need* pockets!"). Just as well that Rinata, the sweet wardrobe lady from Barcelona, dresses her head to toe for each taping in a fusion of Filson and Michael Kors. Sounding always as though she's holding pins in her mouth, Rinata assures RayAnne, "I can thave you from yourthelf."

Cassi's own mien has ratcheted up a notch since last season: a new constellation inked on her neck, one eyebrow stippled, and her naturally white-blond hair cut into a shag with its ends dyed in shades of charcoal and pewter, recalling a dog breed that is on the tip of RayAnne's tongue.

"Odd-looking little thing," RayAnne's mother, Bernadette, had observed upon meeting Cassi, less in regard to her style as to the girl's pallor, like that of a Nilla wafer dipped in milk, with veins nearly the same hue as her light blue eyes pulsing at her temple. Combined, it can all be disconcerting enough, but what gets RayAnne is how *still* Cassi is, so that she's often startled when the postlike form next to her comes to life like a street statue or a surveillance camera, or edges out from behind something like an eclipse.

A staffer to her right barks a cough, and RayAnne shakes herself back into the meeting. Marla's nipples have been given the all-clear, and Cassi moves on to the next potential guest.

"Miranda Anderson of Nashville, Tennessee, has had twelve plastic surgeries to make her look just like her corgi, Dibble."

After some discussion and faces made at the screen, Miranda is deemed a no. As the mumbling dies down, Cassi brings up the next screen. "Here we have Babs Develara, Hollywood body-double whose booty has stood in for dozens of A-list celebs, appearing in numerous Oscar-nominated films and, yes, Golden Globe winners."

The producer smiles and looks around the table with a full stop at RayAnne. "Approved."

RayAnne frowns. "But how about *my* second pick?"

"Morticia of Brentwood?"

Cassi deftly clicks around in her PowerPoint. "Cosmetologist who does glam makeovers on average-looking corpses."

"I've seen her homepage." The director shudders. "Macabre."

The producer leans in. "Those before and after shots?"

"We're a no," says the director.

RayAnne slumps. "But she's so . . . Morticia!"

"Sorry, Ray," Cassi says, chipping black polish from her thumbnail. "Even I have to agree on this one."

RayAnne doesn't claim all her choices are brilliant. She looks around the room knowing she must choose her battles and lets it go, which is easier than arguing with them—they are the sorts of women who have been thin all their lives.

One of the new staffers looks uncertainly from RayAnne to the producer. "Is it necessary guests know how to fish?"

"No," RayAnne sighs. "I'd only end up in an empty boat for lack of guests who can kill a minnow." She immediately regrets her choice of words, hoping they don't trigger another PETA discussion, quickly adding, "I teach the basics before we tape, you know, casting, reeling . . ."

RayAnne is relieved the producers seem eager to move on. They're so optimistic about the second season that they've come up with their own lineup of "bigger" guests. The producer takes Cassi's place at the AV podium to bring up a series of headshots. RayAnne cocks her head this way and that, unconsciously mirroring the various poses of Elizabeth Warren, Miley Cyrus, Jennifer Weiner, Reese Witherspoon—women she would love to interview. But. *Good luck with those,* she thinks as those around the conference table coo and honk. *Aim high,* as Gran says.

It's their second meeting to discuss issues that were not issues last season. She scans the new notes passed to her and upon reaching the second line presses the nub of her pen right through to dent the table.

"Fisher*persons*?" She taps the pen hard. "You want me to say *fisherpersons*?"

The producer leans in. "Well . . . you can see why fisher*men* or fisher*man* might pose an issue."

Issue. She doesn't refer to the guests as *fisher*-anything, so it should be a nonissue. She's been learning lots of corporate-speak from management and marketing—terms like *solutioning* and *incentivize. Way-making.* She was thrilled to learn that there are no such things as *problems* anymore, only *way-blockings.*

Fisherman. She recalls Gran Dot's argument that we are all man: hu-*man,* wo-*man.* Dot, in her odd brand of reasoning, had offered, "Woman comes from *womb,* you see, so given that, isn't it obvious? When it came time to name the penis-wielding version of the species, the Greeks just weren't that inspired, I mean, given what they had to work with."

Fingering the dent, RayAnne quickly covers it. "How about fisher*humans*?"

Cassi clears nothing from her throat until RayAnne looks up

to see the producer is actually thinking about it, smoothing her imaginary goatee.

The PR person so fond of Post-it notes holds one up with the word *Fishers* written on it. RayAnne raises her hand and pulls it down in one motion. "Um, a fisher is a mammal, but I don't think they actually fish."

Cassi adds, "Right, but they do hunt porcupines."

RayAnne turns. "They do?"

"Uh-huh." Cassi taps her pencil. "Also, Fisher is the name of a band."

The producer looks concerned. "What sort of band? The sort *you* would listen to?"

"Sure."

"Oh, well. You're not in our demographic."

RayAnne and Cassi blink at each other as if in code. "Fishers," Cassi says, turning back to the producer. "We can live with that." To RayAnne she whispers, "Nothing says you actually have to say it."

"Trust me," RayAnne mumbles, "I won't."

The producer ahems again. "Do you have something to add?" Both look up like deer and shake their heads, Cassi saying, "No," RayAnne adding, "Ma'am."

After more way-blockings are tabled, solutioned, and swept off like crumbs, the meeting abruptly ends with everyone clamming closed their laptops. RayAnne tentatively rises—there's been no mention of a replacement host, or about the search for one, yet in just a few weeks they are to embark on a new taping season. No one has asked, "Oh, by the way, you up for another season?" Is she to assume it's assumed? When the producer stands, everyone else rises in her wake. Usually RayAnne is amused by this and would give anything for the woman to plunk back down just to see if the others might follow, stadium style, but she's teetering on the precipice of the question about hosting. It's about to tumble from her mouth when Cassi pulls her sleeve and motions for her to hurry. Just as they approach the door, a rap sounds on the table.

"One more thing," says the assistant producer with oddly set eyes, whose real name is Amy but who Cassi calls the Grouper.

Here we go.

"Ah, a small item . . ."

"RayAnne. Wardrobe wants to know if you'll be able to wear a size six by the next taping."

All eyes race to RayAnne's hips like those joke eyeballs on springs. She blinks and opens her mouth but no answer forms. Cassi saves the moment by nodding for her. "Sure thing, Boss, size six she will be."

Amy, who defines bossy, pretends to hate being called boss, though her little eyes glint more greenly when Cassi does.

Well then, there's her answer. RayAnne will indeed be the sub, again—one that will no longer be a size eight, however they expect *that* will happen. As far as she knows there is no diet for big bones, and she's about to say so when Cassi pulls her out the door.

It would be nice just once to leave a meeting without feeling less than, or in this case, more than, with her extra five pounds—the extra-stubborn extra five pounds that look like fifteen on camera. In a previous meeting, the concern had been her general lack of experience in front of the camera, discussed as if she hadn't been in the room: "Should we hire a coach for a few sessions with RayAnne?" The time before that—the only meeting she'd ever walked out on—had been a discussion of the gap in her front teeth: "Should she be fitted for a cosmetic cap?" Cassi reported that it had taken ten minutes before anyone even noticed RayAnne had left.

In the eyes of her employers, these are just a few of her shortcomings.

She'd rather not attract too much attention to herself, because while none of her inadequacies are serious enough on their own to be a threat, they do stack up, and by now someone has probably discovered the fib on her résumé—that she wasn't officially employed on the Alabama cable show *Big Fish,* was instead only a frequent presence in their demonstration videos. Her time on *Big Fish* had been short-lived, in any case, thanks to Sweaty Eddie. Eddie was handsome, like the Baldwin brother she could never name, and sweaty. Married as well, though Eddie seemingly had forgotten that small detail in his bid to engineer something with RayAnne. He would rush in at each wrap to pat her down, ostensibly to help undo the wireless microphone, fixated on RayAnne's fishing vest and its multitude of pockets as if it were an Advent calendar in which he might discover a gift—perhaps a breast. She always beat him to the mic, unclipping and dropping it into his glistening palm while smiling, blinking, and thinking, *In hell, Mister.*

Sometimes she wonders if she was offered the consulting job with WYOY because Sweaty Eddie felt guilty, maybe pulling some strings in hopes she wouldn't make a fuss, or sue, which she had every right to do and probably should have. She's just not interested in revisiting their one incident of physical slapstick, which ensued after he pulled her into the boathouse and tried sticking his tongue into her mouth as if the goal were to have it exit her ear. She'd never actually felt threatened or harassed by him; he was too puppy-doggish. Besides, after Eddie had grabbed her, it was only a matter of seconds before she evicted his tongue and shoved him, arms windmilling comically, into the water. She was out the boathouse door and wiping her mouth, so embarrassed for both of them that the moment hadn't properly registered.

The furthest thing from her mind would have been to make a stink about it. So what if Sweaty Eddie got her the consulting gig with WYOY? Thinking of him sends a shudder up her spine that goes on extra-long until she realizes it's the iPhone vibrating in her pocket.

She may never get used to the phone's raw buzz, reminiscent of her sixteenth birthday gift from Gran, an electric Lady Schick that left her with such razor rash she couldn't lower her arms for days. She fishes for the phone, sees her father's number glow for a beat, then powers it off and deposits it in another pocket.

By taking the stairs, RayAnne and Cassi avoid riding the elevator with the others. They thump down the two flights and make their way out of the building without slowing until halfway across the sunny parking lot.

RayAnne stops. "Size six?!"

Cassi holds up a finger. "No problem. The really expensive clothes lie; they're always labeled a size or two smaller than they really are. Rinata has a list of brands we could never afford on our pay." Cassi shades her pale eyes. "Don't let them get to you."

"I don't really. It's more the attitude, you know? That default *I work for public television so I am better than you.*"

"*You* work for public television."

"Not like they do."

"True." Cassi squints. "But you fished the pro circuit, right? I hear those guys can be brutal."

RayAnne shrugs. "Some. Most were just horny good ol' boys. At least I had methods of dealing with them."

"What? Like mace?" Cassi kicks the air at crotch height. "Karate?"

"You know the trick of imagining the person who's intimidating you is naked when you're not?" RayAnne holds up a curled pinky. "I just imagined a lot of erectile dysfunction."

"Anyway." Cassi inhales. "It looks like we're on again. Whew, huh?"

"Sure, but why couldn't anyone just—"

"*Say* something? Maybe ask if you want to keep hosting? Listen, if they say it, they will have to offer you a contract. As it is, with you being freelance, they're saving assloads on you, Ray. You cost a fraction of what Mandy did. And right now finance is having one eppie after another."

"Still?"

"Same old. Teabaggers wanna slash any federal funding again, what with shows like NOVA spewing scientific fact and Bert and Ernie being so gay."

"Right." RayAnne has no clear idea of what goes on in finance or any of the other administrative offices above the third floor, never actually having been invited. She aims her key fob at the nondescript silver hatchback in front of her. "This is me." When it doesn't bleep she frowns and walks two cars ahead. "Or this." When she opens the hatch, a number of books fall to the pavement. She dips to grab them, mumbling, "Damn, I'm gonna have fines again."

Cassi stoops to help. "Who goes to the library anymore?"

"I do." She glances at the book Cassi picked up. "Oh, that's a favorite. I wouldn't mind actually owning that one."

Cassi watches her stack it atop the rest. "So, why not buy it?"

RayAnne shrugs. "Well, then I'd buy another, and before you know it I'd need a bookcase."

"To own a copy of *The Wayward Bus?*"

"You know what I mean."

"Not really. Just get a Kindle."

RayAnne hugs the books to her chest. "Not there yet."

Cassi scans the book titles. "Were you, like, something else once? Before fishing?"

"Almost. I majored in journalism, then worked at a crummy weekly, but . . ."

"But what?"

"I was kind of terrible at it. I'd be assigned these human interest stories and wind up sort of . . . enhancing."

"What, like fabricating? Like that *New Republic* guy?"

"More like what my gran calls spit-shining. Giving people's stories slightly better spins and angles."

"But in journalism?" Cassi squints.

"I know. It wasn't for me. Facts aren't nearly as compelling as people, and people have so few facts."

"Maybe you should have considered fiction."

"Tell me. Hey, should you even be out here?"

"I'm wearing SPF 90. Wait'll you see my getup for Location—like a beekeeper. You know they make sun-proof fabric?" Cassi slings her bag and heads toward a red Ford Fiesta that looks as though it might have been painted with a brush. RayAnne opens her mouth to ask if it has air bags, thinks better of it, and waves her off, saying, "Drive safe." Which she hopes is heeded as *Don't text*.

Once in her own car, she juggles her phone uncertainly, then assuming he won't be answering since he rarely does, speed-dials Big Rick. She expects to leave a message but is startled when he picks up on the first ring.

"Hey, Baby Ray."

"Dad. You knew it was me?"

"I got this caller ID gizmo. Gotta love that—now I only talk to your grandmother when I feel like a lecture."

"C'mon, Dad, she only nags when you . . . never mind. I should call her myself."

"How's it going up there in TV land?"

"It's okay. Mostly." She can hear the glug of liquid over ice and looks at her watch. It isn't even eleven a.m. yet in Arizona where Big Rick has recently retired with his latest wife.

"What's that noise?"

"Ice. For *lemonade*."

"Only asking." Unable to keep the names straight, she asks, "How's the bride?"

"She's working out okay. At her golf lesson right now. So, you get another season?"

"I'm on again, it seems—with a few conditions. Let's see— they want a pink cancer ribbon on my trolling motor, forget that they're already embroidered on every life vest. I get to ride a fiberglass trout in some parade, and they want me to call guests 'girlfriend' like Oprah does. Oh, and I have to stand around at the Rod & Gun Expo for two days doing promo."

"So, you signed a contra—"

"No, Dad, no contract."

"I told you to go cable, Ray."

Big Rick fished the pro circuit for years and still refers to Ray-Anne as a "faux pro," though she'd taken more trophies in ten years than he had in twenty. Oddly, he's more enthusiastic about the program even though his own fishing show, *Big Rick's Bass Bonanza,* lasted only six episodes. He's hopeful when he predicts his little girl will hit it big and be able to take care of her old man, buy him a new double-wide to park in his "yard," a square of concrete painted grass green on the outskirts of Scottsdale.

"It's just so frustrating, Dad."

"Listen, Ray. You're better off on television—even *public* television—than you ever could be out on the circuit."

"But I placed second in the Heineken Tourney last year!"

"Ex-*actly*, you were smart to get out while you were on top."

"Dad, I'm not sure I'll be here through another whole season. I mean, what if this bombs?"

"You couldn't bomb if you tried! You got a face for TV, and if you're not gonna use it to get a husband, you might try to snag a fu—freaking contract with it."

RayAnne remembers that the current wife is trying to wean her father off bad language. She doesn't respond, just chews a cuticle while he takes a breath—she can tell he's been smoking by the rattle.

"Fish or cut bait, Ray. Stand your ground with those lesbians. Stick to your guns."

She holds the phone away and blinks at it before replying,

"How do you know . . . ?" The lesbians happen to be the most reasonable of the lot. Still.

A vehicle pulls into one of the reserved spots a few cars away—an old Jeep Wagoneer with wood-grained doors. Like Cassi's car, it is so misplaced among the Volvos and Priuses that RayAnne unconsciously thrums the *Sesame Street* tune over her steering wheel: *One of these things is not like the others.* She leans to get a better look at the driver to see if it's someone to avoid but doesn't recognize him. Hardly the public television type anyway. She's about to turn away when he pushes his sunglasses up into shaggy dark hair to lean over and lock the passenger side door.

Manual locks? She absently wonders how old a car would have to be. He's good-looking enough. Eyes the color of . . . what's the color, not corn-fed blue . . . "Oh. Corn*flower.*"

"Corn-what?" Big Rick asks.

"Nothing."

"'Cuz if you're thinking corn-holer, that's a *male* gay, not a lezbo."

"Dad!" When she yelps, the guy looks up again and RayAnne finds herself suddenly eye to eye with him, albeit six car windows removed. While she might normally look away, she only blinks in response (like a cow, she later thinks), taking in the creases that sidle his mouth like charming parentheses. He has the tousled appearance of someone who gets out of bed at noon—like a musician. She sighs, Big Rick's voice bringing her around. "'Cuz they're all the same when you flip 'em upside down anyway."

"Jeezus, Dad. I gotta go. Say hello to Rah . . . Ri—"

"Rita."

"Well, you can't expect me to keep them straight after five."

"Six. It's easy. Just remember B-A-D-G-E-R. Bernadette, Anne, Delia, Grace, Ellen, *Rita.*"

"Nice. Hey, you called me, did you want something?"

The guy is out of the Wagoneer now, headed her way. He's wearing low-heeled boots and well-fitting jeans.

"Nah, just thought you could use some advice."

"You bet. If I do, Dad, you'll be the first person I ask."

He is approaching now and will pass her windshield in a second. His jaw is solid but not jutty like Leno's, more a modified Dudley Do-Right with a shallower divot. What her brother Kyle calls "ass-chin."

"I'm good. Listen, I gotta go."

"Right. Keep your knockers up, Ray-Ban."

"Sure thing, Big Rick." As her father hangs up she actually does adjust her posture, straightening as if thwacked by a nun.

Approaching, the guy slows ever so minutely in front of her car. When he looks straight at her, she realizes the phone's still glued to her cheek. As he passes, the parentheses of his dimples deepen as if he might be fighting a grin. If he really smiled, those dimples would crease into the most alluring ditches—the sort a girl might gladly fall into. Knowing such a smile might liquefy her, RayAnne sighs because it hardly matters, since he's *too* good looking. Plus he carries some sort of instrument case, so of course he is a musician. In her experience, the only bigger pains than sponsors are musicians. As he passes, she whispers, "Buh bye . . ."

The second he's out of sight, RayAnne pulls down the visor to look in the mirror. She loathes, *loathes* her coloring, always pinking up at the slightest thing, like now, as if a glass of Malbec has been hurled at her. She can thank her mother for her Irish skin and her father for the boxer's jaw and right now is doubly annoyed at Big Rick for planting the mnemonic seed that will doubtless make her think of her mother Bernadette as the *B* in his BADGER.

RayAnne frowns, scrutinizing. She has distinct traits from both parents—not a melding but independent bits of each, her face a prime example of how they could never quite agree on anything. She has Big Rick's thick hair and crooked widow's peak, Bernadette's nose and the same slight gap between her front teeth. People tell her she's pretty, but she's rarely convinced no matter what the mirror shines back—though her face is better now than it was in her twenties, she thinks, more formed, more her own.

RayAnne at thirty-four is a late bloomer, as Gran would say. Very late.

2

.
.
.
.

Her shoulder bag thuds to the stack of moving boxes
that has doubled as a hallway table since she moved
in. It's been eighteen months, but to completely
unpack seems like tempting fate—despite the ratings and Big
Rick's predictions, the show could bomb and she'd just end up
going back out on the circuit and having to sell the place. In the
past year, two units in her brownstone row were foreclosed on,
enough to make her and fellow neighbors twitchy about their
investments, so there's that. No help that her brother Kyle thinks
she's made a grave mistake by buying in this "transitioning"
Minneapolis neighborhood, particularly in such an old building.
But it's only a few blocks to the river, and the realtor had lured
her with endless references to character and charm, assuring
RayAnne that young professionals and hipsters were snapping
up whatever came on the market, that there was even a rumor
of a Whole Foods opening two streets over. Truth be told, she
was given a mortgage she'd been unqualified for, considering her
freelance status.

Her grandmother had balked at the neighborhood, naturally, having never seen it. So RayAnne promised Dot she would
definitely get a dog, repeating, "Yes, Gran, big enough to ward

off a linebacker." She did make good on her promise to install a security system—the real thing and not just the fake control panels and yard sign. There's a dead bolt on the basement door and another on the back porch. As an obsessive lock checker and listener to noises, RayAnne knows every complaint of the old house: the yowl of each radiator, the scuttle of squirrels along gutters, which pipes sing in what key, whether it is an east wind or a west wind huffing down the chimneys. Dot's worry gene skipped a generation—leapfrogging over Big Rick, who practices all the caution of an oversugared toddler—to land smack on Ray-Anne's head. When would she have time to even look for a dog, let alone train one?

The row house is her very own. She is a homeowner. The thought makes her smile. The day after moving in, when she sat on the bare living room floor and realized that after years of motels and seldom slept-in apartments and two brief and ill-advised cohabitations, she could paint the walls absolutely any color and hang any picture she wanted to, she wept with joy. Even after a year, stepping into the foyer lit by little rainbows from the leaded glass fanlight gives her a thrill. Mine? Really? There are two fireplaces—one in the narrow living room and another in the narrow front bedroom above, so naturally she'd overlooked the scary cellar, the dearth of closets, and the attached wooden sun porch with its skirting half off like Courtney Love. Since she doesn't cook, RayAnne is unfazed by the Truman-era kitchen with its aqua linoleum countertops and cabinets barely deep enough to hold dinner plates. The floors aren't really a problem; at least when something spills or rolls she knows which direction to chase it.

The house has history—*real* history that dances forth across eras even when she's performing such mundane actions as hooking her bra: imagining a corset being laced or petticoats being flounced (or whatever one did with a petticoat). Opening the old medicine chest, she wonders what the women of the house used for birth control and shudders over what being female might have entailed at the turn of the century with no Tylenol or tampons or twenty-eight-day pill. She wonders what sorts of headache powders and tinctures they took. When aiming her blow dryer at the crazed mirror to clear the condensation, she puzzles over how they ever coaxed their hair into those fat chignons, the odd sausage bangs of World War II, or the mod helmets of the sixties. Did the previous occupants speak in Old Country accents? Were their heads full of recipes for soap and lefse? Had they flirted with the iceman? Had they had back-alley abortions? Were they obedient wives and harried mothers? Did they want more? For all she knows she sleeps in a room that once housed a suffragette, a flapper from some Iowa farm, a war widow, a beleaguered Catholic mother with too many kids and a secret crush on JFK, maybe a pot-smoking Vietnam protester.

The women of this house could have been anyone.

Dashing to the basement to pull clothes fluffy and warm from the dryer, she cannot imagine spending hours laboring over a ringer washer or blotting a brow with a shirtwaist sleeve while working a mangle, a contraption she's read about but cannot picture. Living in the row house is a little like living between the worn covers of a book, each room a story, making her utterly grateful for her Dyson, her icemaker, her microwave. Such technologies free up hours—hours that are then sucked from RayAnne into the glowing tractor beams of her iPhone, laptop, or flat screen. Now that she finally has a home, there's hardly time to just be in it.

When a tinny squeal sounds from the sun porch, RayAnne calls out, "Keep your pants on!" Rummaging through cupboards, she finds a small saucepan with the label still on and fills it with water. Once on the porch, she pours water onto a drooping ficus, a plant you actually can kill, contrary to the greenhouse clerk's claim. More water goes into the trough of the hamster house as she chirps, "Here I am, Danny Boy, home." The rest she drinks herself, standing.

Later, she leans on the counter with Danny on her shoulder, watching her Amy's Asian Veggie Stir Fry pirouette as it heats, drinking boxed Pinot from a juice glass, and wondering if she'll be able to stay awake long enough to read more than a page of Penelope Lively, who awaits her upstairs.

. . .

Negotiating the waist-high tangle of front yard her mother claims is "restored prairie" to keep the city off her back about mowing, RayAnne approaches Bernadette's front door. When she sneezes, the neighbor looks over the hedge of calendula and reedy grasses from where he's scraping something from the bumper of his SUV. As RayAnne hurries along, she feels him glaring. On the porch she hastily hangs her jacket on the outside railing and brings the knocker down. The heavy door swings on its hinges and she's pulled into the house by her trapped index finger.

"Ow. *Ow.*"

"Is that you, RayAnne?"

"Mom! This door's unlocked again."

Bernadette appears in a billow of caftan. "Hello to you, too, dear. Bring that jacket inside."

"No. Last time I was here I smelled like patchouli for the rest of the day—a janitor at the station and some slacker at Cinnabon both made peace fingers at me. You should at least ask who's knocking."

"You do realize that's not even food, RayAnne. Besides, I like to be surprised."

"And you will be someday. By some axe-murdering, dismembering mother-raper."

Bernadette laughs. "I've survived carjackers in Caracas and armed bandits in Algeria, sweetie. I think I can handle Bloomington." This attitude of *safety last* seems to be the sole trait her parents share.

"Mother, did you sticker Mr. Martin's SUV?"

Bernadette pretends not to have heard. "You going to stand there? I'm making chai."

"He was eyeing daggers at me." RayAnne plucks a bumper sticker from a stack on the hall table. "You did! You can't just alienate every . . . at least not the neighbors. Jeez, Mom, 'I'm a Gasshole!'?"

Bernadette nearly claps. "I know! And he is, and the man deserves what he gets. You tell me how a healthy adult male—who runs several miles a day, mind you—can justify driving an Escalade three blocks to buy a quart of milk."

"You're gonna get in trouble. Please, just stick to your causes."

"Skim, by the way. And outing carbon-footstompers *is* a cause. For a bright girl, RayAnne, you really are out of touch."

Following as Bernadette sails to the kitchen, RayAnne ducks under hanging bouquets of herbs, which her mother pronounces with the *h*. While soy milk heats, RayAnne sinks to the breakfast nook, plucking lavender buds from her hair. The little gnarls of roots and twigs spread over newspaper will no doubt be for making teas or poultices or whatever else is being brewed up for the women on Bernadette's Blood-Tide Quests. Her mother is a New Age aging coach—"Life-Passages Doula," according to her Website—and each month guides a different gaggle of pre-, peri-, and postmenopausal women to spiritual locations in Sedona, Burma, and remote Scottish islands, where she leads them through ritual cleansings and farewell-to-fertility rites for which they pay outrageous sums.

"Watch your elbows, RayAnne. Peony root isn't easy to come by."

"Good grief. Why don't they just take hormones and sweat it out in Palm Springs or Lake Forest or wherever, like everyone else?"

Bernadette bestows RayAnne her Look of Ultimate Patience. "And where would they get support, RayAnne? Do you suppose their husbands are going to repeat the goddess chants with them, or help them out of the Viparita Karani pose when they get stuck?"

"You got me there." On the windowsill is an array of brochures touting natural remedies. RayAnne opens *The Maturing Lily* to a paragraph on personal lubricants derived from cactus plants. Disconcerted by the proximity of *cactus* and *vagina* in the same sentence, she slides the brochure away.

"Take that, Ray. There's good information there."

"Mom. I know how to take care of my own . . . stuff."

"Vagina, honey. Can't you just say *vagina*? You sound like your grandmother."

"Vah-JIIY-nahh. And Gran calls hers 'Jinny.' Anyway, I prefer *kipper-mitt*."

"Go ahead, make fun now." Bernadette sets down the chai. "You'll dry up yourself one day and then you'll be grateful for things like yucca lube."

"Thanks, Mom. I'm thirty-four."

"Yes, a long way from old."

"Yeah? The Irish matchmaker we had on last month didn't seem to think so."

Bernadette chirps, "Oh, I thought she was charming!"

"You saw the show?"

"Quite a few people saw it, RayAnne. It was on television."

"But I thought you were in Timbuk-somewhere."

"Oh, but I have TiVo! And I meant to tell you, after that show I got a call from that lovely boy you used to date, Richard—the one with the nice manners? He was a little upset, asking for your phone number."

"You didn't give it to him, though. Did you? Mother?"

"Richard? Why not? He was in touch with his latent female, wasn't he? But really, RayAnne, you never have been able to not . . . *blurt* things. You should learn to restrain yourself, at least on television."

Of course she should. It tops her list of self-improvement

projects. She blurts. She's a blurter. The chai is too hot, and she dribbles a searing mouthful out onto her saucer.

"Awgh!"

"See? Impulsive." Bernadette picks up the remote, and before RayAnne can protest, she zaps the huge widescreen to life and cues up the show. "I do love my TiVo."

"And I do loathe this episode."

"Frankenman," as it has come to be known at the station, is the episode that most makes her want to grab the nearest anchor and jump. Her frozen profile blossoms hugely onto the screen, mouth half-open, one eye half-closed, each nostril as deep as a sleeve and each tooth the size of a wallet.

"What, a little fumbling? It was funny." Bernadette presses play and RayAnne's megaphone-sized mouth erupts: "Maeve O'Donnell is descended from a long line of matchmakers back in County Clare, but these days her Irish dating service has gone online. Today is the American debut of RiverDate."

RayAnne turns back to the brochure and an illustrated page of manual methods to reduce discomfort during postmenopausal intercourse.

The program started well enough with a discussion of Internet dating protocol, Maeve suggesting the word *date* not be used until a first meeting leads to a second. RayAnne asked all the pertinent questions about online safety and keeping identities private. They discussed tactics for gracefully cutting short a nonstarter "meeting" and how to assure a promising "first contact" led to a "date." Maeve cautioned viewers, "Employ sincerity and modesty when creating a profile. Portray yourself *as is.*"

RayAnne was unable to suppress a snort. Maeve eyed her before leaning to the camera. "RayAnne, for instance, wouldn't claim to be busty."

Maeve warned of using Photoshopped or out-of-date photos. "Face it, ladies, if you're pushing forty and posting a picture of yourself at twenty-nine, the jig, as you say here in America, is up." As RayAnne quelled the urge to cross her arms over her chest, they moved on to ideas for public places to meet.

RayAnne offered, "A zoo?"

Maeve sighed, "Too . . . animal." To RayAnne's look of puzzlement, she explained, "Suggestive. We've all seen the back end of a baboon. Would that make a nice backdrop for a first meeting?"

RayAnne swiveled a look to the camera and back to Maeve. "The farmers' market?"

Maeve nearly tittered. "Oh, dear. And smell like a sheep? Or a cow?"

"Actually, farmers' markets here don't sell—"

"A public garden or busy park, yes." Maeve was still chuckling. "A museum, certainly . . ."

When RayAnne began twisting a hank of hair, Cassi's voice squeaked interference. She dropped it as if it were ignited and listened to the next directive: "Announce an underwriter slot in fifteen seconds." Which she did, cheerfully.

"All good advice, Maeve," RayAnne said, turning to camera two, "and I'm sure we'll hear plenty more of it after we drop anchor!"

RayAnne took the wheel, at first easing *Penelope* away, then suddenly opening the throttle, pasting Maeve back in her seat. The shot faded as the boat sped out of frame with Maeve clutching her hat.

Bernadette fast-forwards to the section where they are settled in and actually fishing, Maeve holding forth with a bit she'd obviously rehearsed about how catch-and-release principles might apply to dating, then asking RayAnne who her dream dates might be, if she could pick anyone in the world, like George Clooney.

RayAnne chewed her lip—her list wasn't that predictable. "Um, some of my dream dates are dead."

"Dead?"

"Uh-huh, like Ed Ricketts."

Maeve cocked her head. "And he is, or was . . . ?"

"Steinbeck's marine biologist? Ed Ricketts. Dead. Hot, but dead. Nikola Tesla for sure. Maybe Orson Welles before he ballooned. Dylan Thomas without the bottle . . ." She shrugged at the camera.

"Right. Let's stick to the living for now. What traits would make a keeper? For you?"

RayAnne's technique for stalling is to simply rehash the question: "What would make a keeper . . . for me? Traits? You mean like the best-of from failed relationships?"

"Let's avoid words like *failed*, shall we? How about . . . *previous* or *prior*. Just start with bits of one fellow's this and another's that to construct a sort of ideal mate."

"Construct. Oh, like Mary Shelley?" Before she knew it, RayAnne was revealing the best and worst of her priors on national television. First names only, but still, their real first names. She led with the talent of Lyle, the guitar player with too many substance habits for her comfort. "Talented, and so . . . out of it."

She tacked on the torso of Paul, the cyclist she never tired of watching undress. "Very rude—but ripped."

"And . . . ," Maeve urged. "Personality?"

"Um, Richard. He was so charming and sweet, except I kept expecting him to come out of the closet wearing something of mine." She tapped her lip. "But my Frankenman would have to be a bit smarter . . ."

There'd been Zack, the smart one who was going to do great things, had a bunch of PhDs. Sex with him had been above average, that she remembers. "This one guy, Zack? He spoke maybe five languages." As RayAnne recalled him, she frowned. "So you'd think he'd know better words for breasts than *titties*. So smarter isn't exactly the wor—" She looked straight at camera one, which fed directly to Cassi's monitor. "Wait, can I say *titties* on air?"

From the breakfast nook, watching her own dunderheadedness courtesy of TiVo, RayAnne groans. Postproduction had promised to cut that and didn't, yet they would edit out the removal of a barbless hook.

Bernadette chortles, then recovers. "Oh, wait, did I tell you that Zack called too?"

"No! Tell me you didn't give him—"

"Your number? Why not?"

"Mom, you can't just do that!"

"Wasn't he going to be a doctor?"

RayAnne pivots her attention back to a drawing in the brochure, turning it this way and that until realizing it is a tutorial for perineal self-massage. On-screen, she's busy topping off her woman-made man with the perfect face of Larry, who'd been "about as lively as the marble his jaw was chiseled from." When the camera drew nearer to RayAnne, the slow realization of what she'd just done on national television appeared like a rash. If that hadn't been bad enough, Maeve then pulled out a dating profile she'd written for RayAnne and proceeded to read the teaser to the camera in her lovely lilt.

"Successful . . ."

RayAnne frowns across the kitchen toward the television, piping up with her own commentary, countering, "*For the moment . . .*"

". . . and dynamic,"

"*Caffeinated.*"

". . . thirtysomething,"

"*Clock ticking.*"

". . . independent professional,"

"*Loner.*"

". . . loves the outdoors,"

"*Claustrophobic.*"

". . . fishing in particular."

"*Dweeb.*"

"Height and weight more or less balanced,"

"*Diet Sprite and laxatives.*"

". . . is open to life's possibilities,"

"*Indecisive.*"

"An incredible catch!"

"*Ha!*"

Bernadette turns. "Really, you should hear yourself. And *laxatives?* You never did use that gift certificate for the colonic, did you?"

The camera panned to RayAnne's plastered smile, but just as she opened her massive on-screen mouth to sputter a response, she was saved by a tug on her line. Though the fish was a runt, she made a great show of struggling and reeling as if a muskie had her hook. When she held up the skinny pike, the cameraman had trouble focusing on it, slender as it was, so RayAnne leaned out over the gunnel and held it to the lens, making it loom large. "Okay! Now that we've caught something, ladies, here's one to ponder while we break for a word from Lefty's Bait. Does size matter?"

RayAnne makes a horsey snort as the screen goes black.

"*I* thought it was funny." Bernadette breezes past, bustles around the kitchen, and returns with a bowl of chips. "It was cute, aside from the tattling parts."

"Mom."

Bernadette squeezes RayAnne's shoulder. "Oh, honey. Would it kill you to lighten up? It's just a show."

"Just my career."

So Zack called? She'd wondered where he might end up. What was it again about their split? She'd chalked it up to the usual—being out on the circuit three weeks each month hadn't been great for maintaining any relationship. She absently chews a handful of chips, then spits the gummy mess into her palm. "Gah, Mom! These taste like cheesy seaweed!"

"Well, I should hope so."

In spite of the Frankenman episode being perhaps her most embarrassing performance yet, responses had been overwhelmingly positive. Still, television is hardly the place to practice. She simply has to do better: she talks too much when nervous, compulsively digs in the product-placement packages of Gummy Trout and Choco-Fish. She chews her nails, slumps, squints, and the only time she's truly at ease is when the guest is actually interesting.

She often wonders why the director doesn't coach her, give more direction.

Her mother narrows an eye in her direction. "You look pale, RayAnne; you getting enough sleep? Bags. Under your eyes." Bernadette bustles again and pulls something from the fridge that looks like sod and plugs in her Vitamix. Just as RayAnne is about to protest, the machine roars. She won't bother arguing because the more she resists, the more Bernadette will push, so she merely sits with her eyes shut until her mother floats back to the table with a glass of neon-green liquid.

"Here. Wheatgrass. Neutralizes toxins."

"Now I'm toxic." RayAnne frowns at the acid green but knocks it back, cringing at the taste, like licking the blades of a lawn mower. Bernadette hands over a glass of water to wash it down.

"Good?" Bernadette takes the glass.

"Perfect pairing with these underpants chips."

"Pish. Oh, I forgot." Bernadette pulls a tightly tied bundle of twiggy herbs from somewhere in her caftan. "Sage to smudge your trailer with."

On location, RayAnne will be staying in a newly leased motor home, one assigned just to her, after having shared with Cassi last season, which was a little like bunking with Casper, her white face lit all hours by the glow of her iPad until RayAnne took to wearing a sleep mask. She tries handing back the sage. "It's a brand-*new* RV."

"Take it. Bad juju can come factory direct. How long will they keep you up there?"

"We've got twelve shows to tape, so probably two sessions. I can be home on the weekends in between."

"You know, I met this woman you should consider, an intimacy yogini."

"Yo-what?"

"Yogini, female yogi. Don't tell me you didn't know that." Bernadette paws around in a Guatemalan patchwork duffel the size of a body bag and pulls out a business card.

Gumani Bali, PhD, Ayurverotic Yogini.

The card has a photograph of a diminutive, dark woman with a crooked grin. "Dr. Ruth in a sari?" RayAnne slides the card back.

Her mother sips her own wheatgrass juice as if it is a Bordeaux. "Gumani is amazing. She's enlightened me to a few things . . ."

"Please." RayAnne holds up a hand.

All too often Bernadette offers up intimate minutiae of her own sex life, most of them dalliances, flings that require no more commitment than a drop-in Zumba class. Most recently she'd hooked up with a raw foods chef half her age, sharing details as if RayAnne might want to know what anyone might have tattooed across their scrotum. She breathes the image away. Bernadette claims to be completely free in her own body, using a tone that suggests RayAnne might be a hostage in hers.

"Thanks, Mom, but I don't really have that much say in what guests are chosen. Besides, it's a family show."

"Not for the show, honey, for *you*." Bernadette leans close as if they are not alone. "I've made an appointment for you. For your birthday!"

"You are kidding me." RayAnne unfolds, slowly rising. "Say you are kidding me."

"Oh, the look on your face! Of course I'm kidding."

When Bernadette laughs hard, this hard, it's easy to imagine her young. She'd been born a literal flower child, having grown up on a sunflower farm in Iowa and headed for a life of hippiedom until sidetracked by marriage to Big Rick—her one great mistake and possibly the driving impetus that now compels her to help other women over their own rough pasts and steer them toward happier lives, her own happiness having been derailed by a man.

When RayAnne was twelve, during one of the defining moments of Dahl family history, Bernadette asserted herself over the carcass of a roast turkey on Thanksgiving afternoon. There was Before The Turkey, The Turkey, and *Après* The Turkey.

Sometime during The Turkey, the valve subduing Bernadette's true nature simply blew under the pressures of the holiday when the strain of domesticity, the demands of motherhood, and an unhappy union played out on an urban midwestern stage proved too much. Emboldened by a number of gin gimlets, Bernadette loudly revealed to all gathered that before she had met Big Rick, she'd been engaged to a mostly forgotten folk singer named Rupert Rutherford, with whom she planned to live on an Oregon commune and raise weed and naked babies. Alas, Rupert was arrested for dealing and sentenced just a week before they were to be married on a beach by a barefoot Rastafarian.

RayAnne understands that if life were fair, marijuana would be legal and her mother would have had her folk singer.

Instead, after several months of waiting for Rupert, Bernadette's patience momentarily flagged. She had an ill-advised, unlikely fling with Big Rick, whom she barely knew. Shortly thereafter she discovered she was pregnant, and somehow Big Rick caught wind of it. He hounded and wooed and charmed her into marrying him. She realized her mistake almost immediately and saw her future dissolve like so much smoke from the chimney of the three-bedroom Colonial in the leafy Minneapolis neighborhood she inexplicably found herself living in. Branded with the Scandinavian ethic of lying in the bed one has made, Bernadette put her shoulder to the tasks of housewifery, child-rearing, and suppression of her free spirit while Big Rick spent two hundred days a year drinking and screwing his way across the pro fishing circuit.

Bernadette had risen to standing (a feat, considering) to address those gathered: "I was a moth knocked off course by the glare of a bare bulb, when I was supposed to be navigating by starlight," Big Rick being the bulb—even RayAnne's then-nine-year-old brother Ky got that. Bernadette pulled the carving fork from the carcass, a little flag of limp skin still attached, and pointed it at Big Rick, working to enunciate. "If I could have raised enough money to get Rupert a decent lawyer, I would not be sitting here now, you bastard." She steadied the fork in Big Rick's direction. "*He* let me think he was for Humphrey because I belonged to Young Democrats. I didn't even know until after we were married that he'd voted for Nixon." She spat the name, then wobbled and changed some mental track. "This . . ." Like a conductor, she gestured to the wallpaper and either the drapes or the yard outside the window, or the driveway with Big Rick's Lincoln parked there, or the mod beveled glass chandelier, her sweeping hands seemingly including her family. "*This* is not the life I was meant to lead." She then sat down hard and passed out, her forehead thudding next to the bowl of Dot's cranberry tangerine compote.

That was the last holiday the Dahl family spent together. On countless occasions afterward, Bernadette found opportunities to reassure RayAnne that she was not included in that *This*. Still, the barb was lodged—she had been the cause of her mother's misery, her own teeny fetal existence the only reason her parents had married in the first place.

Why do people marry, again?

"I gotta pee." She edges out from the breakfast nook and is halfway down the hall before hearing her mother call, "Kegel!"

Returning to the kitchen, she leans against the doorframe. "Okay," she says, *okay* being her mantra when worn down or annoyed. She nods toward the fridge. "Okay, Mom, where's your stash?"

"Stash?" Bernadette is so lousy at feigning innocence.

"The Ben & Jerry's. I know you've got Chunky Monkey around here somewhere."

Bernadette caves. "Rec room fridge. Under the goji sherbet and behind the miso pops." RayAnne is already on her way.

As RayAnne reaches the bottom of the basement stairs, her mother shouts, "Grab the Carnal Mudslide too!"

She crosses the rec room, skirting the massage table where the pool table used to be, swinging behind the tiki bar to the old pink Norge. She finds the ice pick and chips at the frost around the freezer door, working it like a bank robber for three minutes before liberating the cartons within, time enough to forget she is annoyed.

Ice cream in hand, she pauses at the base of the stairs and scans the wall of family photos, drawn to a new addition—a shot of Bernadette in full life-passages-doula mode, wearing a llama cape and embroidered cap, posed with half a dozen aging mavens outside a Nepalese monastery. Next to them is a mountain of matched sets of luggage with a troop of Sherpas standing by. Her mother looks very happy in the photo. And probably is, in her plinky, feel-good world that is so easy for RayAnne to scoff at. Maybe that's why Bernadette is so maddening lately. She's so unflappable, so . . . assured.

RayAnne spies the latest portrait of her brother and his family and smiles. Kyle and Ingrid wear teeth-gritting grins while pinning their identical twins in WWE holds as if casually hugging them. Wilt and Michael are darling and indiscernible. Kyle calls them Thing One and Thing Two, not quite joking. To her grandmother, who can't be bothered keeping her great-grandsons straight, they are That Pair of Springs.

There's a glamorous black-and-white of Dot at a linen-covered table leaning against Dead Ted (so called to distinguish him from RayAnne's grandfather on her mother's side, also a Ted, also dead, referred to as Other Ted) in the dining room of their restaurant, Dot looking very Jackie O in her spangled sheath and teased hair. Very glam. Another restaurant shot shows her on the other side of the swinging doors, wearing her chef togs, posing with her kitchen staff, and wielding a whisk the length of her arm. RayAnne is glad that her mother and Dot have stayed close over the years, never having allowed Big Rick or any of the ensuing wives to wedge them apart. Dot still calls Bernadette once a week.

In another picture, RayAnne's grainy seven-year-old face is framed in a Dutch boy haircut. She's raccoon-eyed in the bright sun, having collared her grandmother from behind with dimpled arms. Dot's in her lawn chair with Snicker, the ratty lap dog that RayAnne sometimes bit when no one was looking. The dog is baring its little needle teeth up at RayAnne, but Dot seems oblivious, looking slightly blank and holding fast to RayAnne's wrists, still freshly grieving for Dead Ted.

There's only one family photo that includes Big Rick, a yellowing Sears portrait. RayAnne is pudgy and Kyle twig thin. Their mother is unconvincingly dressed like a suburban housewife in a pastel blouse with shoulder pads and poodle hair, looking brittle and reluctant, nothing like the tanned, open-faced woman two frames away in Nepal.

When stepping back from the wall, seeing the photos all together as a history, RayAnne wonders why she bothers to worry as much as she does. Here, decades of her family gaze out at her—lives lived and survived (or not, in the case of Dead Ted, toppled by an aneurysm on the seventh hole) that make her current worries seem trivial. It's the important things she needs to focus on. She should see more of her brother and his family. She *must* see Dot soon, and not just on Skype.

Bernadette calls down, "You dawdle, it'll melt."

Her hands numb with cold, RayAnne takes the stairs in twos.

· · ·

Sitting with her mother in the jungle of the backyard, digging directly from the carton of ice cream, she muses that as long as she and Bernadette don't look at each other it could be any year at all, any one of their backyard ice cream afternoons—she could be fifteen or twenty-five, but at the moment licking her spoon she feels five again, which is good, because lately she's been feeling fifty.

As if reading her mind, Bernadette aims a spoonful at Ray-Anne and makes an airplane noise.

"Open the hangar, RayBean."

Wind sends a heavy lilac branch bobbing into a birdbath she can remember sitting in as a toddler. She opens her mouth, then clamps hard, trapping the spoon so that Bernadette must wrestle it back.

It's better when they both can laugh.

3

.

.

.

.

It's an insane hour, teetering toward four a.m. Shivering and sitting on her roller bag at the curb, RayAnne clutches a steaming travel mug. The row house windows are mostly dark save those belonging to the resident widows, their lights ablaze.

Don't old ladies ever sleep?

The two widows have bookended the row house for decades. Their porches are framed by peeling columns, and their front windows are crowded with colossal geraniums and violets shouldering the glass as if trying to break out. Their end units are the most enviable, with bay windows on the gable ends and narrow side gardens. Both still use the original pulley clotheslines, where their underpants and house dresses flap in the breeze to announce their figures: Stout is from Kraków and barely speaks English, despite living in Minneapolis for sixty years. Winter or summer, she wears headscarves knotted deep somewhere under her jowls. Scrawny is sweet natured, half-blind, and smiles awkwardly as if with someone else's dentures. RayAnne has been told that local realtors are wild for them both to expire. One of these days she's going to knock on their doors with bakery cookies and ask what the neighborhood was like once upon a time, ask about the women who had lived in her slice of the building.

RayAnne's other neighbors, sensibly dead to the world, are nearer her own age—a few young families, a polite set of Pakistani brothers, and a friendly gay couple who have bravely opened a bistro on the next block in anticipation of gentrification. The only other single female seems to be around about as much as she is. Her young neighbors are all pleasant enough and seem terribly busy with their work: one teaches film at the university, the brothers work in IT, the single has some start-up clothing design firm. When they ask RayAnne what she does, her mumbled answer doesn't include *fishing*, only *public* and *television*, which get approving nods every time.

Though she's expecting it, when the new motor home rounds the corner, RayAnne's jaw drops. Long as a Greyhound bus, it spans the width of two of the row houses. Rolling to a stop, it gives a great hydraulic sigh and settles onto its chassis. One look at the graphics wrapping the side and RayAnne is grateful for the ungodly hour and deserted street. A behemoth trout arches along the length of the vehicle, ready to gobble up a lure the size of a muskie. The entire back end of the RV is taken up by a woman's image—not a real woman but an ideal everywoman, were everywoman an even-featured blonde with blue eyes, perfect teeth, and flawless skin. The tire-sized *O* of her mouth looks ready to fellate the bottle of Mermaid Pilsner she's raising to her mouth while one colossal eye winks seductively. The dual exhaust pipes poke from the front of her fishing vest in perfectly regrettable positions.

This must be who they have in mind for a host? A Big Rick–ism escapes RayAnne's lips: "Kee-rist on a bike."

The door huffs opens and Cassi hops to the pavement. It turns out she has a Class A driver's license, which is somehow not surprising. She clomps over with a greeting far too loud for the hour. "Nice barrels, huh?"

"She's like . . . a whatsit?" RayAnne scrabbles.

"Fem-bot? I think we should name her."

RayAnne ponders the face. "Well. If Betty Crocker had a beer-guzzling, tramp-stamped granddaughter who lived to give blow-jobs, this would be her." RayAnne sucks her sippy thermos while considering a name. "Tiffany?"

"Tiffany Crocker." Cassi nods. "Sounds about right."

RayAnne is eager to get the RV moving—her neighbors probably don't know about the show and don't need to. Here in her neighborhood RayAnne's just one of the regulars at Tough Beans, staring into her laptop like everyone else, insulated against interaction by clunky headphones, chewing hoodie strings while tabbing between open tabs of work, various Websites, or Facebook, or browsing (ironically, of course) the personals on *City Pages,* snorting over such ad banners as "Must Love Knots" or "Ugly but Insatiable Seeking Same."

Along with other neighborhood singles, she does her grocery shopping late, loitering at the freezer section uncertainly as if waiting for pizza to be declared a superfood. At the yoga studio, she downward-dogs and wrestles back farts with the rest of them, dodging arms and legs while attempting to be nothing but breath and movement. On the river path she delays her jogging with exaggerated hamstring stretching before setting out to bob among the others, propelled by a loathing for her thighs. RayAnne bears no resemblance to the idealized Tiffany plastered over the back end of the gaudy RV.

Cassi nudges her. "Look at it this way: they wouldn't have bothered with all this if they weren't considering a third season. She's job security."

"I wouldn't count on it." RayAnne hadn't minded the old RV with its warped wallboard and Barbie-sized stove and propane smell. She's seen rigs like this at the sports shows, has seen the price tags—more than she paid for her house. "I thought there were budget constraints?"

"It's leased courtesy of Tiffany's pimp, Mermaid Pilsner." Cassi's tone shifts to a sleazy voiceover drawl: "One of the most craptacular artisanal beers ever brewed." She grandly motions to the RV. "You gotta see the kitchen, and those pop-out sections expand the back end like Kirstie Alley's hips. All the windows work and you can touch *anything* without getting a shock. And there's an icemaker."

Now that she's found a spot for one, RayAnne regrets not taking one of Bernadette's "I'm a Gasshole!" bumper stickers. Sticking her head in, she sees the RV is better appointed than her house, certainly cleaner, with chrome and leather everywhere and a master electrical console with color-coded switches and a remote. She instantly dislikes it, all of it: the halogen lights, the beige-on-beige decor, and the upholstery with paper runners like at the women's clinic. "We allowed to sit?"

They strap themselves into swiveling bucket seats and Cassi revs the engine, rubbing her hands together. "Hot for some Rod & Gun action?"

Having never been to such an expo, Cassi is actually excited. With no desire to rain on the girl's parade, RayAnne only smiles. "You betcha."

. . .

Hours later she wakes from the sort of dreams one can only have when barreling along in a living room at seventy miles an hour. She sort of remembers the stops for gas and is shocked to see they've nearly reached Chicago. "Was I drooling?" she asks.

Cassi rips off a section of paper runner from under her knee and hands it over. "Some."

At a massive underground garage at the convention center, the RV is taken over by a union driver, who hands it over to a teamster to wash and polish before parking it in the convention hall, where an IBEW electrician will plug it in and hang the monitors, and another union somebody will unfurl its canopy. Cassi and RayAnne are not allowed to do so much as open the legs of folding tables, so they take a shuttle downtown to have lunch and check into their rooms.

After stowing their bags, they walk to the pier, where Cassi eats mini donuts and RayAnne takes the empty bag to breathe in the sugary warm air. They roam aimlessly up Michigan Avenue and enter a store only because their feet ache. It sells nothing but cashmere, the entire store, and they shuffle from display to display of sweaters and scarves and throws, making little noises at every price tag until a clerk gives them a withering look and they move on.

The FAO Schwarz store is hosting an American Girl Doll event, awash in mothers with daughters who all seem to be competing for the title of most slap-worthy. The mothers keep one cool eye on Cassi while RayAnne shops for Lego kits for her nephews. When her head begins throbbing from the lights and noise, RayAnne concludes that if she ever has a child, it will need to be a boy because the banshee pitch only little girls can achieve cuts right through her. Even after they leave the store, her ears ring with the tune of the constantly looping "It's a Small World," wondering how the clerks bear eight-hour shifts of it.

It's still light when they stagger into the hotel lobby, but RayAnne is ready for her room-service chicken Caesar (dressing on the side), an hour of cable, and bed. Some might think being on the road is exciting, but after ten years on the circuit RayAnne would give her thumbs for the sort of nine-to-five routine that sounds like purgatory to most but joyously predictable to her. As she drifts off, the toy store tune wedges into her brain and she hums herself to sleep, wishing the lyrics were true, that it was a small world after all.

. . .

In the morning they arrive at the expo late, everything at the convention center already lit up and going full bore. They hang back in the broad entrance hall, which is rounded like an omnitheater, marveling at the projections of *Planet Earth*–like schools of game fish maniacally charging and gnawing so that it seems they are trying to eat anyone passing by. Some people actually duck and dodge in amusing reversals of predator and prey.

"Imagine standing here stoned," Cassi observes.

"No thanks," RayAnne laughs. She wouldn't dare these days, clearly remembering the twenty pounds she gained in college, prone to the sort of munchies that always landed her cross-legged in front of the open fridge eating straight from the condiment shelves like the scene in *9½ Weeks*. No Mickey Rourke, just olives and Cheez Whiz.

"Interesting getup, by the way." She cocks an eye at Cassi.

Cassi is dressed in one of her ironic outfits: Wellington rubber boots, blaze orange leggings, an extra-long red thermal shirt that doubles as a minidress, snugged at the waist by a kiddie plastic ammo belt. Every garment and each boot is plastered with dozens of bullet-hole decals that look remarkably real. It's all topped with the sort of quilted vest old men wear, though Cassi's has been fashionably cropped like a bolero jacket. In a nod to fishing, treble hooks hang from her earlobes like lethal little candelabras. RayAnne hopes Cassi has thought to file the barbs.

Conversely, RayAnne is head to toe in Filson khaki with numerous zip-off options: putty-colored chamois shirt, fawn-hued cargo pants, lightweight beige utility vest, and olive green billed cap with the show's logo. She feels anonymous and nearly androgynous here in the odd world she was once part of.

Cassi enlists RayAnne to take a video on her cell phone as a steelhead opens its jaws over her head. "C'mon," RayAnne urges, handing the phone back after a minute. "Let's get this over with."

There is a scrolling marquee listing the entertainment and demo schedule at the top of the escalator. A dance troupe called the White Tails is slated for noon. The Mermen Nabbertackle

Choir will be opening for a Billy Ray Cyrus impersonator named Willie Ray Cyrus. The master of ceremonies is the most famous fishing show host of all time, Rob Mack from the Trout Channel, whom RayAnne would have wagered money on having died, maybe more than once, making her wonder if the Trout Channel doesn't trot out a Rob Mack lookalike now and then like CBS did with Lassie. The early evening wrap-up is a fashion show of waders, quick-wicking underwear, and fishing vests from the clothier FishunFashun. Under "Just for the Ladies" is an appearance by beefcake calendar favorite Mr. Northern Tool. Under "Activities," there's Casting for Beginners and a chef's demonstration for cooking freshwater bisque at Lefty's Bait and Tackle.

"Our Lefty's?"

Cassi is taking more video with her phone. "Yup."

"Do we have to go?"

"You should at least introduce yourself to the underwriters."

As they descend the escalator, the scope of the expo is stunning, the size of a small town, a grid of aisles with street signs. It's surrounded by several stages for entertainment, two food courts, and elaborately constructed environments, like the fake blue Mylar lake showcasing yachts and bass boats. There's an archery field where plastic target deer stand in fake grass and shudder each time they are struck with graphite arrows flung from complicated bows. There is a wall of fiberglass cliffs populated with taxidermy elk and rams. There's a long line to get into the Lucite-walled shooting range where the moving target posters are human silhouettes. Gun barrels poke from portable duck blinds aimed at flocks of stuffed mallards and geese suspended from above by wires.

The escalator deposits them on Winchester Avenue, where they are immediately absorbed into a current of men that surges and slows at booths like MuskTang Sally's, where a shivering teen in a fur bikini hands out scratch-and-sniff samples of game scents: Doe Potion Number Nine, Madam Gazelle, and Cari-Booty. There are in fact many products and weapons being proffered and suggestively caressed by scantily clad girls.

Most booths have video monitors looping presentations or infomercials of their products and services, such as the one featuring a chicken pecking at the ground, minding its own business, then exploding after being shot with a new, improved ammunition. The air is filled with the twang of country music, pips of muffled gunfire, and the nattering of three thousand men. Exhaust fans drone but cannot clear the odors of cordite, barbeque sauce, and AXE.

It suddenly dawns on Cassi, and she elbows RayAnne. "We're supposed to solicit memberships for WYOY here?"

RayAnne answers glumly, "You see why I resisted?"

Cassi shrugs. "Well, they have paid for a booth . . . so I suppose it's the exposure that's important?"

"Pragmatist."

"It might even be interesting." Seeing RayAnne's look, she adds, "In a socio-anthropological sort of way, of course. Or maybe we could sneak out early?"

RayAnne has never been able to sneak out of anything. "There're probably sponsors lurking around taking notes."

Along the way they are distracted by a wire enclosure of water spaniels and retriever puppies. "Aw, look."

When RayAnne bends, a boy quickly steps in front of her. "You can't pet 'em, lady. They're bein' trained."

Just across the aisle from the puppies is a demo kitchen where a man wearing a chef's hat and a bandolier of ammo across his chest serves up little samples of game bird he's cooked over an electric grill.

"I'm starving," Cassi says, tugging RayAnne. The chef is explaining how the product, Spice Shot, works, spreading out his cartridges. "You got your Lemon Pepper, Cajun Spice, Traditional, and Teriyaki. All packed right here in this ammo, 'cept there's no birdshot, just rock salt, so nothing to break your teeth on. Just load up a flavor cartridge, cock, and kill. Your bird is seasoned before it hits the ground!"

The smell of pheasant is making the puppies crazy, so that they jump and strain against the fence, yelping and falling back when their shock collars buzz.

RayAnne pulls Cassi along. "Let's just find our spot." She consults her map and in five minutes they've located the RV. It's parked on Astroturf with the back end, the Tiffany end, smack on the aisle, exhaust pipes front and center. "Great."

The tables have stacks of giveaway calendars and logo pens for her to sign with in the event anyone might want her autograph. There's a pair of iPads loaded with WYOY pledge forms and Square to accept donations. They rearrange the booth and look through the promo merchandise, T-shirts and mugs stamped "Get Hooked," "Good Things Come to Those Who Bait," "Catch, Release, Repeat (Sundays at 6 p.m. WYOY)," "I'm a Woman. I Fish. Deal with It." There are a dozen boxes under the table filled with more swag than they will ever get rid of. Cassi checks her watch, saying brightly, "Only seven hours to go."

"Don't forget tomorrow." At least RayAnne has something to look forward to—the day after the expo ends, she goes directly to Florida for an entire week to visit her grandmother, where she will do little more than read, lie around on the beach with her brother and nephews, and throw a party—Dot is turning eighty. RayAnne pulls out a tattered paperback from her backpack, *The French Lieutenant's Woman,* which has been an effective sedative every night for the past week. After two pages she sighs. "What've you got?"

"Piercr." Cassi wriggles down with her iPhone. "It's the steampunker's Grindr." After a half hour, no passersby have stopped, though many men slow to examine the female end of the RV and comment on her barrels. Cassi makes a "Free" sign for the stack of calendars and pushes them closer to the aisle.

Two guys elbow each other and point to Tiffany, one asking RayAnne, "When's *she* showing up?"

"Ah . . . later." RayAnne looks over her glasses. "If you become a WYOY member, you get a mug or one of these T-shirts."

Cassi hands one over. "When Tiffany comes back she'll autograph that for you. While you're wearing it."

RayAnne shoots her a look. "But only if you sign up at the Lunker Level."

The man looks at the literature on the table, including the small NPT sign. "Yeah? What the hell is NPT again?"

"National Public Television."

"And I'm supposed to pay to watch it?"

Cassi crosses her arms. "You pay for cable."

"Point." He turns to his friend and jerks his head at Tiffany. "Al, you ever seen this chick on TV?"

Al shrugs. "Not really. My wife watches this show. It's like Oprah in a boat."

"It is?" RayAnne asks.

The guy takes out his wallet and holds his credit card like he might snatch it back. "I want a mug and a shirt."

By three p.m., the table is littered with empty coffee cups, yogurt containers, and expo swag Cassi has harvested on her forays out into the aisles. She's just arrived with more, asking, "Any more suckahs?"

"Only one since you left," RayAnne says. "That's a grand total of a dozen." She holds up the T-shirt she's signed with a fat red marker—*To Studmuffin Dave, Tiffany!* "We'll just tell them she's come and gone. Here they all are, personalized; we'll tell them it's lipstick."

"To *Steamin' Steven*? That's a lot of hearts."

They go through Cassi's recent score: bullet-shaped candy, logo fridge magnets, billed caps, trout-shaped oven mitts—only one tasteful item, a calendar of old ads for fishing gear from

Lefty's Bait, the single item RayAnne sets aside for herself. Another calendar is from a gun company, featuring half-nude coeds posing suggestively with semiautomatic weapons. Cassi snorts at February and its G-string-clad girl riding a semiautomatic. "So happiness *is* a warm gun?"

August is even more offensive. "Oh, come on." RayAnne frowns. "That cannot taste good."

Cassi is ready to toss the calendar when she notices it comes with a little translucent package. "Look," she says. "A camo-condom!"

"That alone . . ." RayAnne shudders. "That could rocket me over the fence."

Above their heads, a flat screen aimed at the aisle plays a video that no one pays the slightest bit of attention to, probably because RayAnne has set the volume to barely audible. It loops a collection of impromptu shorts and outtakes from the show. In the first, RayAnne is busy outfitting her line and choosing bait, gently pawing through her tackle box, talking as if thinking aloud.

"What draws me to fishing? I suppose the act of it, you know? It's so . . . hopeful. Though I think catching fish is really overemphasized and overrated. I mean, unless you're feeding your family or work on a trawler, getting skunked is no tragedy. Fishing is peaceful, you're in a boat, and the world is back there on shore. For me . . . for *me*, it's a way to think, to relax." She begins doing something that requires both hands, holding the line between her teeth while talking. "Sho there's the occasional triumph, you might get a fighter, shome exshitement . . ." Caught up in the motions of tying her leader, she severs the line with a bite, then, remembering the camera, she looks up and says, "Oh, but don't do what I just did . . . unless you have dental coverage. Where was I? Oh, yeah. Catching a fish can be fun, but the old saying, *Anticipation is the purest form of pleasure?* That's it. Just getting out there is what matters. That's our goal here on *Fishing*."

Such monologues weren't scripted; in fact, most were filmed

candidly when she thought she was merely answering casual questions from the crew. The tapes were dug up after responses from audiences indicated they most liked RayAnne when she was just being herself. She wasn't initially keen on the idea of the videos, but after seeing them edited and strung together, they seemed okay after all, maybe because she meant what she said on them—that at best fishing is merely a sort of meditation with no agenda, how, in a boat, calm has a chance to surface. That sometimes doing next to nothing is important.

RayAnne pops up. "I gotta stretch my legs. Want anything? Coke? Assault rifle?"

"Nah." Cassi barely looks up, engrossed in a new game, boots propped. "Hey, stop in at Lefty's. I told them you'd be by."

"Great. Thanks."

Vendors she passes promote everything from feather-light titanium rods and strap-on depth finders to Ferrari-style bass boats with matching trailers priced many times more than an average car. Expos are geared to portray fishing as an alpha sport, requiring state-of-the-art everything, all designed to tempt males of a certain age with expendable income to own the fastest boat or most enviable rod—men with wallets crammed with bills in higher denominations than their emotional IQs. The place teems with them.

She's a little twitchy passing the booths that sell weapons and handguns and is reminded of Bernadette's philosophy on gun issues. Whenever a school shooting or murder is in the news, Bernadette goes a little rabid. "If only knives would come back into fashion! Murder would be so much rarer. Any coward can shoot a gun; it'd actually take balls to kill someone with a knife, up close and visceral." Her mother has a point. If drive-by killings entailed throwing rounds of knives out of moving car windows, inner city streets would become nursery safe. No one's going to hold up a Kwik Trip with a Leatherman.

No doubt Bernadette would label the men at the expo less

evolved for the enjoyment they take in stalking and killing. Looking around, there is admittedly not much introspection going on at the corner of Glock Lane and Taxidermy Avenue. Near an exit, RayAnne waffles, pining for fresh air, but her vendor tag is back in the booth acting as a bookmark, so she might not get back in the door without it . . . which might not be such a bad thing, except she hasn't got her phone either.

At the concession stand, greasy hot dogs ride little Ferris wheels under heat lamps. She buys the only healthy thing on offer, a smoothie, sucking it down at a stand-up table chosen because it's too small to share. On the way back, she stops in a bathroom but upon leaving turns the wrong way. By the time she realizes, she's deep into the weapons side of the convention hall, dead-ended under a banner emblazoned "Steve and Steve's Kill Cam!"

There's no one in the Kill Cam booth, but on a wide video screen, two men in fatigues stand stiffly with hands clasped over their groins. Steve and Steve bellow in tandem, "Film the kill! Relive the hunt!" They demonstrate how to attach the Kill Cam to a rifle barrel and operate it like a scope. Squinting at their cue cards, they pitch. "One great way to remember a great hunt!" says Steve. "Who says that you cannot hunt out of season?" Other Steve asks. The scene cuts to them reclining in loungers watching a massive flat screen where a felled doe twitches on blood-stained snow.

"Jeezus," RayAnne mutters. "How gr—"

"Grisly?" The low voice comes from directly behind.

Turning, she says, "Gruesome."

She blinks at a face she recognizes but cannot place. It takes a beat. The man frowning up at the screen is the guy from the WYOY parking lot. The dimpled musician, so far out of context she grows slightly flummoxed. He takes a step forward, still fastened to the screen. "You suppose they write their own copy?"

"You assuming they can write?"

"There's that." He has a deep laugh.

"Have we met?" she asks, immediately thinking, *Is that the best you can come up with?*

"Not formally." He grins. "But I've been hoping to, actually. I'm Hal. Hal Bergen."

He says it in a way that makes her think she should know him, but she cannot think why. Offering her hand, she automatically braces to receive the crushing, knuckle-aligning handshake men at these sorts of events tend to employ—the testosterone squeeze, the *you're playing a man's game here, little lady* crush. But his clasp is light and wrong. She looks down to see his hand is half-encased in a sort of brace, like a leather golf glove with stays. After a slice of silence during which she stupidly stares, he eases his hand away, winking. "Bad day at the sawmill."

She laughs, assuming she's meant to. His other hand seems okay.

"How's the show been for you so far?" he asks.

"*This* show?"

She can be such an idiot. Her brother Kyle claims that, around men, her social skills regress to age ten, suggesting she might adopt any approach besides her own. The guy—whose name she has promptly forgotten—is better looking than she remembers, but then she's up close now, wearing glasses (not her lovely new glasses of course, but the clunky Harry Potter ones). Her hair is jammed in a clip; she's not wearing a smidgeon of makeup. He, on the other hand, looks professionally styled to a state of semi-scruff as if for an indie album cover shoot. His hair is a dark mop threaded with early silver. He's got the sort of eyelashes wasted on a man, and his mouth is particularly good, dimples exactly where she would have placed them herself.

Ky claims she's unfairly wary of handsome men because of Big Rick.

"Um, are we supposed to know each other?"

"Supposed to?" He looks slightly puzzled. "Well, no, not . . . Ah, you mean fraternize?"

"I'm not sure . . . what I mean." Now *flummoxed* might as well be stamped across her forehead. As it tends to in awkward situations, her flight instinct kicks in and she surveys the aisle over his shoulder. "Anyway, yeah, I should really get back."

"Oh?" He's clearly disappointed.

She shrugs. "Good to meet you . . ."

"Good to meet you too, RayAnne. See you later, I hope?"

Later? She's halfway down the aisle before slowing. He knew her name? She hadn't offered it. Maybe he works at one of the businesses that share the same building as WYOY, like the alt-rock FM station on the eighth floor, or the wind power turbine distributor. Might he be one of the dozen male viewers watching the show? Remembering where she meant to go in the first place, she pats multiple pockets, but her expo map is gone, probably left at the concession stand. She turns back, hoping the guy might have one, or maybe know where Lefty's Bait is, but he's gone, the only sounds more gunshots erupting from speakers at the Kill Cam booth and more pips of gunfire from the indoor shooting range.

She aims herself past another aisle of weapon booths. At the NRA stage a crowd is gathered to hear what's-his-Wayne holding forth on his ten-point plan to train and arm grade school hall monitors, while a boy wearing body armor walks the length of the stage before turning awkwardly like a model, not quite carrying it off under the weight of the vest and the firearm. She shudders, thinks of her twin nephews, while Mr. LaPierre bombasts. Her brother Ky maintains that when it comes down to it, those who deserve it rarely get gunned down.

A shortcut takes her through the marina, a relative oasis compared to the rest of the expo. At the Evinrude dock she sees Roger Lyndon and instinctively ducks to avoid his radar. Too late—he's made eye contact and one bushy eyebrow has jumped. His voice isn't loud yet it carries his words like cargo on a barge. "Hey, hey, hey. Look who we have here! Miss RayAnne Dahl." Roger is surrounded by the usual interchangeable klatch of minions not yet fired, ready to trip over each other to fetch whatever Roger snaps his fingers at.

"Uncle Roger." It's what she has called him since she was five. Forget that the word *uncle* conjures protective or trustworthy. Roger is nobody's uncle; he's the Don Corleone of pro fishing—if a favor needs doing or a deal needs cutting, it's Uncle Roger one goes to. She feels his gaze ooze across her and somehow take in everything, front and back. RayAnne feels her confidence peel to the floor like some yellow skin to skid on with the next misstep. As he reaches for her, she steps squarely backwards and extends a hand for him to shake. He practically *tuts* and presses her hand aside to pull her into a cloying embrace, ripe with cigar smoke and Old Spice, snugging her too closely and for a beat too long, as if waiting for her to relax into the grip she's already wiggling from.

He lets go and sighs hugely, then smiles with his piano-key teeth. "I hear you're doing good things, RayAnne."

"Do you?" She waits for him to elaborate while stealing wary glances at his lackeys. "From who . . . um, whom?"

"Oh, you know, the old jungle drums, the trapline. So how's Kermit the Frog working out for you?"

"Kermit?"

"Your new boss—public tee-vee. I've heard you've gone over to the Obama Care Bear channel."

RayAnne looks up to the limp port-of-call flags on the fly deck of a massive fishing yacht called *Roger Dodger*. Such boats are only the heel of Roger's bread and butter; he also owns a franchise of fishing resorts called Pikers and three cable channels. He sponsors half a dozen pro sport programs, including *Whoppers* and his Everglades reality hit *Cast-A-Gator*, which features a trio of swamp-dwelling families, three brothers the obvious result of intermarriage. Most of their conversations require subtitles to be understood.

Behind his back, Roger is often referred to as Master Baiter.

"Well, Uncle Roger, I understand our numbers are pretty good."

"Is that so?" He looks at her as if she knows no such thing.

"So I guess Kermit's doing all right by me."

"Six figures, I trust? After all, you're fishing and what? Making girl chat?"

Six figures? "I pay my mortgage." *Girl chat?*

Gran would split a seam to hear such talk—it's so utterly tactless to ask about someone's means, unless of course they are in need. Simply, there are more important things to know about a person than how much they make. If she told Uncle Roger what the public television rate for freelancers was . . .

As if on cue, Roger flips the gold-tipped ivory toothpick he keeps stashed in his mouth and slowly telescopes it out between his teeth until it rests on his wet bottom lip. RayAnne is fastened to the procedure: when he starts talking again the toothpick becomes a tiny baton conducting his every word. "I see they got you driving some old sardine can of a boat twice your age—what's that about?"

"You mean *Penelope?* We're going for a bit of class." She inclines her head to the great fiberglass stern shadowing them. "Style instead of bling."

His mouth presses to a straight line, and for a second she's afraid he might pat her head like he used to. "Well, good on you, girl. You ever want to get back into the real deal, you see Uncle Roger when your contract runs out."

If she admitted she had no contract, he'd probably snort that toothpick right up into his brain, something she'd stick around to watch.

"Bye, Uncle Rodge." All four of the silent sidekicks watch her walk the length of the dock, the hair raised on her neck every step of the way.

. . .

Wielding a Sharpie, Cassi is drawing Snidely Whiplash mustaches on the models in the Mr. Northern Tool calendar. As RayAnne walks up, Cassi is just finishing up with November, who wields a wrench the size of a bat and whose overalls are peeled over his sculpted, grease-smudged torso nearly to his junk.

RayAnne drops her bag. "Mmm, more men."

Cassi looks up. "Do straight guys wax?"

"Models, maybe. I knew a straight guy who shaved his back with a razor duct-taped to a spatula. Don't ask me." RayAnne falls to her knees and digs under the table for her iPad. "I've gotta get out of here."

Cassi brightens. "Hey, wanna get some Thai?"

"Can't. I have a date."

"A what?" Cassi blinks like a doe.

"Don't look so surprised."

"Gawd, not with someone from here?"

"No. Just this guy I used to go out with—turns out he lives in Chicago, not far. Zack Cartman."

"Not *titty* Zack?"

RayAnne sighs. "Yes, titty Zach. He wasn't that bad."

"What time you want me to call in case you need an out?"

"Cassi, I think I can handle it."

RayAnne packs up and girds herself for the trip to the escalator. She's a few steps away before turning back. "Hey, you know of some musician named Al Borden . . . or Cal Herter?"

"Which, Borden or Herter? You've got a little something, strawberry seed maybe, chin."

"Naturally." RayAnne swipes it with her wrist. "I probably have the name wrong." She rarely gets a name right the first time unless she is determined to staple it to memory. If the person has to do with work or is some kind of professional connection, she can retain names like a camel—it's amazing the things she can remember about the women on the show when some days she can't recall what her breakfast has been, even when she's eaten two.

She can remember what Cal or Al or whoever was wearing, though—a blue Henley that strained nicely across his biceps, and gray jeans. And what he wasn't wearing—a ring. Remembering the glove brace, she frowns and wonders aloud, "What musical instrument can be played with one hand?"

Cassi offers, "Besides harmonica? A bongo? Dunno."

. . .

The restaurant is Italian, the lighting low, a very date-y sort of place. Zack is groomed and dressed to impress, wearing an expensive-looking sport coat over a whisper-soft crewneck, identical to one she'd gawked at the day before in the cashmere store. His nails shine, making her wonder if he's had a manicure. He goes for the double-handed grasp, pulling her close and planting a Euro kiss on each cheek. RayAnne looks down to confirm his jeans are indeed not merely ironed but creased. Some things never change.

Zack scans her approvingly, actually pausing at her cleavage before giving a thumbs-up.

Humor? She can't tell but is willing to give him the benefit of the doubt. He looks sort of . . . flawless. She shouldn't have worn the dress; it only makes her appear eager, and this is just dinner. In spite of herself, she feels a quivery little thrill. He had been a really great kisser.

They barely get the wine ordered before he's deep into describing his current work, developing prototype titanium hip and knee replacements and a start-up chain of clinics for the boomers whose joints will all start going to hell around the same time, if he has his way. "You get a crowd of over-fifties all working out? Boom! Spinning class or the 5K run? Joints popping like Orville Redenbacher, and I'll be there, handing out Z's Knees at a hundred K a pop."

"*Z's Knees,* is tha—"

"The brand. Like it? I'm working on the branding with an ad agency—in Minneapolis, in fact."

Reminded suddenly of his knack for commandeering a conversation, she glances at the digits on his watch so that she might time how long it will take before he asks a question directed toward her—about her. He's quite the talker, not boring exactly but definitely long-winded. When he shrugs off questions about his mother and brother, she just nods, remembering that he is his own favorite topic. She elbows in a question. "Zack, I always thought you'd end up practicing medicine or doing research?"

"Naw, hardware is the place to be. I had been working in robotic prosthetics, but when Iraq started winding down—and you *know* the next war is going to be cyber, or at least fought with more drones than combat troops, so there'll be a lot fewer limbs being blown off . . ."

She sets down her fork in the carnage of lasagna she's only half finished.

"Uh-oh, sorry. Anyway, robotic replacement limbs and running blades look like a dwindling market for now. So I'm moving on to corroded joints."

"Are you?"

Which only sets him off again—how he's funding his new venture by courting capital in Europe and China, where apparently his charm and language skills are winning over some big investors. RayAnne sighs. The entire day has had the oily theme of money about it. When the subject finally looks like it might fizzle, she makes a brief allusion to her own work, but the hint fails, so she plants her chin on her fist once again to stop herself from yawning widely. They've wrung the last drops from a bottle of Chianti. In his midtwenties, Zack had been a bit full of himself. Now, closer to forty, he's brimming over.

At the next sentence beginning with "And then I . . ." her

patience implodes and she interrupts. "So, Zack, you called me. Had you seen the show?"

"No, but my sister saw it. Said it wasn't actually too bad."

He hadn't even seen the show? She presses the water glass to her cheek. "Wine, always does this."

"So I recall, Pinky." He tops his comment with a wink. "And not just your face."

She excuses herself. In the bathroom stall she speed-dials Cassi, who answers on the first ring, not even bothering with hello. "Let me guess. You want me to call you with something dire?"

"Yup, but wait ten minutes; I just ordered the tiramisu."

4

.
.
.
.

RayAnne holds her backpack tight between her knees so it won't go flying again. Propped like a tripod on the bench seat of the golf cart, she keeps an eye on her elderly driver in case he swerves again or nods off. Mr. Delmonico is very tan, very wrinkled, and for some reason wearing only a Speedo and a half-buttoned Hawaiian shirt while driving RayAnne from the parking lot of Dune Cottage Village to her grandmother Dot's door. The lanes of the gated community are car-free, allowing only golf carts, Segways, and the mobility scooters her grandmother holds in such disdain, complaining, "Half those lard-asses don't even need them."

Dune Cottage Village is a concentric web of cedar-shake structures all canted toward the gulf, connected to the grassy beach by a number of handicap-accessible boardwalks. Dot chose the place because of its seaside location—"Knock that off my bucket list!"—and its golf course. The smell of lawn fertilizer and the sound of old men hollering "Fore!" were always fond reminders of her dearly departed Ted. Set farther inland beyond the golf course and across the main road are the rambling facilities of the Falls, where the view matters less because it's where most residents from the Dunes eventually go to die. They move back from the sea in increments, first to the assisted-living low-rise apartment building, then to either the memory care center or the nursing facility, and finally the hospice, which is farther back still, with its own driveway so that the hearses can come and go out of sight and more or less out of mind. For those in the cottages—Olympian by comparison—a move to the Falls means the beginning of the end. Or, as Dot says, "The skit before the one with the parrot." Here, the euphemism *crossing the road* needs no explanation.

Dot's little parking space is taken up by the three-wheeled bicycle she pedals to and from the farmers' market, the liquor store, and the beach, the trinity of destinations she claims hold everything she needs in life: a fresh mango, her fishmonger, a bottle of white, and a place to watch the sun set while the off-duty cadets jog.

Twin lemon trees mark Dot's front garden, the size of a carpet, where Mr. Delmonico's golf cart grinds to a halt and he shouts, "Here we are!" as if RayAnne is the deaf one. He jumps out and grabs a net sack of coconuts and bounds up the walk, smoothing his "hair" before ringing the bell. RayAnne wrestles her roller bag to the door just as it swings wide. Dot is aproned as usual, accessorized with a wooden spoon.

"Mr. D, how nice of you to drive her down! And there she is, my RayBee!"

She reaches for her just as Mr. Delmonico steps in so they all meet in an awkward crush with the bag of coconuts. RayAnne leans out of range of the wooden spoon dripping some sort of batter and manages to hug Dot, only abstractly registering that her grandmother's shoulders feel a little bony.

"Oh, thank you for these, Mr. D!" Dot hefts the bag of coconuts at RayAnne and winks. "I'm making a curry that'll burn both ways." To Mr. D she adds, "RayAnne is the one I was telling you about. She's a big television star!"

"Not quite, Gran."

Mr. D grins with teeth that are too small to be false. "Well, if she's anything like her grandmother, she's already a star! Now you call me if there's anything you ladies need. Dot. Miss Dahl. Both you Dahls."

"Thanks for the ride, Mr. Delmonico. It was nice to meet you."

"Call me Mr. D." He turns to Dot. "We'll see you tomorrow?"

"Six o'clock. Wear pants!"

"Wear *pants!*" All the way to his golf cart he keeps turning to chortle. "Wear pants!"

RayAnne is pulled inside with a tug that belies Dot's stature, so that Mr. D's third "Wear pants!" is muffled by the closed door.

"Jeez. What's he on, Gran?"

"Oh, Ensure and Cialis, I imagine. But that's just Dominic." She turns RayAnne by the shoulders and gives her the scan. "My, you're like a zipper! Well, we'll fatten you up."

"Gran. I'm not Gretel."

"Tcht. They better not be asking you to lose weight for that silly show. Men like a bit of ham with their grits."

"Producers don't."

Dot reaches out to cup one of RayAnne's breasts. "You didn't get the push-up gel bras I sent?"

She twists away. "I did. They make me look like a—"

"Trollop? That's the idea, dear. Turn around, let me see your hinder."

She's been in the house less than a minute. "No! Gran, can't you just say hello?" RayAnne tries to ignore Trinket, the frantic Pomeranian jumping at her kneecaps.

Dot forges ahead, pulling RayAnne's bag to the guest room.

"Gran, let me take that. Are Ky and the twins here?"

"The clones? I installed them all in the motel down the beach after those two springs tried microwaving Trinket."

"They didn't."

The dog pokes between her ankles like a duster. Dot picks up Trinket and nuzzles her nose to nose. "Oh, yes they did. Those monsters almost *cooked* Grandma's little angel, didn't they?" She sits on the ruffly bed, patting a spot for RayAnne to occupy. "In my day those two would have been on leashes."

"You might suggest that to Ky."

"I did. By the way, where is that mother of theirs?"

"Ingrid? Probably up to her ears in work right now."

"You'd think a bank teller could find time to mend her husband's jeans."

"She's a bank regulator, Gran, whole different story . . ." RayAnne looks at the wooden spoon, now somehow in her own hand. "And jeans are supposed to be ripped."

Dot is distracted by the dog licking her face. "But the little brutes are gone now, aren't they, Trinket? Smooches for Mama Dot?" She holds the dog out toward RayAnne. "Smooches?"

She can't help but notice that Dot, always a blur of motion, has begun slowing, at least enough to make her easier to track, because she only gets up and down from the table five times during lunch. After her last bite, Dot simply winds down and stops like a music box. Even so, it takes a little urging to get her to lie down for a nap. "You're almost eighty, Gran. Old ladies nap."

"Not when their only granddaughter comes to visit."

"What if I want a nap? We have a whole week." She escorts Dot to her room and folds her to sitting on the bed before prying her shoes off. Dot's eyelids are drooping as she hits the pillow. "Who's my pudgy-wudgy?"

RayAnne sighs. *No one will ever let me forget I was fat.* She tucks the afghan up to Dot's chin and kisses the tip of her nose. "I'm your pudgy-wudgy."

The snoring commences before the door is closed.

She unpacks her things into the open drawers of the guest room bureau, idly glancing at the painting hung above, the single object of great value her grandmother owns. It's a small still life of pitchers and bottles, kept out of sight in the guest room because Dot doesn't want to increase the insurance coverage on her home. RayAnne clearly remembers Big Rick scoffing, "Who the hell would steal something that looks like a retard painted it?" And while some might think it's no great shakes, RayAnne likes it very much. With its soothing lines, nearly monochromatic with no jarring colors, it's the sort of painting that might lower your blood pressure if you looked at it long enough. A few bottles, a flowerless vase, and a couple of squat vessels that could be salt cellars or mustard crocks. Disparate vessels congregated like a small party dressed in similar shades, quiet figures casting quiet shadows. Just right of the group was an earthenware pitcher that always made RayAnne think of Dot, a gleam on its lip as if to suggest a quip.

The provenance of the painting parallels a pivotal time in her grandmother's history—the years she studied cooking in Italy as a very young woman, a time RayAnne often begs Dot to talk about. If she's in an expansive mood, she sometimes will tell how she'd found the painting in Naples, just after the war, back when it was cheaper to study cooking in Europe. "I was quite pretty then," Dot will brag, "but Italians couldn't get their mouths around my name, so instead of Dorthea they called me Dortee." On her daily bike trip to her classes at the *Cucina Napoli,* she passed a tiny gallery, sometimes stopping to look at the little still life in the window. At first she thought it odd and amateurish, sometimes it seemed sweet and innocent, and other times it looked very somber—all depending on the hour of the day and in what light she passed by. After it disappeared from the window, she realized how much she had liked it and missed seeing it. She went in to ask if it had been sold and was relieved to learn it had only been shifted to hang on an inside wall. Dot had never had the slightest interest in owning a painting, and even at postwar prices it was well beyond her reach, signed by someone named Morandi.

FISHING! . . . . . .
72

"But I had some money saved, and the gallery owner saw I was a sucker for it, so he lowered the price by twenty thousand lire and talked me into buying it on installments. I can't honestly say why, but at the time I was willing to give up several months of trolley fares and Italian lessons and even a trip to Lake Como in order to make those payments. I wanted it that much."

RayAnne had looked up Giorgio Morandi, read about his life in Bologna as a recluse, which made sense, given the introverted quality of his art. Perhaps Dot was drawn to the composition in the manner that opposites attract—movement seeking stillness, a restful place to slow her restless gaze.

Dots recounts her time in Italy as a blur of colors and smells and ceaseless activity, each day a small adventure. Every time she tells the story of the painting, Dot adds different details. In some versions she regularly arose at dawn in order to make the long walk to her classes to save the trolley money; in others she bicycled the narrow streets. A conflicting version has her selling her bicycle to make three past-due installments. In any case, RayAnne never tires of the story because it is ever-changing, and because Dot's ramblings transport them both to the steep, ochre-hued lanes where she occupied a room in an ancient Neapolitan house with a tiled courtyard, staggered clay roofs, too many cats, and a tragic landlady who had lost two sons to the war and cursed Mussolini every night in her prayers. On the street side, the butter-yellow stone house opened onto rough travertine steps that were washed every morning and by afternoon shimmered, mirage-like, with the heat. From her room Dot could watch the sunrise tint the neighboring buildings slowly, from the chimney pots down. She had no clock in her room but could tell the hour by which lintel the sunbeam lit upon. The painting had a similar bit of such light, according to Dot, Italian light she could take back home with her to America.

She describes the alleys of Naples, thick with smells of yeast, too-ripe fruit, and olive mash from the presses, skeins of smoke trailing from hand-rolled cigarillos, the bitter tinges of roasting coffee beans and scorched milk. On her way to the *accademia*, Dot ducked under smelly garlands of anchovies strung to dry, dodged sausages curing like cudgels on heavy clotheslines. She portrays the place as the contents of an exotic pantry.

Lire intended for Italian lessons had gone to the painting, but no matter—informal lessons were to be had on the streets for the price of listening. She began to pick up words and phrases on various patios. In the early hours she navigated the lanes among delivery men, trash collectors, boys pushing handcarts stacked with newspapers and fish, dock laborers headed for the waterfront, women carrying braces of doves upside down by their feet.

"And the *puttane,* just getting off shift." Dot always looks pensive when describing them. "Not very tarted up, like you'd expect—more wholesome, like peasant girls just home from working the vineyards. Surprisingly chipper, considering they were whores." She boasts that during her long morning trudges in Napoli, she grew fluent in obscenities and probably broke some record for getting lewd propositions, which, thanks to her keen ear, she could turn down flat not only in Italian but Portuguese and Spanish as well. "I was a rather bold thing," Dot sighs to RayAnne, looking entirely wistful.

She had her share of marriage proposals too—one she eventually accepted. Nico had been a classmate. At first, Dortee believed herself to be in love with the young man, when actually she was in love with the way his neck sat on his shoulders. She also adored the quaint trattoria his family ran and his little dog, Eduardo. Dot and Nico eloped and were married all of eight weeks, during which time Nico's parents, sisters, aunts and uncles, family priest, neighbors, and landlord all railed relentlessly against the union. It was unthinkable that Nico, an only son, would marry a non-Catholic—and elope, at that. More unthinkable was that Dot was a foreigner, no matter that Americans were generally embraced after the war. What gleam the marriage had launched with quickly dulled under the family pressure, until the young couple almost gladly agreed to an annulment, freeing Nico to honor his prior engagement and marry his childhood sweetheart and cousin, Teresina. By the time Dot's own parents had time to react to the jolt of news that their nineteen-year-old daughter had married an Italian cook, it was time to send word home: *Disregard previous telegram. Stop.*

Dot was embarrassed but not crushed. "Nico," she had confided to RayAnne, "wasn't much of a lover—all jutting chin and piercing eyes, but not much else." Which suggested there might have been a size issue, though all Dot would ever offer was, "Put it this way, RayBee, I was practically a virgin on my *second* wedding night."

Dot considers her two years in Italy her one real adventure. "When I was so young, thinking I could do anything, live every moment. It was probably the last time I was truly brave."

RayAnne doubts that very much. Dot went on to marry Ted and must have roused plenty of bravery to get through the loss of their little daughter Betsy, who drowned in the pool of a country club where Dot was briefly the chef. Perhaps after that, Dot lived with less abandon, but she never wavered in her passion for feeding people. She'd worked decades in the restaurant business, opening a string of popular but short-lived establishments. While Dot was loved by her patrons and staff, she was admittedly a terrible businesswoman, rarely writing things down or keeping up on the tedious aspects like inventory and bookkeeping. She'd open a restaurant, fail, start over, and fail again. Finally, Dead Ted gave up his job managing a horse track and devoted his time to the business end of Dot's next venture. Together they finally nailed it and for twenty years ran a supper club near the track, Dorthea's. Dot always described the place as "swank" with a glimmer of pride.

RayAnne remembers Dorthea's deep tufted booths, low

lights, and lounge walls covered with framed photos of celebrities scrawled with accolades to Dot. Mr. Rondo, the maître d', was a former jockey, as were many of the waiters. The matchbooks were embossed with "Short on waiters, long on service." Bar drinks were named for horses, and the dining room featured framed silks worn in winning races. After Ted died, Dot lost heart for the business and sold, but never stopped cooking, usually as a volunteer at shelters, claiming it got her through her first years as a widow better than therapy ever could have. RayAnne might not understand how cooking could be therapeutic, but having been on the receiving end of Dot's talents, would argue that there isn't much Dot's cabbage and spring onion dumplings in chicken consommé cannot cure.

She dusts the frame of the Morandi with the sweaty sock she's peeled off. The painting may represent a wedge of her grandmother's history, but surely not the defining one. And as much as she has tried to take Dot's advice about her own direction, she's mostly just reminded of regrets and false starts. Working for Big Rick on the pro circuit began as a way to pay for college, but after getting lucky and taking a few trophies herself, she lost focus, and the circuit became a place to idle. "Fishing is a whole lot easier than deciding on a future," Dot would hound her. How could she be so clever yet be unable to find something to pursue beyond pro sport fishing? Simply, RayAnne could not imagine what she might be good at. The journalism degree had proved utterly useless: she graduated the precise moment print media began its slide. The idea of working behind the scenes in television news seemed appealing, but networks like Fox were demeaning the whole profession, and even good journalists were caving and going along with the song and dance. When RayAnne had realized the closest thing to fair and balanced on television was *The Daily Show*, she gave up on the whole thing entirely.

Of course she wants to do something fulfilling, contribute

something, like Dot has, like Bernadette does. She hopes *Fishing* might succeed but doesn't dare invest much hope in case she jinxes it.

Looking at the Morandi, RayAnne wonders if the act of creating the little painting made the artist happy, or if shy old Giorgio couldn't be happy until it was finished. Two very different things.

. . .

After changing clothes, she steps outside and squints, unaccustomed to the Florida sun, to walk the beach to Sunset Shore Motel where Kyle and the twins are staying. Looking at her bare feet, she's reminded of a story she'd read on the plane, in which a woman's sandaled heel was described as looking like a chunk of Parmesan.

She supposes it's too late to become a writer.

Next to a stomped sandcastle, her brother lies on a towel facedown, as if felled in his tracks. Before she can spot the twins, they tackle her from behind, each targeting a knee, so that she is first airborne, then tumbling backward over them. In an instant they are gone and she's splayed on the sand with the air knocked from her lungs.

Gasping for breath, she waits for the pain to subside. Kyle crawls over on hands and knees, his face looming into frame above her. "Welcome to my world."

When she tries to speak, only a wheeze comes out.

"That your best hello?" Kyle sniffs. "You're finally here and I *still* have no one to talk to." He rises to his knees and hollers over his shoulder, "Wilt Chamberlain Dahl! Michael Jordan Dahl! Get over here now and apologize to your Auntie Ray!"

Ky's wife, Ingrid, in a postoperative stupor after her Cesarean, had left the naming of the twins to Kyle: "Call 'em what you want, Ky. Just lemme sleep." Kyle, a sports historian and statistician, took her permission quite literally, so that Ingrid awoke to find her sons named for two philandering NBA All-Stars.

The boys shuffle near, each pushing the other forward. They mumble a tandem apology in their language and prepare to launch.

"Whoa!" Ky grabs waistbands before they can flee. "Sorry what?

"Sorree for knocking you down?" Their words emit in stereo.

"And . . . ?"

"Hurting you?"

"That's better." Kyle sits back on his heels and they bound away. RayAnne takes painful little gulps of air while he explains. "New strategy: make them at least acknowledge what they've done. Never stops them from doing it again, but at least I can tell Ingrid I've tried." He topples to the sand next to her. "Don't have children . . . better yet, take one of these and raise it in captivity."

RayAnne is able to prop onto her elbows. "I think I'm okay. Don't kill yourself helping me up."

They spread out a blanket and drink the two warm beers Ray-Anne found in Dot's pantry, watching from afar as the boys tear up the beach.

Kyle scratches his chin. "This trip, their goal is to see which of them can get Trinket's entire head in his mouth."

"Nice. Hey, does Gran seem okay to you?"

"Why?"

"I dunno. I mean I've only been here a few hours, but . . ."

"She's maybe a little slower," Kyle says. "She is eighty." He nods to where the twins are crouched and digging like terriers, sand spewing in bursts from between their legs. "Hey, would you mind watching them for a half hour? I'd kill for a run."

"Go ahead." She's barely answered before he's up and jogging away.

The twins are ginger-blond, lanky miniatures of Ky. RayAnne edges closer, trying to tell which is which. They construct an elaborate maze of sand trenches and driftwood trestles, a labyrinth where their plastic muscle-bound action figures stalk and kill each other in a game with convoluted rules impossible to keep straight. Unless they want something, they are mostly oblivious to her, which she supposes is the way of twins; she would ignore her too if she had a second self to play with. Aside from slathering them with sunscreen and reminding them to drink from their squidgy water bottles, she doesn't do much besides ask if either has to pee. Both look to the surf, then back to her, shrugging.

RayAnne needs to go herself; of course she hadn't thought of that before Ky left. She takes each boy by the hand and steers them to the public toilet, but outside the door marked Women they both halt, digging their heels in like spades. "We're not *women*."

"No. You are not," RayAnne concedes and starts looking around, almost as if there might be some enclosure or pen or something she might tie them to, thinking Dot's suggestion of leashes not so far-fetched. What do parents do? She covers the *w* and *o* on the sign with her hand. "See? It says men." But they don't fall for it. She tries nudging them closer to the door as a mom with a little boy joins the queue.

RayAnne really has to pee. "C'mon guys, please."

The woman with the boy taps her arm. "I can watch yours, if you'll watch mine?"

"Thank you." RayAnne takes a step.

"Stranger danger!" Wilt (maybe Michael) yells, crossing his arms. Three teenage girls and another mother step into line.

"Fine, then you two stay here and watch each other." She winks at the mother with the little boy. "I'll be right out." She's practically hopping. They are at the front of the line now and the door will open after the next flush.

"Dad wouldn't like it if you left us alone."

"We'd have to tell him . . ."

". . . unless you bought us ice cream."

RayAnne blinks at them, speechless. Just then the door yawns opens and a girl edges past, revealing the empty bathroom. Before the boys have a chance to resist she scoops them both up, surprised at her strength, and lugs them in while they holler as if she's dragging them through flames. Before the door bumps shut she hears the woman in line tsk, "Nannies."

After three riotous minutes in the bathroom there is a ten-minute negotiation at the concession stand. Back on the beach, RayAnne waits for the twins to finish their ice cream sandwiches so she can lick the wrappers. Far down the horizon, Kyle appears as a far bobbing speck, growing closer. She squints to blur his image until he reaches the blanket.

Huffing, he peels off his T-shirt and wipes his face with it. "Anybody bleeding?"

"Not yet. That's quite a half hour you took there."

"I owe you one." Ky falls to the blanket.

"They're so cute. But so rotten."

"And are cute precisely because they are rotten, Ray. They have to be, because—"

"This one of your theories?"

"—because if they weren't cute, you'd leave them right there on the floor of Walmart when they have surround-sound tantrums because you won't buy them fucking Skittles. They're cute so that you don't hurl them from the car window after they've dug shit from their Pampers and mashed it into each other's ears and every nook and cranny of their car seats."

"C'mon. It's not that bad?"

"They are cute for the same reasons teenage boys have constant boners and women your age go batshit racing the baby clock. They are absolute proof of evolution: biology tricks us into having sex to make the little bastards, then nature makes them cute to trick us into raising them until they aren't so cute and can fend for themselves."

RayAnne does her best Alistair Cooke: "And that, according to Kyle Edward Dahl, is how our species perpetuates."

"Laugh now. See?" He points to a couple of old guys strutting near where a pair of women sit basting themselves with suntan oil. "Even those old farts are still trying to get some."

"Eew. You're right, they're cruising. And so tan! Like . . ."

"Bacon?" Kyle offers.

"Hey, isn't that Mr. Delmonico?"

"Mr. D? Nah, they all look alike. But I'm pretty sure the old toad's been doing Gran."

"Doing? Ky, that's too gross."

"I swear. He was at her place when we got there, looking all cat-who-got-the-canary. Did you know these geezers get their Levitra prescriptions paid for by Medicare?" Ky nods toward the old men. "They're probably getting more than I am."

"Hey. Don't expect much sympathy from me."

"Right. Lemme guess, no Frankenmen are knocking down your door so they can get their dirty shorts aired on public television?" Kyle ducks to deflect her swat.

The boys are within earshot, so RayAnne only signs a speedy "fuck off" in American Sign Language. ASL was how she and Ky used to communicate over the dinner table or in the car with their quarreling parents. The ASL drove Bernadette mental, even though she'd been the one to insist they attend the Waldorf school. Big Rick assumed they only pretend-signed so would cast his own hand gestures at their "chats."

"It's late. I promised Gran I'd help with dinner. You coming over?"

The twins approach, tugging at the crotches of their swim trunks.

"Nope. I'm hauling the monsters back to the motel, then it's Booger King for us. Right, boys? What's the matter now?"

"We got sand . . . ," Wilt begins, ". . . on our festivals," Michael finishes. They both pull down their swim trunks, swiveling to show RayAnne. "See?"

. . .

While Dot carefully pours in a thread of walnut oil, RayAnne whisks the egg yolks. She has no idea what they are making, only that it's going to be good, because there is thick cream in the bowl along with whatever else Dot slips like mickeys into her dishes. Dot will defend her choice of ingredients insisting, as vehemently as NRA supporters claim guns don't kill people, that butter never killed any of her patrons.

Dot suddenly stops humming and turns to her. "You can seduce a man with food. Believe me—I've done it."

"Gran, you admit that?" She whispers to the eggs, "Trust me, I'm not that desperate."

"Still, it wouldn't kill you to learn to cook. I'm just saying. It's a pity, lovely girl like you. Is there . . . something? You can tell me, you know."

"Something? Like what, Gran?"

"Oh," Dot shrugs. "You know, lesbianism . . ."

"Gran."

"Don't look at me like that. It'd be fine with me if you decide to go gay." Dot has promised RayAnne that once the eggs are beaten she can grate the nutmeg. "I mean, better an Ellen than nothing, right? Are you going to leave your hair like that?"

Mr. D and his grandson, who just happens to be RayAnne's age and single, are coming for dinner. She's been set up. A timer dings and Dot bends to peer in the oven window. She snaps her fingers and says in a conspiratorial whisper, "Hand me those mitts."

RayAnne whispers back, "Gran, are we baking a man trap?"

"Don't be silly. This is for us."

. . .

Dot's cottage is one of the less expensive ones, set back nearer the gates with only a narrow slice of ocean view, but if they push their lounge chairs together on the deck and fuse their temples, they can both watch the waves. Earlier, Dot had pointed out the larger cottages with wide vistas, envy in her voice when describing the kitchens: "Viking ranges and marble counters, wasted on these old farts, that's for sure."

"They don't cook?" RayAnne is surprised. Dune Cottage is known for attracting retirees from the business—restaurateurs, many chefs among them.

"Ha. Old stove jockeys? Last thing they want to do is cook. That lane is mostly widowers; a few others have wives circling the drain over at the Falls. Tony Vecchio lives in that one. He can't so much as look at spaghetti anymore. Howie Gelber went vegetarian the moment his steak house closed."

"Who's hotter?"

"Howie has a Sub-Zero. But Tony has a marble counter, which really is the best for rolling pastry."

Does her grandmother intend to cook her way into an ocean-view kitchen with six gas jets and a pastry slab? "You don't really believe the way to a man's heart is through his stomach?"

"Goodness no. There're other routes," she laughs. "I s'pose I could make a Sacher torte with some of that, whatsit? Viagra?"

"Uh, Gran, do you know what priapism is?"

"What?"

"A condition where erections last several hours. That's what those can drugs do."

"Good heavens. Really?"

Trinket taps her polished nails across the linoleum to growl at her empty food dish.

Dot blinks. "Just a minute, Princess, I'll make your liver toast." Turning to RayAnne she asks, "Hours?"

.   .   .

The dinner is endless. Mr. D's grandson, Allen, is a chiropractor with a monobrow and seems as happy about being set up as she is. RayAnne admits she's never been to an MMA match. "Which is what, again?"

"Cage fighting." Allen admits he's never liked fishing. Ray-Anne asks if he has read anything interesting lately. He looks at her suspiciously. "Like books?"

Once it's determined they have the opposite of attraction, they proceed to ignore each other and leave the talking to Dot and Mr. D. At one point when both men are looking away, Ray-Anne mimes slashing her own wrists and Dot mouths, *Stop it.*

When the main course is finally finished, RayAnne begins to get up to make coffee, but Dot kicks her ankle out from under her. "Now don't you kids move a muscle."

Mr. D stands. "Allen, you should tell RayAnne about the home theater you're building."

Allen looks at her and then his father. "Right."

RayAnne at least tries. "Oh, where you'll watch, what . . . besides cage fighting?"

"NASCAR." He brightens. "You like NASCAR?"

Mr. D collects plates and they are left alone. Not a peep comes from the kitchen. They are obviously behind the swinging doors, straining to hear anything RayAnne and Allen might say to each other. Allen stretches his legs to reveal his ankles and RayAnne smiles, thinking at least he's not a complete wash, somewhat redeemed for wearing Homer Simpson novelty socks.

Dot calls from the kitchen, "We've made a surprise dessert."

RayAnne sits up. "Baked Alaska, I bet."

Allen inhales. "Yup."

To atone for her two servings of dessert, the next morning Ray-Anne hits the treadmill early. When Dot shuffles out to the deck, she's rubbing her eyes. "I heard grunting."

"Just . . . another . . . ten . . . minutes." RayAnne blots sweat from her eyes.

Dot sits on the lounger and shakes her head. "Your generation is supposed to be the one to fix things, so smart, coming up with all that technology, yet . . ."

"Yet what?"

"Here you are killing yourself over a few calories, ready to fall into that ridiculous trap and go around looking like all the other women on television. Why can't you just deal with the fact you have hips, dear? If you do, then maybe the next young woman in your shoes will see that it's okay."

Sometimes Dot makes ultimate sense in maddening ways. RayAnne stops the treadmill and hops off, panting. "So I should get fat and become a role model?"

"No, just don't get skinny. By the way, you were rude last night."

"Maybe. But you ambushed me, Gran. Why're you suddenly trying to marry me off?"

"I only want to see you happy."

"Married or happy? You assume they go hand in hand."

"I suppose I do," Dot says wistfully. "Maybe because my marriage was happy. The second one anyway. I miss Ted, you know . . . still."

RayAnne sits and pulls Dot into a damp hug, "Oh, Gran. Granny-Gran? You're crying."

"I'm not. My eyes are watering. You smell like a man's tennis shoe."

. . .

In the afternoons, RayAnne sits under a palm tree for hours, struggling to concentrate on the book in her lap, rereading pages. She watches the surf retreat and repeat, the bright sun scouring her brain until it feels hollow as a shell. Even in the shade, her body feels limp, as if caramelizing. When she complains about the Florida sun, Ky reminds her it is the Sunshine State, after all, with a warning on every license plate like the surgeon general's warning on cigarette packs. They pull their deck chairs deeper into the cover of broad palms and RayAnne wishes for one of

Bernadette's caftans so she might walk the beach without her back freckling up like a trout.

She rolls to her elbows. "When's Dad due to show?"

"Day before the party. I've got his flight in my BlackBerry." Kyle is silent a minute. "Remember that party he planned for you at that upscale restaurant? Was it Jax's, with the trout pond?"

"Sweet sixteen. Gawd, that dress he got me at the Oval Room, with the pom-pom sleeves?"

"I just remember the front—the Hostess Cupcake Sno Ball boobs. What happened with him that time?"

RayAnne shrugs. "He had more important things to do, like fly to Vegas to elope with . . . which was it, number three?"

"Delia."

"Right, the *d* in BADGER." She rolls back over.

"What?"

"BADGER. Ask Dad when he gets here."

⋅ ⋅ ⋅

Florida is perfect for old people who never seem warm enough. In the evenings, just as the temperature becomes bearable, Dot wraps up in a puffy quilted robe and shivers through the ten o'clock news. On the deck RayAnne looks to the sky and says, "Nothing. For four days I've done nothing."

Dot, suddenly behind her, corrects, "No, you've just not accomplished anything."

"Thanks, Gran."

"Oh, you know what I mean. You're just doing what people do on vacation." Which has amounted to slogging the beach with Kyle, watching the boys, playing Scrabble with Dot on the patio, and eating like a pig while wishing with every bite that she had the metabolism of a hamster. Size *six*?

5

. . . .

Dot's feet are in RayAnne's lap. The nail polish is Posy Pink.

"Gran, you have to hold still."

"But this is so exciting!"

"You act like you've never seen it."

The television is pulled close, and the DVD of the Ida Lott episode is cued up, the first segment RayAnne hosted.

"Oh, pish. You don't look all that nervous."

"I had to wash down a beta blocker with a coffee mug of chardonnay to get through it."

Dot wriggles again.

"Now look what you've made me do!" RayAnne gets the nail polish remover and a cotton ball to clean the smudge across Dot's big toe.

Beginner's luck had been on her side. Ida Lott turned out to be funny and approachable, a chatty grandmother in her early seventies. She could even fish. RayAnne did not have to scramble to fill time or even ask many questions. On land, Ida walked with two canes, having lost half of her toes to frostbite during her ordeal, but seated in the boat you wouldn't know.

Ida cast a line while explaining. "I was on my way to visit my daughter's family when the storm hit. I did just the wrong thing, pulled off the highway to a lesser road because I saw a red blinking light, thinking it might be a plow or police car, but it was only a rail crossing signal. I didn't get much farther before sliding into the ditch."

"Were you frightened?"

"Not right away. I was too busy. While the engine was still running I had to keep getting out to clear the tailpipe. That's when my shoes got soaked. I had snow for water, so that was no problem. I knew I could do without food. But the cold . . ."

"What did you think about?"

"Besides ways to keep from freezing, I thought about life. Mine. What it had meant. I wanted my little grandsons to grow up having something of me—they were too young to even have many memories at the time. So on the second day, thinking about the worst case, I began to write out all the best stories I had."

"Yes," RayAnne leaned in. "I loved the one of how you met your husband while bowling?"

Ida had a twinkly laugh. "I threw such a gutter ball it hit Robert's pins, two lanes over. It was a strike!"

Growing serious, RayAnne urged her on. "But there's so much more than just personal history and anecdotes in this book."

"Yes, the Life 101 chapters. I felt I might impart some wisdom to my grandkids, like how to navigate the rough bits, in case they ever got bullied or felt somehow less than. And in later chapters, I try to address the teen years, you know, teenaged angst?"

"Yup," RayAnne nodded. "I know it."

"So much can go wrong. There were things I felt they should believe for themselves, in case I wasn't around to remind them. I also wanted them to know what I would have wished for them in case I—"

"In case you'd died in that car?"

"Yes. I wanted them to be themselves, love themselves no matter what, handsome or pimply, gay or straight, skinny or fat. Or just odd."

RayAnne leaned in. "To me those were the most touching passages in the book, when you're directly addressing the boys."

"Well, I wanted to prepare them to be, to be . . ."

"Human beings?" RayAnne offered.

"Exactly! And maybe they'll be parents themselves one day too, but I guess there's no way of preparing anyone for that. I needed to leave them something."

RayAnne turned to the second camera and held up a fat stack of jagged-edged brown pages bound together with rubber bands, covered edge to edge with cramped writing. "And this is what Ida originally submitted to her editor."

The camera panned to Ida. "Of course I have a computer file now, but I wanted your audience to see the actual manuscript—I had a stack of grocery bags in the trunk. I tore them into two hundred pages. I wrote until my hands went numb or the pen froze up or I had to tuck my fingers into my armpits to thaw."

RayAnne held up the ratty bundle next to the actual published book, *Five Days on a Chiclet*—its brown paper cover cleverly similar.

"So you had two pens, some water, and one piece of gum?"

"Which I decided I would only chew after officially giving up. And I almost did after realizing how bad my feet were."

"When you started to think about dying?"

"Yes, I wrote my will that morning. It was getting colder."

"And did you finally chew the Chiclet?"

"No." Ida pulled a thin gold chain out from the collar of her cardigan and the camera zoomed in to show a dainty crystal case with the red Chiclet inside.

"This piece of gum saved my life. Each time I felt I might give up, it reminded me to fight."

"How did you?"

"Well, RayAnne, when it got really bad, it seemed to come down to a choice." Ida shrugged as if it were no biggie. "I chose life."

As the credits roll, RayAnne caps the bottle of nail polish. If only all the guests were as well-spoken or interesting as Ida. She blows on Dot's toes. "Ta-da!" She looks up and is shocked to see tears streaming down Dot's cheeks. The second time in two days.

"Gran?"

Dot knuckles away a tear. "I'm just . . . so proud of you."

. . .

Friday is cloudy and cooler. Bad weather, according to a shivering Dot, but a wish granted to RayAnne—the reprieve from the Florida sun doubly welcome, having rendered the beach mercifully clear of sunbathers. After her beach walk, she borrows Ky's rental car and drives Dot to the mall. Neither likes clothes shopping much, but Dot has a good eye and wastes little time. Indeed, at the very first rack in the boutique, she zeroes in on a simple tunic and matching lounge pants in charcoal linen that look boring on the hanger but quite elegant when Dot sashays out of the fitting room in them. Inside of ten minutes she has a lovely scarf and a pair of open-weave flats.

Pleased with themselves, they natter happily right up to the moment the clerk begins ringing up the purchase, when RayAnne slides her Visa card across the counter, intending the outfit to be her birthday gift to Dot.

"You will not."

"Yes, I will, Gran."

"Not." Dot raises her voice.

"But I want to."

Dot tries pulling the outfit from the counter. "Then at least let me pick something from the sale rack."

RayAnne holds fast, laughing. "No! Let go."

"Now don't be such, such a . . . pissant."

"What does that even mean?" RayAnne frowns. "Gran. I have a real job now. I get a paycheck twice a month."

Dot sniffs. "Tcht. For something I'll wear once."

"No. You'll be able to wear this over and over. Anytime."

Dot relents but won't look at her while the clerk wraps everything in tissue, making a great show of nesting the garments in two very fancy shopping bags, taking her time until Dot snaps, "This isn't a tea ceremony!"

RayAnne and the clerk exchange looks. She's never known Dot to be rude, or even impatient, but most of the last week she has been—impatient and a little cranky. Maybe the moodiness is birthday-party jitters, because while Dot loves to fuss over others, she hates any fuss being made over her. And having visitors, RayAnne suspects, is much more strenuous than Dot will admit. Just looking at the twins seems to exhaust her.

At the hairdresser, Dot will neither sit nor accept an offer of iced tea until RayAnne promises to keep her credit cards in her purse and fetch her a glass of water.

"Fine. Cross my heart. What's that you're taking?"

"My calcium pill."

After rummaging Dot's scalp, the stylist declares, "You shouldn't perm—you already have a natural wave." They are able to talk her out of a do and into trimming off the treated hair. "A pixie is what you need."

Dot sighs. "Do what you must." By the time her hair is snipped, dried, and styled, she's herself again, if a little droopy. Turning her head this way and that in the mirror, she concedes, "Well, it's not too terrible, is it?"

All the stylists agree Dot is "just darling" and send her off with a jar of product and a tutorial on how to obtain texture and a tousled look with only a half hour of toil.

∘ ∘ ∘

Big Rick hasn't called, but Dot pretends not to care. He is not mentioned until Thursday, Dot's informal birthday dinner. They all wait for the doorbell, his absence all the more conspicuous for his empty chair and untouched place setting. The twins pivot to Ky, frowning in tandem. "You said Grandpa Rick would be here."

Dot continues to cut her meal into tiny pieces without eating any of them. "RayAnne, would you mind clearing your father's plate?"

She obliges, then slides his chair away and shifts the cake over to cover Big Rick's empty spot. All the while slyly watching Dot, having suspected all week that she's been feeding Trinket food from her own plate to make it seem like she's eating more than she is. Sometimes Dot drops food directly from her fork to the space between her feet; other times she pretends to chew and swallow, then sneaks the food into her napkin.

Dot's been told she's not allowed to cook for her own party, which is a potluck, but she still insists on making just a "few little things": cannelloni, a panettone, and French jam tarts. From her apron she pulls out a list of twenty grocery items, alphabetized beginning with anise, ending with Worcestershire, and hands it to RayAnne. "You asked if I needed anything?"

"Right." RayAnne scans the list. "I *was* going to walk."

"Take my trike; the basket holds loads."

"Sure this is all, Gran? Nothing else you want?"

Dot smiles sweetly and lays a floury hand over RayAnne's. "Just to be a great-grandmother, sweetheart."

"You already are!"

"Puh." Dot waves her out the door.

Navigating the lanes of Dune Cottage Village can be tricky. Most residents are either hearing impaired, vision impaired, lead footed, or all three. Because every corner poses a potential ca-lamity, golf carts and mobility scooters are fitted with computer sensors that warn of approaching vehicles, also triggering a light to blink at the corners, where a digital Model T *ahOOOga* sounds loud enough for the deafest of the deaf. After nearly being clipped by a Segway driven by someone who looked a lot like Rumpole of the Bailey but turned out only to be a matron wearing perm rods and a purple housecoat, RayAnne pedals cautiously toward the intersections, ready to cover her ears.

Nearing the gatehouse parking lot, she spots Ky restraining Wilt by one arm. "No more calling her Grandma Dotty. Do you hear?"

"But you do!"

"Never mind what I do. Where's your brother?"

Wilt points to the entrance, where Michael Jordan is peeing into the fountain, mimicking the arc of the water spewing from the mouth of the bronze frog.

"Jesus Christ Almighty."

"Jesus *fucking* Christ Almighty, Daddy," Wilt corrects him.

RayAnne is almost upon them before Ky sees her. "Finally, a Human Being."

It's something they've called each other since grade school. During the peak year of their parents' battles and the divorce, *Little Big Man* wasn't just a film—it was their alternate universe. Letters to Santa could have been a props list for a Western. Luckily, Big Rick's absentee-parent guilt was so great he filled their toy boxes and closets with enough arrows, feathers, suede fringe, tom-toms, tomahawks, and striped blankets to outfit an entire tribe of Human Beings. RayAnne wore moccasins and braids to school for the duration of eighth grade. Their tents and make-shift teepees were their territories, too small and inconvenient for their father to wriggle into when he would suddenly show up at the house all hugs and whiskey cheer during custody visits. Kyle and RayAnne stubbornly played on their own, backs turned on Big Rick, who would pout until they reluctantly cast him as their Custer, a role for which he was unintentionally perfect, griping just like the general when they refused to follow his orders or play his way. The few times they allowed him to be an Indian, he was always named Talks Big.

After the divorce Big Rick bought a place of his own, a suburban townhouse furnished like a hotel, down to the wall art. Suddenly, he had legal custody for full weekends, and RayAnne and Kyle were dragged from school Friday afternoons to Apple Valley. They hated his suburb of culs-de-sac with no sidewalks or stores to walk to, no trees large enough to climb. The visitations spanned infinity, with only the portal of the television screen and *Little Big Man* on the VCR for escape. When not watching Jack Crabb croak out his story, they played tricks on Big Rick, creeping silently along his colorless carpet to rearrange the contents of his desk drawers, his files, the kitchen cupboards, medicine chest, toolbox, closet, the trunk of his car. They shuffled sections of his Sunday paper and refolded it to appear unread. In their boredom they concocted a dozen ways to irk him. Too late, Ray-Anne realized the annoyance they incited only triggered an inclination to drink more.

They avoided any references to his drinking after Ky's badly aimed suction-cup arrow hit Big Rick's highball glass, spilling it into his lap. Ky defended himself by saying Big Rick drank too much anyway. Kyle was punished for his back talk by being made to stand out on the cold deck while RayAnne and Big Rick ate Chinese takeout from Ky's favorite restaurant. His portions were set in plain sight of the window and later given to the dog while he watched. He'd been sent to bed with nothing to eat save the cold eggroll and two fortune cookies RayAnne was able to squirrel into her pockets.

They were barely civil to Big Rick's girlfriends and definitely not PC, referring to their visits as "casting calls" and dubbing them with names like False Claw for the one with fake nails, or Perch Face, whose eyes were set wide like Jackie O's. Brown Root was a bottle blond, and Swamp Lash was prone to leaky tears.

Less than six months after the divorce, their father began marrying such women, one after another.

Kyle and RayAnne eventually grew out of their *Little Big Man* phase, and the headdresses and chamois leggings and bows were shunted upstairs to the attic. But even now, the first question they pose to each other after they have dated or befriended someone new is "Are they a Human Being?" It's a question that nearly always gives RayAnne pause.

Ky has a pleading look. "I was coming over to ask if you'd watch them for like twenty minutes."

"Another run?" The boys begin circling the trike.

"I just wanna talk to Ingrid, uninterrupted . . ." He glances at a text on his phone. "She's between flights at LaGuardia."

"Why not. I'm surrounded anyway."

Ky walks back to the fountain, phone to his ear. RayAnne lets the boys climb into the cargo well in the back and proceeds to struggle to wheel them around the parking lot. After three times around she's red and sweating but at least has burnt off a few of the morning's French toast calories.

By the time she returns to the cottage with the groceries, Dot is fast asleep in her lounger wearing an oven mitt.

. . .

The hours before the party are humid, and RayAnne feels sticky before her dress is even zipped. As the house begins to fill, it grows even warmer, so that after each round circling with her tray of crudités, she stands in front of the open fridge. Each time the doorbell rings and it is not Big Rick, she flushes another degree. He hasn't even called with an excuse.

Dot looks sweet in her new outfit, which she's elegantly topped off with a rope of tied pearls. When complimented on her melon-colored silk scarf, she quips, "When I'm old I shall not wear purple. Ever."

"Gran, you look beautiful." RayAnne fluffs Dot's pixie.

"With this bird wattle? I'm prehistoric."

"Eighty isn't that old."

"If you say eighty is the new sixty, I'll smack you. I'm so old"—she nods at the iPhone RayAnne is clutching, her fingers itching to speed-dial Big Rick's number—"that when I was a girl and needed to talk to someone, I had to get on a horse." This claim is actually true. Dot was raised in rural Wisconsin on an orchard she called "Apple-achia."

Looking around, RayAnne sees two dozen bobbing gray heads, their cumulative years of life on Earth numbering in the thousands. Many are Dot's neighbors; a few are friends.

Others are fellow volunteers from the shelter where Dot cooks on Thursdays—they brag that Dot packs the center with over-flow diners with her gnocchi in marinara and crusty baguettes. On her day to cook, certain suspiciously un-homeless-looking men shuffle from the direction of the marina still wearing their Ferragamo loafers, Breitling watches shoved out of sight up their sleeves. But Dot serves them anyway, then serves up her donation box, sweetly suggesting they part with bills of large denominations.

A retired butcher, Sid, corners RayAnne and urges her to al-ways buy kosher—it doesn't matter if she's Jewish or not. She promises, if only to stop him describing the correct and incorrect methods of slaughtering a chicken. "Even halal, sweetheart, just promise you won't buy any of that filthy Tyson or Perdue crap. And don't get me started on the ground beef. Pink slime." He winks.

Old Mrs. Cruz and even older half-blind Mr. Cruz were pas-try chefs "when God was a boy" and have baked a lopsided cake decorated with icing roses that look as if they were pitched from a distance. The frosting letters are piped in a telltale Parkinson's hand: Haffy Birtnday DoT.

Not all the party guests are old. Later arrivals include young vendors from the open-air market where Dot gets her produce and fish, a gay couple RayAnne recognizes from the beach, and the guy from the fish taco truck Pescado Loco. Looking at the gathering, it registers that nearly all Dot's guests either grow, produce, or serve some manner of food: the turkey sausage lady, the pair of citrus farmers, the chocolatier and her shrimper husband, and the many retirees who worked in the business. RayAnne has to smile. Dot's social circle could staff some great prep kitchen serving the commonweal of the table. The past is the last harvest, the present is what's in season, and the future is the next meal. Simple.

Mr. D seems to be hosting the event, which is fine with RayAnne and Kyle, who is happy to "let someone who speaks codger answer the door." Dot tries to fuss over her guests, but no one will have it, making her sit as if she's holding court, insisting she open their presents as they arrive. Most congregate at the buffet table, where there is more food than can possibly be eaten, but Dot has had the foresight to provide little takeout containers, which no one seems shy about loading.

Kyle serves drinks alongside one of the tanned cruisers from the beach, a former bartender who cleverly fashions a tiara from bent straws and swizzle sticks for Dot, tickling her to her core when she's crowned with it. The twins are nearly behaving, having been repeatedly warned they will lose the Xbox Kyle was forced to buy them so he can threaten to take it away.

Ky and RayAnne light the eighty candles, the song gets sung, and Dot gets lots of help blowing out the candles from Mr. D, seemingly plastered to her side.

The door opens, then slams. RayAnne hears Big Rick's booming voice before she sees him. He's made it after all—barely, just as the party is beginning to wind down and the early-to-bed crowd have started shaking their pill dispensers and poking themselves into cardigans. Those who had indulged had been slightly loopy after one cocktail and smashed after two. One fellow on his way to the bathroom got a funny look on his face and wondered aloud to RayAnne, "Was that audible?" She stepped quickly out of his range.

Big Rick is toting a giant stuffed giraffe, as if he's passed through some carnival on his way from the airport. RayAnne watches from behind the louvered kitchen door as he makes a big deal of giving his mother this ridiculous present.

She slips out the sliding doors to the deck. For a while the party will be his. Big Rick's presence demands that kind of attention, and she'd rather not watch people fall under his thrall—what Bernadette calls "the Ponzi." His charm is always most effective on those who don't yet know him. RayAnne can only hope he remembers that it is Dot's night.

She can avoid him only so long, and eventually he spots her through the sliding glass doors and sets down the squirming twins he's been holding like two footballs, shouting, "Hey, Baby Ray!" He sweeps his big paw to motion her in. When she doesn't, he makes his way outside. Before he can speak, she holds up a hand. "Some timing, Dad. You were supposed to be here yesterday."

"My flight was canceled."

"Was it? Gran was expecting you. She even made you beef Wellington."

"That steak baked in a crust?"

"Yeah. It was amazing. Ky gave yours to Trinket."

"C'mon, RayAnne, I just got here."

"And I'm leaving bright and early, so that works out kinda perfect."

She is so used to his broken promises by now they shouldn't come as any surprise. There'd been countless no-shows besides her sixteenth birthday. Her tonsillectomy, piano recitals, school plays, and the track meets where she'd be the only girl without a parent cheering at the finish line—her mother too busy "questing" and Big Rick missing in action as usual. Years later, out on the circuit, where she'd set out to prove herself in a place where he'd have to take note, he was nearly as elusive; even during the photo ops during which she'd be given the trophy or handed the check, he'd usually already have sidled off into the marina bar or lodge lounge, depending where they were, to "celebrate." It's one thing to stand her up—she can take it. But Gran?

"Your mother, in case you hadn't noticed, turned eighty yesterday. And you're just now showing up?"

Big Rick breaks from her glare. "RayBee, my flight was canceled; you can call the airline. I was on the first one out this morning, then I had to wait for a rental car . . ."

"Whatever, Dad."

"Cross my heart."

"If you can find it."

She leaves him on the deck and retreats to the bar, which is really just a credenza pulled far enough away from the wall so Kyle can stand behind it and mix drinks. She pours her own gin, adding ice and tonic like afterthoughts. Kyle plunks in a garnish of lime, lamenting, "I wouldn't mind getting shitfaced myself, but Gran says I can only drink beer while on duty."

"For the best. Gin just makes you more idiotic."

"And makes you a gnarly pissant."

"Do you know I have been called that twice in two days?"

"It's a Dot-ism. The boys think she's made up nicknames for them, Piss and Ant."

Dot sidles up and asks for a glass of ice she doesn't need and pulls RayAnne through the door into the kitchen, scolding, "Ray-Anne, I heard you."

"Heard what?"

"You can be awfully hard on your father."

"And you can be awfully soft."

"Our expectations are different. Mine are low, so—"

"So you're rarely disappointed, I know. You forgive him *every*thing."

Dot looks at her hard. "It's what parents do." She steers Ray-Anne out to the deck and takes a deep draught of air. "Besides, he left a voice mail. I got it before bed last night."

"Why didn't you say?"

She points to the ocean, rippled with moonlight. "Remember when you stayed with me summers and we'd watch the sun rise?"

"Yeah . . ."

"You were a neurotic little thing then too. Waking me at all hours like that."

"Neurotic?"

"Okay, a worrywart, or ACDC, or whatever it is you are." Dot wraps her arm around RayAnne's waist and they look out over the surf with their heads together.

"Whatever I am," RayAnne concedes, "I miss you already, Gran. Maybe I should stay a day or two longer."

"Don't be silly. You've been hiding out here long enough. You have an important job now. Aren't they sending you to that lake in the tundra? So go do it. I've packed cookies into your luggage."

"Snickerdoodles?"

"See? Everything's gonna be all right."

6

.
.
.
.

Meet Missy Fox."

"Wow, look what I caught!" Missy is standing in the stern, grinning ear to ear while holding an eight-pound walleye, trophy-size. At thirty inches, it's longer than Missy's torso. She hoists it higher for the camera, turning it this way and that to show angles. "I can't believe this! I've never caught a fish!"

RayAnne is laughing. "Talk about beginner's luck!"

Given her profession, Missy is not at all what RayAnne had expected. Open-faced and freckled, with strawberry blond hair pulled tight in a scrunchie, looking closer to twenty than forty. With her compact frame, she could be a gymnast. She makes kissing motions at the fish's mouth and gives it one last admiring look before releasing it back into the dark water on the lee side of *Penelope*. Earlier, RayAnne had stopped the taping a few moments after the catch to take photos and measurements that Missy might take to a taxidermist to have a graphite model made.

RayAnne turns to the camera. "That was one lucky fish. Missy's typical prey don't get off so easily. Missy Fox is a bounty hunter. She tracks down deadbeat dads for nonpayment of child support and hunts down abusive husbands who have active warrants for arrest."

Missy is casually wiping fish slime from her fingers onto her sweatshirt. "Well, agencies don't like the term *deadbeat dad* since it's not PC. *NCP* is what they use. Noncustodial parent. It's rare, but once in a blue moon, it is a mom who ducks out on child support."

"Mothers?"

"Rare, like I said. The few moms we do deal with usually have some emotional issues or substance addictions messing up their maternal abilities, and most have some abuse in their own pasts. Ninety-nine percent of NCPs are men, and a surprising number are employed, law-abiding, pay all their other bills, but just won't cough up for their own kids' welfare. Did you know that in most states, a person's credit rating isn't even affected by nonpayment of child maintenance?"

"Really? So it's not always like they don't have the money?"

"Honey, some of these guys have seven-figure incomes, but the swine just aren't willing to pony up."

Swine. A term Dot might use. RayAnne looks up from her task of impaling a squirming leech onto a double hook. "What kinds of excuses do these dads come up with?"

Missy, watching the leech procedure, tries the same with her own. "With most nutcups—sorry, NCPs—it's sheer selfishness, or they're out to punish the ex, or just don't give a rat's . . . backside. It's the kids who suffer. What I do is less about snagging the dads as it is about helping the kids."

RayAnne quickly touches the feed in her ear. "I'm sure there are plenty of struggling parents watching who can relate to this story, and we'll be listing a number of organizations and links on our Website, including Missy's agency, Fox Hunt, which has recently reached a milestone of having collected twenty million dollars in child maintenance." She turns to Missy. "The alias, *Fox. . .* ?"

"Yeah. Missy Fox, a total stripper's name. It's my ace in the hole. When I start nosing around for some guy, and his coworkers or drinking buddies see the name on my pink business card, they can't give me phone numbers or addresses fast enough. Some have even offered to drive me to the NCP's house." Missy, having given up on her leech, hands it over. "Here, you seem to know how to handle these."

"What got you started?"

"My own dad took off when I was ten. My mom was a drunk. My brothers and I barely made it through high school."

She says it so matter-of-factly. RayAnne stops weaving Missy's leech and looks intently at her. "I suppose plenty of us grew up in failing families and are scared to think of foisting that baggage onto the next generation?"

"Happens all the time, continuing the cycle." Missy accepts the baited hook and casts her line. "There should be some program like Al-Anon for bad parenting, you know, instead of dealing with alcoholics."

"Parents that are children?" RayAnne asks. "How about Adult Children of Adult Children?"

Missy snorts. "Or Adult Children of Dickheads."

As a soft rain begins to pitter down, both women raise their faces to it, closing their eyes. After a beat, RayAnne turns to the lens and the camera crew beyond, who are trying to shield their equipment and gesturing for her to wrap. "After this word from our underwriter, we'll finish our conversation with Missy back on dry land."

Missy reels in her line while blinking wet lashes. "This is so fun."

On the way back to the dock, RayAnne wonders if Missy would like to join her in the RV later for a glass of wine. Her temporary home is now parked and hooked up, the Tiffany end thankfully backed into a clump of alder. There might be a bottle of wine around somewhere. She's never been very good at making friends, but, as Ky often reminds her, she never really tries.

RayAnne wakes as the last raindrops from the storm drip from the pines, hitting the roof of the motor home in nickel-sized splats. In between is the silence that is one of the best features of being on Location. They can all thank Cassi for scouting it; she has relatives in the area and spent summers on the lake as a kid, so she knows a dozen walleye holes that her late great-grandmother had fished and kept secret from everyone but Cassi. Apparently one of the sponsors has a cabin nearby as well, which helped green-light the choice. Location is leased from the owner of the decommissioned resort next door, its mailbox lettered with once-red paint, *Vacationland*. At first, most of the crew and staff complained mightily about the distance from Minneapolis, but after a week of unrivaled fishing and stunning views, they clammed up. For the next twelve weeks, this bit of the Northwoods will be home to *Fishing*: a little village of RVs and pop-up campers and tents, droning generators and mounds of equipment, satellite dishes, Porta-Potties, a tent kitchen, and the catering truck that arrives each dawn and leaves after dinner.

The nearest town is Hatchet Inlet, just miles from the border in an area of the state Big Rick calls North Armpit and the crew simply refer to as Bumfuck. RayAnne has explored the lake with DNR maps, using her depth finder and Garmin to chart Cassi's best fishing spots, trolling the shores for picturesque spots to film and fish.

This morning the surface of the bay on Little Hatchet Lake is calm as a sheet of foil, unlike the day before, when it was sloshing with whitecaps by the time she and Missy Fox docked. Their glass of cheer never materialized. Missy had to leave right after taping, hot on the trail of another *tool,* this one owing tens of thousands in support for four daughters, all younger than ten years old.

It's safe to say RayAnne's not keen on interviewing that afternoon's guest, Mary Hawley, the psychologist featured in a documentary about juvenile psychopaths, *Why Does Jennifer Kill?*, which RayAnne dutifully watched on her laptop the night before, taking notes, then dragging the scenes along into her sleep. Thankfully, the storm woke her just as the senior prom in her dream was about to commence, and a flash of lightning illuminated the interior of the motor home, alerting her to the presence of not one but two silently frantic bats that had somehow squeezed inside to avoid the deluge. Had anyone been around in the predawn, they'd have been in for some cheap entertainment watching RayAnne dodge and flounder with every light blazing, casting her beach towel like a salmon net, determined to capture and liberate the bats and redeem at least part of her choppy night. If she hadn't been on edge already, the searing lightning and ripping bursts of thunder set the perfect stage for thoughts of pimply murderers lurking among the pines with cleavers. RayAnne didn't normally mind storms, but the RV was a large metal object smack in the middle of majestically tall pines, each a potential conduit for bolts of death.

Once the bats were finally trapped and ushered out, she'd crawled back under the covers, only to hear her phone alarm begin beeping and vibrating itself across her nightstand, landing on the carpet with a thud.

Though it's not yet five a.m., the sky is light—July in the north, with their latitude not so far from the border and the tundra beyond, the subarctic midnight sun only a few hundred miles away. RayAnne bangs and stubs her way from bed to the little bathroom, then to the little kitchen to make coffee, yawning nonstop. After the high ceilings of her townhouse, she feels large and unwieldy in the RV, as if she's suddenly grown extra elbows and knees. But she's getting used to it, and after a week with the windows wide, the toxic new-carpet smell is fading under a mix of campfire smoke, the aerosol sting of OFF!, pine chaff, and fresh air shearing down from Canada. So much daylight.

. . .

Carrying her coffee and a towel down to *Penelope,* she's anxious to see what the rain might have wrought on the docks and her boat. Hurrying, she stumbles on a tree root, coffee trickling down the knee of her chinos.

"Tarnation!" Curses and oaths still sometimes erupt in the crotchety voice of Jack Crabb. RayAnne once read that Dustin Hoffman prepared to play the part of one-hundred-fifteen-year-old Jack by screaming in his dressing room beforehand for a solid hour—something she could easily manage herself some days. In more contemplative moments, she might hear the voice of Old Lodge Skins in her head. When feeling particularly coquettish (which admittedly was not often), her thoughts come in the lisp of Little Horse, the gay Human Being who offers to become Little Big Man's wife.

At the dock RayAnne stops in her tracks. To her dismay, someone not only has unsnapped *Penelope*'s vinyl cover but has eased her from the slip—the same someone who's now standing at the helm with his back to RayAnne, wiping spots from *Penelope*'s windscreen.

By the end of the first season, the crew had come to treat RayAnne less like a Mandy and more like one of them—mainly because she'd gotten to know them and earned some respect by taking time to learn each crew member's duties, the basics of their equipment, and how this relates to that. They're in this together, after all, isolated as they are up in Bumfuck. While she's still a little freaked by the amount of electrical cables lying coiled like cobras over the docks so near water, she's learned what powers what, how the monitors and generators and lights work, and where most of the breakers are. She's careful to step out of the way of the crew's choreographed routines. She does her part; they do theirs.

All she has asked of them is that they leave *Penelope* exclusively in her care. The boat is her responsibility, her domain. And now some interloper has not only powered up *Penelope,* he's all over her, rubbing at her dashboard like he owns her.

Most of the crew have heard the condensed version of how RayAnne found *Penelope,* then towed the wreck fifteen hundred miles to Ogunquit, Maine, where a reclusive restorer took nearly two years to bring her back from the brink, necessitating a hefty loan she reckons will be paid off sometime between clearing up her student loans and becoming eligible for Medicare.

RayAnne juts her chin at the trespasser's back.

"Ex*cuse* me?" She's barely able to keep the growl from her voice. "You're in my boat, mister." She sounds comically like Caroline Crabb, Jack's gun-slinging sister.

The man turns, startled. Once recovered, he says, "Oh, hey. Hi."

The guy from the parking lot—the Rod & Gun Expo guy. Again. His name wells up from nowhere, RayAnne thinking, *Sure, now I remember.* She's able to make his name sound like an accusation: "Hal? It is Hal, right?"

The chamois in his hand drops to his side. He seems as surprised as she is and obviously unaware he's breached some protocol. "Ah. Yes. *Yeah.* RayAnne, am I . . . ?"

"In my boat? Yes."

"Oh." He folds the chamois and lays it on the seat exactly as RayAnne had left it. "Sorry. It was quite a downpour last night and I wanted to check everything was okay." When he hops up to the dock, RayAnne sees he's barefoot, having left his wet sneakers on the dock. At least he's a courteous trespasser.

The carrying case for whatever instrument he plays is next to his feet. Now that they are face to face, the same befuddlement that visited her during their previous encounters roils up again. "Hang on. I'm a bit confused here. You're not freelance, or crew, yet you were at the Expo . . ." She scans his casual posture and bare feet. "And I know you're not management."

He laughs. "None of the above." In explanation, he picks up

his case and clicks the hasp. Inside, nested in compartments, are arrays of fishing lures and jars of the new artificial bait everyone is talking about. The Lefty's logo is stamped inside the lid.

"Oh." Bits and pieces rattling in RayAnne's head fall roughly into place. "You work for Lefty's?"

Lefty's is their biggest underwriter, a growing chain of fishing gear and bait outlets known for its line of quality products and for sourcing them all from Minnesota, their slogan "Bait Locally."

"You could say that." He grins.

"Right." *Sales rep, of course,* she thinks. "So you're here about the PETA complaint."

"Uh-huh." He snails his eyebrows into a scowl and does a dead-on imitation of Robert, the stuffy guy from legal. "In an effort to, ahem, make the show more, ahem, *humane* and utterly sanitized, you will from this day forward use only fake-live bait instead of live, living bait."

RayAnne laughs, her annoyance draining to make room for something smoother. It is a lovely morning, after all; the storm has pummeled the pine chaff and other allergens to the ground. The air is good.

He cocks his head. "Sorry. No one told you I was coming?"

"They did, but I didn't expect *you*-you."

"Well, here *I*-I am, along with my wares. So no more chopping live night crawlers in half with your thumbnail?"

"That got edited out!"

"Not before a test audience saw the dailies." He's able to make the shake of his head seem beguiling. "Fortunately I'm the only one who saw yesterday's footage with Missy Fox. Writhing leeches?" Hal affects Robert's voice again: "Simply won't do." He holds up the lure case as if proffering jewels. "So. Might I interest Madam in some biodegradable vegan chum? Perhaps some gluten-free latex minnow-ettes? A completely bloodless rice-mochi leech?"

"Well," she mimics him, "perhaps Madam should try a few out first?"

"Now?"

"Sure."

When they pull away from the dock, RayAnne at the helm, her hair flying, the bats and broken sleep and pimpled teenage killers are utterly forgotten.

. . .

Once they've baited their lines and have settled in to fish, Hal pulls out a foil packet tucked in his windbreaker. "How do you feel about cold pancakes?"

Suddenly ravenous, she feels great about them. He opens the packet between them to reveal a half dozen rolled frilly-edged pancakes filled with something creamy. He refreshes her coffee with his own thermos.

"Cheers." She tentatively holds her mug to meet the edge of his.

"*Till din Hälsa*. Dig in, before they get warm."

"Is that Norwegian?"

He shakes his head. "Swedish. My grandmother taught me a few words, and how to make these."

"My grandmother taught me that carrying bacon bits in your pockets attracts men." As soon as she says it she feels like an idiot and plugs her mouth with a pancake. The edges are crisp, and the moist centers are slightly sweet, with a hint of something.

"What's that filling?"

"The secret ingredient. Mashed potatoes with maple syrup."

"So good." RayAnne chews, closing her eyes. Things you would never think to put together. She murmurs around the mouthful, "Boy howdy."

Hal laughs and raises his thermos a second time. "Here's to grandmothers."

She suddenly regrets snapping at Hal. "Sorry about back on the dock. I can get . . . I don't usually let just anyone in my boat."

"Well, *Penelope* isn't just any boat, right?"

He's the first person to call her by name. RayAnne smiles. "No, she is not."

"If boats could talk, right? How'd you find her?"

"Oh, long story."

"Yeah?" He leans back and tucks his pole under one arm as if he has all day.

She chews down her last bite. "I wasn't even shopping for a boat. In fact, I was looking for the Porta-Potty in a marina in Michigan. Just behind it was this graveyard of Chris-Crafts and old Crestliners—the sort of place you go to scavenge for parts. Anyway, I only saw the shape of her under a tarp but thought, you know, here's something different. When I saw the fish-scale finish I decided right there. But what a wreck. Carburetor gone, what finish wasn't worn off was gouged, half the decking rotted, no windscreen. Her hull was cracked."

"None of that stopped you?"

"The opposite." RayAnne shakes her head at the memory. "I decided on the spot I wasn't just going to save her but improve her."

"Like a missionary?"

"More like the Six Million Dollar Man." RayAnne reaches under the console to unlock a compartment. It's not as though *Penelope* has an astonishing story—it's just that until now no one's been curious enough to ask. She pulls out a waterproof zip folder thick with papers: log books, slip rental contracts, fuel receipts, license stickers. *Penelope*'s provenance. She rummages through.

"Here. Here she is, the original *Penelope*."

It's a faded color photo with ruffle-cut edges. A woman water-skiing, wearing the sort of shirred swimsuit that looks like there could be a girdle involved. The bottom of the snapshot shows the bench seat in the foreground, the little flags flying straight with speed. The white wake looks like a road of plowed water. Even in the grainy photo the woman is quite beautiful—arched brows, bright teeth, and a figure like Marilyn's. The camera angle is straight on.

"Look at her." Hal holds up the snapshot to align the back end of the boat with that in the photograph. "Like seeing a ghost." He nods to the log book. "This was in there?"

"Yes, it belonged to the original buyer, the real Penelope's husband, Mr. Lancaster, so I looked him up. The boat had been his wedding present to her. Sweet old guy."

"What did he say?"

"Not much on our first phone call. Just that they had the boat maybe thirty years then sold her. His wife had just died that week, but I didn't know that then. Only that he was sad."

"He didn't want this photo back?"

"Said to keep it, that he had others. I sent him before-and-after pictures of the restoration. He sent a long letter back, wrote out the whole story of how they met." She eases the photo gently from Hal's bad hand. As her palm brushes his, she can't help but wonder if it has much feeling. It seems to function well enough, the fingers bend and move in a talk-to-the-hand sort of motion. Would his fingertips experience sensation? If he skimmed them across the downy hairs on her forearm would he feel the goose bumps? Impulsively she wants to pick up this hand and run her teeth over the knuckles.

"Sounds like a nice old guy."

"What?" RayAnne straightens. "Yeah. Really sweet. We write now and then. I even thought about hooking him up with my Gran, since she's forever trying to hook me up on blind dates."

"Will you?"

She shakes her head. "Gran's still grieving. Dead Ted—that was my grandfather—seems to be a chapter Gran's still living thirty years later."

"I'd hate to think of someone mourning me for that long."

"Well, I'd hate to think of someone not mourning me." Ray-Anne laughs, but a small part of her means it. "Anyway, Mr. Lancaster watches the show all the time now, says it does him good to see *Penelope* out on the water—it reminds him of old times. And he seems to think she's famous just 'cuz she's on TV."

Hal just grins. "Imagine that."

They are silent a moment, both looking out over the lake. He elbows her softly. "This show . . . not such a bad place to punch the clock, is it?"

"Nope."

"These women you find, you really get them to . . . they *talk*, and it's not phony. How do you do it?"

Do? She doesn't really do anything beyond asking the questions she senses they most want to answer—or maybe need to answer.

She shakes her head. "I dunno. If I think about that too long, I'll start to wonder myself."

Guests do seem to open up, like strangers do when time is finite and has a scheduled end, like during a flight to somewhere, or a visit to the hair salon, a drink at the bar in a town you're just passing through. The plane will land, the hair gets swept up, the tab paid—you have only so long to tell your story. On *Fishing*, the boat will dock. RayAnne reckons it must seem a safe place to spill.

"They only say the things they're thinking."

She'd like to ask Hal questions but is unsure where to start. Her gaze wanders again to land on his hand.

He leans in, his tone matter-of-fact. "You can ask me about it." He wriggles his fingers.

"What?" Heat blooms across her face, and she begins to stammer. "I didn't . . ."

Just then Hal gets such a firm tug on his line the pole nearly leaves his hand. While he starts reeling, she scrambles to get the net, thinking, *Thank you, fish.*

Saved by a fat bass. Hal expertly lands it, unhooks it. It's sturdy and handsome with a clear stripe. They admire it a moment before he releases it. He leans far over the gunnel, allowing the fish to slip from his hands like an offering.

More fish start biting then, so there's not much chance for real talk. The weights and numbers of their catches even impress the local game warden, who motors over to see what they're up to, with questions about the filming location and the show, and to check permits.

Motoring back later, RayAnne asks, "You don't suppose *Fishing* could actually get real traction, like a commercial show?"

"Like *Fin* or *Dock Watson?*" Hal smiles. "I'd wager it could."

"Well, Lefty's has wagered, haven't they?"

"Um, true." He turns back to the wheel, smiling.

She certainly has wondered why anyone would sink money into such an untested premise as an all-women fishing talk show on public television.

Growing pensive, she watches the tendril of a curl bat against the nape of Hal's neck until they near the dock.

. . .

When RayAnne breezes into the RV, Cassi barely looks up from her laptop at the booth that doubles as the world's tiniest shared office space. "Catch anything?"

"Three bass, a ton of sunnies, and two big walleye." She sees her bed has been made and sighs. No sooner has RayAnne set something down than Cassi has either filed it, tidied it, folded it, tossed it, or eaten it herself. As a defense, RayAnne has unconsciously adapted strategies a sibling might: hiding things, gobbling.

Rinata has sent the wardrobe from Minneapolis. Identical

clear garment bags hang on the rack—sets of two of everything in case she out-sweats a shirt or spills in her lap, occurrences of which are all too frequent. Rather than bare her muffin top to Cassi, RayAnne ducks behind the rack to shed her clothes, humming while sausaging into her Spanx.

Cassi stops pecking her keypad. "Someone is in a good mood. I heard you laughing out there."

RayAnne pops her head up over the rack. "What do you know about Hal? He seems okay."

"I told you about him. You were supposed to go meet him at the Lefty's booth during that Shoot & Kill Expo."

"Rod & Gun Expo."

"Whatever. You looked pretty cozy out there in the boat. I thought you never crossed that line."

"What line?" RayAnne sucks in her middle and snaps the waistband into place, wondering if Spanx's motto is "Breathing Is Overrated." She pulls garments from hangers.

"The sponsor line."

"So Hal is with Lefty's. Big deal."

"He's not *with* Lefty's." Cassi gives her a curious look. "Ray, Hal *is* Lefty."

"What?" RayAnne's words are muffled under the stripes of the boatneck shirt she's wrestling into. She yanks it over her nose. "Hal is Lefty?" She falls to the couch as if shoved.

"Duh, you haven't noticed his right hand?"

"But that's his right hand, why would that . . ." She smacks her forehead. "Gawd, how stupid."

"Yup, *right* hand. Which is how Lefty's got started—insurance money from his accident. It was kind of a big story around here, but I guess you missed a lot being out on the circuit?"

"Sawmill accident?"

"Yeah. It got cut off, and a dog found it in the snow and brought it home nearly frozen, which is apparently a good thing, 'cuz he was able to get it sewn ba—"

"Jeeeez. Cut off?"

"And sewn back on." Cassi holds up her own hand. "Imagine how many nerves and stringy things are in a wrist."

"I got it." RayAnne holds up her own hand and grimaces. "Sponsor?" She hoists herself to standing to finish dressing, jabbing her arms into a khaki overshirt, which, according to the instructions pinned to it, is to be worn over the striped shirt but with only the *middle two buttons buttoned*. Then the pants, also with a note in Rinata's scratchy handwriting, *casually rolled to just below knob of knee.*

Every day, RayAnne wears clothes that belong to no one and is instructed how to wear them. At least the hat is hers. She straightens in the mirror, assessing herself with her most stoic Mrs. Pendrake face, jaw set. The day has taken a turn, and so has the breeze. She sniffs, as if smelling rotting chum. "Well, I guess that's that."

Cassi shrugs. "I don't get it. All sponsors can't be evil."

"Not evil, off-limits. They have agendas." She thinks of smarmy Roger Lyndon. "They literally float the boat, and they can just as easily sink it."

"Shame. You looked sorta right together."

RayAnne pauses before swiveling away. "Dammit."

"Exactly."

. . .

The interview with the author of *Why Does Jennifer Kill?* goes about as well as RayAnne expects, her own dark remarks lending an unintentionally flippant tone to the segment with such comments as "Why didn't she just disguise the poison in yogurt?" and "Maybe he deserved it?"

Motoring Professor Hawley back to the dock, she sees Hal milling just beyond the crew. He gives her a smile and a wave, which she unconvincingly pretends to have missed. He might have been more forthright in the boat, might have offered something less ambiguous than that he was "with" Lefty's.

Once the professor is safely out of the boat and handed off to Cassi, RayAnne shifts into reverse and spins the steering wheel, shifts and roars away with the throttle open—her version of door slamming. She speeds around a promontory that defines the bay until she is out of sight of Location. After dropping anchor in the middle of a small bay, she sits rocking for several minutes. She doesn't feel like fishing but doesn't have enough gas to just tool around. There is something just out of reach that she's hankering for but doesn't know what. When this happens, it's never good to be near food, especially the product placement cooler. She mindlessly eats a little of everything before realizing her hankering has nothing to do with food. Three caramels into the Godiva assortment, she is officially disgusted with herself.

Who is she to grouse? Hosting this show is a dream job. As Hal pointed out, it's not a bad place to punch a clock. Getting paid to fish? Interviewing women who are, for the most part, exceptional and, as often, inspirational? Still, there are days it seems like there should be more of something.

But what?

It's hard to find the door out of such moods. Of course Ky would just say she's pricklier than usual; Big Rick would be more blunt and ask if she were on the rag, and her mother would encourage her to feel her feelings, good or bad. Advice flows unbidden from the part of her conscience Dot occupies, and she can nearly hear her voice: "You do know, RayAnne, that the only person in the world who can make you happy is you."

The last squashed caramel is melting in her fist. Shuddering, she leans over the gunnel and swishes her hands in the lake. The sun beating down reminds her of the warning from Darren the makeup guy about squinting and crow's-feet, so she sets about pulling *Penelope*'s vinyl canopy up, then snaps it into place. A book would be nice, but she's not about to go back to shore to get one. Once *Penelope*'s hood is up, RayAnne curls up on the bench seat, rocking in her floating den.

After ten minutes of flopping this way and that, she gives up on the idea of a nap. There's a full hour before they watch the dailies. The one thing she does have out on the lake is cell reception. She speed-dials Dot, and after five rings nearly hangs up, but suddenly Gran's voice is there, sounding out of breath.

"Hello?"

"Gran."

"Who is this?"

"It's *me*; isn't your caller ID on?"

"Oh? What is it, RayBee?"

"Nothing, Gran, just thought I'd call."

"You never call during the day. Is something wrong?"

"No. Yes. Not really. I'm just a little bummed. There's been another mosquito hatch, and everything wardrobe sends is a half-size too small . . . can you hear me okay?"

"Where are you? Sounds like you're in a blender."

"That was just a Jet Ski. I have to be out here on the lake to get a signal."

"You're not driving, are you?" Dot seems to be mumbling around some obstruction.

"No. You sound weird too."

"Dentist. I've been to the dentist; you should feel the side of my face. Now, what is it?"

"What is what?"

"Whatever you called about."

"Nothing, I just called to say hi."

"Well, hi to you too. Did you sign up with RiverDate yet? You said you would."

She said no such thing. "Gran, I nev—"

"It's a perfectly acceptable way to meet men these days."

"I do meet men. All the time."

"I'm sure you do. But you are such a picky girl, always complaining there's something missing or wrong with them. You never seem to see what's *right*."

"As it happens, Gran, I did meet a guy with a lot that is right."

Dot sighs. "And the wrong part?"

"He's a sponsor."

"Oh, dear."

"See?"

"Remember what that nice Irish lady on the show said? 'We can't always be trusted to know for ourselves what's best for us.'"

She's a little sorry she called at all. "Gran, can we please talk about something else?"

"If you're blue, RayAnne, just stay busy."

. . .

After watching dailies with the crew, RayAnne skirts the clearing where cars are parked. When she doesn't see Hal's red Wagoneer, she decides he's gone and ducks into the catering tent. Absently, she helps herself to a Rice Krispies bar the size of a paving brick and picks up an abandoned copy of *Men's Health*.

With sticky fingers, she's chewing her way through an article titled "Is She Faking?" when a shadow falls over the page. She jolts to see Cassi perched on the adjacent table as if beamed there.

"Jeez! You pop up like a prairie dog."

Cassi holds up a sheaf of clippings. "We're being watched! We made the *O* list!"

"*O* list?"

"Oprah's Favorite Things. Listen: 'Dig out your life vests and sun hats—you'll want to go *Fishing* with RayAnne and her new friends. No big names on this floating talk show, just real women saying real things.'"

"No kidding?"

"And there's more. *Vogue*—this one's short—says, 'Tune in, sit back, and tune out.'" Cassi hands over a few.

"*Entertainment Weekly*." RayAnne clears her throat and skims down the column. "What? 'Is *Fishing* the new book club?' They're not serious?"

They both ponder this a moment before Cassi continues, "*Money Magazine*: 'Heads up on possible boom market niche to outfit this high- to mid-female demographic in sport fishing gear.' We should get some champagne."

RayAnne blinks at the photocopied clip from *More*. "This one titled 'Rod and Real' says, 'Women are settling down in front of the screen on Sundays to do what men have been doing for ages—go fishing.' Where does one find champagne in Hatchetville?"

"Hatchet Inlet."

"Right." RayAnne reaches absently for the Rice Krispies brick. Remembering her manners, she holds it out, offering, "Sustenance?"

Cassi slam-dunks it into the nearest trash bin.

7

.

.

.

.

Her neck kinked from the long drive, RayAnne leans against the kitchen counter; the thought of sitting is unbearable. Home for less than an hour, she's separating junk mail from the bills, lobbing flyers and envelopes toward the recycle bin without looking up, hitting it about half the time. Near the basement door, her empty roller bag is clammed open next to a mound of dirty clothes that smell like Location.

She tears open bills and stacks them next to her laptop, determined that this time she will set up accounts online. Amid the detritus of advertisements and campaign flyers is a fat manila envelope forwarded from the station. Inside are a dozen envelopes, handwritten with return addresses and names she doesn't recognize, likely more snail mail versions of the many emails Cassi is continuously scrolling through: requests for certain guests RayAnne should want to have on the show as much as they do—Pink! Snookie! Some mail has been downright weird, like the marriage proposal to RayAnne from the survivalist who could barely spell but had offered as a dowry one fenced, off-the-grid, two-hundred-acre compound where they would "not be bothured" and a well-stocked arsenal. Obviously in touch with his inner romantic, the man had added that RayAnne was "beutifull enuff" and that he "wuld like a wife that can catch and gut her own diner." She crams the unopened envelopes back into the mailer and stuffs it away in a drawer, reminding herself to ask the mailroom to stop forwarding them.

Checking the house phone for messages, she's informed by Ms. Sprint that she has *forty-six messages,* and RayAnne grows suddenly warm, as if just handed a math test. Instinctively, she rolls the cordless phone from her palm into the junk drawer. For good measure she tosses in her cell phone and shuts it with her hip.

Messages can wait. These days off for the long Labor Day weekend are the only real free time she's had all month. She's itching to do nothing—soak in the tub, read a few books, spruce up her yard. She and Cassi have worked their tails off to produce eight decent episodes so far this summer, taping twenty-four segments, interviewing twenty-four women. Of those, at least a third were great, most very interesting, and only a few duds. There's just one more session of taping—a mere two episodes to go.

RayAnne has to admit, since the thumbs-up from Oprah, she's dared to let herself think her career might actually go somewhere. If nothing else, it's beginning to feel a little like security— that this house might remain hers as long as she's pulling in a couple of decent checks a month. Still, she need only surf cable channels to be reminded that a show being good doesn't always translate to its being renewed.

For the moment, the hard work has earned her a break and time—time to get excited over such mundane tasks as choosing blinds for her bedroom, finding a planter for her front stoop, or assembling the patio furniture still boxed in her garage stall. Most people go north and fish to relax. But to her a weekend in the city and a trip to Home Depot for mousetraps and oven cleaner sound like vacation. On the drive home she'd daydreamed of puttering in her garden, and while not entirely sure what that entails exactly, she imagines one must need a hose to hold while doing it, so she'll buy one of those too. RayAnne gazes out the window to her tiny yard, much of it taken up by the trunk of a stately oak, its branches spanning over the fence to shade several neighboring porches. Given the lack of sun in her yard, she can't consider flowers—perhaps she'll plant ferns? Does one plant ferns? Do they start out as *frondlings*? All things to learn.

There's nothing to eat or drink in the house, but the very idea of getting back into the car makes her lower back ache. Movement is what she needs. Eyeing the wheels on her suitcase, she decides to pull it to the co-op and roll her groceries home like the neighborhood widows do with their old-lady carts. She makes a list, empties sand from the suitcase, and grabs her wallet.

At the front door, her hand is nearly to the knob when someone jabs the doorbell, making her jump back a yard. The bell is the old buzzer type, raspy and jarring enough, but standing right under it is like being bellowed at. She's about to squint out the peephole when a muffled, tuneless, familiar whistling commences.

No. Can't be! She looks to make sure, holding her breath. Sure enough, there's his forehead, shiny with perspiration and big as a melon in the fisheye lens. They haven't seen each other since Dot's birthday. She hasn't heard boo from her father—unless he's left a message or three among the forty-six on her phone. Covering her mouth, she turns into the house and yells into her palm, "Coming!" When she looks down at her suitcase, the idea comes to her and she counts to five, waiting for the next jab of the bell, when she swings the door wide.

"Dad?"

"Ray-Ban!"

His red Lincoln is parked at the curb, dull with the dust of several midwestern states. "You drove here?"

"On the road since Wednesday. Aren't you gonna invite your old man in?"

"Dad, I didn't even know you were coming to town."

"You don't check your voice mail?"

"Well . . . I just got back."

He nods at her roller bag. "Looks like you're just leaving."

"Yes! I am. Just this minute, actually."

For a moment each looks at the other's suitcase, tight to their sides like dogs at heel. She bites her lip. Showing up in Minneapolis is one thing; had he expected to stay?

Big Rick clears his throat. "Where you headed?"

"I, uh . . ." She hadn't thought that far. Before she has a chance to come up with something, he nods. "No problemo, RayAnne. I should be heading over to Ky's anyway. Here, at least let me help you with that." He grabs her suitcase to hoist it over the doorjamb. Nearly weightless, it almost sails from his grasp.

"Dad." The jig up, she sighs. "I was only going to the grocery store."

. . .

He sits at the kitchen table while she makes him lunch from the contents of the wrinkled Super America bag he'd dragged in from his car—bologna, white bread, Doritos, and nearly expired milk. He hasn't said how long he might be staying. She clinks a knife around the bottom of the mayonnaise jar. "So how's . . . what's the animal I'm s'posed to remember? BEAVER?"

"BADGER."

"Right." RayAnne nods. "How is Rita?"

"Meh. A little strict these days. Laying down laws, no this, no that."

"No what?"

"Oh, you know, no red meat, no sodium, no Sean Hannity or Laura Ingraham on the TV."

"Sounds like it's for your own good." She turns back to the breadboard and catches a flash of action in the reflection of the microwave window—he's pulled a flask from his pocket and is dashing a shot into his milk. She inhales and forces herself to finish cleaning the knife. In the time it takes to turn and face him, the flask is hidden.

He leans back. "How's your mother? Still pied-piping those rich prunes through Timbuktu and Southeast Asshole?"

"Yes, Dad." Still clutching the butter knife, she plants fists on hips. "Why are you really here?"

"I told you. Felt like a road trip. Can't a father get a hair up his ass to visit his own daughter?"

"She's kicked you out, hasn't she? Rita's kicked you out!"

Every time Big Rick bails on a relationship or is evicted from one or finds himself between wives, he returns to Minneapolis on the premise of visiting his kids and grandchildren and what pals he has left in the area. But soon enough his old habits kick in and his subconscious agenda becomes clear: he's really revisiting the fringes of his first marriage, like a criminal drawn back to the scene. Invariably, he sets out to make a play for Bernadette and an ass of himself, as if not understanding that, with his original ex-wife, *no* means *never*. It's pathetically obvious to everyone except him: he only pursues Bernadette because she is the one woman he will never have.

RayAnne inhales deeply. "Dad . . . not again?"

Big Rick holds his wide shoulders steady, but she knows his jaw is squared to hold back any quaver that might betray him. He looks old. He looks tired. She puts the sandwich down in front of him and pours more milk. Five days—she has five days before heading back to Location Tuesday morning. Other than the domestic agenda she'd planned for the weekend, she cannot think of any excuse, any valid reason she can't handle her father for a few days. On Sunday he can become Ky's problem.

"You can stay here a *few* days." She holds out her empty palm. "On one condition."

After a ten-second stare down, he relents, sighs monumentally, and digs the flask from his pocket and hands it over.

* * *

"Gran?"

Dot stage-whispers right back, "Now where are you? In some car wash?"

"My basement. The washer and dryer are running."

"Well, turn them off!"

"Dad's upstairs."

"I know he's there, RayAnne. We spoke this morning."

"Oh? Did he tell you he's drinking?"

"No, but I could tell. Is that why you're calling, to tattle?"

"No!"

"Well, I'm glad you did anyway. I've been asking around about the kind of dog you should get. Did you know people are less likely to approach a dog that has pointed ears? I suppose because they look alert, though I can't imagine anyone being scared off by a Chihuahua or a corgi. German shepherds are maybe too big, though you want to be able to pick up the poop in just one grab. Trinket's poop is like little pebbles."

"I'm sure. Like precious trinkets. You're changing the subject."

"Yes, I am. Now, boxers are great, but they do have that VA business."

"VA?"

"Visible anus, dear. You may as well spare yourself that."

"I'm really not there yet, getting a dog—"

"Spaniels have a menacing bark, which is a plus, but they shed like crazy."

RayAnne is nearly jumping in place. "Gran, I'm not ready for a dog."

"You promised you'd get one. Huskies can look quite vicious."

Promised? RayAnne recalls agreeing it might be a nice idea down the road but doesn't remember promising. Dot's really exaggerating now. If only to stop the momentum, she caves.

"I will get a dog. Just not right away."

"Soon?"

"Yes! Soon! There're only a few episodes to tape, then it will be autumn, then I'll be here at home working at the station and that will be a great time, a *wonderful* time to get a dog, Gran." She tries to steer the conversation back. "You do know number six has kicked him out?"

"Well, sweetheart, we all knew that was only a matter of time."

"Don't you even care?" RayAnne chews a nail. "You know what, Gran? I'm a little tired of being the adult in this family."

"Good Lord, climb down from that cross, RayAnne. No one has ever asked you to be so responsible. You make so much work for yourself! Let your father ruin his life, if that's what he wants. That's what he does, over and over. We can't go around telling everyone what to do."

"Hello? Dorthea Dahl, can you hear your puppy-pushing, blind-date-ambushing self?"

"Oh, now that's different. That's for your own good. Now, it's only a few days with your father. Can you just try?"

She will. Try. Try to just be a daughter whose dad is in town visiting for the weekend. While making up the futon in the spare room, she racks her brain for places they could go that might prove neutral ground, where he won't embarrass himself or her—places nowhere near alcohol, and certainly not the state fair, with its beer concessions on every corner.

On Saturday morning they head for the farmers' market, but nearly the entire way Big Rick sings, changing the words of the old Jimmy Buffet tune to "Granola-ville," which would make anyone want to rip their own ears off.

They roam the stalls, filling her basket with enough fresh produce that the salad she's planned for dinner will practically make itself. Big Rick grabs a small container of organic microgreens from her.

"Jaysus, RayAnne, six bucks? They grow this stuff in gold dust or what?"

FISHING! . . . .

"Dad . . ." She quietly elbows, nodding at the grower. "He's right there."

"I don't care if he's hoeing cornrows in my hair. Hell, you can buy a whole meal, burger and fries and a salad at Mickey D's for less."

She gives him her look. "I don't eat at Mickey D's." Almost true, but because even routine interactions with Big Rick require taking a stand, she takes exaggerated, towering stands. Ky often coaches her to pick her battles with their father. The problem, simply, is that there are so many to choose from she doesn't know where to start.

At a stand selling grass-fed ground beef—eight-fifty a pound!—the idea occurs to her, a simple father-daughter day fraught with activity and so tailor-made she nearly claps with glee. She asks for two pounds.

Once home, she fetches her tools and drags the long-unopened boxes of patio furniture and a barbeque grill out to the yard. Big Rick is nothing if not handy. He can assemble her out-door table and chairs and grill, and later he can flip burgers for dinner. They will dine alfresco. That should consume most of the day. By tonight, she'll have every minute of tomorrow planned. She hums while prying open the boxes. Big Rick elbows in, rolls up his sleeves, takes one look at her screwdrivers, and shakes his head sadly. "Christ on a cracker, RayBee. This made-in-China crap isn't gonna cut it."

And so there is a trip to the hardware store, which should eat up at least another hour. Big Rick shifts into action mode, determined to outfit her toolbox with decent, American-made replacements.

He resists going in her more practical hatchback, balking. "That Oriental pie tin? It's got zilch headroom." What he won't admit is that he hates being driven by a woman.

"Asian, Dad—*Asian* pie tin." She climbs into his Lincoln, and after a half mile gives her father what he deals.

"How many gallons per mile does this Sherman tank burn?"

"It'll get a lot better mileage once the pipeline protesters quit their eco-whining."

RayAnne does not bother trying to process that logic, and they manage to get to the hardware store with neither barking. Following him down the narrow aisles, the urge to annoy is too tempting, and she picks up a hammer. "Jeez, Dad, twenty-six bucks for a hammer? Heck, when rocks are free and pound a nail just as well?"

"Hardy-har, RayAnne. There's two things in life a man shouldn't skimp on."

"Tools and . . . ?"

He scratches his head. "Dunno, I'll think of something." When he's just being himself and there's no one around to impress, he can be funny.

A red-vested clerk approaches. "You folks finding what you need?" When he sees the screwdriver set in Big Rick's hand, he nods approvingly.

"Yessir." Big Rick holds them out. "Wives leave. Trucks break down. These tools are forever."

RayAnne looks from her father to the clerk, who responds with a phony baritone, "Some days a good wrench is the only friend a man's got."

She's afraid they might break into song in some odd flash mob of two plotted for her benefit. "Huh?"

The clerk shrugs. "Ad campaign."

Big Rick adds, "Stanley."

RayAnne sighs. "Where are the propane tanks, please?"

At the garden section, Big Rick makes a show of choosing a gift for her, a small electric lawnmower—in spite of her having just told him that Bernadette bought her a new rotary push mower as a housewarming gift. Big Rick laughs the notion off. "'Course she'd buy you some hippie-dippie thing like that. This'll mow your lawn in half the time using less juice than your blow-dryer does, so the grid ain't gonna be drained cutting that scrap of lawn."

"Exactly, Dad. You've seen the size of it." It's no bigger than the square of Astroturf they're standing on, but Big Rick cannot pass on a chance to one-up Bernadette. Just as RayAnne readies for an argument, Dot's proverbial finger stretches from Florida to tap her forehead. In midsentence, she swallows her protest and cuts herself a silent bargain: *Just. Play. Along. Return it after he's gone.*

"Okay, thanks. But don't bother gift wrapping it."

In the process of making the purchases, Big Rick tells both clerks that his "not-so-little" girl is a homeowner now, which makes an opening for him to mention the show, which conveniently creates a lead-in to mention his own show, which fortunately one of them is familiar with.

"Sure, I remember *Bass Bonanza*. Back in the nineties, right?"

More chitchat and backslapping ensues in the parking lot, where the men stand jawing and absently watching as RayAnne manages to cram the mower into the trunk of the Lincoln between two sets of golf clubs.

Back home, Big Rick commences puttering. He wrenches and screws the faux wrought iron furniture into shape while she weeds around flagstones and tidies the edging around the trunk of the grandfatherly oak tree that Big Rick says should be cut down in order to keep squirrels off the building. She pats the bark and whispers, "You didn't hear that." Making a show of mowing her tarp-sized lawn with the new mower, she wears headphones to drown out the giant insect drone.

Once the yard work is done, RayAnne tosses the salad and opens a jar of the Boston baked beans Big Rick likes, then slices pickles, onions, buns, and tomatoes. Her father bundles up all the cardboard boxes and starts rearranging her garage stall until she demands he stop and sends him upstairs to shower.

When he comes down, she sees he has shaved and put on a clean shirt. While he fires up the grill, she changes into a summer dress.

Stepping out the back door and into the warm evening, she's met with the smells of burgers searing, freshly cut grass, and tiki torch oil. Her father is at the grill wearing an apron, whistling and sober, *trying*.

Dot is right. She can be pretty hard on him. She lets herself get so riled even when she knows half the time he's only joking. Everyone else in the family seems to have a method for coping with Big Rick: Dot accepts, Kyle ignores, Bernadette lets go. The only approach she can manage is to adopt some sort of auto delay in her reactions—to take a breath before responding, develop patience or something approaching it. Whatever, she knows it won't be long before she has cause to employ it.

Dinner goes well enough; both are so hungry there's not much chatter. He puts another burger on for himself, and while it sizzles they take up one of their safe topics—food—and reminisce over the slapdash dishes they used to invent when she and Ky joined him on the circuit during summer vacations. They would cook on the portable grill or the little harvest gold three-burner stove in the Airstream Big Rick towed from one fishing tournament to the next. TotDish had a total of four ingredients: hamburger, onions, and cream of mushroom soup, topped with frozen tater tots and cooked at four hundred degrees until gurgling.

IncinerRice was invented by accident after a pan of buttered rice had been left on the burner. The bottom turned crusty and so hot that the eggs Big Rick broke over it set almost immediately. When eaten, the yolks oozed down into the crackly parts. It is a dish RayAnne still cooks on rainy days, adding her own gourmet flair of Kraft Parmesan. The smell of scorching rice brings her right back to the damp closeness of the Airstream, its floor perpetually sandy and the radio always tuned to either a baseball game or Paul Harvey.

Big Rick slaps the table. "Remember S'more Volcano?"

The mention of it is enough to make RayAnne salivate. S'more Volcano was a pie tin filled with honey graham cereal topped by a mound of colored mini-marshmallows and strewn with chocolate chips, then centered over the embers in the Weber until the thing puffed up and browned, threatening to blow pastel lava and rivulets of chocolate. RayAnne still bears the scar where a glop of molten pink spewed across her forearm. Their end-of-week meal they called Shipwreck or Crapshoot was composed of leftovers and bits of this and a jar of that or a heel of cheese all added to whatever cold pasta or potatoes or eggs were on hand, then baked into a casserole—sometimes the result was awful, but occasionally it was quite good.

They finish their burgers in silence, remembering better days.

When Big Rick points upward, she follows his gesture from the canopy of leaves to where the North Star is blinking to life. From the distance come sounds of kids hollering, soccer balls being kicked, dogs barking, and the unmistakable rolling growl of a Harley Davidson. It's summer in the city. Not bad here in her own yard, RayAnne thinks. She is actually getting along with her father. If this is normal, it doesn't suck. Just as she's about to say something, she realizes Big Rick hadn't been pointing out the North Star at all, but her loose gutter. "How old did you say this place is?"

"Built in 1890."

"Looks it too. Hell, Ray, for what you paid for this place? You coulda got yourself a brand-new townhouse out in Eagan or Roseville."

"Well, Dad . . ." *One Mississippi, two Mississippi, three . . .* "I suppose I could have. But I don't want to live in Eagan or Roseville. Or even in a new house."

He gives the back of the brownstone a onceover from the

foundation up—the missing porch skirting, the flaky mortar of the brickwork, the snarl of cables where the electric enters the building. "Have it your way. But with an old dump like this? You better prepare for some headaches."

"I am." She stands and takes his plate. "I am having it my way." While she's at it, she might layer on a second coping tactic: diversion, the old bait and switch. "You want dessert?"

When she comes out with coffee and a plate of Oreos, she makes him promise, "You won't tell Gran?"

He chomps a whole cookie. With crumbs on his lips, he mumbles, "Mum's the word." As he lifts his coffee cup, RayAnne notices his hand shake slightly.

She wonders what he'll do next but doesn't ask. From her house, he'll go to Ky's for a few days, or until her brother's had his fill. Anybody's guess after that. Her father is not very good at being alone. Usually, she steers clear of his love life, but showing up like this, appearing almost needy—this is a first. Maybe it's occurred to him that serial marriages aren't the answer, no matter how many times he goes to bat.

"What happened, Dad? I mean, with you and Rita."

He sighs hugely. "Nothing much. The usual control stuff." He shakes his head. "Why is it women always need to control things?" He looks at her as if she might answer and after a beat looks at his watch. "Guess I'll go fire up the tube."

"Sure you don't want to sit out here awhile longer?"

"And miss *Fishing*?"

"Oh, right." It doesn't occur to her to watch the show on TV since she sees the episodes in segments after each is taped and edited, before they get quilted together. She rarely sees it as a whole like a viewer would.

He rubs his hands together. "Who's on?"

RayAnne grins. "The usual, a bunch of controlling women. You'll love the last bit."

. . .

The day of taping had been gusty with whitecaps frothing the lake, forcing the crew to set up in a narrow, less choppy bay. Still, it was a nightmare for the camera operators, who had to stand on the rocking pontoons with Steadicams strapped to their middles and crew on either side to keep them from toppling. Audio had been a challenge too; the mics, clad in gray fake-fur muffs, kept poking in and out of frame, like indecisive squirrels.

"On board today is Helga Knutson, also known as the Bra Viking, whose Minneapolis shop Valkyries has women queueing up for months to get a custom fitting."

In a video visit to the store, viewers pass under crossed broadaxes wielded by two plus-size mannequins wearing sinew-stitched leather tunics, chainmail leggings, and hammered pewter D-cup bras. All that's missing are horned helmets. Cassi, who had accompanied the crew that day, had been crestfallen to learn the leggings were for display only.

The shop's lighting is also medieval, the wattage ranging from tea candle to oil lamp in the inner sanctum of the fitting rooms. Helga's customers walk in looking nondescript—the sort of women you barely notice in line at the pharmacy or in Target. But what a difference a bra makes. Emerging from their final fit, harried soccer moms and midlevel managers seem transformed, wearing the custom bras for which they've shelled out hundreds and waited six months. They appear taller, more about them uplifted than just their breasts, and walk with assurance. As the crescendo of Wagner's opera serenades them out the door, these women look ready to pillage something.

This all absorbs Big Rick's attention until he realizes that, for all his patience, he's not going to see an actual fitting, just chitchat between Helga and RayAnne—no chance of a nipple.

After the pledge break, she leaves him alone to watch the second segment, ostensibly to make popcorn, but actually she'd rather avoid listening to any comments he might make regarding her interview with the organizer of a marriage equality event called the Big Gay Walk. Cassi has been able to sneak in social issues that hover near the no-fly zone for WYOY by cleverly concentrating on the lighter aspects and cute quotients, handpicking edited footage—in this case, children parading their dogs in rainbow costumes, with a charming clip of redheaded sisters holding dolls dressed to match, spinning their costumes for the camera, declaring, "Our daddies made them!" The camera operator focused on other families with two mommies who look like any other busy mothers; edited out are shots of mullet-haired lesbians draped on each other and drag queens waltzing past in heels with bulges in their fishnets.

Back in the living room, RayAnne hands over a bowl of popcorn and muses, "We'll see gay marriage legal in every state, Dad, just watch."

"Texas? Louisiana?" Big Rick grunts. "When hell freezes over."

By the time she settles back down on the carpet, the final guest is already in the boat.

"Kathleen Carter has worked as a marine mammal trainer at such amazing aquariums as the Shedd in Chicago and the Monterey in California. After her first marriage ended, she realized that the training she did by day with seals and dolphins might be adapted to her human relationships."

Kathleen is a round, pleasant-looking woman with apple cheeks. "The basic premise is soooo simple, RayAnne. You just turn away from bad behavior—ignore it—and reward what you perceive as good behavior."

"But how?"

"With positive reinforcement!"

The boat rises and falls in the swells. Neither is holding a pole; it's too choppy—they each just hang on to their bench seats or the gunnels.

"Okay." RayAnne bobs, thinking of Ky. "Say your child is throwing a fit on the floor of Walmart because you won't buy him Skittles?"

"Easy. That child should get nothing. And here's the important part: besides no Skittles, he should get no acknowledgment of his ploy. The less reaction on your part, the more successful you'll be. The child will eventually see you're not going to give in to your own anger or frustration, the very buttons they are trying to push."

While this soaks in, RayAnne nods and holds up a copy of *Very Good!* "In your book one of the chapters is titled 'Exude Indifference'; might that be perceived as a little . . . um, cold?"

"Think *detached*, RayAnne. Sometimes cold is the best defense we've got."

"Where do most people go wrong in relationships?"

"That's easy. They bargain—as if it's a good idea to cut deals with a crying child or irrational partner in the midst of a tantrum or argument." Kathleen turns to the camera to wag a finger directly at viewers. "Do not bargain!"

"Right. You don't actually use the term *behavior modification,* but it's implied." A strand of RayAnne's hair escapes to lash her face and stick to her lip. "You claim you can train a partner or child from the beginning?"

"Absolutely."

"But how about in preexisting relationships, like with siblings, or . . . parents?"

"Now that is a bit more difficult. You're born into the dynamic of multiple sets of behaviors, what we know as *family.* Not hopeless, but not easy."

"No kidding." RayAnne touches the feed going into her ear and turns to the second camera like a train switching tracks. "More with Kathleen after a short break to thank one of tonight's fine underwriters, Lefty's Bait."

RayAnne is dismayed to see herself grinning so stupidly on camera. She'd been thinking of Hal. She looks to her father to see if he's noticed. He hasn't.

Kathleen's wrap-up focuses on getting behaviors under control and standing your ground. "And next time your child is very good, offer nonmaterial rewards, such as a trip to the park, playing a game, watching a film, or just having some one-on-one time alone. And if it's a partner—anything from a date to a favorite meal, or, well, a favorite position."

RayAnne presses her back to the couch. As is so often the case when taping, she's so consumed by the mental gymnastics of forming the next question while processing the answer to the previous one, it's hard to tell how well or badly a show is going until after the fact, when it's committed to digital and too late. This episode isn't half bad.

With the swell of a wave lifting the *Penelope,* RayAnne asks a final question: "Kathleen, which is easier to train, a difficult partner or a dolphin?"

"A dolphin, of course."

Big Rick gives her shoulder a little nudge with his foot. "Nice one." As credits begin to roll, he stretches and reaches for the remote.

"Hold on, Dad. The best part's coming."

It had been Cassi's idea to run outtakes at the end of each show. So far this season, flubs have included a wind-borne Post-it note plastering itself over RayAnne's eye like a pirate's patch, a cameraman valiantly fighting a battle with his balance before tipping off the dock, RayAnne laughing so hard she doubles over and hits her forehead on the steering wheel, and a long shot of *Penelope* at speed with a guest's hat blown from her head to skip along the wake behind like an errant wheel.

The outtake chosen for this show is a confused heron. Just behind the final credits, a heron clumsily lands on *Penelope's* foredeck. It struts across, talons clicking like high heels while RayAnne and Helga the Bra Viking watch, mouths agape. When they burst into laughter, the bird gives them a look, then launches from the boat, pulling along its chopstick legs. The final outtake is of *Penelope* rising and falling in the swells, RayAnne, alone in the stern, facing the camera as it steadies and tests focus. The swells are high enough that RayAnne's head goes up and down, in and out of frame, and her voice is heard, mimicking the Verizon guy, drolly repeating, "Can you see me now? Can you see me now?"

A really good show, and she's made it through a day with Big Rick with no fits, sulking, or growling. All in all, a pretty decent day.

Not that it's over.

As soon as Big Rick is asleep, his snore ruffling through the ceiling grate, RayAnne is fastened like a moth to her laptop, trolling for activities in hopes of filling every moment of the next day.

Kathleen Carter was right, of course: the notion of rewards for good behavior makes ultimate sense. She looks for something, anything Big Rick might enjoy—a car show, a river cruise, a Segway tour of the Mill District. The microbrewery tour is not an option for obvious reasons, and the Walker Art Center is just a bad idea—modern art and Big Rick do not mix: "This Motherwell joker's got nothing on my grandsons—at least they can color in the lines."

There are sheep dog trials, which RayAnne would like to see herself, but unfortunately they are too far in the opposite direction of Ky's suburb, where they will be heading for supper.

A Twins baseball game seems like a safe bet. Of course there will be Budweiser, but a few beers never make her father quite as stupid as Scotch or brandy does, neither of which are available at the stadium as far as she knows. Because it's so last minute, she can't get great tickets, but it's about the game not the view, so she presses the Buy button.

At midnight she drags herself up the stairs. Pleasantly worn out from the yard work and lightheaded from holding her breath much of the day, she sleeps like the dead.

. . .

In the morning she leaves the baseball ticket printout next to Big Rick's coffee and watches his face when he sees it, pleased that he's pleased. After a drawn-out brunch over the Sunday *Star Tribune,* they head for Toys "R" Us so he can buy gifts for the twins. Leaving the store, she makes a mental note to remind Kyle he can thank her for nixing Guitar Hero and steering their father toward the pair of walkie-talkies.

Traffic to the stadium is the usual snarl, with Big Rick growing testier by the minute. It occurs to RayAnne that by this point he probably physically needs a drink. Still, he should be able to maintain for the next half an hour until he has a beer in his hand. No sooner are they seated in the nosebleed section—the best seats RayAnne could get—than he buys two Miller Lites from the roving vendor, one ostensibly for her, which she knows he assumes she will not drink, so he can then down it himself. She makes an exception and manages to chug it despite the taste, winking at his dismay. "My father's daughter, right?"

At the start of the second inning, Big Rick spots an old acquaintance while scanning the stadium with his binoculars. He hands them over, pointing to the window of a private box. "Over there, down two levels. You remember Al Faring."

Al Faring was a client back when Big Rick was at the top of the pro guide roster—fishing guide for hire by the moneyed— usually to exclusive fly-in posts in Canada or ranches near streams in the triumvirate of trout states: Idaho, Montana, and Wyoming.

Just as RayAnne adjusts focus on the binoculars to make out Al Faring, her father practically pulls her up from her seat. "Hell, he's got a box. We don't have to sit up here in the trailer park."

On the way down, he tells her all about how rich Al Faring is, how his family owns half of Saint Paul, how they might be good people for RayAnne to meet. "Yeah, Dad, I know. I've met them more than a few times."

When they reach the door of the box suite, she hangs back, certain Big Rick will make an ass of himself. Sure enough, when Mr. Faring opens the door, there is barely a glimmer of recognition on his face. His wife, Jeanette, comes to the door, graciously containing her annoyance, until she looks past Big Rick to where RayAnne is hoping to be absorbed into the wall.

"Rick Dahl. And, look, here's his daughter, RayAnne! Ray-Anne, come here this minute. Why, all the gals in my book club are watching your show!"

"They are?"

They are urged inside, Big Rick pretending to object, saying he only stopped by to say hello even as he's stepping inside and pulling RayAnne by an elbow. The box is sleek as a Hotel W suite, with a bank of plush swivel chairs overlooking the field, two flat screens for instant replay, and its own bar, of course. RayAnne sags.

Jeanette Faring pulls her to a love seat. "Talk about coincidences, my friend Donna—she's on our committee for the Children's Diabetes Gala—anyway she's just back from Sedona on a trip with your mother. Oh, she didn't call it a hot-flash tour . . . but a whatsit . . . ?"

"Blood-Tide Quest?"

"Yes! Your mother! Oh, Donna absolutely adored her."

RayAnne nods.

Jeanette flutters her heavily ringed fingers. "I've signed up for one of her trips. One north, at some sacred Native American place . . . Saca-something."

"Sacajawea Springs."

"That's right. It looks fabulous on the Website. And did I hear Bernadette is writing a book?"

"She might be." A vague memory of a mention, her mother talking about taking a class at the Loft Literary Center . . .

"Oh, you should have her on the show!"

"My mom?" RayAnne laughs. "That would be . . . ah—"

"Fabulous, right?"

"Nepotism?" A wave of cheers and a thousand fans jumping to their feet disrupts their conversation. Jeanette sighs. "Oh, I suppose we're winning?"

After the uproar settles, Big Rick commences doing what he does, reminding the Farings how fantastic they are, asking all the right questions while RayAnne wriggles through the third inning, toggling between watching the action on the field and politely answering Jeanette's questions about the show. And while she does not look back at her father or Al, she is acutely aware of each bottle cap pried, every foamy pour and clink of a beer glass.

As empties accumulate, Al seems to remember more of the old days, prompted by Big Rick, whose versions are certainly embellished. By the fourth inning they are great buddies enjoying a reunion. To celebrate the eighth home run, Al pulls a liquor bottle from his personal stash while explaining, "Gift from a colleague. Can I interest you in a sip? It's twenty-year."

When he sees the label, Big Rick grins. "Talisker?"

At this, RayAnne swings around and glares. Big Rick composes himself, chuckles, and says, "Gosh, I dunno, Al, Miss Gestapo here keeps pretty tight reins on her old man."

Mr. Faring clucks at her, "Ach, he'll have just one, then." Mr. Faring has begun sounding like he's just off the boat from the Scottish Highlands.

"A course I will," her father says loudly, in RayAnne's direction, perfectly imitating Al's accent. "But just one."

Through her teeth, RayAnne mutters something unintelligible and turns back to Jeanette and the game. When the other team scores, the stadium erupts in boos, and RayAnne whispers, "Yes!"

Jeanette just laughs and pulls a fat paperback from her crocodile Prada purse. "I only endure these games to keep an eye on Al." She lowers her voice and smiles wearily. "Usually I just sit here and read whatever's on tap for book club. See?" She drops *Fifty Shades of Grey* back into her bag. "Thank God you're here. A real person! And your show! So clever. We just love love love it."

Big Rick is as good as his word and has only one Scotch, but since it is sloshing in a sea of beer, he is cheerfully loud all the way back to the parking ramp, where they argue over who will drive. He doesn't relent until she refuses to get in the Lincoln, and he tosses her the keys, muttering, "Jaysus, RayAnne, such a schoolmarm."

8

∘

∘

∘

∘

The streets of Ivy Dales, Ky's outer-ring suburb, are not streets; they are Trails, Places, Ways, or Lanes, all named for great institutions of higher learning, though Ky would wager that few if any residents besides Ingrid have matriculated from schools like Oxford (Lane) or Trinity (Circle). The Dales are laid out in such a manner as to defeat anyone as directionally challenged as RayAnne. She's forever finding herself on Wellesley Place when she should have turned on Wellesley Trail to reach Ky's faux saltbox on Wellesley Way.

Unaccustomed to maneuvering a vehicle as large as Big Rick's Lincoln, she ignores his colossal sighs while wrestling the wheel to turn around and drive back the way they came. Ivy Dales is a maze. The last time she was this turned around was on a city walking tour she took with Dot during her college graduation trip to Prague, when their guide had wound them around the cobbled streets of Old Town, explaining that when the Germans marched in to occupy the city, wily residents took down all the street signs to confound and confuse the enemy troops.

The same afternoon, she and Gran had visited a museum of art made by children of the Holocaust. She remembers thinking she had never seen Gran so quiet for so long, probably thinking of her own little girl, Betsy, who, had she not drowned, would have been an older sister to Big Rick, an aunt to RayAnne. Wouldn't it have been nice to have an aunt? RayAnne wonders if her father might have been a different person if he'd had a sister, a different childhood.

After that gray trip to Prague, RayAnne could have kicked herself for choosing the former Eastern Bloc when they might have done the Mediterranean. It had been her graduation gift from Gran, the destination left up to RayAnne, who had been reading Milan Kundera at the time, so of course they'd slogged through the history of Wenceslas Square, ate awful meals, and got scowled at by sour-faced charwomen in the restrooms for never leaving the right amount of coins in exchange for the few sheets of rough toilet tissue. They could have gone to Italy, toured Naples and the Amalfi Coast with Dot as her guide. They should go now. Why not? She decided to bring up the idea at Thanksgiving.

"There!" Big Rick cranes his neck. "Jesus, Ray-Ban, you've passed it again!"

She had to back up to the cul-de-sac. In Ky's driveway the town car settles low when coming to a stop, like a boat.

Not everything on Wellesley Way is as it seems. The reason the split-rail fence surrounding Ky's yard looks perfectly weathered but in an oddly repetitive way is that it's made of wood-grained composite. Upon closer inspection, the fieldstone foundation is a little too glossy for real stone and has seams. And while the shingled house is designed to look New England old, its interior is as beige and new as the suburb itself. Ky has grown to hate it all—the fakeness, the isolation, his riding mower, the homogeneous skin tones of every neighbor. Ivy Dales is a wooded, more expensive version of the suburb Big Rick lived in after their mother kicked him out.

Ky is particularly rankled at being the object of curiosity and good-natured ribbing as the only stay-at-home dad in their neighborhood. He laments moving from the cramped inner city duplex he and Ingrid started out in, where junkies sometimes peed into the mailbox, but at least there was a coffee shop within a few blocks, a decent bowl of Vietnamese pho, and a sidewalk to walk to it on.

Ivy Dales may feel like Ky's purgatory, but to Ingrid it's a haven. After her arduous workdays spent working in DC or Manhattan, weekends at home are spent soaking up the chlorophyll green and the rambunctious silliness of her sons, so refreshingly real compared to the mind-numbingly predictable and seemingly soulless investment bankers she deals with.

Because it is Sunday evening, Ingrid is gearing up to catch a red-eye after the boys are in bed. RayAnne finds her sister-in-law in the master bedroom, folding fine washables still warm from the dryer into her garment bag. Ingrid's everyday married-lady underwear is sexier and nicer than RayAnne's best lace demi-bra and thong that she only wears on third dates.

Her sister-in-law is tall, beautiful, and weirdly smart in all the ways RayAnne isn't. Terribly accomplished and professional, she is also endlessly and genuinely amused by the entire Dahl family, doling out warm indulgences for even their most asinine behaviors. "You guys are something else" is often her take. She adores them as unconditionally as she does her unruly litter of two. "Wow," she will say, giggling. "Nobody has to guess what anyone in this family is thinking!" Her parents were born in the Faroe Islands, where to smile showing teeth or to frown enlisting an eyebrow is considered losing it. Ingrid's veneer is equally composed, but not at all chilly—when she breaks reserve, it is to cry, "You guys!"

RayAnne had thought the fishing circuit was misogynistic, but Ingrid has told stories about big banking that could curl her hair. The richer they are, Ingrid claims of the investment executives she investigates, the more engorged their sense of entitlement, the bigger their boners for owning everything, even everyone, in their sight lines, whether they actually want them or not. Ingrid reckons there are as many sex addicts and acquisition-alcoholics in banking as there are steroid abusers in the Tour de France. She claims most men she encounters actually despise females, uttering the word *woman* in the same tone they reserve for *Democrat*.

"Trust me," Ingrid will say, shrugging. "The same thing that makes these guys desire a woman is the same thing that makes them hate one. I mean, they'll get women, they'll own them, but somewhere in their psyche is probably some little boy with a horrid mother who used to slap his peepee when he wet the bed or locked him in a cupboard if he touched himself."

Ingrid can seem a little world-weary to RayAnne.

When Ingrid's firm steps in to evaluate a bank or investment group, those under investigation expect big guns in power suits girded by troops of number crunchers and assistants. When they see the emissary is a mere woman without even an assistant at her slender side, they breathe a sigh of relief—their first mistake. Their second is misreading her Scandinavian reserve for shyness, assuming this winsome blond with a disarming Faroe accent is what she appears.

There is an entire staff poised behind Ingrid's back. She's a strategist, and like those she's paid to take down she holds a Harvard MBA and has *The Art of War* down pat. But her résumé also includes degrees in economics and philosophy. She's considered an expert in statistical analysis and is in a pool of talking heads sought out for think tanks and comments by the press. Her resolve to see Citizens United abolished is downright ferocious; Ingrid does not want her sons to grow up in an America puppeteered by corporations. There's been talk of her teaming up with Elizabeth Warren for the fight, but whenever the subject of moving to Washington is broached, Ky sticks fingers in his ears and hums. He loves Minneapolis as fiercely as he dislikes its suburbs.

Ingrid's work wardrobe—components of it laid out on the bed RayAnne lounges on—appears utterly feminine but has a strategy as serious as a heart attack. All skirt hems land one inch above her knee, revealing precisely the amount of leg that incites a desire to view more. She'd never "go in" wearing pants: "So Hillary! And oh, does the boys' club hate her."

Ingrid's gabardine and pinstripe Hugo Boss-y underwire creations are a collaborative effort between her and an effeminate tailor in Saint Paul named Tran. Tran and Ingrid meet twice a year to cut up *Vogue* and *Esquire* fashion spreads, pairing one image of a stunning dress with another of a man's Italian cashmere suit, or a herringbone number with razor pleats. Despite the language barrier, Tran seems to understand Ingrid's mission perfectly, shaping various elements into designs and adding his own dragon lady flair. The end result is sexually charged yet utterly untouchable, the power broker's wet dream, detonating their instinct to either pursue Ingrid or resist her, both win-wins for her team.

"My armor," she calls the wardrobe, keeping it all in a separate closet. "I'm rarely manrrupted wearing Tran's creations."

"Manrrupted?" RayAnne is examining a suit jacket; its tailoring reminds her of Helga the Bra Viking's Valkyries.

"Interrupted by a man." At home, Ingrid manages to look elegant in yoga togs and scuffed ballet slippers.

RayAnne catches herself in the mirror; her own weekend ensemble is plaid cutoffs and a tank top not quite covering the shoulder straps of her jogging bra. If clothes announce an agenda, hers would be *Don't mind me.*

After Ingrid's garment bag is locked and loaded, RayAnne glances out the window to the house across the street, which looks like an afterthought to the four-car garage that dominates it. She drops the diaphanous underpants she'd been unconsciously fondling and falls back onto the pillows. "Come back to the city, Ingrid." RayAnne pleads, "Come back and live closer to the Human Beings." Meaning her, of course.

"Ky's always saying the same thing; so is Bernadette," Ingrid laughs. "You guys!"

. . .

Big Rick takes the twins out back with the walkie-talkies, and RayAnne follows Ingrid to the boys' room, where Danny Boy is happily reclining in his cage among candy wrappers. The boys have been hamster sitting and have been promised that if Danny Boy makes it to the end of September, they will be given a pet of their own. After two months, Danny Boy is fatter and probably diabetic, but beggars can't be choosers, and she had begged Ky to take care of him while she was working on Location for the summer.

"Sorry, Danny."

In the kitchen, they watch Big Rick and the twins through the vast windows. The back of the saltbox is nearly all glass. "Like a dollhouse," RayAnne muses, prompting Ky to shift in midstep to become a stiff-legged Ken doll. The kitchen is larger than the entire first floor of her row house, and many times brighter, with lighting that seemingly glows from nowhere and bounces off an institutional amount of stainless steel.

They crack pistachios and rehash the plan they will pose to Big Rick over dinner—that he go back to Arizona and make up with Rita. Ky suggests reverse psychology.

"You know, challenge the old ego, maybe suggest Rita won't take him back?"

Ingrid calculates this risk in her actuary's brain and shakes her head. "Wrong approach."

"We could . . . ," RayAnne ventures. "We could encourage him to go back to her like we're concerned for his well-being, you know, his happiness."

When Ky and Ingrid both blink at her, she surrenders her palms. "Well, I don't know."

"He can stay here for four days." Ky leans back, crossing his arms. "Max."

Ingrid frowns. "Why not till next weekend? That way I can see him again."

They look at Ingrid as if she has special needs, then back to each other.

"Do you think he'll really go back?" Ky looks dubious.

RayAnne shrugs. She has to feel sorry for number six. Rita, like the others, is younger than Big Rick by decades. "I wonder what they have in common to even fight about."

"And that's probably the problem." Ky is tossing pistachios and catching them in his mouth. "I doubt he invests much in husbanding, anyway. So what's to fight about?"

"Point. Maybe he yelled himself out with Mom."

RayAnne and Kyle grow quiet, as if beamed back to the past when Big Rick would arrive at the house after a trip like a train pulling in, when he and Bernadette would roar and screech so loudly that RayAnne and Ky would crawl under their beds or creep like a *Little Big Man* Pawnee to the top of the stairs. Given their mother's lousy aim, the glassware and pottery pitched at their father's head rarely hit the mark, and though Big Rick never struck Bernadette, there always seemed to be the possibility, the threat that one of them would win one day on some level, meaning the other would lose. They sometimes feared their mother might drop the pottery and pick up a knife. For the year or so before the divorce, RayAnne mused that at least a slap would be specific; blood would be a definite something.

Ky had once tried to explain the family dynamic to Ingrid, but she hadn't grasped the notion, responding rationally, "But Kyle, alcoholism is a disease. Surely your father didn't mean to be horrid."

He may not have meant to be, but he was. At the time, the

word *disease* would have meant nothing to a couple of kids clinging to a stair banister in the middle of the night, pajama sleeves
wet with tears and snot.

"Well, he's promised."

The three stand at the open trunk of the Lyft. The driver is
itching to get going. RayAnne will ride along to the airport and
catch the light rail back to her neighborhood. Big Rick has agreed
to stay a few days with Ky and the boys, then go back to Arizona
and give it another go with Rita. In the meantime, he'll send
flowers and a conciliatory email, which Ky will help draft.

Her father stands at the open door with a twin on each shoulder, both waving as the car backs away. Ky is in the driveway, giving RayAnne a look as they pull out, knitting his fingers to sign,
"I'm fucked."

Ingrid, on the other hand, is optimistic Big Rick will keep the
boys occupied so that Ky might get some hours of research in on
his latest project, a book on the early years of the NHL. Ingrid's
mania for hockey is as deep as Ky's and Dot's. During the Stanley
Cup, they all wear the same jerseys and talk hockey ad nauseum.
RayAnne leaves them all to it for the duration of the playoffs.

It's all settled then. Big Rick is squared away. RayAnne can
drive up to Location in the morning with only the show to worry
about.

She leans back into the seat and considers Ingrid's profile,
so serene, yet always pinballing between her family—the der-
vish twins and neurotic Ky—and the pressure cooker job that
requires her to be battle-ready and utterly confident.

"How do you do it, Ingrid?"

"Do what? Oh, you mean everything?"

"Yeah."

"It's kind of a cliché but it's true—the calmest place? It usually is the eye of the storm."

. . .

After her second six-hour drive in five days, RayAnne pulls into Location and brakes to a skid just as she sees Hal driving in the opposite direction with a beautiful woman in his passenger seat. She remembers he had volunteered to drive the guest, the climatologist from the educational nonprofit Norah's Ark.

Cassi is already set up in the trailer.

Banging in and dropping her duffel, RayAnne asks, "Where's Hal taking the ark person? That is the ark builder, right?"

"I'm great, thanks. How was *your* weekend?"

"Don't ask. My butt is flat from driving. Yours?"

"Ass or weekend?" She taps her travel mug with green fingernails. "Hal's probably taking Norah over to Schmancy Camp."

"Johannson's?" RayAnne frowns. The fancy resort is where guests are sometimes housed since there's nothing like a decent motel nearby. Johannson's is expensive and often overrun with honeymooners. Some guests complain it's almost too romantic; others swoon over the monogrammed everything and little pine tree soaps. RayAnne has only ever been in the resort's bar, next to the lakeside restaurant that does not list prices on its menu. Dot knows all about it; apparently she stayed there with Ted back in the day, when it boasted a Michelin-rated chef.

"Yup."

"He staying there too?" RayAnne chews a nail.

"How would I know?"

"They seem cozy?"

"You really want to know?"

"No. Yes."

"They laughed a lot. But I haven't caught them, uh, *doing it.* What do you care? He's a sponsor."

"Right. And . . . sponsors should act professional."

The next morning she's on the dock tapping her foot, waiting for Norah to be delivered by Hal. They are late.

"Where are they?"

Cassi rolls her eyes. "Three minutes late, Ray, keep your knickers on." Winking, she adds, "Maybe they overslept."

RayAnne harrumphs, digs out her phone as if she has more pressing matters, and walks to the end of the dock for better reception.

She calls Ky to check in. He reports it's going well enough. "I'm hiding in our bathroom with my laptop, actually getting some work done."

"He's okay with the twins?"

"They're five. Easy to impress. Yesterday I had the whole house to myself. He took them to Canterbury Downs to see the horses."

"The track? You let him take your children to the track."

"Three hours of uninterrupted alone time, Ray? Of course I let him. He promised upon pain of death he would not touch a drop. Besides, I strapped a cell phone with GPS to Michael Jordan just in case."

Cassi sidles up and nods toward the road where Hal's Wagoneer is approaching, ticking through the trees. "Ky, I'll call you later."

"Before I forget, Mom called from some yoga camp, Cripple-you?"

"Kripalu."

"Anyway, she said Gran called her, worried you were stressed out or something, so Mom called me. She thinks you're too busy to be bothered."

"Who, Mom or Gran?"

"Gran."

"Why would she think that?"

"Dunno. Have you called her lately?"

. . .

RayAnne smiles brightly for the camera, maybe too brightly. "Four years ago, climatologist Norah Smith bought a Winnebago and turned it into a rolling classroom equipped to teach awareness of global climate change. Hoping to spread that knowledge across southern states, she outfitted her RV to look like an ark on wheels. Today she brings the facts of environmental science to thousands of kids in schools where creationism is taught and evolution is banned from the curriculum. We'll talk with Norah about global warming, the state of melting polar ice caps, and the fate of our coastlines. Norah, welcome aboard."

The camera pans to Norah, a younger, much hotter version of Meryl Streep.

"RayAnne, I'm so glad you asked me." Her accent is a genteel drawl.

She imagines Hal is glad as well. Sponsors do love to worm in, get their thumbprints on things, then hang around the sets and act the big shot. Or, in this case, sniff around resorts where guests stay and chaperone them. RayAnne shakes herself back into the moment, takes one look at Norah, and feels suddenly so dowdy she could be a different species. Of course he would pick someone this gorgeous.

Unprompted, Norah begins, "My goodness, I am so thrilled, I just love this show. I can't believe I'm on it! And RayAnne, you are even prettier in person."

Messing with her, surely. "Well, that's very . . ."

"And all this nature. Lordy, we've nothing like this down in Alabama!"

RayAnne sneaks a look at the notes written on her palm. She'd had the entire weekend to study the guest materials, but Big Rick had monopolized every waking moment. "First, Norah, congratulations on your genius grant."

"I know. So exciting! Now I can build an actual boat, so the classroom can float right there on the gulf, a real Norah's ark." She pronounces it *auk*.

"I hear you had some trouble at some of the summer church camps?"

"Oh, yes, the Jesus camps. Once the Baptists discover I'm teaching climate awareness, my welcome can wear out reeeal quick."

"And you were even escorted to a county line?" RayAnne frowns convincingly. "Have you been threatened?"

"Well, I've certainly been discouraged and called some names—everything from 'the Devil's Handmaiden' to, well, you can imagine." Her laugh is like glass chimes, and when Norah stands and readies to cast, her reel spins a perfect line, making RayAnne wonder if Hal spent any time teaching her to fish. She imagines him close behind Norah, arms around her, his hand covering hers on the pole . . .

Cassi's canned voice in her ear catches her in mid-drift. "Snap to, Ray."

Brightening, she asks, "And the ark was vandalized?"

"Scorched some. Nothing a little elbow grease and paint couldn't fix."

As Norah talks about the science behind climate change, Ray-Anne scrutinizes her. This woman is the very type she admires, smart and warm, yet tenacious, like her mother, Dot, and Ingrid. When she looks to the camera boat, Hal is giving a thumbs-up, and RayAnne smiles before realizing he's looking past her to Norah, who is gushing statistics about the end of the climate as we know it. "And all these lovely spruce and birch will die out in two or three hundred years or be underwater from the melted polar ice." She looks around. "Shame, isn't it? These pretty lakes are so romantic."

RayAnne smiles tightly. "Are they?"

"Oh!" Norah's eyes widen. "My, I think I've hooked something . . ." She starts reeling. "Just a little nibble," she nearly giggles. "Like a love bite."

While Norah flirts with her fish, RayAnne faces the camera. "When we come back, is keeping up with fashion draining your bank account? Ana Kozlak is the creator of Pockets, a label designing custom uniforms for busy women. We'll have a runway show on the dock featuring Ana's uniform creations for a florist, a writer, a teacher"—she pivots to camera one—"and even a fishing show host. Here's a sneak peek of what's in store."

Footage from that morning features a number of models sashaying across on the dock, RayAnne bringing up the rear in a knee-length fishing-vest dress with perhaps fifty pockets. Overkill. Her bit will be edited, she hopes, at least the moment when the toe of her shoe stuck between the dock boards and she stepped out of it to continue down the runway dock with one foot bare.

After taping, RayAnne finds Norah at a picnic table, lighting up a cigarette. To RayAnne's inquisitive look, she shrugs. "Well, we're all gonna die from something . . ."

"Hmm, I wish I could think like that. The things I would eat. Does Hal smoke?"

"Ha, I don't know about smoke, but he sizzles some."

"Huh." RayAnne grins. "Speak of the devil."

As Hal is coming up the path, Norah crushes her cigarette and fluffs her hair, wondering quietly under her breath, "I s'pose he's married?"

"Hal?" RayAnne feigns indifference. "Hmm, I might've heard that. Probably has kids and the whole shebang. You didn't ask?"

"No." Norah is looking past her, suddenly looking annoyed. "Oh, there's that girl who pops up everywhere like a prairie dog."

"That's just Cassi."

Before Hal has a chance to reach them, Cassi has cut in front, giving RayAnne a curious look. "Ray? Um, I think you should . . . there's been a development." She points up to the satellite truck, where a tall man with a familiar posture is talking to Randall, the camera guy.

She squints—from the back he could double as Big Rick. "No. That's not my . . ."

"Yup."

Not possible. Her father is supposed be on his way to Arizona this minute to reunite with Rita. He should be halfway through Iowa. If he's spun another of the 180s he's so famous for, she'll smack him. Or maybe something is terribly wrong? She immediately thinks of Gran and swallows.

"Go find out what he wants," RayAnne asks Cassi.

RayAnne pushes her hat down and steps out of Hal's trajectory to clear the path to Norah. She scuttles across the picnic area and up the path leading to her RV.

She is inside less than five minutes when she hears Big Rick call her name, not a something-is-wrong tone, more in the lucky-you-I'm-here register. Peeking between the curtains she sees him on the path, Randall pointing in her direction. She drops the curtain.

Patience. She breathes in; she breathes out. *Patience.* Looking out again, she mutters, "He cannot be here. Can. Not. Be. Here." She flattens on the couch so no shadow of her is cast. *Eye of the storm,* she thinks, like calm Ingrid. Eye of the storm. His knock is loud and persistent, as if he knows she's there.

Just when she's ready to cave, footsteps retreat.

Ten minutes later when Cassi raps on the door and steps in, RayAnne states, "He cannot be here." As if saying it will make it so.

"I asked what he needed, if everything was okay; he said he was just passing by."

"Passing by!"

"Well." Cassi shrugs. "He's here. You want me to tell him you're not?"

"Yes. No. I'm sure he's seen me."

"I could say you've left?"

"My car is right there."

"Should I tell him to leave?"

RayAnne considers it, then shakes her head. He's driven six hours, more if he'd actually set off for Arizona then turned around. Maybe Rita redumped him by phone, or text. He wouldn't drive this far for nothing.

As if reading her mind, Cassi shrugs. "He's your dad, right?"

When she ventures to the catering tent, Big Rick has already made himself quite at home and is eating dinner with the crew. Most of them hang on his every word: he's certainly found the right audience to regale with stories about his fishing show days. His broad gestures—like a white pine in a wind—along with the biblical volume of his voice are two sure signs he's been drinking. The crew guffaw and chuckle at his stories, so well-worn RayAnne could step in and finish them should he pass out. It occurs to her that not everyone can detect what she does, not only that he's drunk, but to what particular degree. She hangs back at the door, observing like a human Breathalyzer for three minutes until deeming him to be at least two drinks beyond sensible and in no shape to drive. The person most glued to him is Amy the Grouper, scaling him with her gaze, as if figuring how to best climb him. RayAnne backs out of the tent and sits on a picnic table to wait, chewing a cuticle and glaring at the tent flap. When he finally comes out, she's unable to keep the hysteria out of her voice. "Dad! What are you doing here?"

"Another helluva hello from my girl!"

"You were headed home."

"I was." He waves away her words. "But then, the Rita situation? You know. I thought about who needs me more, so I turned right around and drove up here."

"Who needs you more? Dad! Not me." Immediately regretting her tone, she adds, "You know what I mean, Dad. I don't need you *here*."

He blinks and gets that look, like his fatherhood has been

dashed to the ground, stomped, and kicked back at him. "Aw, RayBee, I thought you'd be happy to have your old man around, help you out here on this deal."

"That's the thing, Dad. This is my deal, and I don't need help. Really. I'd ask if I did."

"Right." He squares his shoulders. "You're right. You've got it covered." He nods, pensive, for as long as it takes to worm himself another opening. "But that crew? Shit. They couldn't find their own asses in the dark with both hands." He aims himself back to the catering tent, following his chin, as if looking for better reception.

RayAnne watches his back, her jaw an open pot of words stewing. *Incorrigible, infuriating, relentless.* Her father is nothing if not relentless.

By dark, the wagon train circle of Winnebagos and pop-up campers housing the crew has budged open to make space for her father to pitch his own tent. From the booth in her galley kitchenette, she can't make out individual words from around the campfire, only the ebbing and rising of laughter, making it evident Big Rick is providing a diversion, a good time, a yabba dabba doo time. Normally she would sit awhile with Cassi and the others, but now it would only seem to endorse Big Rick's presence. She finishes her notes and prepares questions for tomorrow's taping under the dome light. When laughter hoots, she finds the headphones for her iPod and cranks the volume of *Serene Ocean Waves.*

An hour later, Cassi brings a lettuce burrito and a report, having been asked by RayAnne to spy, just a little. It seems that though Big Rick has attracted the laser-like attention of Amy, he's not reciprocating: Amy is batting her big Grouper eyelashes, but Big Rick is not batting back. Cassi also reports he has arranged a poker game among the crew.

"Great." RayAnne inhales. "Now someone's going to lose their shirt."

9

· · · ·

In the catering tent, Hal sidles into the breakfast line next to RayAnne with his tray. Neither has had coffee yet. She barely makes eye contact. "Did you get Norah off?"

He looks at her curiously. "Um, I dropped her off. At the airport."

"Right, that's what I meant." *Idiot.*

Hal nods to where Big Rick has a number of the crew hanging on his every word. "So, your dad is Big Rick from *Bi*—"

RayAnne finishes, "*Big Rick's Bass Bonanza.* Yup."

"I watched his show when I was a kid."

"You and dozens. It got canceled during the first season."

"What happened?"

"What happened?" RayAnne frowns over the array of breakfast offerings. How is she supposed to lose weight when the caterers flaunt mac-and-cheese waffles and artisanal maple sausages? She settles for a feta and spinach egg-white omelet, taking the moment to stall in the face of Hal's question. "Actually?" She decides to tell it straight up. "Actually, sponsors happened."

"Oh? *Oh.*"

She inhales and it all comes out, seemingly in one breath. "I don't remember every detail, just the plot: my dad—married, of course, to my mother—got involved with the wife of the CEO of TroutLocker. Apparently only one of his affairs. Anyway, Mrs. TroutLocker left her husband and pulled a *Fatal Attraction* and followed my mom and us around for a few weeks. There was a restraining order and all that. So my dad got fired because of the scandal, and it made all the newspapers, and my mom went understandably nuts for a while. Dad sued TroutLocker and won, so naturally no underwriter would touch him after that. You know, the usual stuff." Why was she telling him all this?

Hal's mouth opens, as if wondering the same thing, then he recovers, grabbing a cream cheese pastry to offer her. She shakes her head, making her fat-cheeked fat face.

"Ah, sorry." He drops the pastry onto his own plate. "That must have been pretty rough."

"Well, it was no trip to the so-dee fountain."

"Pardon?"

"Sorry, it's this scene in—"

"In *Little Big Man*." Hal grins. "One of my favorite scenes, Jack playing with the elephant spigot while Mrs. Pendrake is in the storeroom getting . . . you know. But yeah, I see what you mean. Ouch."

He has favorite scenes from her favorite film? Now she's staring at him like she had that first day in the parking lot. The moment is interrupted when Amy walks up, dressed as if for an eighties disco instead of the backwoods. She reaches between them to grab a fork. They both turn to watch as she slowly sashays past Big Rick's table to her own, where a fork is clearly visible. RayAnne and Hal exchange looks. He nods in the direction of an empty table and she follows.

Over breakfast Hal brings her up to speed on all the goings-on she's been avoiding since Big Rick's arrival. As she'd suspected, her father has indeed ingratiated himself to the crew, always there to tote some case or coil some cable. Hal reports he's even shown Randall a few tricks for filming on big water, like how to anchor a Steadicam onto the oarlocks, jury-rigging this, devising that.

"Sounds just like him, always ready to lend a hand." Always a hearty chuckle for everyone's bad jokes, a refill, a buddy-thump to the back, another cold one. All with names dropped here and there from back in the day when he guided for the rich and famous.

Glancing over at her father, she strains to hear what he's saying, while at the same time trying to listen to Hal, who is talking about some pierogi or polka dinner at the Hatchet Inlet town hall. Big Rick is telling a story about taking RayAnne out on the circuit when she was a teen.

"Yee-up, thought she'd teach her old man a lesson."

She swivels and coughs to make her presence known. Once she has her father's attention, she dares him to go on with such a searing look, he stops midsentence and pretends to have something stuck in his throat. He may have finagled his way into Location, but family history, her history, is off-limits, especially some tired story about the day he was supposed to take Walter Mondale fishing but she'd superglued all the tackle boxes shut.

God forbid he's around when they tape the segment on the Birkett twins, who for obvious reasons are known for never appearing on television or granting interviews. As it turns out, they've asked to be on the show—it seems both are crazy about fishing.

When she turns back at the sound of a scraping chair, Hal is already standing, lifting his tray. "Seems you're kind of preoccupied."

"Oh? Sorry, what were you saying? Wait."

But he's already backing away with an injured grin. "I think I was asking you out."

Cassi's fists are planted on her hips. "What do you mean? He either asked you out or he didn't."

"Well, he started to, I guess."

"Argh, Ray, why can't you pick up on—"

"On what?"

"Signals. It's like you've got two bars of reception when it comes to yourself—when it's three feet away staring you in the face. Where's your radar?"

"I'm not a bat." RayAnne sulks.

"Bats use *sonar*. That thing you do so well with the guests?"

"What?"

"Listening. Give it a try but, like, to yourself?" Cassi checks her watch. "We better move; the twins are probably here."

RayAnne faces camera two.

"Kira and Kit Birkett are happy, healthy, twenty-four-year-old twins. Unlike other twins, they are irrevocably conjoined at the breastbone, sharing major vascular components. They will never be surgically separated. Having just finished their premed education, they are preparing to intern in the fields of dermatology and plastic surgery."

RayAnne had been jittery with a combination of anticipation and dread, worried about Kit and Kira's arrival, how they might be regarded or treated by the crew. She was concerned enough about how they'd get around on Location, never mind getting aboard *Penelope*. She was also worried about her own potential missteps and reactions; what if she stared or asked the wrong question?

But she had worried for nothing. Kit and Kira waltz around Location with more grace on four legs than she could on two. Still, though he's hanging a respectable distance back, she's convinced Big Rick will make some stupid remark, one of his brutishly honest slips, or worse, make some joke with the word *Siamese* in it or challenge them to a sack race.

But here they are, cheerfully reeling in small perch while discussing the challenges of their upcoming medical residencies. RayAnne asks how they will manage two at once.

They laugh. "We manage everything two at once."

After twenty minutes in the boat, RayAnne has almost forgotten their uniqueness, possibly because Kit and Kira seem to think nothing of it and don't consider themselves anything special. "You know, besides the freak factor," offers Kira.

Kit says, "We just have a different 'normal.'"

Indeed, from their ribs up, they seem like average sisters with very different personalities.

"I'm night," says Kira.

"And I'm day," Kit finishes.

They debate about what to use for lures and wager bets over which of them will catch the biggest fish. They are quite competitive, they confess. "Our priority right now," Kit tells RayAnne, "is to tackle med school."

"We've even dumped our boyfriends."

Before RayAnne can get her head around the idea of them having boyfriends, Kira leans to the camera as if sharing a confidence. "You think *your* love life is complicated?" She rolls her eyes Kit's way. "My sister is the biggest dope about men."

In response, Kit makes the universal gag-me gesture. "Gawd, the things I overhear!"

They tell her that, like a lot of people, they listen to loud music when they clean their apartment, but since they have wildly differing tastes, each wears headphones. The result, Kit says, is something people would probably pay to see, them bashing about, mopping and scrubbing to different beats and dance moves, Kit swiping the mirror along to Trampled by Turtles while Kira lip-syncs Adele at a toilet-brush microphone.

Many of the questions RayAnne had planned to ask about the logistics of their lives fall away under their chatter. Both are talkers, both opinionated and quite candid about their limitations and their advantages. "I always know where to find her," quips Kit.

"I'm never lonely," Kira adds.

RayAnne carefully poses her next question: "Do you ever want to be alone?"

They look at her as if she's asked if the moon is made of Swiss cheese. Kit says, "Why bother wanting something—"

Kira finishes, "That you'll never have?"

They appear to expect an answer, but RayAnne can only muse, "True." Moving on, she asks, "Do you ever fight?"

"Do we ever fight?" They fold with laughter, batting at each other's knees.

Other, deeper laughter sounds across a short expanse of water, and RayAnne turns, mortified to see Big Rick planted in one of the camera boats as if he belongs there.

Toward the end of the interview, there's a more serious moment when Kira looks from her sister directly to the lens. "You see, neither of us is a freak until someone sees our difference as being . . . *relevant.*"

Kit nods in agreement. "I'm a freak when you decide I am, but that's your deal."

It's a bit of introspection that seems very Dot-like to RayAnne.

"That," Cassi says as the twins scramble out of the boat, "was awesome. Maybe one of the best segments we've ever taped."

The twins insist on having their picture taken with RayAnne and Cassi—who seems to intrigue them both. Kit drapes an arm around RayAnne and Kira snuggles into Cassi. "Good thing we like attention, huh?"

Kit sweetly plants a peck on RayAnne's cheek.

Her stupid grin lasts through the good-byes, and as they are driven away by Hal, RayAnne's fingers drift to where the girl kissed her. In the delight of the moment, it occurs to her she might just have the best job on Earth. Not even the shadow of Big Rick in the periphery can dampen that. She makes a mental note to call Gran the next morning: *Make sure you watch this one.*

. . .

But, just as Gran says, where there's a bloom on the rose, there's usually a pile of horseshit nearby.

RayAnne is working over *Penelope*'s bow with a tin of paste wax and a cloth diaper when Cassi finds her. Since this morning's news, she's been avoiding the crew and staff, most gone apoplectic since the final scheduled guest of the season canceled at the last minute—the math teacher with the nose transplant, something about sinuses and airplanes. Now they are frantically scrambling to find a replacement so the show can wrap. As it is, the Grouper is already wound like a spring with Big Rick ignoring her. The season wrap party is slated for that evening, and a bunch of sponsors are due to converge on Location.

RayAnne had been totally prepared for the math teacher and her newly constructed nose, had voraciously read the notes and drafted questions into the wee hours. Rebecca Standish had been hiking in the Badlands in a lesser canyon with a Milky Way bar in her shirt pocket. When something huge stepped into her path, she'd barely known what hit her. The next thing Rebecca knew, she was sitting in her bra, her shirt torn away save a single sleeve, watching the rump of a grizzly shambling up the trail—the rest of her shirt stuck to the bottom of his rear paw like toilet paper. In shock, she began laughing uncontrollably, slow to realize her nose had been clawed into sections until her mouth filled with blood. Her laughter drew the attention of a troop of Eagle Scouts, who thankfully had cell phones with GPS. A medevac helicopter team was able to land and lift her out before she bled to death. But while Rebecca was being rescued, there would be no saving the supermodel on the lip of a canyon only a few miles away. The model (whose name is well known, but for her family's sake will not be mentioned in the interview) had just plummeted to her death during a photo shoot after the photographer's assistant asked her to take just one more step back into better light. The model had been a donor, but with the impact of her fall, most working organs had been rendered useless. She had landed on her back, though, sparing her face.

RayAnne is disappointed, having worked hard gathering both women's stories. But not everything pans out, and she needs to learn to roll with such setbacks. So no guest yet—but Cassi and others are working on it. She can either tend *Penelope* or pace, so she takes Dot's advice and stays busy. Besides, there's nothing to be done; she can hardly prepare for a last-minute replacement when she doesn't know who it might be, or when they might come. Could be today, could be tomorrow . . .

A ghostly form appears as a reflection on the windscreen. RayAnne spins. Cassi.

"What. What is that look for?"

For a moment the girl just stands with a pained smile.

RayAnne sets down the wax. "Spit it."

Cassi points through the trees to the parking area. "You saw that bus-thing?"

"Uh-huh." A few minutes earlier, a luxury touring van with loaded luggage racks had pulled into Location. RayAnne assumed it was the shuttle of sponsors due from Minneapolis for the wrap party. "Great, so they're, like, five hours early?"

"Well, that's just it. They're not the sponsors."

"Not them? Well, then who?"

"You better come with me, Ray."

Yam, lavender, and patchouli. She can smell her before even rounding the end of the van.

Bernadette spins. "RayAnne!"

"Mother?"

RayAnne is caught off balance, too dumbstruck to raise her arms. Bernadette catches her midsway in the embrace of a boxer stilling his training bag. Over her mother's shoulder, she sees the troop of her mother's Blood-Tide Questers milling, pointing, frilling their bejeweled fingers in little waves. *Toodles.*

"And you've brought all your—"

"My girls, yes! Isn't this fantastic? We're just on our way to our retreat up at Sacajawea, you know, the sweat lodge spa? And I realized how close we were, so I thought, why not stop by? See you in action? Get the tour!"

RayAnne's focus shifts to a face just behind her mother's—Jeanette Faring.

It's quite enough having Big Rick loitering around Location. She's only putting up with him because it all ends soon and everyone goes home, or in his case goes somewhere. But both parents on top of the crisis of the canceled guest? Not to mention the sponsors.

It all simply, suddenly exceeds RayAnne's reserves. She cannot risk Bernadette getting a whiff of Big Rick, or vice versa, yet cannot fathom how such a collision can be prevented. Panic dampens her underarms. It's possible none of the staff or crew has seen the bus yet. It's lunchtime; those not in the catering tent are busy thumping laptops and iPhones, scrambling to replace Rebecca Standish.

Her mother's sudden appearance leaves RayAnne mouthing empty air like a trout, completely lost for words. Bernadette must take her mavens and retreat from Location as quickly as they materialized. As if reading her mind, Cassi attempts to herd several back to the bus, but a number seem to have quested off on various paths.

Just as she takes a breath to implore her mother to leave, RayAnne sees the Grouper bounding down the path. RayAnne grabs Bernadette's caftan sleeve and yanks her behind the trunk of a large cedar. "Mom, listen, I'm really sorry, but this just isn't a good—"

The Grouper, swift as a deer, suddenly appears on the path only yards away. Her nasal trill cuts RayAnne off. "I thought that was you!"

RayAnne drops her mother's sleeve, unable to form any coherent explanation as to why Location should suddenly be overrun not only with both her parents but a tribe of inquisitive women.

Bernadette leans from behind the tree. "Amy? Amy Harris!"

"I was right! Oh. My. God. Bernadette! I haven't seen you since Burning Man!"

RayAnne looks confoundedly from one to the other. "You know each other?"

Amy smile-scowls at RayAnne while giving her mother a squeeze. "RayAnne, you never mentioned Bernadette Mills is your *mother!*"

"Well, no. I wouldn't have . . ." RayAnne blinks upward to a low scudding cloud as if it might offer some explanation for the turn her day is taking. Her mother and Amy commence catching up, yammering, hugging.

Cassi, halfway to the van, turns and drops the elbows of two of the mavens to watch a moment before calling to RayAnne, "Should I take them on a tour?"

RayAnne closes her eyes. "Yes."

A diversion might at least keep them out of the way until the next thing that will invariably go wrong.

But there is no waiting. A chortle of a particular baritone booms from the path leading to the catering tent. Lunch is over. Bernadette's ears prick up, and she swivels her head like an owl without moving her shoulders. Her eyes grow round at RayAnne and her normally soothing tone of voice climbs to a raptor's pitch. "That cannot be who I think it is."

"Actually." RayAnne feels the burning buzz on her lip that usually forewarns the eruption of a cold sore. "It is." In addition, the talons of a headache have begun squeezing the base of her skull. It's not even noon. Both parents are here, she has no guest, and Location is about to be inundated with show sponsors and the higher-ups in NPT, the people who will decide if *Fishing* is worth the risk.

Backing away, she fights the urge to run. "I'll be. In my trailer. Going to. Lie down."

.   .   .

Of course she can't lie still. She paces Tiffany end to end, the length of which is exactly—surprise—thirteen strides. When someone opens the door unannounced, she freezes.

Cassi sticks her head in. "Ray?"

"Are they gone? Tell me they're gone. You got my text? Did you find anything for my lip? Was there any trouble?"

"Yes. And yes." Cassi hands over a tube of Carmex, saying, "As far as trouble? Your parents only saw each other long enough to fling some nasty looks. In other news, we're on for three o'clock. Amy's found a guest to replace Nose Job."

"Thank God." RayAnne turns to the mirror and dabs at the glowing bump on her lip. "At least something's going right. Who is it?"

"Hang on to your bobbers."

"Who . . ." RayAnne catches Cassi's eye in the mirror and pivots. "*Who* is the guest?"

"Bernadette Mills. New Age aging coach to the menopausal rich."

.   .   .

RayAnne is aboard *Penelope* and far out on the water when the expected van from the station arrives loaded with sponsors. Everyone on Location is to be at peak performance, ready to answer questions, make nice with those who have come to inspect the operation and meet the people behind the scenes, check out the bang they're getting for their bucks. The Wallets—Big Rick's name for sponsors—are expecting a catered petting zoo with an open bar. She aims her binoculars through the windscreen, zeroing in on the steep slope where paths zag down the hill. Staffers

FISHING! . . . .

169

are leading sponsors on a tour to the dock, the beach, the picnic area. Bernadette's mavens crawl the place like it's an ant farm. Up on the plateau, she can make out a party rental van and a delivery truck. Some workers string lights under a large temporary canopy while others bang together a small stage for the band. One guy tries unsuccessfully to poke tiki torches into the stony ground leading to the parking lot, his obscenities carrying across the water.

RayAnne's been given a pass for the moment; she needs to prepare for her impromptu guest, after all. Out on the lake in *Penelope*, she stares at the water while gingerly tapping the growing bump on her lip. The boat rocks in the wake of fishermen zipping around from one bass hole to the next. She thinks idly of the song "Mad Dogs and Englishmen." No fish worth its scales would bite in the noonday sun. Abstractly, RayAnne feels like pounding these fishermen for their stupidity and for disturbing her concentration.

But as Bernadette says, there's no man more hopeful than one holding his pole.

She can't stay out here much longer—as tempted as she is to fire up *Penelope* and defect to Canada, she's going to have to go back, buck up, and interview her mother.

Interview my mother.

Gran will know what to do. RayAnne speed-dials, but Gran isn't answering—probably out watching the sweaty cadets jogging in packs or has her Vitamix set to epic and can't hear the phone.

When RayAnne was young and things went badly and she'd fall headlong into one of her yellow funks, Gran would pull her close, insisting, "Tell Gran all about it," then patiently listen to RayAnne's whimpers and petty grievances as if they were the most important and vexing problems facing the world. RayAnne cannot recall what sort of dramas she'd have played out at age six, or ten, or seventeen, but Gran's response was always the same, patting the place on the couch next to her, coaxing, "Tell." Then she would stroke the nape of RayAnne's neck and smooth her hair while RayAnne gnashed and gnarled and eventually talked herself out, exhausted. She'd finally roll her head back across the pleats of Gran's skirt to blink up at the woman who made it all better by saying practically nothing.

When the answering machine kicks in, she leaves a message: "Okay, Gran. It's only me. We'll talk later?" After hanging up she repeats, "Okay," as if things are.

RayAnne turns the ignition, and *Penelope* rumbles to life. RayAnne spins the wheel in the direction of the shore. She manages a quiet docking, and with the stealth of a Human Being takes the lesser paths and shortcuts to her trailer. Once inside, she shouts into a bunched-up beach towel for two minutes, then does her best to compose herself. They tape in an hour; once that one single, final interview is in the can, the season will officially wrap, and Location will break down and pack up like a traveling carnival. There's a twelve-week hiatus before it all starts up again, at least the planning stages—that's months. Were Gran here, she'd be assuring RayAnne as she would before a dentist appointment. *You just get through this one next thing, then celebrate it being over. We'll have ice cream!*

Icing the carbuncle on her lip, she can only hope Darren down in makeup can work some sort of magic. She covers it as best she can with concealer, then changes into the same outfit worn the day before while interviewing the twins, because as far as the camera is concerned, it's still yesterday.

If only.

She tucks Cassi's notecards into a cargo pocket and steps out, inhaling the piney air and reminding herself to breathe. Halfway down the hill at the fork, she takes the steeper, more dangerous path.

10

.

.

.

.

RayAnne can see her mother walking along on the path below, still wearing her paper makeup bib and following Amy to the dock. They are on the trail that eventually shortcuts through the picnic area. From her high vantage point, RayAnne can also see the picnic tables where Big Rick is holding court with three of Bernadette's girls, his arm casually slung over the shoulder of one. Their giggles waft up the hill, sounding more like teens than card-carrying members of AARP. On the table next to them is an open bottle of wine and an empty one, tipped on its side.

When Bernadette and Amy emerge from the path to cross the clearing, Big Rick grins widely, dispatches wine into two fresh Dixie cups, and holds them aloft at their approach. RayAnne presses her foot to the ground as if it's a brake that might stop time moving forward.

His greeting is expansive. "Ah, two more beauties come to join in our little bacchanalia!"

Amy practically skips forward. Bernadette blinks like she's just stepped indoors from bright sunlight, taking in Big Rick's unbuttoned shirt, the amount of wine left in the standing bottle, and the now-giddy trio of women who have strayed from her troop.

Big Rick booms, "C'mon, have a drink with me and the cougars here."

RayAnne covers her mouth, praying her father will shut his.

Bernadette faces Big Rick. "Richard. You might get that mouth checked; it appears to be leaking."

"Oh, right. I guess that wasn't very P-frickin'-C of me. Sorry." He cocks his head and offers, more formally, "'Dette, please join me and your *meno-pals* here for a glass of cheer. Whaddya say?"

She looks to the women, tipsy and grinning, then back to Big Rick. "Don't you have a new model at home? Or has her freshness date expired?"

"Ah, the ex officio is irate!"

"Please. I doubt you even know what that means. Listen, Richard," Bernadette tears off the makeup bib and crumples it. "You can go ahead and ruin this for me, but if you screw this up for RayAnne . . ."

"My, my, Miss Inner Quietude is sounding pretty hostile there, Bernie-dette."

Bernadette's voice is loud enough to travel, not just up the slope but to everyone milling on the paths and the crew on the dock waiting for them. "Why don't you just leave RayAnne be, leave us all be?"

He's no longer grinning. "And why don't you go get your ears candled, or your chakras rotated, or whatever the woo-woo hell you do."

"Richard, so help me—"

"So help me what? So help me, Gandhi?"

The women abandon the picnic table one by one, no longer charmed, giving Bernadette apologetic looks for their temporary treason. Bernadette's clenched fists fall from her hips. "You know what, Richard? You can just . . ." Words rarely fail Bernadette, but they do now. "Just kiss my ass."

As she starts walking, Big Rick calls after her.

"Yeah? Maybe I should—might do you some good!"

When particularly nervous, RayAnne tries to imagine addressing viewers one at a time and so speaks as she would to a single person. She thinks about how she might engage some busy executive, distract her enough that she sets aside her papers to shift closer to the television, or entertain the mother of young children who is nabbing an hour to watch *Fishing*. Or get the attention of a college girl, tempt her to look up from her ramen at the sound of the theme music, and give her chin a wipe. RayAnne speaks with an implied conspiracy because she knows busy women watching television have stolen the time to do so. When she says hello and winks at the beginning of every show, the takeaway is *Forget the twenty things vying for your attention—for the next fifty minutes, it's just us.* RayAnne has an abstract awareness of her audience, but as easily as she can imagine them as individuals she can compact them like a zip file to stash neatly in the outline of Cassi, because Cassi always stands behind camera two for each taping, her silhouette the focus of RayAnne's intentions—her *drishti,* in Bernadette-speak. When RayAnne hears "Roll!" she imagines dozens of women whooshing into Cassi like a colony of bats to a cave. She'd never realized how much she relied on that visual device until she notices the second pontoon puttering from its moorage, and Cassi's not in it. She's been left on the dock and is taking off her life vest.

"Whoa, Cassi! You're missing your boat."

"I got kicked off to make room for the guys from Laguna and Cast-Away."

"No!" RayAnne swivels and shades her eyes. Indeed, the pontoon is loaded with sponsors. In Cassi's usual place sits Hal, flanked by a rep from Mermaid Pilsner and the CEO of Jailbait. The other boat has even more, too far out on the lake to make out. She waves and whistles to the pontoon to no avail.

"No . . . ," she moans. Everyone else is bent to their tasks, oblivious to her plight. The gaffer is gaffing; the sound guy is clipping a wireless mic onto Bernadette. Darren is checking continuity by comparing RayAnne's clothes and hair to iPhone shots of the previous day's shoot.

"Don't worry, Ray," Cassi says, handing over RayAnne's earpiece. "I'll be right here. Got my monitor all plugged in, see?" Frowning, RayAnne screws in the earbud. Cassi presses the live button and says, "Check, check," sounding gritty and tinny in RayAnne's ear. People are waiting for her to get in the boat.

"Go," Cassi says, directly into the mouthpiece. "Go, go, *go*."

. . .

"Weren't Kira and Kit just amazing? The twins are a true inspiration, especially for those of us that think *we* have challenges." The camera zooms out to show the boat rocking and RayAnne sitting across from Bernadette, who sways a little like a Weeble on the bench seat, her face flushed nearly to the shade of *Penelope*. RayAnne hopes she's not still fuming from her run-in with Big Rick.

"Our second guest"—RayAnne must maneuver each word past the sore on her lip, now raised like a lump of broiled cheese—"is life-passages doula Bernadette Mills." She stutters on -*dette*. "Thousands of you follow her blog *Blood Tides,* and over the years many have participated in her ritual Meno-Trek pilgrimages to spiritual destinations. One of our own staff has even been questing with Bernadette in the Nevada desert."

Not sure which direction to turn, she pivots to camera two, which is wrong, so she's signaled to turn back and does so, haltingly. "My own journey with Bernadette began over thirty years ago." Resisting the impulse to tongue the cracking pancake makeup covering the cold sore, RayAnne mumbles, "Bernadette Mills is my m-mother."

The ensuing pause is far too long.

Not once before has she had to rely on notes on camera, but

as for what to say to her own mother, she's at a loss. She awkwardly holds a number of index cards with questions Cassi has come up with. It doesn't help that she's stayed intentionally out of the loop of Bernadette's career, remaining diligently neutral for fear of giving into her snarky side and scoffing at her mother's New Agey-ness, what she and Ky refer to as her *optimistyness*.

Bernadette's smile is pasted, as she waits for some cue or a question, casting uneasy glances far across the rough water to the dock, to land.

The prompts on the index cards are written in Cassi's tight handwriting so that RayAnne must squint. She shuffles them out of order until one gives itself up to the breeze to blow into the water off the stern. They both watch it float for a second, then Bernadette pats RayAnne's knee. "No matter, honey. We don't need the cards. If it helps, I can just tell the audience a bit about the Blood-Tide Quests and you can ask me questions from there."

"Mom." RayAnne covers her mic and speaks without moving her lips. "Please don't give me advice about my job while I'm doing it." She looks to camera one. "You'll edit that out? Sorry everyone, can we start over?"

And so they do. The notecards are useless. She falters through a few uninspired questions, and it all begins a slow slide downhill. Every time she looks to camera two expecting to see Cassi, her point of focus is filled with the disconcerting visage of Hal.

She should have insisted Cassi be on board. Why doesn't she stand her ground?

To make things worse, it's too windy to fish. Being so accustomed to holding a rod and reel, she doesn't know quite what to do with her hands. She decides to sit on them, forgetting they might come in handy when needing balance. *Penelope* isn't just rocking now; waves begin tugging the boat this way and that as if trying to unmoor them.

RayAnne's frustration gives way to nervousness, and in her nervousness she keeps repeating her mantra of "Okay."

Bernadette does her best to salvage the interview by more or less asking herself questions and then answering. Inside five minutes—and they need an average of thirty to harvest a decent ten minutes for an interview—the interview seems to be going nowhere. They each make an effort to revive the conversation, which only results in them talking over one another.

"Okay, okay. Can you tell me about the rituals—"

"I thought I'd talk some about the rituals—"

"Okay, go on, Mom." RayAnne cringes—she had been determined not to say *Mom,* meant to be professional and use *Bernadette.*

"No, you start."

"No, *you,* okay?"

RayAnne's desperation intensifies while swells under the boat lift it to a stomach-churning height. Over the next twelve minutes, the interview devolves into a rehash of ancient mother-daughter dysfunction, while those looking on watch it all. The camera operators keep making eye contact with Amy the Grouper, who signals for them to keep taping. In her feed, RayAnne can hear Cassi's voice, quiet in a way it rarely is: "Stop now, Ray. Stop the interview."

But RayAnne does not, at least not until one very surprising revelation is out of the bag. Sponsors and crew look on while the interview culminates in a grand finale that includes tears and ends with a flourish of vomit.

The last thing RayAnne barks at the camera is "Please turn that off! This isn't some fucking reality show!"

* * *

Throughout the trip to shore, Bernadette keeps her eyes scrunched shut and clutches the gunnel. RayAnne speeds toward land to outrun the boats with sponsors and crew. *Penelope's* bow plows over swells to crash down again and again, her stern bucking out of the waves so that the propellers whir uselessly in the air, like a plane in a tailspin.

Once docked, she yanks off her microphone and tosses it to the decking. In spite of repeating "Sorry, Mom," she leaves her for someone else to take care of. She pounds across the boards and without a glance passes Cassi, who scurries to help Bernadette.

Striding through the picnic area, Big Rick catches up to her, but RayAnne twists away when he reaches for her arm. "Fuck off, Dad."

Her mother is trying to catch up as well but is still wobbling on her sea legs, looking quite green. When reaching Big Rick, she gives up the chase and pauses to catch a breath. "Indeed, Richard. Fuck off." Her hands hang in their caftan sleeves and she gags a little on the words like she might throw up again, but after a woozy sway she only sighs and plods forward. "Oh, RayBee."

. . .

RayAnne sprints, not toward her trailer but up the rougher path to the old scout camp, fleeing Location altogether. Stopping to tie her shoe, she regrets not rinsing her hands in the lake. Ripping some soft leaves from a low plant, she wipes the vomit off her palms and from between her slimy fingers. She marches and stumbles along overgrown paths around the old campsites, repeating figure eights, a little like Danny Boy in his Habitrail.

The interview wasn't just a failure. It was humiliating and the opposite of professional. She can only imagine what the sponsors are thinking. Backing up against a birch, she slides down to the mulchy ground, where she mindlessly strips more plants of their leaves. There she sits, struggling to think of anything but the events of the last hour.

Only when her bottom is numb and her pants damp from

sitting does she rouse herself to slog back to Location. Rounding a corner, she waves her way through a cloud of gnats. When one suddenly zooms into her ear, she yelps. Stopping in her tracks, she shakes her head, trying to dislodge it. When shaking doesn't work, she bends down and thumps the side of her skull with her palm as if it's a ketchup bottle. Behind her, a male voice calls out, "RayAnne!"

Great. She doesn't respond, just keeps stumbling forward until her arm is grabbed.

"Ray. Hold on!"

She spins to face Hal with wild eyes and bangs her temple again. Why does it have to be him?

"Bug. In my ear."

"Oh." He looks relieved. "I thought you were having some sort of seizure." He steadies her jaw and squints into her ear. "Can you hold still?"

She writhes. "Get it out? Please."

Hal looks up the path and back, then steers her along. "C'mon."

"C'mon where?"

In answer, he guides her to the windowless old well house, where he shoulders open the door and pulls her in.

"What? Why in here?"

"You'll see."

The door slams, veiling them in darkness and dank humidity. She cannot think straight with all the buzzing, which is like having an Alka-Seltzer plopped in her ear. "It's dark!"

"That's the idea. Just hang on."

She hears clothing rustle and the distinct sound of a zipper.

Has he lost his mind? She begins to struggle, her voice verging on screechy. "What are you doing?"

A square of blue light suddenly illuminates their faces from underneath. "Getting my phone. For the flashlight." Even in the dim light it's apparent how offended he is. "Now stop squirming." He holds the beam up to her ear. "The bug will come to the light. It'll come out."

"Will it?" She doubts it. The insect seems to be pinballing the chambers of her head. Soon it will tunnel down her throat.

"Quiet. Please?"

The perfect way to end the season: triple and quadruple the humiliation. Just heap it on.

"RayAnne, please, stay still." A moment passes, and another. The insect seems to have at least calmed, probably considering its next plan of attack. She settles enough to hold herself steady. Hal lowers his voice, saying, "You didn't really think I was going to . . . ?" They are close enough that she can feel his breath on her temple.

"To ravage me? Yes. No. Sorry, I can't stand this." She fights the urge to shake her head again.

Hal lightly holds her jaw. "Don't. Move."

They stand silent in a pool of darkness, both barely breathing, waiting. When they do speak, it's to whisper.

She sniffs. "Oh God, my mother . . ."

"She's fine."

"I'm fired, aren't I?"

"No. But—"

"Wait. No, I don't even want to know," RayAnne groans. "Gawd, it's *buzzing*. Is she still here? My mother?"

"Last I saw, she was herding her group to their bus—what does she call them?"

"The Mavenhood."

"Right."

She cannot see Hal but can sense he's smiling. "Quite the pair of parents you have, Ray."

"Hardly a pair." RayAnne flinches. "Never a pair; that was the problem."

"Well, interesting, anyway."

"Interesting?" RayAnne stiffens. "My mother's head is shoved so far up her happy place . . . and he's just a big toddler with a sippy cup of bourbon."

"Well. Sure. They are who they are, but you wouldn't be you if not—"

"Don't do that." She raises her voice. "Don't patronize me. I've made a hash of it. Let's agree to agree on that. You've seen the mistakes." RayAnne shudders. "I mean besides just today."

"I don't know what you're talking about. Listen, you were authentic out there, you were real with your mother, and actually? Sixty percent of it was fine."

"Losing my shit on camera. Nice season finale."

"Okay, forty percent. The worst will be edited out, Ray."

"The sponsors all saw. How does editing fix that?" The buzzing gets louder, and her voice rises with it.

"Trust me, it will."

"Right, like you can fix it."

Hal pauses, as if carefully choosing his words. "What if I can, actually?"

"Just leave it."

"You've no idea, do you?"

"Of what?"

"Of . . ." He shakes his head. "Wait, I can see it. Here it comes." All is quiet as Hal delicately dips his pinky into the bowl of her ear. "Got it!"

Finally. "Thank God." She slumps in relief, then looks up. "I have no idea of what?"

He still has her chin cupped in his hand. "Of how good you are at this—how bright, how natural you are. And, and how . . ."

She opens her mouth, about to object when he begins lowering his face to hers.

Is he going to kiss her?

He is. He's going to kiss her.

In spite of herself, in spite of it all, RayAnne feels a sweet, elastic tug. Admittedly, she's wondered just what kissing Hal would be like. Perhaps since the moment he walked past her car in the parking lot, flashing that grin. And on the morning they'd gone fishing when he'd fed her pancakes and was so easy to talk to. The thing about Hal, she realizes, is that he's effortless. To be around, to joke with. There's no agenda. Show or no show, she doesn't need to be anything but herself around Hal.

And now he's going to kiss her. Here in the satiny, musty darkness of the well house with the smell of bay rum and mild sweat like a tonic. As if her next breath is of helium, her body lifts lightly off her heels. His lips are a delicious inch away from hers. This is it.

Then the scritch of the needle as the soundtrack halts and she remembers with horror the canker sizzling on her lip. Her hand zip-lines to her face just in time for Hal's mouth to connect with her knuckles, which, having been recently vomited on, reek.

His eyes pop open. "Ah?"

RayAnne steps back. "Oh, God. I'm sorry—I forgot about this . . . this." She stupidly points at the cold sore, as if he can see in the dark.

Hal steps back. "Oh, I didn't mean to—"

"No!" Of course, what she means is yes. Of course she would kiss him if not for the growing monstrosity on her lip and her vomit-caked fingers, which not only smell but now burn. "Wait. I can't see. Something . . . my hands," she holds them out and even in the darkness can tell something's wrong.

He shines the phone at them and she gasps, "What the . . . ?" Each finger is swollen and pink, as if her palms have sprouted bundles of wieners. Seeing them acts as a panic switch, her fingers consumed by itchiness.

"I wiped them with those leaves. Oh, God! Is this—?"

"Oh, boy." Hal grimaces. "Poison ivy—afraid so." As they both look at her hands the beam from his cell phone flickers, then peters out, sinking them back into darkness.

He exhales. "Battery. You'll need calamine. And don't touch yourself; don't spread the oil."

In living, stinking color, it's all rather more than RayAnne can handle. For the third time in one day, her flight instinct roars to life. She gropes for the door with her burning catcher's mitts, barely managing to turn the handle. Hal reaches to help and the door slams open. Evening sunlight pours into the cocoon of space. She ducks out from under Hal's outstretched arm.

Ten yards down the path, Cassi is walking with Amy. As the well house door bangs open, both stop dead in their tracks and watch RayAnne spill from the dark interior, followed by Hal, both blinking in the sudden glare. Clearly disheveled, RayAnne trots in the direction of her trailer.

"Be sure to wash that off!" Hal calls after her.

She calls back over her shoulder, "Do you have a bottle of that stuff?"

"Yes! You have ice?"

Amy's jaw drops. Cassi's face remains smooth; only her eyes are snorting.

. . .

Anemic strains of the wrap party float into the windows of Ray-Anne's RV. She hears the flat drone of attempted conversations and the out-of-tune band. The klezmer trio, which had sounded like jazzy gypsies during rehearsal, now plod along as if they've played one bar mitzvah too many.

There is a distant scooping of ice and pffting of bottle caps being pried. She'd seen the caterers stocking the bar earlier; there's enough booze for fifty Big Ricks.

Until this, *Fishing* had been going pretty well, even in Ray-Anne's nothing-if-not-critical estimation. But the sponsors have now judged firsthand the "talent" their investments and efforts are backing. She can practically imagine the texts: *debacle, cancel, failed.* She plunges her hands in a sink of ice water.

When she had not answered Hal's earlier knock, he'd waited a full five minutes before saying, "Right, have it your way." He'd wedged the bottle of calamine between the door and the screen and left.

Once it's dark and RayAnne's hands have slightly deflated, she ventures down the path to the shore and treads quietly to the end of the dock, where she can get three bars of reception on her phone. She'd sooner motor out onto the lake, but *Penelope* has already been floated onto her trailer and pulled up the hill.

Dot's not answering. RayAnne counts down the six rings, imagining the phone on its cradle in her grandmother's empty kitchen. The recording chirps, "This is Dot, here I'm not! Leave a message."

"Gran. I just . . . it's kinda bad. Mom showed up and was on the show. And it was . . . well, awful doesn't quite cover it." She stops to breathe. "And you should see my hands." Her voice is nasal with tears. "Dad's still around here somewhere. Drunk, if you can imagine. And this guy, Hal . . . oh, never mind. But anyway, you must be feeling better, 'cuz you're not home. Okay, season's over, so . . ." She manages to inject false cheer into her voice. "Dismount! I can go home tomorrow. Maybe even tonight." Words just seem to evaporate as they come out, meaningless. "Okay, Gran. Wuv yooou."

After hanging up, she nearly wishes for a bug to take up residence in her other ear—something to knock aside thoughts of the interview with her mother, seeming to loop on replay in her head, no matter what else she tries to think about. Thankfully, Bernadette and her mavens would be deep in their yurts by now, *rituaing*, which Cassi informs her is now a word. At least she's among her own, chanting farewells to their menses and probably drinking glasses of Beaujolais. If only Bernadette could forget the worst bits, as if it all were only a barf-shrouded dream.

She bends stiffly forward like a Barbie and swishes her itchy hands in the cold lake water. The swelling has gone down, thanks to ice and calamine. Still, she must fight the urge to chew the skin from her hands.

In the night sky above, the northern lights have begun to shimmer in and out of focus. Shafts of neon green pulse over the mirror of the lake, as if the heavens have gargled with Scope and are spewing it at Location. She sniffs and gets to her feet, muttering, "Big aurora-boring-alis deal."

. . .

After her things are packed, she applies a fresh layer of the calamine and watches it dry like spackle over her pink knuckles. It had been outright rude to refuse to answer Hal's knock. Just one of the things on the list of *too late*.

It's not quite midnight, so the day isn't over, and while it's not quite tomorrow, the thought of waking up here—in the aftermath—is unbearable. She needs to put as much distance as possible between herself and Location, her father, and *Fishing*. Rehashing the more spectacular moments of the day, she sinks minutely into the couch cushions, as if gaining weight by the minute.

The party has fizzled, the camp gone quiet.

This is the sort of bottom she'd hit during the holiday season of seventh grade, when her parents split. It was just after the scandal and cancelation of *Big Rick's Bass Bonanza* went public. A classmate had been thoughtful enough to post a newspaper article to the bulletin board detailing the court case and the troika of Big Rick, Mrs. TroutLocker, and the Fishing Channel.

Bernadette—between bouts of rage and the shock of realizing her family had been stalked by Mrs. TroutLocker playing the role of Glenn Close—had met with RayAnne's teachers and counselors to alert them to the weirdness. It had all blown up in the run-up to Christmas during the post-turkey weeks after Thanksgiving.

RayAnne was sent away with Dot for the holidays on a hastily arranged Amtrak trip to Chicago, ostensibly to celebrate grandmother–granddaughter Christmas, like it was a thing. They stayed at the stuffy Drake, where RayAnne and Dot had a pathetic tabletop Christmas tree in their too-hot hotel suite, where the sheets were too tight and gave RayAnne torpedo feet in spite of Dot's insistence there was no such condition. When venturing outside along the broad Chicago avenues, they experienced an entirely new brand of cold somehow more biting than any in Minnesota. They fought the wind between department stores and museums, shivered along the pier, and ducked away from the windows atop the Hancock Building as glass rattled in the wind. At the ice rink, her new skates were on her feet all of ten minutes when a gust shifted off the lake, working up a wind that set Dot declaring that such cold could "tear the tits off a mare." Over Christmas dinner, RayAnne bawled over her plate of greasy roast goose and told Gran all she really wanted for Christmas was permission to legally change her name. It was all picked out, a name she thought sounded like a writer's, *Margot Danforth*—the sort of continental-sounding name she might move to another country with, like Australia or Canada. If her parents wouldn't allow her a new name, the least they could do was allow her to attend a different school.

At twelve, she was too selfish to care what sort of time Gran or her parents might be having. Big Rick had taken up residence in a motel near the Minneapolis airport. Bernadette was attending the women's divorce support retreat that would become the grit in the oyster of inspiration for her future career of Blood-Tide Questing.

Ky, ten and clueless, was spending the entire school break skiing in Montana with a classmate's rich family, having the time of his life.

As if it were possible, the weeks after the holiday were even worse for RayAnne. She struggled daily but could not keep good thoughts in her head. Home was a fun house of Bernadette's triumvirate of moods: weepy, furious, and giddy. School felt like a trip down a cinder path on hands and knees. Usually an eager student, RayAnne suddenly hated school, felt the sniggers behind her back. She couldn't open her mouth without her cheeks flaring apple-red, earning her the name "RaygedyAnne."

Which was exactly how she felt then. And now.

· · ·

She starts at the sound of van doors slamming in the distance, gravel crunching as vehicles depart to transport sponsors back to Schmancy Camp.

Once assured all is quiet, RayAnne steps out into the night with her backpack and rolls her heavy suitcase carefully over tree roots. Parts of the camp have already been broken down, the docks cleared of equipment, pontoons motored back to the marina they'd been rented from, the satellite truck telescoped down and driven away. Looking out over the lake, she sees the northern lights are still on and idly wonders if her awe has been shut off.

As she nears the party tent, a set of voices and footsteps move inside. Most tiki torches have burnt out, but one in the tent casts flickering silhouettes of two men like shadow puppets: one unmistakable and bulky, the other slim. Their forms move to the stage, where a few folding chairs are still set up. Her father stumbles as he steps onstage. "Shit, this thing moving?"

"You okay there, Rick?" Hal's shadow reaches out to steady her father's.

Realizing there's no way they can see her, RayAnne edges closer.

"Yee-up, all good. Thanks. It's Cal, right?"

"Close enough."

Big Rick thuds onto a chair. "Some party. That horn player? My grandsons sound better blowing toilet paper rolls."

"Oh, I don't know, they weren't so bad. Might've been a better party, though. Shame RayAnne couldn't join us."

"Safe to say she's avoiding her old man. That one can nurse a grudge."

"Well, today wasn't exactly—"

"Ha! You don't know my daughter very well, fella."

"Maybe not as much as I'd like." He clears his throat.

Her father shifts and fishes in his pockets, and she hears car keys jangle. "Well, Cal." Big Rick slaps both thighs. "Time to get a move-on."

"Pretty late to be on the road, don't you think?"

"Nah. Besides, I already broke down my tent. If I start now, I can be in the cities by morning."

Hal pauses. "Listen, I've got a fold-out you can bunk on. That way you can get some sleep and have some breakfast before heading out."

Keys dangling from her father's fingers drop to the stage. Hal is quick to pick them up but doesn't hand them back.

"All settled then: you bunk with me, say good-bye to RayAnne in the morning before you leave."

"Oh, I dunno. She's a pretty tough nut."

"Maybe not so tough, Rick." He helps her father to his feet.

She watches them leave like she might watch a scene in some film, Hal bent a little under the weight of her father. *Well*, she thinks. Another lost to Big Rick's charms.

Halfway to her car she stops caring about the clatter she's making, wrestling her roller bag over gravel as best she can with her stupid, itching flipper-hands. She shoves her luggage into the hatchback, jams herself behind the wheel, and turns the key with difficulty, like a parody of starting a car. Tires skid as she peels out of the parking area with as much peel as a four-cylinder Scion can manage.

*   *   *

A few hours later she stops at a Motel 6 north of Duluth. At reception she requests two ice buckets and then must ask the sleepy desk clerk to wrangle the credit card out of her wallet because her fingers are too swollen. She spends the rest of the night propped in bed, flanked by the buckets with her hands submerged like twin *Titanics,* listening to the champion snorer in the next room.

As she drifts, she recites the slogans of every hokey inspirational poster she's ever seen: *Hang in there! Losing Isn't Not Winning!* After the second dose of Benadryl takes effect, a more reasonable voice finally incites her to sleep, Old Lodge Skins, distant, but resonant: "Sometimes the magic works. Sometimes it doesn't."

11

•

•

•

•

Teresa Hedley of K9ResQ is all business during her inspection, poking into RayAnne's rooms and closets, scribbling cryptically on a clipboard. The interview is so in-depth, RayAnne wonders if adopting a child might be easier. She's had to defend her motivations for getting a dog in the face of a dozen questions. An entire week has been spent making the house dog friendly—a canine haven replete with a bone-shaped fleece dog bed, basket of chew toys, the double stainless dish in its own stand so no one has to down-dog for meals. Upon entering the kitchen, Teresa eyes these items warily.

"You understand there's no guarantee we can partner you with a dog right away." She squints at the pantry, separated from the kitchen by the novelty beaded curtain RayAnne spent an entire summer making. "Are those fishing lures?"

RayAnne edges in front. "The barbs have been removed."

Teresa makes another note.

RayAnne is not deterred—it's all about getting a dog. Since her return from being on Location, she's busied herself with all things dog—reading dog books; surfing dog sites; investigating breeds, their habits, behaviors; the longevity and health issues of French bulldogs versus Hungarian vizslas. Were Teresa to suddenly give a pop quiz on hip dysplasia in shepherds, Ray-Anne would ace it. Perhaps she shouldn't appear as determined as she feels. "Right. I'm in no rush or anything. I'm just getting prepared, so . . ."

"A dog." Teresa's pen is poised. "Why now? Why have you chosen this point in your life to adopt?"

"Well, I'm on break from work, so I have time to devote to training and all that." She rattles the curtain of old Rapalas and shrugs. "It's not like I do craft projects all day."

It's almost a relief when Teresa simply gets to the point. "But why, exactly, do you want a dog?"

Her honest answer, *I'm sick of humans,* is swallowed. *Fine, don't let me have a dog. I'll find someone who will.* She gives up the posturing and wearily admits, "I just want one. And I promised my grandmother I'd get one."

"Well then!" Teresa is suddenly animated, pulling doggy dossiers from her files and spreading them across the kitchen table. Once her papers and doggy portraits are arrayed, she says, "Sit!"

RayAnne sits. Most of the photos show mixed breeds, but a number are purebreds. The first photo is eye-catching: a cocker spaniel blurred in midair while jumping over a hurdle.

Teresa nods in approval. "This is Harry, a real active boy."

"What do you call what he's doing?"

"Agility. Harry is also a great candidate for dock diving."

"Would he jump out of a boat?"

"Maybe."

"I'm not really set up for flying dogs."

The next picture is of a pit bull. "Bob is a special-needs case."

"I see." Never having seen a dog with an eye patch, RayAnne bites her lip. The cold sore has healed, finally, as have her Mickey Mouse hands.

Teresa whispers over a picture of a handsome if droopy-looking red retriever. "Roscoe. Very quiet."

RayAnne checks his sheet, stopping when she gets to his age and whispers back, "He might be sort of . . . old?"

"Well, yes, but. Okay, that's good. You're in it for the long haul, then? We have Mitzi here, blue heeler cattle dog. She's just two, and super smart, but as you can tell from the picture, she's recently whelped." Mitzi does look sweet but is weighted by a dozen low-slung teats like half-full water balloons. "Of course we'll spay her once the pups are weaned and provide all the puppy chow until they are pla—"

RayAnne shakes her head, sliding the picture aside. Underneath is a glossy shot of two blue-eyed Australian shepherds, both tilting their heads at the camera at identical angles.

"They're awfully cute. And that's a smart breed, right?"

"Gracie and George. Brother and sister, not to be separated."

"Oh."

Teresa lays down three photos with a flourish, each with a four-month-old Brittany spaniel puppy, all with curly liver-and-pearl coats and faces to melt icebergs. RayAnne steels herself against the images—no puppies. She knows how this one goes: you fall for their looks, but they're utterly unproven; no one can vouch for them save their mother, who only speaks dog. Looking at puppies is like being in a bar at last call wearing what Ky calls beer goggles, when the wrong guy looks fantastic enough to drag home. She stands firm. For one thing, puppies chew, and she's fond of the few nice things she owns, like the rugs from Gran's old house, and her new motion-balance shoes, which, while ugly, would ideally remain paired—forget Big Rick's snipe that even nuns wouldn't be caught dead wearing them.

If she were ready to take on the kind of commitment a puppy required, she'd have had an actual child by now. At least the traits of dog breeds are somewhat consistent; human children are the unpredictable mutts.

Teresa is clearly disappointed when RayAnne shuffles the puppies' pictures under the others.

She pauses at the next picture, a tricolored face furred in Starbucks hues of caramel, cream, and espresso. His name is Rory. His coat could be part poodle for its soft wave, but his ears are peaked, one flopped at three-quarter mast like a border collie's. One of Rory's eyes is blue; the other is the color and clarity of a wet butterscotch Life Saver. Fringing his muzzle is a Scottie-like scruff that makes him look a little like a dog in disguise. His bicolored gaze is cocked warily at the camera.

"Who's this guy?"

"Breed-wise he's a Heinz 57 but has some herder in him for sure, maybe a bit of Aussie or border collie with that eye. He's a . . . different fellow." Teresa begins moving along, but RayAnne plants her palm on the sheet, pulling it closer.

"Different how?"

"He's a surrender. His owner brought him in complaining he was thunder-shy."

"Is that bad?" Seems reasonable to her.

Teresa shrugs. "Well, actually, most loud noises set him off."

"Off, as in?"

"Off and running—usually to the nearest tight space. He needs to feel safe."

Safe. She can relate to that. "What else?"

Teresa is squinting at the page. "Yes, see, *herder tendencies*." She points out a red circle-slash over the silhouette of a toddler. "He should not go to a home with children or other pets."

"Other pets." Danny Boy flits through RayAnne's mind but is as quickly dismissed, since Gran insists rodents do not qualify as pets. "Because . . . ?"

"He would herd them into corners and places where he can keep an eye on things. A child or cat might find such behavior frightening or threatening."

RayAnne scans his stats and profile. Rory is two years old, neutered, his shots are up to date, he is chipped, house-trained, knows basic commands, scores four out of five on leash manners, and weighs forty pounds. Under "Breed" is the happy-sounding understatement "Variety!" Over the bottom of the printed sheet, someone has handwritten and underlined *smart.*

Smart. Smart is good. With the exception of certain promising bright guys in her past who turned out to be duds. On the show, matchmaker Maeve had observed that women often confuse intelligence in a man with integrity—a mistake RayAnne has made, and not just with Titty-Zack.

But a dog? Surely a smart dog could only be a good dog. Puzzling over an odd term on the page, she asks Teresa, "What's a *Velcro* dog?"

A ringtone of French horns interrupts them, emitting from the junk drawer as if a tiny brass ensemble is wedged in amid the pencil stubs and dried-up Sharpies. Teresa looks around curiously before zeroing in on the closed drawer. RayAnne ignores it; having assigned various ringtones to her contacts, she now knows who is calling.

The calls announced by brass tones are all from WYOY. She's read the polite texts left by producers and staff, requesting she get in touch *at her convenience.* She figures the longer she stalls, the more chance her performance with Bernadette has to recede down the queues of producers' inboxes and memories. Bernadette's ringtone is "Over the Rainbow" in pan flutes, but her mother hasn't called, surely sorry she'd ever agreed to appear on *Fishing.* A phone call would be too casual on either of their parts. Likely Bernadette is not even in range. RayAnne has driven by her house only to find it dark. No doubt she's off questing somewhere. A letter seems best when it comes to her mother, but Ray-Anne keeps writing and deleting, typing and deleting.

Ky's ringtone is Queen's "We Are the Champions," Gran's is *West Side Story*'s "Jet Song." "I Am the Walrus" announces Big Rick, not that he would dare call.

Teresa nods to indicate the ringing drawer. "Shouldn't you . . . ?"

"Answer that? Nah, I pretty much don't these days unless it's my grandmother." RayAnne immediately flashes a grin, not wanting to be perceived as some crank or eccentric. "Can I set up a time to meet Rory?"

At the door, Teresa casts a scrutinizing eye over her, and for a moment RayAnne fears she's going to change her mind and reject the application on the spot.

"You look awfully familiar."

RayAnne sighs in relief. "I get told that, like, all the time."

"But, I'd swear—"

"I know. People think I'm someone, but I'm not."

. . .

There was something the Birkett twins had said, something she'd thought enough of to paraphrase in pink chalk on the kitchen hall blackboard: *Choose who you are.*

Kira had said, "We didn't choose how we are . . ." and Kit had finished, "but at least we can choose *who* we are."

This directive confronts RayAnne every time she bangs in the back door, and for as much as it sounds like something her mother might say, she has to admit, it can't hurt to try. She will choose who she is, now that she has the time to figure out how. Her only real plans are getting a dog and making a road trip, driving the scenic route all the way down the Mississippi River then east to Florida for an extended stay with Dot over Thanksgiving. In the meantime she's just hanging. She has ordered a cord of fireplace wood and plans to enjoy every spark and ember of it.

Rory is being fostered in Wisconsin. Sunday she gets up at dawn in order to get there before the family goes to church. Barely out of Minneapolis, RayAnne realizes she's going to be ridiculously early. Exiting the freeway, she takes the scenic route meandering up the St. Croix Valley. The late September sky is wiper-fluid blue, with golden aspen leaves pirouetting in the breeze. Oak leaves hang tight as if knowing they're in for another Minnesota winter.

RayAnne is trying to give Bernadette's axiom "live in the moment" a go. She's enjoying the scenery. Living in the now, according to the author of her favorite new blog, *Doggerel,* is the number-one best thing about interacting with a dog; you've no choice but to be in the moment with them—their moment. It's been a relief to dig into the topic of dogs after those months of trolling through notes and bios of women she'd wanted to interview for the show. Since wrapping up the season, she's spoken to Cassi once to ask if she was going to be fired. Cassi had insisted not but sounded cagey, saying there would be a few changes, that "wheels are turning." RayAnne interpreted this to mean producers have begun looking for another Mandy and more celebrity guests to drum up the sorts of underwriting they wet themselves over, like Toyota or Wells Fargo. Wouldn't it be ironic if Cassi's prediction actually came true and *Fishing* became a Coke show after all?

She pulls into a scenic overlook. The waterfall sends up a fine mist, and a stripe of fog rises just above the river's surface. Because of the hour, she has the place to herself, but it's a little like watching a movie alone when it would be better to share it with someone. It might be too early for tourists and Sunday drivers, but it is an hour later in Florida, and Gran will be up and baking something by now.

"Morning, Gran."

"My, you sound better."

"I am. Great, in fact."

"Hmm." Dot sounds unconvinced. "*I* thought you were doing a marvelous job."

"Of course you'd say that, but Gran, I'm not who they had in mind in the first place. I mean, a camera-shy talk show host? Plus, it wasn't exactly professional of me to haul along the family baggage, lock, stock, and battling parents. And it wasn't exactly stressless."

"Well, then, good riddance to the headaches, right?" Gran yawned.

"I totally jumped in without thinking, just like Mom says I always do. I was just so flattered to be asked to fill in, you know? But I was so . . . out of my depth. I sure won't miss producers looking at me like a cut of meat that just needs a bit trimmed off."

"Now you're talking. Are you eating enough? You're not buying those servings-for-one frozen things."

"No, Gran, I'm cooking every meal from *Mastering the Art of French Cooking*."

"Don't be smart, dear."

"Besides, it's not like I had much say in the show. How many times did Cassi and I discover the perfect guest, then get shot down in favor of some glamoramus or somebody selling some gimmick?"

"So everything's fine."

"Mostly." After a silence RayAnne asks, "Gran, is Dad on a bender somewhere?"

Dot pauses. "Maybe he's just holing up, like you're doing."

"I'm not holing up. You make me sound like some prairie dog."

Dot sighs. "Speaking of, did you get that dog yet?"

"I'm working on it."

. . .

Once over the bridge from Taylors Falls, she watches for the county road sign and follows a paved road until it turns to gravel. The hobby farm is easy enough to find with its yellow barn. She needn't have worried about the early hour—the couple is outside bagging leaves and gathering sheets off the clothesline, as if they've been up for hours. The husband wipes his hand across the front of his jacket before shaking RayAnne's.

"Call me Earl."

A woman comes up from behind. "I'm Mary." They have the obligatory weather chat while walking to the barn.

The yellow building has wide rolling doors on either end, both open. Inside, Rory is circling a small gathering in the middle of the cement floor, a number of plastic bags buoyed and shifting in a vortex of breeze. When one cartwheels out of the swirl the dog pounces, returning it to the fray and dropping it among its mates.

Earl shrugs. "Silly fella thinks they're sheep."

Mary smiles and, in a voice eerily like Dot's, adds, "Neurotic little thing."

Upon hearing his mistress, Rory reluctantly abandons his chore and scampers over. When he sees RayAnne, he detours to trot directly to her. He sits, meets her eye, and tilts his adorable head as if to ask, "Who have we here?" When she reaches to pet him, Rory presses his skull upward into the perfect-fitting cap of her hand, his silky fur tickling the spaces between her fingers. With a stupid grin, RayAnne drops to one knee to look Rory in his mismatched eyes.

"Well," she says. "Hello there, dog."

He assesses her, then nuzzles in to smell her neck. At first she thinks she's imagining it, but then she feels it again—the ever-nagging band of tension between her neck and shoulders beginning to release. Rory rests his chin on her shoulder, sighing hugely, as if he's just located some beloved old rag.

"Huh," grunts Earl. "I guess that's that."

After coffee and Mary's cake, the folding kennel and leash are stowed in the hatchback, and the plastic-bag sheep are rounded up. Earl hands over the bin of much-chewed Lincoln Logs Rory is particularly attached to. There is only a moment of hesitation when it comes time to leave. Rory leans hard against Mary's leg and looks up at her with as near to a shrug as a dog might muster, as if to say that he, like RayAnne, really has no choice. He hops up into the passenger seat. Ready for what's next.

. . .

Who knew so much time and space could be taken up by a forty-pound animal? RayAnne happily puts up with behavior she would never tolerate in a man. She's learned to plow around the house rather than lift her feet to avoid being launched ceiling-ward by one of the Lincoln Logs scattered everywhere, including the stairs. She hadn't intended to allow Rory upstairs, but already there's a second dog bed in her room, along with more Lincoln Logs. If she's not vigilant, a nighttime trip to the bathroom could easily turn into a skit.

The kitchen table has been shoved aside to make room for the folding kennel and bowl caddy. She's offered Rory chew toys and a Kong stuffed with treats, but he doesn't acknowledge these other than to drop them on the sheepskin he's designated as his island of misfit toys.

The sheer volume of dog hair makes her wonder if the stuff could be spun into yarn and knitted into sweaters, and not three minutes into a Google search, she discovers the cult of dog-hair sweater knitters and weavers and an article on a designer who has woven a Samoyed cape for Kate Middleton. Another knits her golden retriever sweaters made from its own fur. In the living room, a stack of dog-training books spills from the coffee table. Having now reconsidered bookshelves, RayAnne has topped the pile with an Ikea catalog.

"Oh, to be a dog," she muses to Gran on the phone.

Gran sighs on the other end. "I imagine you're regretting all those times you were mean to Trinket now."

"Um, no."

She tells Dot about their lessons at Citizen Dog. Tuesday and Thursday evenings, she and Rory attend Obedience One with twelve other dogs in varying degrees of good dog, trainable dog, and bad dog.

"Dagmar says there's only two kinds of dog owners, dumb and dumber."

"Oh, that's a good name for a trainer. Sounds no-nonsense."

"She looks exactly like her mastiff, Gran. Five times a session she yells, 'Obedience is work!' We actually get stars next to our names for good work."

One of the dumber owners and a complete newbie, RayAnne is willing to admit her ignorance in full—knowing nothing, she follows every instruction, figuring she and Rory are both in training. And since her social life is nil, there's all the time in the world to master sit, heel, stay, and down.

"I think I can do this, Gran."

"Of course you can, dear; did you think you couldn't?"

"Well . . . I didn't know dogs had so much personality. When others come around he pulls me away before I can pet them, like a jealous boyfriend. And he hates Danny Boy. When he's out of his cage and on my shoulder, Rory just faces the wall and sulks."

"What goes around comes around." Dot's laughter sounds a little thin. "You used to mope just like that."

Rory's eyes flash with happiness at monosyllabic offerings of "Walk?" or "Car?" or "Treat?" When she lifts his leash from the hook he beelines to her left knee and sits at the ready. *I'll go anywhere! Do anything! No questions asked! No need to explain your motivations to me!* The fawning drivel she leaks back at him would make anyone gag: "Who's a handsome devil? Who is the handsomest devil-dog in the world? Who has the softest, softest fur? Fur like butter. Yup, you lick that thing. Lovelovelovelovelove you!"

In the backyard, his urinal of choice is a horseradish plant she's been unable to kill no matter how deeply she hacks at its roots. Now, as Team Radish, their mutual goal is its death. Each time Rory lifts his leg at it she sings in her best Elmer Fudd, "We're hunting horse-waadish, we're hunting horse-waaadish."

His herding instinct seems reserved for inanimate objects. His primary task is keeping a bead on RayAnne, constantly updating her precise coordinates. If she's in the bathroom, he's on the other side of the door, nosing the crack as if sniffing out her every move. When she sits, his paws are placed one inch from each of her feet, adjusting and shifting as she does. If she's at her desk, he's under it. Of course this is what they meant by Velcro dog. When she's out of his line of sight, she can sense his unease, his need for her to be back in it. She wonders if this is what having a stalker is like.

He is not the watchdog Dot would've hoped for. When the doorbell rings he gives a girly whimper and hightails it for the space between RayAnne's calves. If there is no space, he carves one with his damp snout. Teresa was right; most noises are a challenge, anything loud or abrupt, the garbage truck, the mail slot. One ding of the microwave and he is sitting on RayAnne's toes so she might protect him from whatever is coming to kill and eat them both. She is supposed to ignore this behavior, but it's hard not to laugh. Rory loves peanut butter and makes snarling faces when trying to lick it off the roof of his mouth. She takes a picture of him in the act of baring his teeth and sends it to Dot, texting, "Nobody's gonna mess with this bad boy!"

. . .

Somewhere along the line, Rory's confidence was damaged. RayAnne doesn't know his history and prefers not to think of what cruelty or neglect he might have endured before the nice hobby farmers fostered him. He hates being leashed to a railing or post, even for the minute it takes to pop into the library to toss books down the return chute, or to duck into Walgreens for shampoo or the coffee shop for a dark roast to go. Whenever she pauses near a doorway or shop window, he acts like he will be left to starve on the pavement. Dagmar reckons some previous owner tied or chained him, probably for a good portion of the day.

RayAnne needs something to go right, and training Rory might be one thing she can do properly. If she does everything Dagmar says, they'll test into Level Two Obedience, and she will have accomplished that. They will have. Reading the dog books, she learns many things. He raises his eyebrows when she excitedly informs him of such tidbits as "Did you know dogs have no sense of their own size?" This explains his trying to burrow into an empty flowerpot when the aluminum stepladder crashed to the patio.

Perusing a chapter on canine eyesight, she puts down the book and looks deeply into Rory's eyes, saying, "Get this. Dogs' eyes have different cones than human eyes." His butterscotch eye winks, she swears. "You see about as well as a color-blind man." She makes a mental note to buy a blue leash. Dogs apparently can see blue.

Outings with Rory are measured in the miles racked up on her Stepz app. They walk both sides of the Mississippi, investigating neighborhoods in the Warehouse District, St. Anthony Main, lower Northeast, Boom Island. Dagmar suggested taking him north to the metal scrapyards on the river or the rail yards where there is constant clanging and crashing. He needs to get used to noise.

Such places have always intrigued RayAnne from a distance, but having a dog in need of tough love now makes them a destination. Her pockets are smelly with high-value treats—pork jerky and little plastic bags of steamed chicken bits. RayAnne leads him toward the environs of rust and crashing chaos, the loading and unloading of barges, the *ca-thunk* of trains switching tracks. They find a patch of grass near the cranes that hoist and bash shipping containers into stacks, and she lets Rory overtake her lap, feeding him chicken bits each time he stops trembling or whining.

Autumn has peaked. It's her favorite season, though entirely too short. Each day grows a degree or so cooler, the sky a shade bluer on clear days, a shade grayer on cloudy ones. Evenings shorten by a minute or three each night, but weirdly, RayAnne finds herself staying up later—eating dinner after ten and seldom climbing the stairs before two a.m. She once read that a healthy body, if left to its own devices, will sleep just the right amount, during the hours that best suit it. The right amount for her is apparently ten or eleven hours. The darkness suits her waking hours, and her new routine is a complete reversal of summer on Location—no more dragging herself out each dawn to catch the first fish.

When not walking Rory, many of her hours are spent reading. On crisp afternoons she's sunk low in a chair on the coffee shop patio, bundled in sweaters and the gloves she's cut the fingertips from, Rory wedged under the wrought iron on sun-warmed patio stones. There are books on the front seat of her car in case they get caught waiting somewhere. Her sling bag is abandoned for a backpack that will accommodate hardcovers and Rory's accessories. Throwing caution to the wind, she has begun buying books. Her growing library is a variety of the sort found at rummage sales: *The Island of the Colorblind, Travels with Charley, My Life in France, The Thin Man, Valley of the Dolls, The Shack*. For five dollars at a thrift store, she'd scored a shopping bag of 1950s detective and romance novels. Not a discriminating reader, she picks up whatever's next on the pile, and if it doesn't grab her in the first pages, it is abandoned. A story should engage with twists or interesting characters, occupy her mind's lanes of thoughts to keep them clear of her own. She's discovered a recent crime series by a Scottish writer and downloaded the audio versions to her iPhone so she can listen while jogging with Rory. There's not much she won't read, save books with covers that feature partial women—female limbs, a torso, bodiless hands holding some thing or each other, legs from the knees down or a face from the nose up, women from behind gazing into the distance. Why always from behind? She wonders why writers don't revolt when publishers can't endow their characters with more than a jawline or a suggestive shoulder.

There's been a message from Hal. "It occurs to me you don't have my number, so here it is. Things to talk about, right? So, whenever . . . wait, scratch that, *not* whenever. Call soon. Please."

She stares at the phone, unable to imagine what "things" might be.

12

· · · ·

The weekend blows in with an early northeaster, hurling leaves across the window planters to plaster themselves on the screens of the porch where RayAnne sits reading, wearing something that is neither a sleeping bag nor a onesie, as the Koucharoo infomercial insists, but both! It has a hood, and when laid flat it looks like a sleeping bag for a human-sized starfish. It has pouches designed to hold chip bags and television remotes. Ky must have trolled late-night cable to come up with this hit on his parade of most hideous Christmas gifts—a contest he's won every year since childhood by virtue of being its sole competitor. Perhaps if he knew RayAnne actually wears her Koucharoo, it might put a stop to the beer can hats, antigravity shoes, the rubber Big Mouth Billy Bass on a plaque singing "Take Me to the River," and the cape embroidered with scenes from "The Twelve Days of Christmas" with blinking LED lights—the sort of crap that clutters a closet until pitched into the Goodwill box.

After hearing the mail slot clang, RayAnne puffles down the hall to find a few pieces of mail for Big Rick on the tile amid the junk mail. The envelopes are forwarded from Arizona by Number Six. RayAnne wedges them behind the lamp on the hall table. If he does show up, she'll shove it back through the slot, unable to imagine opening the door to her father anytime soon—especially since hearing from Ky, who'd heard from Gran, to whom Bernadette had confided that when she and her mavens were leaving Location, Big Rick stood in front of the van, blocking the road, and mooned them all. This was witnessed by half the crew, a number of sponsors, and Hal.

She hasn't erased Hal's messages but will. That morning he had left another: "It's me. Again. I'm, ah, just wondering if you're still—what does your email responder say? 'Gone fishin'?' But season's over, so . . ."

Replaying it, she stands outside watching Rory rove his small domain, peeing along its perimeters. Finished with that, he herds oak leaves swirling on the patio, pawing at those falling in midair. Should she call Hal back or not? She lets Rory decide, holding out the phone for him to sniff. When he only drops to the flagstones and covers his snout with both paws, she retreats to the porch to resume thumbing her paperback. Maybe later, after their walk, she and Rory will drive down to the storage facility at the marina where *Penelope* is parked, just to check on her.

After three pages, the book she's trying to read falls limply to her lap.

Such are the days, she thinks.

.   .   .

Shadowed by shame for her laziness, Sunday morning RayAnne vows to do something constructive. After traipsing around IKEA for two hours, she has not only justified her meatball lunch but now has a project.

A burly, helpful IKEA guy had loaded the cartons into her hatchback. Once home and eager to get started, she realizes there is no burly, helpful guy on this end, where the boxes are too heavy to wrangle from the car herself. No small problem. She momentarily considers calling Ky then decides against it, knowing Ingrid's weekend hours at home will be dwindling. She tries lifting again, then wonders about Rani and Patak, the Pakistani brothers next door. But having shied away from all her neighbors this long, it would seem entirely too rude to ask for help now. She stands looking dumbly down the street, deserted in the middle of the afternoon—people are out doing Sunday things, off to museums, to the mall, dinner at the in-laws', choosing paint at Home Depot, at home watching a Vikings game, whatever.

The unmovable boxes pose a pickle, but not a huge one—one Gran would call a gherkin.

After poking around the garage, RayAnne returns to the car with a utility knife, climbs in to straddle the console, and slices open the short ends of the boxes. She repeats the attack from the hatchback end and wrangles individual shelves out a few at a time, cursing like a longshoreman. The more manageable loads are then dragged inside. An hour later, the curb looks like a cardboard truck has tipped over. Fighting the wind, she retrieves the pieces along with the dozen flying instruction sheets with the mute little *show-don't-tell* IKEA man. Once all is in the living room and brown paper is peeled from the shelves, she hears Gran's ringtone and scrabbles around to find the phone.

"Hey, Gran. Guess what I'm doing?"

"Knitting?"

"Building bookcases! Well, not building, but IKEA, so same-same. What are you up to?"

"No good, as usual. Say, I'm looking at my calendar and wondering about that road trip; did you settle on a date?"

"I'll get to your place the day before Thanksgiving. And stay for three weeks?"

"You think that's a good idea so late in the season? You don't want to be driving through snow. You could come earlier."

RayAnne laughs. "I can drive through snow, Gran. Why, you eloping with Mr. D or something?"

"Ha. No reason." Dot chuckles. "Just . . . the driving. You know me, worrywart. Get your brother to help you with those shelves."

"Nope. It's DIY all the way."

"Well, you get to it, dear."

"I'll send a pic once I'm done. Smooches."

After laying out the shelves and examining the little hexagonal tool that looks like it could snap like a twig, she gets the tools Big Rick bought and finds a more substantial version of the same diameter. She's rather proud of how smoothly the operation is going. She can totally manage this. Just as she's thinking it, her elbow jostles the utility knife set too close to the edge of the mantle. She fumbles in slow motion to catch it and does—the blade she forgot to retract plunges into the ham of her thumb, nearly to its hilt.

"Mmmmotherfucker!" It happens in an instant. The knife wobbles an instant before the weight of it cranks her hand downward and it clatters to the floor, followed by an impressive spurt of blood. "Shitshitshitshitshit . . ." Rory is at her heels in a flash, sniffing the knife. Just as he's about to lick the blade, she kicks it under the couch. Stepping over him, she rushes to the kitchen sink to run water over the cut to get a better look. It's deep. The sight of muscle—of her own meat—contracts her stomach to a lump. Pain bolts up her wrist and arm. Stitches. It will definitely need stitches.

Remembering the blade had a few rust spots, she moans, knowing she's in for a tetanus shot as well. "Damndamndamnit." Once she has fumbled open the first aid kit and starts ripping things open with her teeth, she realizes there aren't enough gauze pads—each time she moves her thumb, more blood spurts. There's no way she'll be able to drive herself to the ER. After poking numbers into the cordless to order a ride, she wads paper towels into her palm and makes a fist around them. Seeing the orange dog-poo bags on the counter, she's inspired to shove her hand into one to hold everything in place and keep the blood from dripping. She scatters a few rawhide chews for Rory before shutting the front door on him. Waiting outside for the taxi, she holds her hand high, managing to look crazy.

She'd imagined a late afternoon on a Sunday at the ER would be slow, but the halls of Hennepin County Medical Center are ablaze with light, noise, and all the chaos of a paycheck Friday, a full-moon midnight. She is categorized "priority" by the woman at admissions after she listlessly notes the amount of blood in RayAnne's bag, now nearly enough to float a goldfish. RayAnne is given a number, pointed to a large waiting room, and told simply, "Wait."

Nearly every molded green and yellow chair is occupied. The sick and injured comprise a disparate mix of young and old, crisscrossing all strata. A seductively dressed, heavily made-up mother whispers to her pregnant teenage daughter, who stares straight ahead and only snaps gum in response; a rheumy-eyed Hispanic man is flanked by two younger men who could be his sons, all three dressed as if for church. At first RayAnne settles across from a young mother with two toddlers, but both commence croupy, barking coughs and ooze rivulets of green snot. She moves on, ostensibly looking for a magazine. A tanned fiftyish golfer type with a gold watch and diamond ring holds a cold pack to his ankle. Passing a Vietnamese family, she notes all their eyes on the ER double door, as if waiting for someone to be wheeled out. She can assume the two teenage boys—one holding his arm, the other with ice on his knee—have been skateboarding, because one still has his foot planted on his board, toeing it in and out from under his chair. A graying pair of suburban lookalike sisters watch CNN on the corner TV. A teary-eyed, well-dressed blond holds her jaw and turns away from anyone looking at her. Beyond them are more rows, all full of hurting people, all waiting. Many stare into the screens of their phones.

She has forgotten hers, of course. In her rush to get out of the house, she'd only grabbed her wallet. She finds a table where there's a pile of magazines and blinks at the incongruity of the titles: *Dressage Digest, Wine Spectator, Cigar Aficionado,* and *Yacht,* obvious rejects from the doctors' lounge. Across from her, a tattooed, asthmatic-sounding hipster in a duffle coat holds his eyes closed, as if concentrating on teleporting himself to a better waiting room in a better hospital. Her hand hurts.

Off to the side is a short corridor of vending machines. One is being repeatedly kicked by an angry little bald man. She's got no book to read and only about three dollars in cash. The pay phone in the tiled hall looks broken, but even if she had quarters, who besides Gran would she bother with this?

A half hour into the wait, the only patients called up so far are the woman and her leaking children. One of the identical sisters gets up on a chair to change the television channel from CNN. When she skips past the Vikings halftime show, a few men moan, one imploring, "C'mon, lady . . ." They are rewarded with the final minutes of a documentary about wolves. No one complains, but no one is enthused either. The television is a place to aim their eyes, something to blink at besides their phones or each other.

RayAnne lifts her bloody bag. The bleeding has slowed, maybe even stopped. She's wondering how Rory is handling her sudden absence when she realizes the tune emitting from the television is the theme song for *Fishing.*

She freezes. Her eyes swivel to see who looks up at the TV before she dares to. There she is, welcoming the entire waiting room to climb aboard *Penelope.* The pregnant girl's mother stops badgering her long enough to turn to the screen. One of the sisters says, "Shhh," though no one is talking.

"Today on *Fishing* we'll go to the gym with Leslie Jordache." A photo fills the screen, showing an obese, pretty, caramel-skinned young woman sprawled on a lawn chair that looks like it might snap. "At thirty years old, the only thing Leslie Jordache was lifting regularly was the two-gallon ice cream bucket from her freezer." The picture changes to one of Leslie looming large in an altogether different way, braced under a set of huge barbells, a silver medal over the spandex singlet covering her muscular chest, much of her great weight shed, the rest shifted and muscled more tightly to her frame, owning it. "Today, a hundred pounds and ten years later, Leslie is the reigning Canadian women's weightlifting champ. We'll talk to Leslie about her journey from couch potato to Olympian." She looks to the other camera. "Later in the show we'll fish with Captain Angie Jones from the tall ship program High Seas, where she helps chemically dependent teens literally sail through recovery. Captain Angie teaches seafaring and nautical skills on a floating rehab ship." RayAnne looks directly at her audience, adding, "Blimey."

There is a mild shuffling in the waiting room as a few people adjust their chairs for better angles. RayAnne picks up a *Golf Digest* to watch from behind the cover of an article titled "Is Tiger Grrrreat?"

Leslie Jordache is seated in the usual guest spot, the bench seat, but the gaffer had had to place several sandbags across from her to level *Penelope* in the water. Even before RayAnne can ask Leslie what her inspiration and motivation were to get up off the couch, Leslie is leaning forward ready to bust with all she has to say—another of those guests who can carry the show, RayAnne's presence barely needed.

"My motivation? That was self-preservation, RayAnne."

"For your health, your psyche? Survival?"

"All of the above. My first husband, Jimmy, was a piece of work. When he'd come at me swinging, I used to have this fantasy. I'd close my eyes and imagine grabbing him before he could make a fist. I had a vision of lifting him off his feet and over my head to throw him, just chuck him . . . at a wall, the TV, his damn dog, anything—I just wanted to *throw* that man."

A number of people laugh.

On screen, RayAnne chuckles. "And one day you . . ."

"One day I'd just had enough. I said to myself, 'Leslie, stop being this man's fool. Stop dreaming about things being better and make them better,' and so I did. I started going to the gym that very day. I didn't know how long it was gonna take, but I was gonna do it, I was gonna work out and train until I could lift two hundred and forty-seven pounds."

"Jimmy's weight? And did you ever get to—"

"Clean and jerk him? Nah, by the time I was snatching two hundred pounds I realized he wasn't worth the breath it would take. He sure as hell wasn't hitting me anymore."

One of the ladies in the row in front of RayAnne hoots. A male voice from behind her says, "Go, Leslie."

RayAnne sneaks a sidelong glance at the woman holding her jaw. She's dry-eyed now and fastened to the screen. It's not just women watching; it's the younger Hispanic men, both the skateboarders, some guy in scrubs and surgical booties, and an old man nearby holding a urine sample.

The conversation between RayAnne and her guest continues over the short video of her visit to Leslie's gym. The dubious look on RayAnne's face when Leslie motions her down to the weight bench is funny, but when RayAnne tries lifting up the barbell with its pair of thirty-pound weights, the camera zooms to her face, eyes bugging while she mouths, *Help.*

Laughter ripples across the room.

RayAnne laughs too, because she remembers worrying she might fart on camera.

"See, RayAnne," Leslie encourages her, changing the weights to twenties. "It's easy—you just aim for impossible, then work your way up."

In fact, earlier in the day when faced with heavy IKEA boxes, it had been the thought of Leslie that had inspired RayAnne to not give up. She smiles into the pages of *Golf Digest*. In a way, she has Leslie to thank for this trip to the ER.

When the underwriter slot commences, a few people mutter; they'd clearly been enjoying the show. RayAnne looks around. She wasn't imagining that. And now several people are even talking about it.

"Number thirty-three? Number thirty-three? RayAnne Dahl?"

"Oh. Me." RayAnne gets up too fast. She sways; the magazine slides to the floor. Her nearest neighbor, the guy with the urine sample, reaches over to steady her, but she rights herself and waves him off. "I'm good, thanks, just dizzy."

He dips to grab the magazine and offers it, but she shakes her head, holding her bagged and bloodied hand. One skateboarder turns to the other. "Hey, man, that *is* her. I told you."

Heads turns as the skateboarder points to the television, then to RayAnne. "It's her. This lady here is that fishing lady."

"No shit?" Urine guy gives her a wink. The woman who'd changed channels swivels from her front-row seat, saying, "Well, I'll be." Her sister gives a wave. "Great show, RayAnne."

"What happened, some fish bite you?"

Blushing deeply, RayAnne approaches the nurse, now nodding. "You really are the fishing gal on that show?" A few people clap as she's led away. "I guess you must be. You're famous. You rich too? Is that funny?"

The nurse makes a big deal about telling the doctor, an impatient woman who looks as if she has more pressing matters than sewing up another DIY gone wrong. "Honestly." The doctor shakes her head, looking at the wound. "Sundays are the worst." The injection of a numbing agent into her hand hurts so much RayAnne thinks she might leave her body.

"I should have signed out an hour ago." The doctor sounds

peeved, but when she looks up, she's grinning. "This is the second Sunday in a row I haven't made it home in time to watch your show."

My show? Once her hand is an unfeeling lump, she turns away from the procedure of the cut being cleaned and stitched—just three sutures, the cut is deep, not wide.

"My father and I usually watch you together." The doctor snips the suture. "He says it's a nice break from *Antiques Roadshow*." She flips up the magnifier clipped onto her glasses lens. "That should do it. You won't be casting or reeling with that hand for a few weeks."

"Thanks."

After stripping off her rubber gloves, the doctor adds, "I'd ask for your autograph for my dad, but you won't be writing much either."

"I'm left-handed."

"Ah," she pulls a prescription pad and pen from her lab coat pocket. "In that case, his name is Norm."

RayAnne smiles. "Spelled like it sounds?"

Once home, she calms Rory, who alternately whimpers and glares at her, sniffs the bandage, and sulks. When she opens the back door to let him out, he won't cross the threshold.

Who can blame him? She'd slammed him on the wrong side of the door already once today, leaving him for hours. Stepping out into the dark yard herself, she goes to the horseradish plant, where she cradles her hand and waits for him, humming like Elmer Fudd. He comes along warily and pees, refusing to look at her.

There's dried blood streaking the IKEA cardboard and the kitchen counter, but any that had dripped on the hall and kitchen floors had all been lapped up by Rory. While filling his bowl, she eyes him. He's tasted her blood. She has read that a team of sled dogs will eat their master if he falls ill or is injured to the point of defenselessness. While Rory crunches kibble, she takes two of the painkillers she stood in line for at the hospital pharmacy. Reading the bottle while the second capsule snails down her gullet, she realizes the dose was only one.

Surveying the shelves and hardware strewn across the living room floor, the scope of her little DIY project dawns. She couldn't put the shelves up now if she wanted to. But there's more: sunk into the upholstery of the nearest chair while the painkillers kick in, she realizes she hadn't considered the uneven floors. Does she own a drill bit large enough to make holes in the plaster for the butterfly bolts? No. Had she measured correctly? Probably not. What she'd optimistically thought might take up an afternoon—assembling a simple wall of bookshelves—has already necessitated a trip to the hospital and suddenly looks like a life's work. Nothing she'll accomplish anytime soon.

She slides from the chair to the carpet. Rory whimpers and lays his head on her knee. Sniffling, she considers him. As awesome as Rory is, some days a dog just isn't enough. As she drifts into a buzzy unease, she wants Gran. Wants her mother. Mostly she doesn't want to be alone.

But getting up to find the phone is too colossal an effort. Besides, a call won't cut it this time. She could use a face-to-face dose of her mother, or an hour with Gran, who would whip up some antidote—one of her favorites, like the lemon zest bars with a dusting of powdered sugar, the crust mined with crystalized ginger, or those hazelnut meringue cookies with chewy centers. Normally RayAnne would salivate at the thought of Dot's two-bite cherry turnovers, flaky and oozy at the same time, but the painkillers have dried her mouth like a wind sock.

Bernadette would suggest she meditate on something, a smooth pebble, a cloud, one of those serenity fountains that make her want to pee. Or she might suggest that RayAnne teleport herself to a safe zone, a happy place that is not in bed under the duvet, hugging her body pillow.

Where is her happy place these days, besides *Penelope*? This house? It's close, but somehow not quite. Do people ever really find their happy place?

A minute goes by, then two. The narcotics thicken her thoughts until she muses aloud to Rory, "What was I looking for again?"

13

. . . .

It was as if she were right there, on the day of the final shoot. The camera panned from *Penelope's* rocking bow to the captain's seat. Smiling tightly, RayAnne asked Bernadette, "So you created the Blood-Tide Quests because . . . ?"

Since settling in the boat across from her mother, RayAnne kept thinking back to the months after her thirteenth birthday when her parents separated and the post-divorce fallout hit the height of family dysfunction. She was supposed to be thinking of questions a host would ask, but what she really wanted to know is what her mother could possibly have been thinking. What sort of perimenopausal state incited Bernadette to round up other fever-pitched middle-aged women to tromp the New Age spiritual landscape of sacred wells, shamans, yogis, and homeopaths just when she and Ky had needed her most? Weekends they were left in the care of Big Rick and his bimbo-of-the-month or their bug-eyed neighbor Mrs. Leeper, who parked her impressive backside at the dining room table with gluey scrapbooking projects, only occasionally rousing herself to open a can of soup or scorch some Hamburger Helper.

"Why did I create the quests?" Bernadette cleared her throat.

"Twenty years ago, we didn't talk much about menopause, at least not publicly. We do now, thank Goddess, but before *The Silent Passage* came out, menopause was mostly silent. Bringing it out of the closet, gathering women to embrace their life changes? To break the cycle of shame society imposes on women's bodies? That just seemed like a cause to get behind."

Facing her mother, RayAnne chomped a sharp incisor into the sore on her lip, the pain like voltage—her eyes welled instantly. On either side of *Penelope,* attentive sponsors bobbed in all-too-close proximity. Why couldn't they have shown up the day before, when the Birkett twins had been so compelling?

A question better swallowed fell from her lips: "Weren't your children a cause?" After a half second she pivoted to the camera boat. "Scrap that." Back to Bernadette, she scrabbled. "I mean . . . wasn't it difficult to sacrifice so much family time?"

Bernadette looked affronted. "Meaning?"

"Meaning going off, doing all that questing . . ." Her inner idiot prompted her to add, "Like, all the time."

"Oh, honey, I wasn't gone all that much."

RayAnne leaned in. "Every weekend?" It was as if she couldn't stop herself. She fought a sudden desire to jump ship.

Invoking her Tone of Ultimate Patience, Bernadette frowned. "RayAnne, these women needed me even more than you did."

"More? Mom. Seriously."

A wave passed over her mother's features, and when she continued her voice wobbled. "I was a stay-at-home mother for twelve years!"

"Sure, but . . ." RayAnne caught the sudden look of panic in her mother's eye. "Mom? You okay?"

"No!" Bernadette gulped, an edge of hysteria in her voice. "I'm seasick."

"What? You don't get seasick!"

"How would you know? You've never seen me in a buh-*boat.*" Bernadette grasped both armrests and tilted as if set to launch.

"I have so." Could it be she'd never seen her mother in a boat?

Bernadette exhaled. "Now, there's an omen I didn't heed. Why would a woman who is afraid of water marry a man who spent half his life on boats?"

"Why didn't you ever mentio—"

"A lot of good it would've done!" Bernadette's cheeks sucked in and huffed out, Lamaze-style. "You three were always out fishing, sailing, swimming, or whatever. You all love the water. I . . . just don't. I never said anything because I didn't want to be the killjoy."

RayAnne shook her head. "But I'm your daughter! How could I not know you're afraid of water?"

"Maybe because you never paid attention!" Bernadette's eyes darted, as if seeking some escape, but everywhere was water, pontoons bobbing, and cameras aimed at them like cannons.

Amy made frantic hand gestures they both ignored. RayAnne suddenly yanked free her earpiece, and Cassi's distant voice fell to her lap, squawking like some tiny mouse.

"But then why?" RayAnne cast a Vanna White palm to showcase the great expanse of water now frothing with whitecaps. "Why are you out here now?"

"To help you!" The pitch in her mother's voice climbed as *Penelope* lifted on a sizable swell. "You needed a guest! Here I am!" Bernadette looked then like she might vomit. When RayAnne realized her mother indeed would, she quickly scanned the boat for some receptacle, but there was only her tackle box.

Next came the moment, recorded for posterity from two different camera angles, when she had formed a bowl with cupped hands so that her mother, the shade of pale lettuce by then, could vomit into them. Not only did Bernadette vomit, it kept coming—her breakfast had been a kelp-and-kale Green Monster smoothie, which upon coming out looked and smelled remarkably like it had going in. RayAnne had to gulp back her own meal of Special K and soy milk to keep from joining the revelry.

And there, cast in HD digital vividness, was the triumphal, final moment of RayAnne's last interview on *Fishing*.

. . .

If only it had been a dream. It's dark when she stirs on the living room floor, hand throbbing, stomach growling, and Rory snoring lightly next to her. She peels her cheek from the bubble wrap she'd been using as a pillow and gets to her feet, shaking the leg that's asleep, mumbling to herself in a Jack Crabb rasp, "Pick it up, girl. Git it together."

And she will. At the moment she will get it together with another painkiller and something to eat. Turning her back on the living room mess, she pulls the pocket doors closed and follows Rory to his bowl in the kitchen, where the only light is the microwave blinking its perpetual 12:00, never having been reset after the last blown fuse. Not that time much matters; she eats when hungry and sleeps when tired. She downs a pill and with some difficulty unwraps a Lean Cuisine pizza and slides it in the microwave. She plows her good hand through kitchen drawers in search of the corkscrew, and when she pulls, it snags a fat manila envelope that falls from the drawer to the linoleum to spill its contents, a dozen handwritten envelopes. Those viewer letters she'd meant to give to Cassi weeks and weeks ago.

As RayAnne scoops them up to toss them back in the drawer, the microwave dings a distraction and she sets them on the table. Cutting the pizza will be a problem, but why bother with silly refinements when she intends to eat the whole thing? She cannot manage the corkscrew either, so gives up and locates a cheaper bottle with a twist-off cap.

Dinner served, she finds the dog-eared page in her current paperback and holds it open with her elbow, keeping her hand elevated while eating.

Reading during meals was never allowed at Dot's house. A

book on the table was a crime against civility. Gran claimed meal-time was sacrosanct, family time, and also, she wanted the meal to be the center of attention, fishing for all the compliments her dishes deserved.

Defying the rule in her own home usually makes RayAnne feel like an adult, each splat of tomato sauce on a page a mark of independence. But now, snarfing through a tasteless Frisbee of pizza and leaving greasy prints on the pages of a mediocre story, she wishes for someone to press her book aside and demand to talk. It's a silly book, chick-lit with sappy characters, and exclamation points, and the font seems suddenly too small. Rory follows her every movement until the pizza is nearly gone and he noses in, hoping for crust. She caves. "Fine."

It dawns on her that wine and painkillers might not be a great combo, because she feels woozy. Picking up one of the letters, she focuses and reads the return address and name aloud to Rory. When his ears prick up, she pulls a few more close and opens them with a fork and her teeth.

Dear Miss Dahl,

My name is Eleanor. Your show with the grandmother lost in the blizzard really got to me. I read her book twice. It occurred to me that my grown daughters and grand-daughters might like to hear something of my history as a Rockette and a mobster's mistress, so I wrote a few stories and had them bound into books—they said it was the best gift ever. Thanks for the inspiration and keep having great women on your show!

E.B.

"Exactly," she says to Rory. "That is the type of viewer Cassi and I were hoping for—women who could relate to the guests, with stories of their own, right?"

Dear RayAnne,

> *We don't see much TV with real people (unless you*
> *count reality shows that have real awful people), but your*
> *guests seem so interesting, and real, like you. I kept telling*
> *my friends to watch, but the show was on the same night*
> *as our Zumba class, so we convinced our instructor to*
> *change it. Now we all watch you. Keep it real!*
>> *Jenny, Chris, Kelsey, Mark, Jennifer, Jenna & Meg*

Included is a picture of a smiling thirtysomething group in work-out togs, all giving a thumbs-up.

"Rory, we have fans."

There are more letters with the same bent of "Keep it up and keep it real" accolades.

Those people in the ER liked it. She looks to Rory. "The ER was yesterday, right?" she says and offers another bit of crust. The letters are packed with the sort of praise and encouragement that staff and producers have been so stingy with. Still, it might not be too late for her to salvage the host's seat at WYOY. Maybe she should march down there and apologize for the unprofessional meltdown with her mother and her father's drunken behavior and ask for a second chance. She's just not so sure that going back to being the fishing consultant will be enough—like that song Gran sings, "How you gonna keep 'em on the farm once they've seen Par-ee?" The fact is she wants to host the show. And if not this show, another one. Uncle Roger had offered her a shot, hadn't he? That might not be so terrible—if she could talk Cassi into going along with her. But every time she thinks of Roger, she finds herself drifting to the nearest sink to wash her hands.

She picks up the last envelope. It's thicker than the others, containing an unsigned card and a stamped envelope—the letter is written on a page torn from a spiral notebook, the handwriting reminding her of Ky's teenaged scrawl.

Dear Fishing RayAnne,
> *I'm in ninth grade and live in Madison. I have two
> sisters. My mom likes your show and I'm hoping you
> would sign this card for her—I've included a stamp and
> put our address on the envelope. Mail really cheers Mom
> up—she has ALS and was in the hospital a lot but now
> we have a hospice lady come to our house. My mom's
> name is Maggie.*
> > *Yours truly,*
> > > *Ryan Edward Olson*

She'd been about to take a sip of wine but sets her tumbler
down. Looking at the date, she swallows and slowly pulls out the
enclosed card, the sort she would normally laugh at—a photo
of a kitten looking mischievous, posed next to a spilled pot of
geraniums.

Ryan Edward Olson. This boy couldn't be more than thirteen.
He's gone to the trouble of searching out the address of the station and writing to her—a total stranger—in a bid to lift his dying
mother's spirits. She knuckles away a tear, then another, then lets
herself go, shoulders shaking, until she's honking into her napkin. Here she's been feeling sorry for herself—wallowing, just as
Gran said—while out in the real world others carry on with all
manner of hardships. Boys try to cheer dying mothers.

RayAnne catches her red-eyed reflection in the kitchen window and shakes her head, muttering, "Pissant."

Ryan mentioned hospice. Hoping it's not too late, she reaches
for a pen, lays open the card to the blank space—the field of
white. *Her name is Maggie.*

Dear Maggie,
> *Your son Ryan took the time to write and let me know
> you are a fan of our show* Fishing. *I'm so glad you enjoy*

*it. It's been thrilling to meet the inspiring women we have
as guests, I feel so lucky to be able to interview them, and
to share their stories with you.*

RayAnne taps the pen.

*Ryan seems like a wonderful boy, but I imagine you
already know that. I don't have children myself, but if
I ever have a son, I hope he'd be as thoughtful as Ryan.
He tells me you are ill, and I'm so very sorry to hear that.*

The pen stops. She is out of her league here, wholly inconse-
quential in the scheme of things—as if anything she could say
might make the merest dent in the suffering of a family three
hundred miles away in a house with a hospital bed and medical equipment and death waiting at the center of it. She stares
at the half-written card and remembers one of Gran's well-worn
mantras: "When in doubt, grab the nearest truth." Gran is right,
of course. Always is.

*I understand you and your family must be going
through very difficult times, but I also imagine you are
all very brave. Ryan's note reminded me just how precious
family is, and that we need to pull close those we love.
It was so sweet of him to write on your behalf.*

Out the window, RayAnne catches sight of a snowflake drifting
across the patio light. Then another fluffy flake. First snow of the
season.

*I hope you are enjoying beautiful moments with your
children; I hope you are watching the first snowfall from
your windows.
All my best to you and your family,
RayAnne*

She'll put it in the mailbox this minute. Standing up, the combination of wine, pain pills, and emotion sway her, but at the same time she feels a vague sense of a weight shrugged off—perhaps the self-pity she's been buttoned into like an ugly dress. Whatever she has shed feels like it's pooled at her feet, something she can step out of and kick aside.

Outside her front door, she breathes in the night air deeply, clearing her head. She walks to the corner in her slippers and drops the card in the mailbox. It could be three a.m., it could be six p.m.; it gets dark so early these days. She stands a moment, registering the frigid temperature and holding out her bandaged hand to catch flakes of swirling snow.

By the time she's reached her door, RayAnne is revived some by the chill. Again, she hears the voices of the Birkett twins—perhaps you can, indeed, choose who you are.

. . .

She's set her alarm for the first time in weeks and is up with the first light. A chalkboard-gray sky lidded with snow clouds greets her when she yanks the shade. Her head pounds in rhythm to the throb in her hand. In the kitchen she sets about making coffee, clumsily, thinking of the mental list she'd fallen asleep to:

Letter to Mom: Apology
Cassi: Apology
Amy: Apology
Visit Ky and the boys
Craigslist: Handyman for shelves

And once that's all done? She's saved the best for last:
Google-map the route to Gran's. If Gran wants her to come earlier, she will, perhaps as soon as next weekend.

Scooping kibble into Rory's dish, she is determined that the end of her week will look nothing like the beginning. Halfway through her first cup of coffee, she's plugged her laptop in to charge, has found her phone and a legal pad, and is ready to listen to all her messages—when the doorbell rings.

Rory has made progress: instead of yelping and welding himself to her leg, he merely uses her as a human shield, following to the front hall on her heels. Assuming it's FedEx with Rory's new activity cube, which will reward him with a treat each time he successfully flips it over with his snout or paw, she doesn't bother with the peephole, just swings the door wide.

It's not FedEx.

It's Hal.

His unexpected presence incites a sort of brain-stutter. He does have a knack for popping up completely out of context—at least her context.

The chill swirling into the foyer makes her shudder. His hair is a bit longer, a curl tugged across his forehead by the sort of wind that had rattled the windows all night. Snow dusts the shoulders of his gray plaid jacket, the backdrop of the clouds and colorless trees all so dull his eyes seem that much bluer, like the gas pilot on her stove.

"Hello." He shifts from foot to foot. "I was . . . *not* just in your neighborhood; I've actually driven quite a lo—what happened to you?"

"Long story. DIY." She shrugs like it's nothing. Her bandage is similar to his brace; her fingers are free, but her wrist and thumb are immobilized.

"May I come in?"

Since seeing him with her stumbling father on Location, RayAnne has tried to neutralize all thoughts of Hal. Her performance with Bernadette was one thing, but she's loath to think of those moments in the well house—the near-kiss and her vomit-scented knuckles are incidents to be categorized under Moments to Forget.

But now the cornucopia of events of what had possibly been the worst day of her adult life comes spilling into the door along with Hal, her own personal-worst Groundhog Day, but of course there is no going back to fix things, and now here is Hal on her doorstep, a manila envelope casually tucked under one arm.

He flashes an imploring smile. "*Captain*, may I? It's freezing out here."

"Of course. Sorry." She steps aside.

Rory loops around her legs to get at Hal, wagging his entire back end and making that rare, joyful moan he makes when finding something ripe to roll in.

"What a good-looking pooch."

"This is Rory."

"What a face you have. Aren't you a handsome boy?" Hal bends down, and Rory, who does not lick faces—unless one has egg yolk or peanut butter on its chin—is all over Hal, lapping him up while his tail lashes at RayAnne's shins.

"Weird." RayAnne straightens, her arms drifting to cross over her chest. "He doesn't usually . . ."

Hal sets down the envelope and drops to his knees in order to ruffle Rory's ears and neck. "Doesn't usually . . . ?"

She shrugs. "Fawn."

Hal immediately devolves to dog-speak. "What a good dog! Rory? Such good name for a good dog!"

Feeling suddenly possessive and a little invaded, she quips, "Well, you can't have him."

Why, oh why does she blurt? Thankfully Hal seems to have barely heard her with Rory all over him. Well, he's caught her off guard, hasn't he? It's not that she can't handle the unexpected; it's just that some advance warning would be nice, a little time to prepare. As it is, her thoughts swirl in a clear dome.

Hal looks up and says, "I tried calling again."

He's got her there. "Everybody has."

Motioning him to follow, she moves into the kitchen and sets about finding him a mug, blowing the dust from one and rinsing it under the tap. Her silence, which he'll likely misinterpret, isn't intentional; she's simply out of the habit of speaking much to anyone human. Trying to remember if she'd washed her face or even mined the gunk from her eyes, she takes a quick look at her reflection in the window over the sink, baring her teeth to check for toast bits. When she turns back to give Hal his coffee, he's looking down at the letter she's reread half a dozen times—Ryan's letter. Caught, he looks at her. "Sorry, I don't usually—"

Ready to volley, *Gawk at other people's private mail?* RayAnne stops herself. "Well, it *was* just there." Handing over the mug, she smiles weakly. "That one really got to me."

"Yeah. I can see why. Jeez. Poor kid."

RayAnne sits. "I only hope my reply is in time." After a few beats, she looks down. The manila envelope he's set on the table has her name on it. So he's here to deliver something. "Is that more viewer mail?" She's not sure she can handle more right now.

"Nope."

"What then?"

"Your contract."

Her laugh comes out more as a bark. "Contract?"

. . .

Half an hour later she's still blinking in disbelief. Skimming the contract a second time, she zeroes in on certain sections. "*Two seasons? Really?*"

"Really."

"As host?"

"Yes, as host."

She sits back. "I don't understand."

He frowns. "You haven't been watching?"

"No. Well, I sort of stumbled upon the show with Leslie Jordache."

Season two had begun airing weeks before. Of course she'd known, but these days the only television she watches is pet-themed, like *Rescue Ink, Animal Planet, DogTown,* or the show with the doe-eyed dog trainer with two first names, Zak George. Having no desire to be reminded of her near-career, she'd pointedly avoided the Sunday evening WYOY slot for *Fishing.*

"But the episode with my mother . . ."

"Is the one we led with for the season, actually—you two in front of the segment with the twins in the second half. It's gotten the highest ratings yet."

"You're joking." Which part of her on-camera pissant hissy fit could possibly have garnered any ratings, let alone high ones?

He says something that sounds like a remix of his words in the well house that day: "You were real out there, you *and* your mother."

RayAnne pulls a face. "It was a disaster."

Hal sighs. "I told you the worst would be cut. I sat in on the editing to make sure."

"You did?"

He frowns. "Well, I generally do what I say I'm going to. You do know Cassi and the crew followed your mother up to that sweat lodge retreat the next day?"

"No."

"She got a really great ten-minute piece out of it. Mostly of Bernadette in action. We can thank Cassi for saving the segment."

"They cut out the throwing-up part, right?"

"The actual moment? Don't worry, it only shows your face while she's doing it."

This time he is kidding—his laugh is deep, while hers sounds like a sort of punctured-tire hiss.

Hal's hand settles firmly on her shoulder. "Hey. Give yourself some credit. Give us all some credit."

Her eyes fall back to the contract. Two seasons. The document is a six-page scroll of legalese she can barely grasp. When his hand falls away from her shoulder to turn the page, she feels a slight trail of disappointment. She looks again at the amount they will be paying her. It's probably a fraction of what Mandy got, certainly less than a cable show host might get, yet more than she's used to making—quite a decent sum, in fact. She re-reads the terms. "Wait. This figure, that's not for two seasons?"

"No, see, *annual*. That's what you'll get for each season."

"No way." It's three times what she'd made during her best year on the circuit. Images of PAID stamped over her student loans, her Amex, and the final bills for *Penelope's* restoration flit through her mind. It's an income Gran would call "comfortable enough." Comfortable enough that RayAnne could take Gran to Italy. *I could take Gran to Naples.*

But she's getting ahead of herself; besides, it's not like she's signed anything yet. There are still unanswered questions.

"And Cassi?"

"Producer."

She squints hard at Hal with Caroline Crabb's snake-eye. "For real?"

"Cross my heart."

She's still not convinced it's all real. "Why'd they send *you*?"

"They didn't. I sent myself."

"Because . . ."

"I wanted to? Crazy, I know—because Lefty's, because *I*, signed on as an underwriter for the duration of your contract."

Perhaps Dot is wrong after all; opportunity can come knock-ing. It's a lot to take in. A week ago she was reading crime novels in bed in the afternoon, eating meals of red licorice and Cheez-Its.

"You have a pen?"

"Sure. But don't you want to have your lawyer look it over first?"

Would admitting she doesn't have a lawyer make her seem like a total rube? She chews her lip. "Seems you've looked it over a few times."

"Just making sure you get what you deserve."

She signs the document. "That works for me." She holds her good hand out to his and they solemnly shake in a left-handed deal.

RayAnne recalls the morning they'd gone fishing, the ease they'd had with one another; sitting here with him now feels like sitting in the boat that day. She shrugs, adding, "Boss."

"Nope. None of that. Collaborator, more like. Think you can stop thinking of me as a sponsor?"

"I can, I think. It's not so much—when I think of sponsors I'm always reminded of something Old Lodge Skins said, 'There is an endless supply of white men . . .'"

Hal finishes the quote. "'But there have always been a limited number of Human Beings.'" He sighs. "There's two strikes against me: I'm a sponsor and a man."

"And white."

"Well, mostly. My father's mom was Lakota, so . . ."

"You *are* part Human Being."

Rory is turning circles under the table. "Ray. I'd—"

She cuts him off, thinking that maybe enough has been said, at least for now. "We should celebrate sometime."

He brightens. "Sure. Sure, you'll need a bit to let this all sink in."

Hal is still wearing his coat, but it seems too late to be a good hostess and offer to hang it up. Besides, he's right; she has still not taken it all in—the turn of events, the scope, the *thunk* of life abruptly switching tracks. The contract in her hand is real.

Hal nods. "Make sure you send that registered mail. You really didn't think you'd be signed on?"

"Not as host."

.   .   .

One of the boots Hal had heeled off in the foyer is missing; Rory's been in round-up mode again. She opens the pocket doors to the living room and sure enough, the boot is in the middle of the carpet among a small herd of RayAnne's own footwear and bits of discarded bubble wrap. Hal looks around at the chaos of cardboard and stacks of shelves.

She holds up her bandaged hand. "The offending DIY project. Seemed like a good idea at the time." RayAnne picks up his well-worn Frye boot and hands it over.

He takes his time putting it back on, his gaze assessing the wall and the shelves stacked against it. At the door he seems hesitant, as if word-shopping. "I could . . ." He seems to be weighing an option. Nodding to the wall, he offers, "I could bring my tools over and tackle these bookshelves."

"That's really nice, but—"

"Seriously. You'll need some shims with these walls. I could bring some, maybe order takeout from Szechuan Village? We could celebrate."

Chinese does sound good, but she nods to the window where snow is accumulating on the sill. "Will they even deliver? It'll be amateur night on the roads."

Rory is suddenly sitting on her foot, as if to remind her how much he likes to herd empty takeout containers.

"I can pick it up. I just put snow tires on the Wagoneer."

"Oh, well then, Chinese *and* shims."

"Dan-dan noodle? Spicy pork."

"Perfect."

"Great." He grins, suddenly boyish.

After the door shuts, she clamps a hand over her mouth and manages not to squeal until hearing the door of Hal's Jeep slam. She braces her back against the wall and slides to Rory's level, clutching her copy of the contract like a bouquet. Thoughts dart and jump as she reels them in. She's got a contract. They have a show.

All the ideas she'd shunted to the background come edging back—the potential guests she and Cassi had talked about after their long days of taping, their plots to circumnavigate those producers loath to take risks, brainstorming a wish list that included Amy Klobuchar; Janet Yellen; Malala Yousafzai, the girl shot by the Taliban for daring to go to school; hysterically funny feminists Caitlin Moran and Amy Schumer. RayAnne and Cassi would collapse on Tiffany's couches and hatch show ideas that kept entertainment value high while being relevant, admittedly with an agenda. They wondered if Lizz Winstead from Lady Parts Justice League might agree to come on. RayAnne's generation has been taking women's rights for granted, states like North Dakota have been banning abortions, and trolls like the "legitimate rape" guy and scary Paul Ryan pop up across the political landscape like stinkhorn mushrooms. They'd considered booking the young woman who'd defected from the Brattleboro nutcase church who pickets military funerals with "God Hates Fags" signs. There are so many challenges out there. RayAnne was interested in the author of *Doing Nothing,* a chronicle of the social costs and insidious fallout stemming from the seemingly innocent tradition of women changing their names upon marrying, how doing nothing can instead take back power, diffuse the underlying message. If women don't value their own identities enough to keep them, why should society?

She will dig around in her notes and call Cassi later. *Producer.* She has to laugh.

Amazing.

.   .   .

Hal's only coming over with Chinese food for DIY, hardly a date. Or is it? He can't have shaken the calamitous, vomitus near-kiss any more than she can. RayAnne shudders—it's almost too mortifying to think about. Really, she should be questioning the wisdom of even a friendly meal with him, especially on the heels of signing a contract.

The show. A real salary. Would Christmas be too soon to take Dot to Naples?

14

.

.

.

.

Unlike certain first kisses, the first snow is always the best snow. Fluffy, with no ice lurking beneath. Taking Hal's advice, RayAnne is letting things sink in. Walking off some of the buzz, kicking through the ankle-deep snow, snug in her official winter uniform of mukluks and the gray down jacket that makes her look like the Michelin Man rolled in soot. As she looks skyward, flakes sting across the bridge of her nose like cold freckles. Rory sniffs as if trying to remember where he's smelled snow before.

After a mile at a brisk pace, she slows, her head a little clearer, her pulse only cardio-fast, not racy. The throb in her hand has lessened some, thanks to the cold. She allows herself to be absorbed by the weather, which for the moment is magical in its novelty. A snow day, a school-closer.

When she and Ky were little and woke on snowy mornings, they would race for the television to wrestle for the remote and channel-surf the weather reports, shouting out the running ticker of school closings like manic bond traders. They would cheer for their own school. There would be time for real oatmeal instead of instant. They would pull their sleds to the hill above the rink, part at the clubhouse gate so as not to be caught dead together, and locate their friends. Those days felt just like this, except now she's gripping a dog leash instead of a sled rope.

Rory tugs ahead on his leash when they near the gate of the dog park as if to say, *Walk on; nothing to see here, folks.* It dawns on RayAnne that he only goes because she drags him. She is learning to pay attention to what he wants but until now has only been leading him through her world, giving him no choice but to go along to whatever's next. She pulls all the strings when he's probably thinking, *Would a side trip to this telephone pole kill you?* Normally, every walk with Rory is an opportunity to learn, à la Dagmar, but rules do not apply on snow days. Rory pulls her along on his own diversions, cutting through the park, sniffing at every hydrant. He chomps at flakes, paws them from his snout, blinks them coquettishly from his lashes, making RayAnne snort. He is hesitant about rolling in it until RayAnne drops to the ground to show him how.

On her iPhone, she makes a short video to send to Gran— Rory bounding through the snow and skidding to a stop at her feet to jar the frame and focus, RayAnne unsteadied. "Here's Rory in action, Gran!" She sweeps the viewfinder to the snow-frosted trees. "This is winter!" She turns the camera on herself, fogging the lens with her own breath. "This is me! See you soon! I've got a surprise for you—I've got news! Smooches!"

She presses *send* and trips after Rory, veering off on a side street, plowing right down the middle. They wind their way up Central Avenue and pass Afghan Pizza, where a woman she recognizes is sweeping the stretch of sidewalk clear, wearing a letter jacket over her long skirts and earmuffs over her headscarf. How long it must take for a person from a hot climate to get used to Minnesota, a place that can be cold in more ways than one. She wonders whether Muslim women who wear traditional clothing also wear long underwear or leggings underneath. It occurs to her that a good theme for the show might be to invite women from various cultures to explain traditional garb and its significance in regard to tradition, faith, and society—a hijab she sort of understands, but she could use some enlightenment when it comes to the full burka.

Outside Abdallah Bakery, she ties Rory to the bike rack. When she reaches for the door, he whines and strains as if she has tethered him to a grizzly. Inside, she hastily points to the first items in the glass case that might make acceptable desserts to follow her takeout dinner with Hal—baklava and a dozen squares of yellow taffy-like confection with almonds. Rory barks the entire time she's choosing and paying, which is annoying, and it occurs to her that separation is even more distressing for him when he can see her through the windows. Nothing is so yearned for as that which is just out of reach.

They stop at the coffee shop, its windows so steamed she can barely see inside. Coats and scarves dry on chair backs, and radiators have created a tropical microclimate. While looping the leash to a snow-domed patio table, she weighs how much yowling Rory might broadcast against how badly she wants a latte. The barista clearing tables inside wipes clear a circle in the condensation and raps the glass, motioning for her to bring Rory inside.

RayAnne sticks her head in the door. "You sure?"

"Day like this? Screw the health inspector."

The moment he's inside, Rory shakes, pelting all in range with fine snow and icy droplets. Fortunately, the snow-day atmosphere has affected even the grumpiest patron—the café suddenly goes viral with good cheer. Several people pet Rory, sending his tail wagging and back end wriggling so violently his rear paws threaten to slip out from under him on the tile. A woman offers to hold his leash while RayAnne orders and pays.

"He thinks he's shy," she explains.

Back outside, it occurs to her that she might have easily been describing herself. She's able to get halfway down the block before it sinks in all over again and she bursts out, "We've got a show!"

. . .

Back home she stands in front of her open closet for a long time. What to wear for a DIY session with a colleague? Jeans and a sweater, she supposes, but not the light-weave snug sky-colored V-neck she might wear on a date, too low-cut for hanging shelves. Safer to choose one from her sturdier stock of Hildegard numbers shipped every Christmas from Gran since she'd outgrown dolls. They are thick Scandinavian pullovers and cardigans with geometrical patterns knitted in red, cream, black, and green, with snowflakes, trees, and reindeer, as if Dot remembers Minnesota as some vast ski resort. The sweaters have armorlike pewter closures and hasps, and not one is remotely alluring. She chooses the most festive—a pumpkin and sage number with cream snowflakes. While buckling in, RayAnne employs reverse psychology: *If he likes me in this, he'll like me in anything.*

. . .

Considering the weather, Hal arrives earlier than she expects. Opening the door, she steps back from the blast of snow over his shoulder and takes the bag of takeout he hands her. "Jeez, still coming down?"

He stomps. "I can't remember a first snow like this." He ducks out again to return with a toolbox. The takeout bag is leaking a garlicky-smelling ooze. RayAnne licks her fingers. "Mmm?"

"Seafood fun."

Rory follows the takeout bag as if fastened to it, and Hal follows Rory with another bag. Once in the kitchen, he pulls out two growlers of beer from a nearby brewpub, holding them up for RayAnne's vote.

She cheerfully points. "That one."

The kitchen table is nearly set. RayAnne had reasoned that the dining room would feel too formal for an occasion that is definitely casual. She and Hal move carefully in the small kitchen, easing around each other like shy dance partners. The music she has chosen is low-key, her iPod queued up with Bon Iver, Regina Spektor, Mumford and Sons, Low Anthem, the Eels, St. Vincent, and the Owls.

She'd set out forks, unsure if Hal could manage chopsticks, but he pulls them from the bag and sets them next to each plate. Once they dig in she sees he has a better grasp on them than she does, able to pick up one of the slippery dumplings while she can only manage to slap one to and fro like an oiled puck. Hal grins at her quandary, clamps one, and aims it at her mouth. She tentatively bites, their eyes meeting.

RayAnne has never been so aware of the sound of her own chewing. His dimples crease.

They are close enough she can smell the drying wool of his snow-dampened shirt cuffs. She drops her gaze to his wrist, to the scar where his hand was reattached, the line so uniform and neat it looks like a thin rubber band snugging his wrist, the slightest pause interrupting the dark, seal-sleek hairs. Of course there would be similar sleek hair up his sleeve, likely across his chest . . .

She swallows the chewed dumpling with an audible gulp and they both laugh.

Hal winks. "Nice to see a woman actually eat."

"Ha." She steers the conversation to the show, telling Hal about encountering the Muslim shopkeeper and her idea regarding garments and culture. "Do you think the producers would go for—"

"Sure I do. I think it's a great idea." Without breaking her gaze, Hal crosses his chopsticks into an X and holds them up. "But would you mind if we call a moratorium on shop talk? Just for tonight?"

"Oh?"

"Yeah. I'm just the handyman, ma'am."

"Of course." But she has so many questions. It only occurs to her now, that while she's been avoiding the station, Cassi and Hal must have been hard at work behind the scenes, assuring that the show will go on. He's done a lot of work on her behalf, and he does run a rather large business to boot—tonight is probably a break for him.

Hal locates the studs by gently rapping his knuckles across the wall with his ear flat to the plaster. He hangs a plumb bob and makes marks along the length of the string. He taps the pencil against his chin, considering.

His ears are small and close to his head. When RayAnne imagines taking one of his earlobes between her teeth—who knows from where such urges spring—a falling-elevator sensation travels her spine.

Between the ensuing drilling, anchor bolting, and fitting, there isn't much opportunity for conversation. During the pauses between attaching and adjusting one shelf and leveling the next, they volley light questions about recent books read and films watched, eventually veering, for some reason, to cartoons.

"Favorite animated character?"

He doesn't pause. "Pepé Le Pew."

"Why?"

He tests the cordless drill. "Such optimism. Pepé never gives up, does he?" After drilling a hole, he holds his hand open for the bolt, and she snaps it into his palm like a surgical nurse. "Thanks. Plus he's got no idea of his own smell. Clueless. You gotta pity the guy." He turns to her. "Your favorite?"

"Mine?" She grins. "Rocky the Flying Squirrel."

"Why?"

"Well, he can fly."

They hold up the next shelf together and fit it into place, the heels of their good hands touching.

"Point. Least favorite?" Hal huffs at the stray curl that has unfurled to dangle near his eye.

She wants badly to reach up and tuck it into place but forces herself to concentrate on the question.

"Foghorn Leghorn, I guess."

"Because?"

"So bombastic."

"Good word."

"Isn't it?"

Hal offers, "I've never liked Wile E. Coyote."

"Not very wily, is he?"

"Never learns from his mistakes." The body of the drill suddenly jerks forward and takes Hal with it, pulling his elbow to the wall. He mutters under his breath, "Shit fuck *shit*." A section of plaster has caved under the pressure of the drill.

They watch chips and dust fall while listening to the cascade of plaster inside the wall. RayAnne recalls the first time she'd seen the room. "Oh, this is something I should have remembered." During the Sunday open house before sending in her offer, she'd seen a broken wall sconce dangling from the very spot, before the owner had the walls patched and primed. Now there's a jagged two-inch hole and a dent the size of a soup bowl, no lath behind to support it.

"Damn. Sorry."

RayAnne chews a cuticle. "This is what they call a setback, right?"

"Yup."

"Well, it's for the best; I was just thinking of the noise— all this pounding and screwing, with my neighbor just a wall away."

"Right." Hal bites back a smile. "Looks like I'll just have to come back with some drywall patch and screen. Would tomorrow work?"

"Sure." They stand back to at least admire the three shelves that are in place, eyeing the bubble in the level. RayAnne says, "Perfect." They are shoulder to shoulder.

Hal nods. "Only twelve more to go."

"Actually, one would hold all of my books."

"Right, I almost forgot." Hal goes to his coat and pulls out a package wrapped in the Sunday comics. Handing it over, he apologizes, "I didn't have any wrapping paper, so . . ."

"A book?" She tears the paper, ripping *Family Circus* in half. "Sooo, you've brought me a copy of . . . Wow." It's a vintage edition of *The Wayward Bus* in perfect condition.

"A favorite of mine."

"Is it? I love Steinbeck. How did you—"

"Cassi told me."

"Did she?" RayAnne lowers to the couch, pretending to read the flap while wondering what else Cassi might have told Hal. A hiss of windblown snow sprays the window and they both turn to look.

RayAnne gasps. "It is really piling up out there."

Hal frowns. "Ray, I better get on the road before I get stuck here." Catching his poor choice of words, he says, "I mean stranded. Not that that would be so bad."

Wind rattles the fan window above the front door. There's no attempt of a kiss, just a cheek-scrape and hug that is merely wool to wool and buckles to buttons.

She stands at the window, watching as he starts the Jeep and brushes several inches from the windshield. The only vehicles crawling along the road are a tow truck and a lone fishtailing cab. Once he's moving there's a bit of tire spinning, but he manages enough momentum to pull away, no time to slow and wave.

Five minutes after he's gone, just as she's running the dishwater, her cell phone rings. Probably him, maybe spun out or gotten stuck? Maybe on his way back, maybe decided stranded is the better option. By the time she finds her phone, it stops ringing. Checking the number, it's one she doesn't recognize but is the same Florida area code as Dot's. She plugs the number into a reverse search. Just as it comes up as "St. Agnes Medical Center," her landline begins ringing from the hallway.

She bolts toward the phone, something like a cold fist beginning to clench in her gut.

15

.

.

.

.

RayAnne rushes along the moving walkway of the nearly deserted concourse, poking at her cell phone. She has landed at O'Hare and is between flights and between gates, but the weather has tailed her from Minneapolis, now bearing down on Chicago, and cancellations are beginning to fill the flight monitors. She may not be able to stay ahead of the storm. Leaving one message after another, her voice is growing increasingly panicky.

"Dad, wherever you are, call."

Then, "Ky, call now. I'm at O'Hare, getting my connecting flight." She speed-dials another number and is ready to leave a message when Cassi picks up.

"Ray! I just got your message. How awful . . . is your grand-mother okay?"

"That's just it—I don't know. The nurses don't say much, and they're paging the doctor. I don't know what's wrong with her." RayAnne struggles to concentrate. "Listen, about Rory?"

"Of course I can watch him, no problem."

"But how about getting to my house?"

"Again, no problem, I've just pulled my skis out of the base-ment. I'll be there in like half an hour."

"Thanks. Rory's not used to being alone. Listen, I've only got five minutes until boarding. You got a pen?"

"Yup."

"Key's in the mailbox. Rory's food and treats are on the counter, so are poop bags, vet's number, and his chip information. I'll be at St. Agnes Hospital—I've left the number. Keep trying Kyle while I'm flying, would you? And my dad? Their numbers are on the inside of the kitchen cupboard above the sink. I've only just gotten a text from Ingrid; she thinks my mom is off the coast of Scotland on an island with some pagan cult. Look up *bloodtides.com* and see if you can find any reference to Findhorn or the Wicker Woman, the Isle of Iona. Maybe there's some emergency contact number."

"Sure thing," says Cassi. "But will your flight even take off? I just saw Chicago on the news."

"Fingers crossed. Thanks for doing all this. Listen, he might not answer you."

"Rory?"

"No. My dad—well, actually both. Just check under the daybed on the sun porch for Rory. I have to go."

She speed-dials her brother again. "Dammit, Kyle, answer your phone. Please!"

When the flight announcement drones over the PA, RayAnne strains but can only make out a gargle of numbers followed by "Now boarding." She runs, reaching the gate as the last passengers are lining up. Still digging in her shoulder bag for her ticket and ID, she steps in line. When the flight attendant holds out her hand, RayAnne still hasn't found it—it's painful to dig with her bandaged hand. "I just had it, sorry. Hang on."

The wearied flight attendant sighs. "Step aside, miss, and let passengers who have their tickets through."

She could swear she'd put it in the side pocket. "But it was just here." She's fighting tears. The woman behind touches her arm. "Your bag has got turned, dear." Indeed it has, and there's her ticket poking out of the pocket of the flip side. Hastily thanking the woman, RayAnne notes she's about Gran's age. Her eyes sting and fill.

The attendant grabs her ticket and reads it. "Fine. Ms. Dahl. You may board." She squints at RayAnne and then the ticket. "RayAnne . . . RayAnne Dahl?"

"Pardon?"

The attendant literally whips her frown upside down and says in a conspiratorial voice, "You're the *Fishing* RayAnne." As if RayAnne might not know.

"Yes."

"Well, we're not supposed to do the fan thing, but . . ."

Two other late arrivals have rushed up behind them, breathless. RayAnne pinches the bridge of her nose to keep from crying. "Listen, I don't mean to be rude, I just need to get on. My grandmother . . ."

The flight attendant gives her a closer look, sees the tears welling, pulls her aside, and says, "Hang on." She quickly takes the next tickets, practically pushing the late passengers down the Jetway before turning back to RayAnne, noticing her hand.

"Are you all right?"

"I'm not, actually. Something's happened to my grandmother. There was an ambulance, but I don't know." Nothing else comes out, just the sensation of heat where her voice was. She shivers in the draft leaking in around the Jetway.

"Oh, hon, that's *awful*." She taps her nametag, lettered "Heather." "C'mon, follow me. You need anything, you let Heather know." Heather frowns and winks at the same time. "Oh, look, some idiot's put you in coach. Let me fix your seat assignment."

Though she is the last passenger to board, she is the first to be given a blanket and a hot drink. A different attendant brings her a packet of tissues. "Lucky you caught this flight, Ms. Dahl; next one's already canceled." Before backing away, she whispers, "I just loved that episode with the nun that jumps for Jesus."

To RayAnne's great relief, the seat next to her is empty—she won't have to talk to anyone. While she's distractedly thankful for the bump up to business class, being recognized and given preferential treatment adds a waxy layer of unease to her distress.

She needs to get to Gran now and could kick herself for not demanding more information from the nurse at the ICU desk, who would only report that Dot was unconscious, that her condition was serious. As far as what that might mean, RayAnne's imagination is doing its worst. One does not land in the ICU for nothing. About all she could wring out of the nurse was "Your grandmother has had an incident." What's an incident? Had she misheard? Had she said "accident"? She thinks of the narrow lanes of Dune Cottage Village and how the golf carts just barrel through, oblivious. Dot could've been thrown from her three-wheeled bike or T-boned by a mobility scooter.

She supposes *incident* might be reserved for events like a stroke or heart attack. RayAnne is pressed back into the upholstery as the plane takes off. Usually, the first five minutes of a flight make her rigid with tension, since most crashes occur in that window of time, but in her state, she's only vaguely aware of takeoff until they are rising high above the city.

Only when she's calm enough to think—think back on how Gran has been sounding during their recent conversations—does she realize. Gran is sick, of course. Sick-sick. How is it she hadn't caught the clues during her last visit, or their phone calls since? It's all so obvious now. When she'd questioned Dot's tinny-sounding wheeze the week before, her grandmother laughed it off, blaming the cordless phone. Usually the one gabbing on for an hour, lately Gran had taken to being the first to say good-bye, sometimes just trailing off, sounding distracted or tired, making RayAnne vaguely wonder if this was the beginning of Dot seeming old. Of course she'd never let on to anything; at most Dot might admit she was maybe "a titch under the weather" or had eaten something that hadn't agreed with her. When asked about the constant throat clearing, she would only grunt, "Dairy."

As it all adds up, RayAnne sinks. She rifles back to the last few conversations and cringes, remembers complaining yet again about Big Rick and his performance at Location, how he'd made such an ass of himself: "And, Gran, I know you know he mooned Mom's mavens!"

Dot had chuckled. "Well, you can't pick your family, can you? It's the luck of the draw."

"Gran, even Mom was pretty shrill."

"Honey, your mother can't be all *namaste* all the time. I imagine even swamis lose it now and then."

"But Gran . . ."

"Sweetheart, what your parents do isn't your doing. Stop worrying and just embrace who they *are*."

"So you're Dr. Phil now? It's not that simple, Gran. It happened on Location, with a dozen people watching . . . I mean, that was my career."

There were rummaging sounds on Dot's end. "Exactly. It's your career, so take the reins. What is it your mother says, just man up and do it? Or is it *vagooge* up?"

"Va-what?"

"Your jinny, RayAnne. *Pussy*."

"Gran!"

"Well, you have to admit it's fitting. Listen, you know how I hate to give advice."

RayAnne laughed and Dot joined in, having actually heard herself. "But I have just recently figured out this one teeny thing."

"What's that, Gran?"

"That all we have is who we have . . ." Her voice had an airy, punctured-tire quality. "Warts and all."

"Who's the drama queen now?"

Gran didn't seem to be listening, mumbling, "Oh, here it is."

"Here is what, Gran?"

"My thermometer."

"Are you sick?" She sounded sick.

"Heavens no. My meat thermometer."

And their very last conversation, in which Dot had dropped hints that RayAnne might consider making her trip to Florida sooner, using the winter driving as an excuse.

But maybe that's all coincidence and she only has some elderly-sounding malady like bursitis or pleurisy. Whatever it is, RayAnne has been too busy and self-absorbed to notice Gran has not been herself, and now she's ill to the point of unconsciousness? The nurse hadn't said *asleep*; she'd said Dot was unconscious.

The plane shudders. She barely registered the turbulence and now looks out at the speeding sleet and chaos of the storm, as if ordered up to reflect the occasion, the plane blindly tearing through the clouds as RayAnne picks back through static memories. Lightning pulses in.

You only hear and see what you want. How many times had Gran accused her of that, of daydreaming, living a selective reality, in la-la land. Just bumping along with her head in the clouds.

As if on cue, the plane banks high and lifts from the storm clouds and turbulence, shrugging them off. Her ears pop as the plane levels out and aims toward a blue-black yonder, a clear night pricked with an infinity of stars. RayAnne rolls her forehead on the cool glass. All is cold and pristine, while below the weather churns. In the distance, a perfect crescent moon hangs like an ornament. Clinging to the sight like a buoy, she is stilled by the beauty and forgets for a merciful moment why she's on the plane. When she reaches out to touch the glass, each fingertip makes its own little hoop of frost. Her eyes close; she drifts.

She manages to sleep a little, but it is a fitful, open-mouthed sleep that dries her tongue until it feels like a chunk of bark. In her dream, she's pedaling Dot's three-wheeled bike along the beach, but it's barely moving. One of those dreams. She looks back to where Big Rick is sitting in the wicker cargo basket, and she yells at him to get out, which he does, grumbling that he's not dead weight. But the bike still won't go, and she absolutely has to get somewhere. Looking down, she sees the tires are sunk deep into the sand. Realizing she must beat the incoming tide, RayAnne abandons the bike to run from the sea. Though she cannot see it for the fog, she knows it will soon come like a tidal wall. Running backwards, she falls and cannot get up. Flat on her back, she rolls to her side just as Dot sits down next to her, wearing her best nightie and shaking a hospital wristband like it's a bangle.

"Here we are, RayBee."

"Gran. What are you doing out here?"

"I live here, goose!" Dot pats the sand that is now a bed, urging RayAnne to climb in and lie back. She taps RayAnne's forehead like she used to when either imparting something important or scolding her.

"You know to not be on top after you're thirty, don't you?"

"On top?"

"Unless it's dark, of course." She taps. Tap tap tap.

RayAnne has no idea what Dot means, cannot think with the tapping. "Dark when?"

"During *intercourse,* of course."

"What?"

The attendant is tapping her. Not her forehead, but her shoulder. "Ms. Dahl. Ms. Dahl? Sorry to wake you. We're about to land, and your seat back needs to be upright."

Blinking in the bright cabin light, she straightens. In a flash, reality resumes, she stiffens.

. . .

A humid breeze follows RayAnne from the cab into the hospital foyer and the information desk, where the woman looks her up and down, taking in her snow boots, parka, and Norwegian cardigan in which she's basting in her own sweat. She is directed to the east wing; the elevator takes her to the third floor and dumps her out at a kiosk where three nurses all lean into their computer screens, their backs to the console where patients' call buttons flash. RayAnne must clear her throat to be acknowledged.

To RayAnne's many questions, the Jamaican nurse shakes her head. "Yes, Dorthea Dahl is in dis ward. No, she cannot be seen just yet. Not till attending physician can be paged."

"But what's wrong with her?"

The nurse comes out from behind the station and steers Ray-Anne to a waiting area, saying only, "Doctor, he will explain the situ-a-shun."

Left alone, RayAnne peels off her parka. In the nearest bathroom, she takes off her heavy sweater and mops her armpits with cold water and pink foam from a dispenser. The brown paper towels she tries to dry herself with fall apart on contact. Feeling no fresher, she settles in the waiting room to fidget. She considers prowling the ICU corridors to find Dot on her own—stick her head into rooms until she finds her—but decides against it, in case the doctor comes looking for her.

After ten minutes, she checks back at the desk, where she is reminded that it has only been ten minutes since she was last there and is shooed away. Around the corner from the waiting room, she stands in front of a bank of vending machines, rubbing quarters together for another three minutes until she forgets she's supposed to be choosing something to drink, then stands awhile longer, eventually choosing nothing. The third time she visits the desk, the nurse's patience quickly expires and she gives RayAnne a look. "He is coming, girl. Trust me."

By the time the doctor finally shows, she has flipped mindlessly through the pages of two issues of *Good Housekeeping* and one *AARP*. RayAnne rises from the aqua vinyl couch when she sees the white coat coming her way. Even at ten paces she sees the doctor is wearing the sort of solicitous look that can only mean bad news. "Miss Dahl?" He clamps her damp hand between his two dry palms, a gesture that makes her swallow hard. "I'm Dr. Phillips."

She searches his face. "When can I see my grandmother?"

"In a while, Miss Dahl." The doctor motions for her to sit and seats himself just across. "Just as soon as we go over a few things." He speaks with a drawl, so maddeningly slow each word might be strained through molasses. "Is there anyone here with you? Any family?"

"I've been trying to reach them." RayAnne pulls the phone from her pocket and shakes her head at it. "My brother's been trying to get on a flight from Minneapolis. My dad, Big—*Richard*, Dot's son—is probably off on a bender somewhere." She fights the quiver of her chin. "And my mother's on some Druid island with no cell reception. So, yeah, it's only me."

He makes a hammock of his hands between his knees. "That's a shame. You shouldn't be alone for this news."

"News? She's not . . . ?"

"No. No, but your grandmother is not simply unconscious either. She's in a coma."

"A coma?"

"Yes. A coma caused by an insulin overdose."

"Insulin? But that's not . . ." RayAnne frowns. "Gran's not diabetic."

"No, she is not." Dr. Phillips is knitting together each word. In the duration of their conversation he might have crocheted a hot pad. She wants to hit him.

"You said *overdose?*"

"The probable reason she overdosed—the likely reason— would have been intentional, and not so surprising, considering her cancer is stage four."

"Wait." RayAnne feels a wave of relief. "You've got the wrong patient. My grandmother doesn't have cancer. You've confused her with anoth—"

He shakes his head. "Miss Dahl, I'm afraid your grand-mother, Dorthea Dahl, does indeed have cancer. I've been treating her for months."

She looks now and sees his nametag says "Oncology." "I don't . . . *what* cancer?"

"This is what I was afraid of. She didn't tell you. Your grand-mother was diagnosed with pancreatic cancer several months ago. Her prognosis was—is—not good. As I said, stage four."

"I don't understand." The air surrounding RayAnne begins to pixilate.

And just like on television, the doctor lays a comforting hand over her arm. As she looks at his slender fingers, he says, "Miss Dahl, it doesn't get any worse. I'd just begun the process of setting her up with hospice care. This sort of cancer—"

"You keep saying cancer, and overdose . . ."

"Yes. I'm sorry, Miss Dahl. This must be a terrible shock. The insulin overdose was very likely intentional, meant to cut her suffering short, to spare her loved ones the sort of rugged ending that is so typical with this disease—to spare you."

Spare? Nothing, but nothing, is making sense.

"If the ambulance had arrived ten minutes later, your grand-mother would have probably died as she'd intended, sitting in her deck chair."

"Died as she intended?" RayAnne's voice is someone else's, a flat drone. "But wait . . . how did she get here?"

"She is only here because her dog woke a neighbor, who went over to see if everything was all right. They called the ambulance." He stands and nods toward a glass door and window halfway down the hall, offering his arm. "Shall we go see her?"

RayAnne grasps his arm to pull herself up as much as to steady herself. "But. When is she going to wake up? She *is* going to wake up?"

He faces her, and as he answers the question, she stands in a glitch in time, his words slowly ricochet and shift in the light and angles of the shadowed corridor. Two minutes later, she lets go of his sleeve. Dr. Phillips spoke softly, words punctuated with varying pressure on her hand and the blinking of his kindly eyes. Though she had clearly heard the words *brain* and *function*, RayAnne erases them from her mind and deconstructs his sentences, editing and striking out words to meet her own urgent need—to know that her grandmother is alive.

He guides her down the corridor, supporting her elbow in the palm of his hand. "This is her room." Once inside, he lets her go but hovers just behind, as if she's on training wheels. She takes cautious steps to the side of the bed with the fewest machines and cords and hanging bags of liquid. Once her hands are on the bedrail, Dr. Phillips backs discreetly out, leaving her looking down at the slight mound on the bed that is Dot.

Forcing herself to look closely, RayAnne takes in her grandmother's powdery face, white, as if made up for Kabuki.

"Gran?"

When she neither moves nor responds, RayAnne looks to the monitors as if they might blip some response. "Gran?" The glowing green lines travel landscapes of hills and valleys, with ticks of neon that indicate her various functions. The line showing her heartbeat is shallow as a scallop of lace. The schuk-schuk of another machine fills Dot's lungs. Numbers that mean nothing to RayAnne flash slowly. The breathing tube is held in Dot's mouth with tape, a sight that on its own is enough to start RayAnne's shoulders quaking. Not trusting her legs, she pulls a chair tight to the bed and sits. Careful of the IV, she takes Dot's hand, which at least looks enough like her grandmother's hand, though it is bonier and more crepey than she remembers. "Oh, God." Wide-eyed, she stares over the bedrail at Gran's profile.

"Oh, Gran. What've you done?"

16

. . . .

RayAnne faced the camera, not with her usual smile but a solemn expression. "Filmmaker and photographer Lynette Hanson was already an antiwar activist when her son Josh, a NATO worker, was killed in Iraq. After his death, she spent five years making the film *One Hundred*, which premieres at Sundance this January."

Lynette had already been interviewed dozens of times on her tour to promote *One Hundred*, and it shows. Her focus was impressive, wearing a look RayAnne translated as a sort of armor worn when facing a camera. Settled in *Penelope*, they'd been fishing near the reedy shore where cattails swayed, most of their interview layered over with images of silent film footage.

"*One Hundred* is structured like a Ken Burns documentary, in that it's composed mostly of stills interspersed with video or film. Each segment stands alone—is that right?"

"Yes. Each one-minute biography documents one of a hundred lives—one hundred of the tens of *thousands* whose lives have been lost in the Middle East."

RayAnne added, "The film has no delineation between sides. Equal weight is given to all."

"That's right, because this has been everyone's war."

"And with no narration, the film possesses no single language."

Lynette's smile was Mona Lisa sad. "Loss is often beyond language. The decision to not apply words to these images was very deliberate; I wanted the imagery to say everything."

While they'd been talking, five lives had played out across the screen in as many minutes: an Iraqi teen, a Canadian nurse, an American soldier, a rebel soldier, and an elderly Muslim woman. A typical visual biography commenced with a baby picture, followed by snapshots of childhood or school photos, video snippets of life events such as cake candles blown, bikes ridden, kites flown, diplomas grasped, brides kissed. Each life distilled to the length of an American television commercial. The final shots were the last photo taken or last known photo of the deceased, sometimes a framed portrait held in the lap of a family member, sometimes set upon a grave, propped on a coffin lid, or, in the grisly instance of the teen, laid flat on his dead body. Few images besides the video segments are on screen more than a few seconds. With no music it was more silent than a silent film, a layer of hollow eeriness rendered across the images. The only sounds rang at the end of each life—the spare tone of a single chime delineating one from the next.

The camera panned from Lynette's determined and prematurely lined face to settle on RayAnne's, just as a tear she'd been holding back broke to make its way down her cheek, clearing a channel in her makeup.

After the shoot, RayAnne had stood with the crew in the catering tent, watching herself cry on camera. No one spoke. As soon as the segment was over, Amy began making a face, as if sniffing wet litter. She cleared her throat. "So political, and honestly . . . waaay too sad. Viewers aren't going to like it. We can't air this."

Cassi swung around to Amy, who had begun to get up. "But you admit it's powerful?" To see emotion on Cassi's face was a rare thing, and she was emoting daggers.

"Of course, Cassi." Amy said. "But we're not reporters. *Fishing* is supposed to be entertainment. As far as war and death? Well, some of our sponsors might even—"

"I've checked." Fully expecting Amy to balk, Cassi had prepared. "Only two have military contracts—OspreyVision is a supplier of night-vision goggles, and DryStash makes body bags."

Like Cassi, RayAnne had been determined on this one and spoke up. "I say we watch it again. And if you still don't agree, we'll ask the CEO of JailBait; he lost a son in Afghanistan."

Before Amy had had a chance to protest, Cassi had queued up the segment from the middle, RayAnne addressing Lynette.

"It's easy to understand why you were motivated to make this film, but I wonder how you found the wherewithal to do it? To do the research and collect photos and videos from grieving families. How did you bear it?" The silence between RayAnne's question and Lynette's answer was laced with the incongruous sounds of Location—lake water patting *Penelope*'s hull, birdsong, distant motorboats.

"RayAnne, as painful as the process was, it was easier than doing nothing." She looked directly into the camera. "As any mother or grandmother out there understands, doing *anything* is easier than facing the grief of losing a child."

. . .

Thinking of that episode now, sitting next to Dot's hospital bed, RayAnne cannot shake the memory of Lynette's film, and no sooner does she close her own eyes than vignettes of Dot's life leech into her consciousness: the hand-colored photo of Gran as a frowning child, bangs cut ear to ear and her head crowned by a huge ribbon; a teenaged Gran laughing on a bike. Some images RayAnne can recall for herself: Gran's face blurred behind a proffered spoonful of something, Gran refusing to meet RayAnne's eye after she'd managed to attach dozens of clothespins to the tail and ears of one of Gran's lap dogs. Gran slapping down a poker hand before raking in the coins. Her dropped jaw at the zoo when they saw a bull elephant's erection and dissolved in laughter.

She cannot, will not allow silent images of Dot to be followed by the single low chime. RayAnne drifts in and out of a fitful half sleep, sitting straight up in the chair, almost glad for the jolts, the interruptions of a hundred voiceless hospital noises.

. . .

Around the time the sun comes up, the same Jamaican nurse who had been so cranky during the night cheerfully bustles into Dot's room, her shift nearly over, humming as she opens the drapes. She seems surprised to find RayAnne still there, yawning and knuckling her eyes. The nurse's tag reads "Deborah." She steps deftly around RayAnne to check machines and fluids, all the while texting notes and levels into a sort of BlackBerry device.

She pockets the device and says, "You should go get some rest, girl. Eat some food, yes?" She pulls the sheet taut beneath Dot, rocking her little body on the mattress.

RayAnne winces, shaking her head. "I'm not hungry."

Deborah urges, "Go. She be the same when you get back."

RayAnne does need to pee, badly. "Leave?"

Deborah lays a clean gown on the bed and briskly rolls Dot to her side. RayAnne reaches out in a panic, as if Gran might roll right off the bed. Deborah unties the loose knot where the gown ties at the back of Dot's frail neck. "Miss, dis little lady isn't going anywhere."

RayAnne hesitates, wanting to lean in and help but at the same time knowing she cannot handle watching Gran be trussed and turned like a chicken. Cradled in Deborah's sturdy brown hands, Gran's arm looks like a sleeve of waxed paper. The nurse persists. "Off you go. You got a motel room? Someplace to take a nap, maybe a shower?"

She hadn't thought that far. "I suppose I'll go . . ." RayAnne frowns. "To her house."

"You go there, then."

RayAnne looks hard at Deborah, her good-bye catching roughly in her throat as she backs out of the room.

. . .

In the cab to Dune Cottage Village, RayAnne is almost relieved to discover her cell phone is completely out of battery. By now her family will all know to come and will be arriving when they can. She's saved from making calls she's too tired to make to say things she cannot trust herself to voice. This is something no one can fix—not her mother or Kyle and certainly not Big Rick. RayAnne is now cut off as much by distance as by the wall of confusing terms and heavy facts the doctor has stacked in front of her. How could she relay Dr. Phillips's news when she cannot believe it herself—that Gran is barely Gran at all?

Not quite in the present, RayAnne feels herself suspended just under it, coming up for air now and then, long enough to wonder at the automatic motions she's been making. Waving down a taxi; or drinking from a Styrofoam cup, only realizing it is coffee once she drinks it, unable to recall how it got into her hands; or looking out the cab window at palm trees; or reading the names of stores when passing the strip mall, names she's seen a hundred times that only now strike her as ridiculous. *Toys "R" Us, Steak Escape, Dollarmania, Dressbarn.* She wonders how she can be doing such normal things when Gran is floating somewhere that isn't quite life but not quite death.

She keeps hearing the word in Dr. Phillips's drawl, his three-syllable *ca-ahn-cer.* As for his conviction that Dot attempted suicide, he's wrong. She wouldn't. As the cab rolls on, RayAnne watches people walking on sidewalks and driving along as if it's just another day. When she pulls up to the gates of Dune Cottage Village, RayAnne does not wait for her change but dodges out and jogs as best she can in her snow boots to Dot's door, her sleep-deprived brain musing that this could all be a joke, and not a very funny one. What she needs right now is to open the door and find Gran standing in her kitchen.

RayAnne lets herself in with the key duct-taped under the seat of Gran's going-to-market trike. She stands in the foyer, shedding her parka and the boots that have been on her feet for incalculable hours. Taking several breaths before venturing in, she tentatively pokes her head into rooms that are far neater than normal, as if Dot had been expecting company. In the guest room there's a stack of fresh towels on the bed. In the hall RayAnne takes off her clothes, bundles them into a ball, and lobs them toward the laundry closet.

Sitting in the bathtub, she lets the water run until it's up to her chin. While soaking, she watches her weird reflections in the chrome handicap bars bolted to the tile. A half dozen warped circus versions of herself stare back in a sort of visual onomatopoeia, her face looking exactly how she feels. When she thinks of Gran, something inside warps as well.

Her big toe fits perfectly in the faucet, a cork to stop the drip. When she'd been about ten or eleven and staying with Dot one summer, they'd watched an old rerun of *The Dick Van Dyke Show,* one with a particularly silly bit in which Laura Petrie gets her big toe stuck in the spigot while locked in the bathroom. Rob came to her rescue, of course, but when he went to break down the door, he covered his eyes, which seemed to RayAnne to be more like something a brother or fireman would do. She wondered why a husband would be afraid of seeing his own wife's body, because Rob Petrie seemed afraid. During the commercial, RayAnne wriggled up from the floor to the sofa, looked Gran in the eye, and asked, "Gran, did Grandpa Ted ever see you naked?"

Dot sputtered some of whatever she'd been drinking and laughed. "Just twice." The answer confused RayAnne until much later, when she heard the punch line to the old Catholic joke—once for each child conceived, implying sex was only for making babies. Odd she can remember such detailed moments of a decades-old afternoon of watching television but can remember nothing of her cab ride from the hospital.

An hour later, toes and fingers completely pruned, RayAnne plods back down the hall, unsteady with exhaustion. Something is off in the rooms she passes, something she had only vaguely registered when she'd first come in—small flags of pastel paper or stickers stuck to objects: pictures, lamps, and furniture. Closer inspection reveals them to be Post-it notes. In Dot's bedroom her gaze settles on the bureau, where the velvet Mikimoto box is clammed open with her grandmother's pearls laid out in a neat spiral, the matching earrings clipped to a pale yellow Post-it.

Her eyes shutter closed. She cannot imagine Dot laying out her treasured jewelry for the last time. The idea makes her knees feel like glue. Her grandmother going room to room, ill, moving from possession to possession, alone with her awful secret, attaching little tags to the precious belongings she was leaving behind.

RayAnne goes down softly to the carpet like a puppet, in sections. After a few minutes she crawls over to Dot's bed and climbs in, burrowing, covering her head with Gran's pillow, smelling Gran's smell.

. . .

You can be too tired to sleep. It's afternoon when she finally gives up. She pulls on a pair of Dot's elastic-waist pants, which settle low like hip-huggers, long in the crotch. She abandons them in favor of a skirt that she can cinch with a safety pin, then blindly pulls on a T-shirt. Wrapping herself in a lightweight cardigan, she doesn't notice until stepping into the glare of the bathroom that the sweater is covered in Dot's hair.

Had she had chemo? RayAnne already has a dozen more questions for Dr. Phillips. Most of the hours tossing in bed were spent reconstructing what the last few months might have been like for Gran. She needs to know exactly how long her grandmother has been ill, if there has been much pain, what her symptoms and suffering have been; she wants to see her chart and more than anything wants to ask the question Dr. Phillips likely cannot answer: *Why?*

With ultimate care, she plucks individual hairs from the sweater. When she finishes the front, she takes it off and arranges it on the counter to pluck the back. Gathered up, Dot's silvery curls look like a mound of smoke. Staring at the little wastebasket, RayAnne knows tossing them is not an option and looks around for a place to put them. Inside the medicine chest is a half-empty aspirin bottle that she opens with her teeth. After the tablets cascade into the toilet, she stuffs the hair into the clear bottle.

The medicine chest has been cleared except for little wrapped hotel soaps and Pepto-Bismol. There's nothing in the wastebasket. It seems any pharmaceutical evidence of the previous months has been cleared. Dot's nightstand is empty as well, not even a ring of dust to suggest bottles and vials—all obliterated, as stealthily as a Pawnee sweeping away her own footprints.

RayAnne had forced Dot to sit through numerous screenings of *Little Big Man,* got her to admit Old Lodge Skins was pretty sexy for an old guy. It never failed to make Dot laugh when the old chief inquired about Jack Crabb's relations with his wife: "Did you mount her with pleasure?"

Absently slipping the aspirin bottle into the skirt pocket, she looks to the mirror, blinking. Noticing the writing on the T-shirt, she frowns: "It's my birthday. Spank me!" She remembers how Dot had laughed as she'd held it up to her chest, modeling for all to see while wagging her backside like Trinket wags her tail.

. . .

Out on the patio, RayAnne stands in the late afternoon sun while the salty breeze bats the hem of the skirt against her knees. The deck chair had been pushed to the middle, where Dot's slice of ocean view glints between the other cottages. *The* chair. Dr. Phillips had said that if the ambulance had been ten minutes later, Dot would have died as she'd intended, *sitting in her deck chair.*

Draped on the arm of the deck chair is Dot's afghan, damp with sea air. The little side table has nothing on it, cleared by someone, maybe the paramedics. There is no sign, no physical evidence of yesterday's scene (just yesterday?). Even as she's thinking it, a reflection catches her eye, something stuck between the decking, cylindrical, glossy, and difficult to make out in the shadow. Squatting, she wriggles a finger in to pry it out and yelps.

She's been stuck—it's a syringe.

"Oh. *Oh?*" The bleeding finger is jammed into her mouth. With her other hand RayAnne pries the syringe loose by the plunger end. When she'd asked Dr. Phillips how he was so sure Dot had meant to kill herself, he'd said the paramedics had collected four empty insulin syringes. Well, here is a fifth. This time she fights to control her knees and lowers slowly to sit where Gran had, facing the narrow vista of the sea, straining to hear the distant shush of surf.

To live on the ocean had been on Dot's bucket list for years. She could have moved here much sooner, but she wanted to stay near Minneapolis while Kyle and RayAnne were still young. But then, when they were teens, she lingered, kept changing her mind, modifying her plan until it included staying to see them graduate from high school. Then she argued with no one— *What's a few more years?*—and stayed on until both RayAnne and Ky had finished college, when Ky went out of state to graduate school and RayAnne starting working for Big Rick and hit the fishing circuit. Only then did Dot go live her dream of a little old cottage by the sea, even though it's not quite a cottage and not very old.

Dune Cottage Village was a developer's scheme to crowd in as many units as possible; outwardly they are meant to look like quaint fishermen's houses, complete with floats and nets hung as if to dry on the gray shingled exteriors, while inside the handicap-accessible rooms are as beige and boring as any senior housing.

RayAnne wonders what else was on Dot's bucket list. Gran never wrote anything down—would only rap her temple, saying, "If it's not important enough to stick in here, it's not worth keeping." Indeed, as far as RayAnne knows, none of Dot's recipes was even committed to paper. When Dorthea's supper club became popular, a publisher approached her about writing a cookbook, but Dot only scoffed, "You can't describe to someone how to debone a quail; you have to *show* them!"

RayAnne rises from the lounger and takes two steps when a horrid squeal announces her bare foot coming down on something soft and fuzzy. Rodent? Mouse? A shudder of revulsion travels her entire body. But it's only one of Trinket's chew toys, and as RayAnne instinctively kicks it away, she remembers, *Trinket!*

Where is the dog?

Dr. Phillips had mentioned that Trinket alerted a neighbor by barking unceasingly, which is only what Trinket always does.

Looking around, RayAnne supposes that whatever neighbor called the ambulance might have taken the dog in. Trinket could be in any of the dozen cottages clustered around Dot's, or maybe roaming loose. She walks down the boardwalk, calling in a loud whisper that comes out more like a hiss, "Trinket, *Trink*-et. Trinket, you little . . . *come!*" She supposes she could knock on a few doors, but there's no time to waste looking for a neurotic Pomeranian that is the exact color of sand. She has to get back to the hospital.

In the house she collects herself, calls a cab from the landline, and pries on the only pair of Dot's shoes that fit, the thick-soled orthopedic trainers she'd worn on the treadmill.

Hurrying through the little lanes of cottages, RayAnne feels light-headed and remembers she has not eaten anything since peanuts on the plane, a thousand hours ago . . . or at least twenty. That was then. Before what is now. A whole different life. Since seeing Dot, moments have stretched sideways and flowed parallel to real time, badly out of sync.

When she reaches the main gate, her cab isn't there yet. The dispatcher had said ten minutes and it's been almost fifteen. A step-van idling near the guardhouse emits a discreet half honk, and a wizened arm beckons from the driver's window. It's an El- derCab, replete with wheelchair lift. Shunting into gear, it creeps toward her. True to the company brand, the driver is an elderly cabbie, and considering the volume of his radio, his hearing aids are in need of batteries. When she shouts the name of the hos- pital, he nods at her mouth as if lip-reading, then declares, "You are not from here, yes, miss?" His license says "Enrico Zagate."

"No, Minnesota." Enrico better not want to talk. She's almost glad for the pounding salsa beat coming out of his speakers.

"Minnesota?" He points to the radio, shouting. "You hear about the storm they havin'? Radio says Middlewest get hit real hard." He chuckles.

She shouts back, "Did they say anything about the airports?"

"Oh, they been closed down."

"Chicago?"

"Closed. Blizzard like they not have since 1967."

When she whispers "Goddammit," he seems to hear perfectly.

"No reason for blaspheme, miss. Maybe God up there say it is *time* to deliver a whopper!"

"That's not really funny." Her tone seems to shut him up. Enrico has a crocheted cross of acrylic yarn hanging from the rearview mirror and a rosary wrapped around the visor. The dash is plastered with illustrated postcards of Jesus in various Jesus-y poses, such as emitting holy rays from his palms, surrounding himself with lambs, blessing the heads of rainbow children, and leaning waggishly on a crook, gazing from the hooded eyes of a gigolo shepherd.

The taxi seems to run on the blare of salsa. RayAnne watches the rosary sway with its tiny Christ pinned like a bug. Do people really believe God tests humankind by doling out things like snowstorms and cancer? People believe in a lot of things, a lot of awful things.

"Mr. Zagate?"

"Call me Enrico!" He turns the radio down. "Yes, miss?"

"You believe in heaven, right?"

"*Sí*. Of course."

"Why?"

"Why?" He looks in the rearview and eyes her as if she's just asked if the world is flat. "Because . . . when you die? It's either heaven with the angels, or the devil in hell."

"You believe that?"

"Oh, yes, miss. Heaven or hell."

"But Enrico." She sits back as they approach the hospital. "What if it's neither?"

17

．

．

．

．

There are messages for her at the ICU desk: Kyle confirming Enrico's claim, all flights are canceled, the airports closed. She calls Cassi from the phone in Dot's room.

"Any luck finding my mom?"

"Yup. A monastery on the Isle of Iona. The next ferry isn't until tomorrow, but then she'll still have to make her way across another island and another ferry, then a cab from someplace called Oban to the Glasgow airport."

"So how soon?"

"She'll land in Sarasota in thirty-six hours—if she makes the flight."

A day and a half. With her eyes closed, RayAnne wraps the phone cord tight around her fingers. She really is alone.

"Ray?"

"Here."

"She sent a message . . . breathe."

One of the platitudes that RayAnne usually finds so annoying. This time she tries to obey, only to find breathing isn't as easy as it sounds.

． ． ．

The second-shift nurse hands RayAnne a sheaf of papers. "Dr. Phillips wants you to go over these and says to call him with any questions. He'll be by to check your grandmother during late rounds. You can talk with him then."

In the room nothing has changed except Dot's gown and the IV bag. She is still a shell on the bed, the ventilator forcing her breaths: *shuck-shhhh . . . shuck-shhhh*. RayAnne watches the machine for ten minutes until nearly hypnotized. Shaking herself to, she sits and looks at the sheaf of papers. One is a Do Not Resuscitate order. Another is an organ donor form; a third donates Dot's body to science. Stapled to them is a brochure with a dreamy photo cover of a foggy country road, "The Five Stages of Grief." RayAnne quickly shuffles the papers one behind the next, as if to stanch the blur of print.

She looks to Dot, trying to remember if they had ever had a conversation regarding death. It was not spoken of when growing up—she was so young when Grandpa Ted died that she'd been fed the lines about angels and heaven and sleeping. Mostly, death happened to other people in other families, or in the distant past before she was born, like the drowning of Dot and Ted's little daughter Betsy, a tragedy that to RayAnne has always been taboo, the name an ancient wound barely mentioned for fear of tearing it open. Suddenly, RayAnne feels terrible for never having asked about Betsy, asking Dot to tell in her own words. RayAnne had wanted to offer some comfort, useless or not, but the moment had never come.

The tape holding Dot's breathing tube has been reapplied in a clumsy manner, making a fold in the flesh of her cheek. The skin under the tape is red with irritation and is the only color on her pale face. RayAnne peels away the tape as gently as she can, thinking of a moment months before, during their last visit, when she'd reached across to thumb away some excess powder from roughly the same spot on Gran's cheek. Gran had laughed,

"Promise you'll come wipe my face when I'm over at the Falls in my wheelchair?"

RayAnne, unable to think of Dot as anything but her energetic self, pinballing around her kitchen or careening along on her big trike, had joked back, "Yes, Gran, I'll wipe your face, but that's all."

Right now she'd give anything to see Gran at the Falls in a wheelchair.

A male nurse sidles in and injects something into Dot's IV line. He checks and charts her vital signs, all the while taking surreptitious glances at RayAnne, sitting stiffly in her chair, arms like scaffolding propping her upright. He catches her eye and ventures, "You can talk to her, you know."

"Pardon?" RayAnne frowns. "Talk to her?"

"She might be able to hear you."

She frowns. "With brain damage?"

"Who knows." The nurse shrugs. "If nothing else, you might be able to hear yourself."

Watching the respirator, RayAnne concentrates on Bernadette's advice. With the help of the prompt of the respirator she's soon miming the same level breaths that Dot's machine makes. Watching the nurse's back as he leaves, she scowls.

Idiot. Talking to Gran's inert body is the last thing she feels like doing. Talk about what, anyway? She's never been so angry with Dot as she is at this moment. Shaking, she stands and paces to the foot of the bed, and in spite of herself RayAnne does speak to Dot, whispering, "I cannot. Can. Not. Believe you've done this, Gran." Whispering and muttering, at first. Then in a raised voice, nearly shrill. From the hall, anyone looking in the window would see RayAnne facing the bed, speaking angrily and using halting gestures, her face red as a scrape.

Half an hour later, her tirade gives way to tears, and after tears she paces more. She will hyperventilate if she cannot calm herself. She settles back to mimic the respirator, now relying on it.

The best thing about the exhaustion is that it numbs. She cannot take her eyes off Dot, because what if she does wake up? What if the machine tracking her brain waves has been broken all this time, is wired badly, is faulty? She slides down in the chair, exhaustion netting over her. Though she fights it, sleep overtakes her within minutes.

. . .

Where did the night go? She is aware of someone leaving the room and of sunlight coming through the slats in the blinds to slash at her face. She blinks, startled, and stands too quickly, nearly collapsing on her leg, which has fallen asleep. While Ray-Anne stomps her foot to wake her muscles to action, a young aide with dreadlocks corralled into a hairnet appears at the foot of Dot's bed with a tray.

She frowns. "What?"

The youth is sullen. "Breakfast."

RayAnne turns. "Seriously?"

"Yup." He checks the computer-generated tab. "Dorthea Dahl?"

"She can't eat."

"Well, this slip says she can." He plunks down the tray and leaves.

Whoever had been in earlier had changed Dot's gown and combed her hair.

"Look, Gran." She lifts a lid on the tray to a mound of cold scrambled egg whites and cold wheat toast. There is a cup of drying grapefruit sections and a bowl of runny yogurt. "See what you've done? Landed yourself someplace with total crap food."

She stares at Dot's hand while her own picks up the fork and maneuvers it robotically from the eggs to her mouth. Between swallows, she shakes her head. "If you were awake, I'd make you eat this yourself." The coffee is lukewarm and bitter.

"This is worse than mine."

Gran would laugh at that. She would.

When Dot's index finger twitches, RayAnne sets down the coffee.

At the desk she learns Dr. Phillips had come and gone while she'd been sleeping. When she insists Deborah track him down to come back, the nurse plants her hands on her hips, but before she can object, RayAnne lies, "It's about the Do Not Resuscitate form."

When he comes, she excitedly tells him about the twitches she'd seen her grandmother make.

"Well, yes, you can expect some movements. But you know most are involuntary reactions." When he adds, "Miss Dahl, now is not the time for hope . . . ," she simply turns away, remaining silent until he leaves the room.

She closely surveys Gran—watches her hands, the little mounds of her blanketed feet. She scans her eyelids, but the orbs beneath do not move in their sockets. Nothing happens. She caresses Dot's arm, lightly running her nails across her inner wrist. She lays a palm over the papery forehead like some healer and demands, "Wake up, now, Gran."

.   .   .

There's a desktop PC with Internet in the ICU family waiting room, where she looks up some of Dr. Phillips's words and phrases: "brain stem death," "persistent vegetative state." She Googles "pancreatic cancer" and reads symptoms of the final stages.

When Deborah comes on shift, she finds RayAnne leaning gray-faced into the computer screen. Deborah is pushing a cart with antiseptic, gauze, and tape. Scanning the Web page Ray-Anne is glued to, she presses a hand on her shoulder. "You don't

FISHING! . . . .

275

need to know all this, I can tell you. There are better ways to go, and your grandma'am knew that for sure. That why she do what she done, girl. Now I'm gonna change the filthy dressing on dis hand of yours." She sits.

RayAnne holds out her hand and Deborah gives her wrist a kindly squeeze before bending to the task. What Deborah says may be true, but there are certain things she needs to know for herself.

"You sign those DNR papers yet, hon?"

"No."

"You read them, at least?"

"No."

Deborah swabs around the wound. "Looks healed up nice. You want me to snip those stitches?"

When RayAnne nods, Deborah glances at the waiting room door. "Don't tell anybody. Downstairs this costs you four hundred dollars."

Once the stitches are out and the much smaller beige bandage is secured, RayAnne stares at it. "Thank you."

"You gotta look them papers over. Dr. Phillips need those."

Once Deborah leaves, RayAnne does go over the papers. One document gives permission to donate Dot's body to medical research. The next, the Do Not Resuscitate order, has a red stickum arrow aimed at the signature blank.

She picks up the organ donor form, skipping to the middle of the page:

The Florida Uniform Anatomical Gift Act . . . authorizes any examinations necessary to ensure the medical acceptability and viability of gifts that may include heart, liver, kidney, pancreas, intestines, skin grafts, heart valves, bones, eyes, corneas, and soft tissue.

At "eyes" she feels the roiling in her stomach, and by "soft tissue" she's swallowing knots of bile. From what she's learned online and from Dot's charts, her organs are not viable, diseased as they are. And her eyes have always been weak. Her body, RayAnne concludes, would be best donated intact for cancer research. She reaches the bathroom just in time. It all comes in one violent rush. The breakfast, which had gone in so cold and tasteless, comes up hot and vile.

After rinsing her mouth and swamping her face with the coldest water she can bear, she forces herself back to Dot's room and takes the little hand resting on the bedcover, twining her fingers with her grandmother's the way she used to when something was frightening or difficult, like waiting in the dentist's office for her name to be called, navigating the revolving door at Dayton's department store, or panicking on the family sailboat when Big Rick would nearly keel the little vessel over. Looking back, there had not been all that many times in her life when Dot was not there to reach out to—if not her hand, at least her voice on the phone.

Gran is always there.

From the hanging IV bag, clear drops of fluid drip into the tubes to hydrate Dot, traveling through her body to flush her kidneys, eventually ending up in the urine bag at the bottom of the bed. RayAnne stares at the bag, feeling a tug of unease. It's only a bodily function, but the sight of it—the ginger ale color of it, diluted, as Dot now is—feels too intimate. She does not want to be reminded that Gran's body is merely a system, a structure of bones padded with flesh and fluid. Tubes and connectors baste her to machines; electric cords meet in a fat cable that plugs into an oversized outlet that accommodates the oversized plug that keeps it all going, keeps Gran alive. Until now, RayAnne has not noticed how the machines surround the bed like a flock of vultures.

It begins to rain outside: plops, heavy random drops.

There would be a note. How has she not thought of it before now! There has to be a note. Dot wouldn't have ditched her family without explanation . . . she would never have just left them.

· · ·

She takes the bus back to Dune Cottage Village. When she walks in the door of Dot's cottage, a Post-it disengages from the umbrella stand to float to the floor like a feather.

The pastel-hued Post-its are plastered to so many of Dot's things—blue, yellow, pink, and green. They flag her best belongings and bits of fine furniture: in the living room they are stuck to the antique pair of leaping ceramic trout, the Waterford carafe with the hairline fissure that reminds RayAnne of lake ice, and the Victorian rocker with upholstered arms; in the bedroom, on the little carved jewelry chest, the Empire highboy, and Dot's pearls. They're everywhere, yet they say nothing, no names or instructions.

In the laundry alcove, RayAnne strips off Dot's clothes and shoves them into the washer with her crumpled jeans. All she has besides her socks, bra, and panties is the awful five-pound Norwegian sweater. Setting the temperature to hot, she tosses it in too, knowing it will shrink to the size of a tea cozy. Naked, she walks down the hall to the guest room, where a chenille robe hangs on a hook. Here are more Post-its—stuck to an etching, an Art Nouveau figurine, and of course the Morandi painting above the dresser. The Post-it on the painting is yellow. RayAnne lifts the frame from its hook and turns it, expecting to find some note or message attached to the back of the canvas. There's nothing.

On the credenza in the little dining room are neat stacks of papers and files, all topped with blue Post-its. She paws this pile of insurance policies, bills, bank and 401(k) statements, Social Security forms, and mortgage documents. No note. Systematically moving on, she rifles desk drawers, the bureau, the bedside table, and anywhere else that looks like a place to hide a suicide note. That hiding a suicide note would be counterintuitive does not occur to RayAnne as she shakes down photo albums and the old scrapbooks kept for RayAnne and Kyle. She shuffles class pictures, crude handmade cards with phonetic spellings: *Be my Valintine, GranMa! A Vary Mary Crismass.* She tucks away a thank-you note written in crayon on lined practice paper and sets the scrapbooks aside to look at later.

There could be a safe-deposit box somewhere?

Rummaging in shelves under the television, she comes across a VHS tape of *Little Big Man* and absently puts it in the player. It resumes playing where Dot had last stopped, with Old Lodge Skins speaking skyward, challenging his maker: "Thank You for making me a Human Being! Thank You for helping me to become a warrior! Thank You for my victories, and for my defeats! Thank You for my vision, and the blindness in which I saw further! You make all things and direct them in their ways. I am gonna die now, unless death wants to fight. And I ask You for the last time to grant me my old power to make things happen."

And then Old Lodge Skins dies, sort of.

After a moment, rain dropping on his forehead, Old Lodge Skins opens one eye and props himself on an elbow, nodding toward Dustin Hoffman, adding, "Take care of my son here. See that he doesn't go crazy."

Old Lodge Skins gives death another go but fails to die. He gets up from the ground and walks slowly off into the rain.

She moves into the kitchen, where a single white Post-it is stuck to the refrigerator door, the only one with any writing, Dot's hand in blue Sharpie ink: *Eat Something.*

A reminder to herself?

Both refrigerator and freezer are stocked to the gills with foil packets and Tupperware containers. A list taped to the crisper has little round stickers the same color as the Post-its, and each sticker is followed by a name. The list is a key. RayAnne is yellow (naturally, being Dot's Ray of Sunshine, her Yellow Bee). Big Rick is blue, Bernadette pink, and Kyle green. Their name colors correspond with the stored food and the many Post-its around the house that obviously designate what items are intended for whom. Taking out a container with a yellow sticker, she leans against the counter, peels the lid, and stares. It's a snack she hasn't seen in decades, one she and Dot used to make together—celery sticks filled with chunky peanut butter and topped with raisins, a creation they called "turds on a log."

The peanut butter is difficult to swallow, but she chews dutifully. She looks again at the single Post-it instructing *Eat Something,* a diminutive square on the field of brushed stainless steel. In a slow dawning, RayAnne realizes this is it. The suicide note.

Eat Something.

The many things Gran prepared and tucked into her fridge are meant to be good-byes.

RayAnne backs up against the dishwasher and slides to the floor, cross-legged, cradling the open Tupperware, blinking up at the note. Her choked laugh catches on the chewed celery. She picks up another stalk. It has a vaguely astringent taste and the strings catch in her teeth. Salt from her tears mingles with the sweet taste of raisin.

. . .

When the phone rings, she peers at the caller ID. It's Ky. She doesn't answer because she has nothing to say. Instead, she goes to the den and makes up the pullout bed for him. The guest room is already set for her father when he shows—if he shows. RayAnne calls the motel down the beach and reserves a room for Bernadette.

Searching for an extra pillow, she opens the cedar chest at the foot of Dot's bed, but there is no bedding. She paws through a few tissue paper–encased layers of old clothing in clear zipper bags. Curious, she unpacks a few, each individually wrapped, with little packets of lavender and cloves to keep the moths at bay.

As she unfolds the clothing and lays garments across the bed, she understands they all somehow belong together. A one-piece seersucker jumper with a skort, a shirred bathing suit with disintegrating foam bra cups, an eyelet-hemmed linen shift. There are accessories too—strings of beads, a pair of pearly rimmed Ray-Bans, huarache sandals, a pair of white pumps, garish clip-on earrings of Bakelite pineapples, a lace-edged nightgown with matching bed jacket.

She has seen the black-and-white images of most of these things in photographs. In the living room, she pulls out the ivory wedding book from a shelf and totes it back to the bedroom. These are Dot's honeymoon clothes, her trousseau. RayAnne leans against the cedar chest with the album on her lap. On the first page is a tanned and smiling young Dot standing in profile on a Cuban beach, wearing her complicated swimsuit and rhinestone sunglasses. She has a lovely figure, which RayAnne does not recognize as being the mold for her own. In another snap, Dot kneels on a blanket with her hands busy in a wicker picnic hamper, her bare heels peeled from the huaraches. In one of the few colored shots, Dot is sitting on Ted's knee at a table set under a palm, wearing the seersucker jumper. An evening shot captures them both at an outdoor café in Havana, Dot in the yellow linen shift with matching bolero jacket, legs primly crossed at the ankles, drinking from a tall glass, cigarette in hand. RayAnne forgets how handsome Ted was. In the front of the album is the wedding portrait of them on the steps of the courthouse. Dot in a tailored suit with a corsage of lilies, looking at the camera as if she cannot believe her luck; Ted, clutching her hand but leaning away, as if to get a better angle, looking at his bride the way a cat looks at string.

RayAnne lays the album aside and digs deeper in the chest. The wedding outfit is there. She unrolls the jacket—dusky-blue nubby silk with amber-colored piping and a row of spherical tortoiseshell buttons. The belt buckle is also tortoise, as are the tiny buttons on the back of the amber silk sleeveless top. The skirt is slit down the back. RayAnne stands in front of the mirror and holds the jacket over her bathrobe. Dot had been exactly her size, once upon a time. She turns this way and that. The suit is the sort of versatile finery women wore in the postwar years—elegant enough to marry in, dressy enough for a party. There is a pair of elbow-length gloves of tawny doeskin. The ensemble is modest enough for church, demure enough for a christening, and, it occurs to RayAnne, somber enough for a funeral.

The thought is like a switch, flipping her back to the automatic mode that has enabled her to function without thinking. She meticulously soothes creases from the wedding suit, finds a padded hanger in the closet, and dresses it, counting the many buttons as she does. Finding the task rather restful, almost narcotic, she finds more hangers for the other outfits, pushing Dot's regular clothes far into the dark recesses of the closet. Once the honeymoon trousseau is spread across the closet rod, she matches the footwear casually underneath, poised as if they might just spring into step. Corresponding little purses are slung across the shoulders of the garments, and she wraps scarves around the stems of the hangers' wire necks. On the shelf just above, Ray-Anne places two of the summery hats to crown the diorama of Dot's best past. The closet is now populated with a wardrobe of best memories.

Back at the cedar chest, she digs to the bottom to find a gift box from a fancy, long-defunct department store. RayAnne opens the lid to a collection of letters, matchbooks, postcards, ticket stubs, announcements, birthday and anniversary cards, pressed flowers, notes, bits of glitter and ribbon. A few dozen tissue-thin blue envelopes are addressed to Dot in Ted's hand. The box is a repository of her grandparents' courtship and marriage. RayAnne quickly puts it back—the idea of pawing through this part of Gran's past is too much like some scene from a sappy novel.

"Okay," she says aloud, rising from her knees. "Okay," she

admonishes the lid of the cedar chest as she closes it. "Enough."
In the silence of Dot's house, RayAnne's voice is like a drip, just
words falling from her lip like an unreliable faucet.

RayAnne returns to the closet and lifts the hanger dressed in
the lacy nightgown and satin bed jacket.

. . .

Her forehead rests on her crossed arms on the edge of the hospital bed. She could be weeping or asleep. Lights in the room and
hall have been dimmed for the night. Sniffling, RayAnne turns
and burrows her head into the warm palm stroking her hair. Suddenly she opens her eyes. Dot is sitting up, her old self, smoothing the bangs away from RayAnne's damp forehead.

"Gran?" RayAnne blinks slowly, raising her head.

"Wasn't supposed to happen like this, sweetheart." Dot's looking around, frowning at the many machines. "There I was, all
ready to go—and now this business."

RayAnne follows her gaze. There are twice as many machines
as there were before, but instead of beeping, they now chirp quietly like songbirds. The digital screens no longer blink and glow
in a neon green but with a mellow, warm apricot light. And how
lovely Gran looks. Color in her cheeks, her hair glossy and pearly
white. Her blue eyes are bluer, clear and shining.

"But you can't just leave us, Gran."

"I have to go sometime, don't I? So I found a way. At least I
thought I had." She sighs. "That goddamn dog."

"Why . . . why didn't you give us any time to be with you, to
say real good-byes?"

"And put you all through some *Terms of Endearment* hoo-ha?
I certainly didn't mean to go trussed up like this." She rattles the
hospital bracelets, which, like the machines, have multiplied to
dozens on each wrist.

"Oh, Gran."

"Listen, pet, if I had told you, it would have been too hard, and you wouldn't have let me go, would you? Not the way I wanted to. Admit it."

"But killing yourself?"

"I preferred to think of it as beating my pancreas to the finish line. I couldn't tell you, because you'd have kept me here, so ill." Dot reaches out to knuckle away a tear from RayAnne's cheek.

"RayAnne."

"Yes?"

"Remember when we used to call you Rayliable? I swear, you are the only sensible person in this family."

"Sensible?"

"Well, sensible enough. And capable. We could always count on you to do the smart thing. Now I need you to do the right thing."

"What do you mean?"

"You know very well what I mean."

"But—"

"But nothing. I've had a life, RayAnne. I loved your granddad so much. We worked so hard and we had such fun. So many friends! And your father—oh, he was a holy terror, of course, but such a funny little boy. Shame you didn't know him before he got so full of himself. And my little Betsy, so much like you . . . I've never told you that, have I? Like twins, you two—when you were born it was like getting her back—so sweet." Dot shrugs. "And Ky? Who can help but love Ky?"

"But—"

"You'll be kind to Mr. D?"

"Mr. D? Gran, did he have anything to do with this?"

"Shush. I've had every good thing in life and then some. And now I'm done, RayAnne. Stick a fork in me—who said that? Some martyr on the spit . . . never mind. Don't let the others see me here—it's bad enough you've had to. And by the way, I'd rather not die in this awful room." She cups RayAnne's jaw with a warm palm and tilts, forcing RayAnne to look her in the eye.

"Say good-bye, now, RayAnne."

"No. No."

Gran's eyes challenge, like a stare-down. One of them will have to blink, and RayAnne understands that it will be her.

"Say good-bye, sweetie."

. . .

RayAnne wakes with a start. Dot's hand falls open on its side. Machines hum; the heart monitor bleeps. The breathing tube is still in place. Gran is the same pale shell she was an hour before. The dream had been so real. Tears pulse from somewhere at RayAnne's core, like some aching sponge being wrung.

At the nurses' station, the clock reads three a.m. when Ray-Anne slides the signed Do Not Resuscitate form across the counter to Deborah. "Can you page Dr. Phillips?"

Deborah looks slowly from the form to RayAnne. "You're not going to wait for your family?"

"This can't . . . she can't wait." RayAnne shakes her head.

"You sure, hon?"

RayAnne nods. "Can you help me with this?" She hands over the dry cleaning bag with Dot's lace-edged nightgown and bed jacket. "And there's one more thing."

There is a balcony terrace on the west end of the wing with a few tables with umbrellas meant for guests and ambulatory patients, though she's never seen anyone but orderlies there, smoking through their breaks. "The terrace. Can we wheel her out there?"

Deborah holds the nightgown and bed jacket as if they are jeweled and meets her eye. "Sure thing, girl."

. . .

Dot is in her honeymoon nightie and bed jacket. Her pearls are in place and her hair is neatly combed and tucked behind her ears. The bed is no longer flat but cranked to a reclining position.

Dr. Phillips unhooks the machines himself while Deborah sees to other details.

They gently motion RayAnne out of the room to remove the breathing tube. Dr. Phillips explains, "There might be . . . sounds."

When RayAnne returns she sees there are no more wires tethering Dot to the terrible machines, to *life*. Even the little finger clamp is gone. When she whispers, "Thank you," it sounds loud in this new quiet with the machines turned off.

It's just Dot, asleep.

At her nod, the orderly swings the bed from the wall and pushes it out the door; Dr. Phillips steers with the side rail. They make an odd procession along the dim corridor, pausing briefly at a recessed wall grotto, where Deborah snaps two canna lilies from a floral arrangement and hands one to RayAnne. The other she tucks into place under Dot's hand.

The bed is wheeled through the double doors and onto the terrace, where the orderly sets the brake and Dr. Phillips drags a patio chair close for RayAnne, then lowers the bed rail. Deborah makes the sign of the cross over her wide bosom and gives RayAnne a teary smile before backing away. The bed faces the direction of the sun, which will rise within the hour. Dr. Phillips discreetly closes the glass door, leaving them alone.

RayAnne sits and takes Gran's hand. Now it's only a matter of being here, waiting for the sun, waiting with Gran, who is alive but slowly growing less so. Dr. Phillips had warned about the possible rasping or gurgling, but even wending toward death, Gran—never one to demand attention, except in the kitchen—is quiet. RayAnne has been told the actual going will probably be a mere matter of a lack of oxygen, the heart slowing, and then eventually stopping. *A mere matter.* She presses Gran's hand to her cheek.

Night is just letting go its grip. It's not a dramatic or particularly pretty sunrise, more of a shimmy. No sunbursts over the horizon to light the scene; the sky simply grows lighter by degrees as Dot's pulse grows more faint.

She counts the satin-covered buttons on Dot's bed jacket several times, then ties and reties the little ribbons at the neck, unable to settle, because if she actually stops fidgeting long enough for Gran to die, then she will.

RayAnne edges onto the bed, stretching out next to her grandmother's side, instinctively needing to absorb the last of her warmth. With her face near Dot's neck, she closes her eyes, taking in the scent. Very gently she lays her palm over the quilted satin covering Dot's breastbone, feeling the shallowest of heartbeats. After a few minutes she is straining to feel anything, pressing her hand more firmly, but the rhythm of Dot's heart has faded from quiet to imperceptible. Like the end of a song.

For several minutes, RayAnne is stock-still, fingers twined in Dot's pearls, tears darkening the satin of the bed jacket.

How many times in thirty-four years had Gran dried her tears, hoisted her into her lap, rocked her, sung to her, scolded her, laughed with her, given in to her, colluded with her? Made a thousand other gestures, whispered a thousand comforts.

She can barely form the word and force it past her lips, but she must comply. Gran had asked only one thing of her: *Say good-bye now, RayAnne.*

"Good-bye, Gran." When she was small and it was time to leave, she would press against the car window or doorway to wait for the inevitable kiss to be blown from Gran's hand.

"Good-bye, Granny Gran."

.   .   .

There is nothing to do but ease away from the bed and set her feet to the solid terrace. Before turning away, she takes in the details of the scene as if studying a photograph, committing it to memory. The morning light is kind. Gran's features have settled lightly and smoothly across the bones of her jaw and forehead.

As trite as the saying is, RayAnne cannot help thinking it: her grandmother does look, for all the world, at peace.

Dr. Phillips rises at her approach and tucks a clipboard under his arm. He'll be recording the time of death. They do that in films, and this moment is no more real than a film. As they pass one another at the door, she can only return his nod and register the weight of his hand on her back.

She watches until he reaches the bed. He looks intently at Dot's face and touches her cheek with the back of his curled fingers. Straightening, he eases a pen from his breast pocket. RayAnne shuts the door before his thumb can click his pen and begin writing.

18

．

．

．

．

There are details to be seen to, but she does not stay.
Outside the hospital's front doors, the sky is now
bright. Still, it's too early for cabs, so RayAnne walks
to the main road and turns south, making her way across a few
thoroughfares in the sparse traffic. Closer to the ocean are blocks
of houses and apartment buildings. Closer yet are the beach-
front homes and estates, most of them fenced or surrounded
by stucco walls. Unable to find any public access to the beach,
she trespasses through an open gate, blind to the gardener who
pauses in his raking to watch her cut across the grass and walk
the length of a wall covered in bougainvillea then across the lawn
to the beach.

A haze welds the sky to ocean so there is no horizon, just a
vast expanse. Once she is within a few strides of the water, she
lets go, lets the sobs come in waves.

It takes two hours to walk the one-mile stretch of beach to Dune
Cottage Village. Later, when she's clear-headed enough to recon-
struct the morning, she will muse that Gran's dying hadn't been
horrible, as she had expected. The actual event had felt quite natural; the reality made much more sense than the concept. The

horribleness had come in the void, the emptiness that kept stopping her in her tracks, when she had to regroup her suddenly clumsy limbs and force them to move forward.

Ky is sitting on the cottage stoop, red-eyed, mindlessly sweeping the flagstone between his spread knees with a stalk of pampas grass. His carry-on bag leans against the door. When he sees RayAnne, he stands, his arms useless at his sides. "Sis?"

"She's gone, Ky." RayAnne digs for the key.

"I know. I've just come from the hospital. I'm sorry I wasn't there, Ray." His face crumples and he reaches blindly. "I'm really sorry."

She numbly submits to a hug. Once inside, she goes directly to Dot's bedroom and locks the door behind her. Opening the closet to the wedding trousseau, she drops to her knees, crawling in under the swaying hems to lie on the carpet amid the shoes. Sliding the door shut, she closes herself in, leaving just enough light to make out the patterns and shapes of the dresses above. She reaches up to touch the different fabrics: silk, seersucker, jersey. She gathers the sandals to hang on to, weaving her fingers into the straps. The dry leather of Dot's huaraches creaks in her grasp.

It's nearly evening before RayAnne emerges from Dot's room. She'd been hearing noises all day, surfacing now and then from her dreamless sleep in the closet to register distant sounds of Trinket barking, the radio droning, and Big Rick's voice, less booming than usual.

And the phone ringing, again and again.

Her father sits at the dining room table, his eyes red behind his Ben Franklin reading glasses, Trinket whimpering in his lap. A folder from the stack on the credenza is opened before him. As RayAnne nears, he closes it and she can clearly read the label, lettered with Dot's schoolgirl script *My Funeral!*—a little doodle of a daisy anchoring the exclamation point.

Ky's sprawled at the table, his hand arranging and realigning a spill of salt along the wood grain with his index finger. Seeing her, he raises his head from the crook of his arm.

She leans over the table and glares at her father. "Where the hell have you been?"

He's unshaven; tear tracks have dried down through his five o'clock shadow. "Jesus, Ray. We're here now, aren't we?"

"We?! Ky has an excuse, Dad, a blizzard. What's yours?"

She understands this is the moment they are all supposed to be hugging and crying but damned if she's giving the time of day. She wants answers.

Ky reaches for her. "Ray . . ."

She roughly shakes his hand off. "No. I want to hear this. What's your story, Dad? Just where were you that you couldn't be bothered to answer your fucking phone for two days? While I was at the hospital dealing . . . alone, while I watched Gran die?"

Big Rick blinks, his anger revving. "This isn't the time to climb down my throat—"

Ky sweeps the salt from the table with his arm, clearly shaken. "Cut it out. Both of you."

RayAnne controls her voice. "Just tell me *where* you were. What bar were you in, who was the bimbo this time?"

"I was in treatment."

"Treatment." Her jaw stalls open. She looks at Ky and back to Big Rick. "Treatment. How many times does that make, *five*?"

She doesn't wait for the answer but wheels into the kitchen through the swinging doors. Twenty seconds later she backs out with a quart of Jameson and three lowball glasses. She lines them up and pours. "Interesting that you should bring up alcohol, because I was just thinking I could use a drink myself."

When Ky stands, she whacks the back of his chair. "Sit down." He sighs and drops.

RayAnne pushes the nearly full glass to within one inch of Big Rick's hand.

"Cheers, everyone." She holds up her whiskey and looks to her father. "Skol? Bottoms up? Down the hatch? Hair of the dog?"

"It's not funny, Ray."

"Right, I forgot. To Dot!" She tips her glass skyward before taking a heavy swig. It sears going down and stings her eyes, but she takes another before setting the glass down hard. Looking from her brother to her father, she says, "What, nobody thirsty?"

Ky stands. "Listen. I know you've been through a lot." He gets up and aims himself at the patio door, taking up his glass. "But when you're done being such a twat, you can find me on the beach, okay, Ray? I'd really like to know what's happened the past few days."

After the door is shut, Big Rick slides the full glass of whiskey to the middle of the table, next to the bottle.

"I've been at Birchwood." He stands and scoops up Trinket, who for once is not yipping or snarling. "I know how much you loved your grandmother." He steps away toward the hall, heading for the guest room, his voice wobbling as he turns. "I loved her too."

RayAnne opens her mouth, but then frowns, narrowing a distracted eye toward the dog. "Wait. When did Trinket show up?"

"Some skinny old fella dropped her off."

· · ·

Mr. D answers his door wearing only golf shorts and dress socks. After leading her through his cottage and to the back deck, he turns on the patio lights and excuses himself. He's back a few minutes later, having added a Hawaiian shirt and slippers, carrying a tray with tea and cookies, insisting she sit in what is obviously his chair.

Of course he'd known all about it. He wasn't surprised there had been no note.

"Your grandmother tried to write one—tried for weeks. Then

she finally gave up and decided on cooking her good-byes." He'd been helping Dot the whole time, running to the market with her lists, collecting extra Tupperware, getting the little colored stickers.

"What else did you help her with?"

He sets his elbows on his knees and looks down as if addressing his feet. "This and that. I drove her to the drugstore across town to get the insulin with a phony prescription."

"But did you . . . did you *help* her?"

"Inject her? No." He meets her eye. "I offered, but she said no. My part was to call the ambulance. We had a nice meal at her place; she wanted to walk down the beach and back alone. We had a glass of wine on her deck and said our good-byes." Tears leak from Mr. D's wrinkly eyes. "I left her there, with Trinket on her lap."

"Then?"

"Then I came home. I think I turned on the television, tried to watch *Dateline* or something. Then I heard Trinket barking. I went as far as the gate and lured her with treats and took her in here. I didn't want her barking anymore, attracting attention. I waited a half hour before calling the ambulance." He faces Ray-Anne. "I didn't wait long enough. I'm so sorry." His face crumples. "I fouled the whole thing up, and you had to go through . . . *you* had to . . . and that was just what she was trying to spare you in the first place."

RayAnne cannot think of any response. She edges next to Mr. D, but he won't look at her. She gently shakes his knee. If he hadn't called the ambulance, Gran would've died on her patio, and she wouldn't have had the opportunity to be with her in the hospital, to have had the good-bye she did. "It's okay, Mr. D, it's okay."

When he walks her to the door, she asks a last question. "What did you have?"

"Pardon?"

"For dinner. What was Gran's last meal?"

"Oh. Um, shrimp scampi, endive salad. A very good bottle of . . ." He seems to be having difficulty remembering. "It was chardonnay. We had . . . grapes, yes, grapes, a baguette, a wedge of Tilson. A simple meal, really."

RayAnne nods and turns.

He adds, "Oh, and cake."

She turns back. "What kind?"

"We had chocolate cake."

On the way back to the cottage, she sees Big Rick coming down the boardwalk and sidesteps behind a palm. He's headed to the beach, pulling Trinket along on her leash. She's barely thought of Rory since arriving in Florida and is pressed by a wave of loneliness for him. How good it would feel to pull him into her lap, sink her face into his ruff.

In the morning she gets up early, determined to be out before her father gets up. After jamming her few things into a market bag, she changes the motel reservation for Bernadette from a single room to a double, then remembering the food Dot prepared, changes it to a kitchenette. When the clerk mentions the price, which normally she would balk at, she says, "Fine." Back in the murky world of life—somewhere on a different planet—there is a job awaiting her, with a contract, and she can now afford such expenses as a motel in which to mourn the death of a loved one. She upgrades her upgrade to a double oceanside kitchenette with a sitting area and balcony. Bag slung over her shoulder, she heads for the kitchen to pack up some of Gran's edible farewells when her gaze is pulled to the dining room table and the *My Funeral!* folder.

She runs her finger across the words, trying but failing to imagine what it might have been like to write them. Within the folder is a preplanned funeral packet from a mortuary called Chesney's, which sounds to RayAnne more like a bar and grill than a funeral home. Dot had taken care of everything in advance: listed the crematorium, chosen and circled an urn in Chesney's catalog, a nonfussy raku ginger jar with an engraved brass label. There's a mix CD of the songs Dot had chosen and a request that in lieu of flowers donations be made to the wetlands conservancy and a nonprofit group supporting sustainable fisheries. The church and the minister's phone numbers are listed along with the time for Saturday, booked at the Unitarian church down the road.

Dot had not only planned her own funeral; she'd chosen the date and time, had done everything save write her own obituary. A delivery slip for rental folding chairs and linens confuses RayAnne until she realizes they are to be delivered for the reception—one of those awful cake and coffee hours to mark the stretch of limbo between Dot's funeral and life without her.

RayAnne lets the folder, the script of Dot's final days, fall to the table.

Atop the pile of papers her father has been working through is a business card over which she does a double take, blinking along the embossed letters of *Hal Bergen*. On the backside is *Birchwood,* and another number, *private line,* all in Hal's handwriting. Without pausing, she snatches up the phone and paces while punching the numbers. When he picks up on the third ring, she does not bother saying hello.

"Hal, why does my father have your business card with Birchwood written on it? What's that about?"

"RayAnne." There's a silence on the other end as Hal collects himself. It's an hour earlier in Minnesota; he'd have been asleep. "First, please just let me say . . . Cassi called. I'm so sorry about your grandmother."

"Later, okay?"

He inhales. "Right. What do you want to know?"

"What is my father doing with this card?"

"I gave it to him. Listen, I know you must be—"

"When?"

"The morning after the wrap party. You were already gone; he was sobering up in my trailer, and the more he remembered from the day before, the more upset he got. I told him I have a friend at Birchwood who might help."

"Treatment was your idea?"

"No. Yes. Ray, maybe you should ask him about this?"

"So the night you came over to build shelves, you knew he was at Birchwood? You knew that?"

"Well, I assumed he'd checked in. I'd hoped he would but figured—"

"And you didn't tell me?"

"I figured it was for him to tell you."

She's silent.

"RayAnne, I wanted to tell you. Anyway, I didn't get the chance, did I?"

It's as if she's in a tunnel. Any emotion that is not grief feels invasive, to be deflected. Staring out the window, she wonders what else Hal might be withholding.

"Ray, are you there? Are you okay?"

The welling anger is almost a welcome respite. "You weren't kidding when you said you have my back, were you? How did I really get that contract, Hal? Was that you too?"

"Absolutely not. I was just looking out for you."

"What was your plan? Get Big Rick fixed? Then fix my career? Fix me?"

"No. I—"

"Well, I'm not your project!" After slamming the receiver to its cradle she blinks several times in the dusty morning light before quietly exhaling. "Shit."

She's halfway to the kitchen when the phone rings. Clearing her throat, she waits a few rings before picking up. "Sorry, but just let me tell you what I don't need—"

"RayAnne?" Bernadette sounds alarmed. "What's going on?"

At the sound of her mother's voice, she bursts into tears. "Mom!"

"I'm here, sweetie. I'm here, at the airport."

. . .

Bernadette, rumpled after traveling forty sleepless hours, is wrecked, but RayAnne falls onto her as though she's a beanbag. Through an hour of blubbering, RayAnne can only half register her mother's words of comfort. All that matters is that she is here.

After both are bawled to exhaustion, RayAnne helps her mother unpack, and Bernadette shoves the beds closer to make room for her yoga mat and settles into Shavasana pose.

RayAnne goes to wash her face, and before she can pat her chin dry, Bernadette's rhythmic Pranayama breathing has morphed into an adenoidal snore. RayAnne covers her mother with a shawl and watches her sleep awhile before finding a pad and pencil and retreating to the balcony, where she'll try to wring out a few thoughts on the obituary and eulogy.

After an hour of doodling and pencil tapping, the pad on her knee still hasn't got more than a few words on it. She hears her name called from below and leans over the railing to see Ky on the sand, shaking Dot's handbag. "Guess what's in here?"

"Shhh. Mom's asleep. What are you doing with Gran's purse?"

"Looking for extra house keys. C'mon. Guess."

"I don't know, Ky." Though she can guess: the same essentials that have always been in Dot's handbags tucked into their proper pockets. When Gran would say, "Get Gran's purse, Ray-Bee," she always knew she was in for some small gift—anything from a single wrapped peppermint to a found agate, a shiny fifty-cent piece or crisp five dollar bill. The handbags were always the clasping kind, never zippers (they only break) or buckles (who has that kind of time?). The contents invariably included a hankie, Life Savers that tasted like perfume, a coin purse, plastic rain hat, and Rolaids that smelled like perfume—odd since Gran never wore any.

"Note?" RayAnne bolts forward and leans over the rail. "Is it a note?"

Ky makes a face. "No. Sorry. Not even close." He snaps it open to show a large baggie, tightly packed with a mossy green herb. Even from the balcony the smell is unmistakable.

"Weed? You're kidding me."

"Medicinal, I s'pose."

"Oh." RayAnne frowns. "For what? Nausea, you think?"

"Maybe. Or not. It hardly matters now, does it?" He's got Gran's picnic hamper and a blanket folded over his arm as well. "C'mon, I've packed munchies and rented a dune buggy. It's out front."

"I have to write the eulogy."

"Bring it." Ky points to the yellow legal pad. "We'll do it together."

.   .   .

Empty Tupperware containers litter the beach blanket. Ky's index finger plows through the contents of one.

"What was that again?" RayAnne licks her lips.

"Chive and cheddar mashed potatoes." He transfers a glob from his finger to hers and she plugs her mouth with it.

"I can feel my underpants getting tighter."

"Some suicide note, huh?"

"Leave it to Gran." RayAnne peers into a container. "I think I know exactly what she meant by this mango chutney."

They both find this hilarious. An old man walking his dog looks over and smiles. "Something must be funny."

"Our grandmother." RayAnne swallows a giggle and blurts, "Just *died*." She and Ky both crack up with laughter.

After the old man walks on, she feels bad and would chase him down to explain, but she could not get up if she wanted to.

Ky looks to the almond toffee biscotti in his hand and says, "You think you're baked?"

Managing not to sob, she tells her brother everything that's happened over the past three long days, from the first phone call to walking away from Dot on the hospital terrace. She relays it all in disorder, all the while digging a large hole in the sand with a plastic spoon still sticky from a dessert called ambrosia. After finishing, she looks up to Ky's face, flat with grief.

She's thought of no one and nothing but Gran or herself all this time, just now realizing how frustrating it must have been for Ky, held captive by the blizzard. She takes his sandy hand. "Guess it's sucked for you too."

"Not the best of snow days."

"Remember before you could spell and you wrote that letter to the Abdominal Snowman, begging him to send a blizzard to Edina? Gran kept it. I saw it in one of her scrapbooks. And that rain dance you'd modified for snow, when we were powwowing for school to close?"

"Yeah, well, we finally got the mother of all blizzards, didn't we?"

When he'd gotten RayAnne's message, he recruited a neighbor to watch the twins in exchange for his seats at the first NHL playoff game. Once at the airport, he watched as flight after flight was canceled. Ingrid barely made it home on the last flight from Newark, but he wouldn't go home with her in case some flight going to anywhere might take off. When his phone battery quit, he'd begged strangers to use their phones, but having never memorized RayAnne's number, stood in the middle of the concourse holding a stranger's phone and uselessly repeating "Call RayAnne" at it until the person eased it from his hand and backed away.

He had found a pay phone and tried to track down Big Rick, who obviously had not gone back to Arizona. When Ky reached Rita, she had been boiling. "If he shows up here, you'll know about it, because the headlines will read 'Lying Bastard Slapped to Death.'"

He'd discovered their father was at Birchwood after actually listening to his older phone messages from Big Rick; one was a week old, asking him to come to some event called Family Day. He'd been checked in since the day after the debacle on Location. On the day of the blizzard, he was just gearing up to sign himself out and embark on the ninety meetings in ninety days routine.

"Apparently that Hal guy picked him up from rehab and drove him to the airport."

RayAnne dropped her sandy spoon. "He did what?"

"And Dad made him promise not to tell you, by the way. He's been calling the cottage; you're going to have to listen to the messages."

"Drove him . . . ?" Ray grows quiet, prying her sandy toes apart with the plastic spoon.

Down the beach they can see their father wading in the shallow surf, his pants rolled up, Trinket under his arm.

Ky takes the spoon from her. "Dad promised Gran he'd go to treatment. After she heard about the blowup on Location, she put her foot down and made him promise to quit drinking for good."

"And?"

"He says he has."

"For the moment," RayAnne grunts.

"Well, he's not drinking this minute, right? Can you maybe give him credit for that?"

"Sure, until he starts again."

Ky gets up and starts collecting empty containers. "Fair enough. Until he starts again. And in the meantime, you might remember he's just lost his mother?"

"Where you going?"

"Ingrid and the boys. Their flight lands in an hour."

. . .

Though the motel room has two queen beds, RayAnne curls like a seahorse next to Bernadette. When RayAnne cries, her mother cries, endlessly smoothing her temples, saying, "That's it, honey." Or "Cry it out."

RayAnne takes five baths in two days, various bits of Dot's Tupperware lining the edge of the tub, morsels of food dropping now and then to bloom in the water. Meringue cookies float. Lemon bars do not. When not soaking, she's within handcuff range of Bernadette, who lends RayAnne a caftan. They walk endless miles up and down the beach, billowing like jibs.

Ky brings more food from Dot's kitchen and they stuff the kitchenette's dorm-sized fridge. They heat things in the microwave or eat them cold while sitting on the balcony, staring at the waves. If *Eat Something* was Dot's deathbed directive, RayAnne is doing her best to oblige, even when not remotely hungry, as if chewing might wring forth Gran.

She stays clear of Big Rick, whom she assumes is busy taking care of details like the funeral or Dot's will. The donation of her body had already taken place—there will be no remains, no cremains in the urn Dot picked out for herself. It will be filled with steel-cut oats instead, Bernadette's idea. Other than going once to the cottage to get Dot's wedding suit and the honeymoon album, she hasn't seen her father. According to Ky, he's been dragging Trinket around like a stuffed toy, half the time using her as a handkerchief.

"Dot would like the idea," Bernadette says, snapping off a thread with her teeth, "of you wearing this." All the buttons have been shifted over half an inch to fit RayAnne. Her mother holds open the jacket. "Arms, sweetie."

Bernadette took care of the obituary, but they've gotten nowhere on writing the eulogy. The day before on the beach with Ky, she'd been too stoned to hold a pencil. Ky's been working it over on the little motel table while RayAnne sits dumbly next to him. They've spent the afternoon hashing over what words to honor Gran with, knowing full well that words won't cut it.

When not blinking at the laptop screen or mindlessly picking at the hem of her borrowed caftan, she focuses on the Morandi painting Ky had toted over, thinking it might cheer her. She pulls a thread from the hem, half listening to Ky mutter as though through a shell.

The painting does help. Looking at it, RayAnne muses that she now owns something she'll never part with, despite Dot's frequent directives to one day sell it: "Buy a nice house, or put your children through college if you ever uncross your legs long enough to have some. Maybe start a business, like a bakery or dress shop. Why are you laughing?"

RayAnne's gaze triangulates between the painting, the window, and the glowing screen on Ky's laptop. Each is neatly bordered by frames and edges, unlike the edgelessness of loss, which seeps and spills, blurring across everything.

Their mother has offered to read the eulogy at the service. RayAnne wonders what, if anything, their father might have to add.

Ky reports that Big Rick has found an AA group at a nearby Shriners temple, and he attends two meetings a day, driving back and forth in the rented golf cart.

Bernadette sits in her makeshift seamstress-yogini corner, where she's now taking down the dual hems of Dot's skirt and its silk lining to accommodate RayAnne's longer legs. Occasionally she will offer up a platitude in hopes of helping with the eulogy. Mostly they just blink away her suggestions until Ky loses patience and rubs his face, muttering, "Mom. No more Kahlil Gibran or Thai Buddhist monk stuff. Gran wasn't . . . woo-woo."

For the first time in days, RayAnne gives way to a smile; her grin is tight with disuse.

What can she write? Even the rosemary breadstick in her

hand dipped in roasted red pepper puree holds no inspiration; though she understands it to be delicious, she's not really tasting much. Mostly the food evokes memories, which she supposes is the point. Many times RayAnne helped Gran prepare the puree, standing at the grill and turning the glossy peppers over the coals until they blackened and collapsed on themselves. The dish has all of three ingredients—the soft, fleshy peppers, olive oil, and salt—that all make a scarlet vortex in the food processor.

That was Gran, she thinks. Like the puree—simple, uncomplicated. When Ky heads to the bathroom with an issue of *Wired,* she plops over into his chair and bends over the keyboard. She inhales mightily and, in what seems like one exhalation, types a flurry of lines, fingers flying. By the time the toilet flushes and Ky comes out of the bathroom smelling like the Glade PlugIn and hotel soap, she's tapped the last period of a decent paragraph.

She grabs her beach towel.

"Hey, where you going?"

"For a walk."

"Hang on." Bernadette parks her needle in the fabric of the skirt. "I'll just be a minute."

But RayAnne is gone, the door shutting behind her. She's nearly to the water by the time her mother catches up. They sit on the dune for several minutes, and both just stare at the ocean.

RayAnne makes a square frame of her fingers and blinks through it to the horizon. "What is the point anyway? I don't see it."

"Point of what?"

"Life. The point?"

"Oh. That's grief talking now." After a beat, Bernadette scoops up a palmful of sand, sifts it between her fingers, and says perhaps the only appropriate thing there is to say, paraphrasing Old Lodge Skins: "Your eyes still see. But your heart no longer receives it."

19

. . . .

While Kyle and Ingrid take the twins shopping for funeral clothes, RayAnne is led on another walk by Bernadette. After pulling the pedometer from folds in her caftan, she proudly reports that in the past three days they have logged thirty-two miles, which explains RayAnne's aching calves. Her mother is a big believer in the meditative quality of walking. When retreating with her mavens, she deviously leads them the long way around to every shrine and holy well on their itinerary. She allows them to get lost, meaning they must tromp an extra mile or more between their taxing routines of yoga sessions and emotive Blood-Tide rituals. After climbing sacred ruins and mincing over miles of ancient cobblestone or jungle paths, they collapse into the beds of their yurts or deluxe tree houses to sleep the sleep of zombies, snoring right through their own hot flashes and night sweats. RayAnne is aware Bernadette has been walking her ragged in the same manner and doesn't mind; exhaustion is helping her sleep.

When grief pulls the rug of momentum out from under her, she sinks to the nearest dune or patch of seagrass. She will turtle into her borrowed caftan, closing her eyes and burnishing one foot with the other like rubbing a genie's lamp. As she drifts, she clings to a very early memory: she was three years old at most, sitting in Gran's lap after swimming. The physicality of this memory is intense, tugging her back in time like some elastic nerve, Gran's chin powdery and soft on her bare shoulder, the whole of RayAnne small enough to tuck into Gran's curve as she clasped RayAnne's feet to warm them. This one recollection has been housed in her body for more than thirty years.

For a while there is nothing but that memory. In her sunlit cocoon of batik cotton, she is just a pair of small feet nestled in her grandmother's warm hands.

. . .

The day of the funeral dawns breezy and cool. From the balcony, RayAnne watches puffy clouds roll while eating Dot's butterscotch pudding, which contains actual Scotch. The service isn't until late afternoon, with the reception slated for happy hour. Leave it to Dot.

At two o'clock, she dresses in her new Walmart bra and panties, carefully slipping into Dot's sleeveless silk top. She raises her arms to see how stubbly her armpits are and shrugs; she has no razor of her own, and Bernadette hasn't shaved since the Reagan administration. Zipping and buttoning herself into Dot's garments, she absently notes there's room after all. In fact the waistband is actually loose, which under different circumstances might incite joy.

Not even for Dot will she endure pantyhose or heels, so she laces her bare feet into a pair of rubber-soled glittery gold Keds found on the sale shelf of the local Foot Locker. In the mirror, the overall effect is as if she's dressed for a Mr. Rogers memorial.

Bernadette steps behind and tugs smooth the shoulders of the jacket. "You look so like her."

"Do I?"

Her mother is outfitted in the gauzy sari worn during her rituals, pure as an unused tampon. White, in Bernadette's personal Wiccanry, signifies the ceasing of the menses and the stanch of the flow. Of course, it's also the color of mourning in many cultures. The wreath of tiny white orchids in her hair is a ringer for the one worn by the Mother Nature of old margarine commercials.

They walk to the cottage to meet Ky, Ingrid, Big Rick, and the twins. No one says much as they file out to join the small knot of people silently gathered at Dot's gate. Big Rick holds Trinket; the topknot of fur between her ears has been clumsily done up in a black satin bow. Small things are beginning to penetrate RayAnne's caul of mourning to allow the present to register: the image of her father fumbling a satin ribbon with his ham-hands gives her pause.

They all line up behind a lone jazz trumpeter. RayAnne immediately recognizes him as the elder cabbie, Enrico Zagate. All commence walking slowly as he plays "What a Wonderful World" in a mournful key, moving at about the same tempo as the song. They slow at the doors of various cottages, and Dot's neighbors come out to weave themselves into the procession. All seem well versed in the choreography of farewells. Enrico changes tunes as they continue on. By the time they reach the last lane, they are forty people swaying to the tune of "St. James Infirmary." A few go only as far as the gate, but most continue on to the motorcade of four limos and twelve golf carts swagged with black netting. Mr. D's cart is the first in line. Once Mr. Zagate puts down his trumpet, the only sounds are the doors of the limos opening and shutting and the putt-putt motors of golf carts idling. RayAnne wonders if all funerals at the village commence so appropriately.

RayAnne is surprised to see the parking lot of the church is nearly full. Dot had chosen the most unchurchlike church she could find, a blond brick Unitarian A-frame with cubist stained glass. The few adornments inside are a stainless steel chalice and a Danish-modern altar. Pews are packed shoulder to shoulder. At Dot's request there are no flowers, but an abundance of white candles flicker across every surface. Family members are led to the front by ushers that RayAnne cannot help but notice are all quite short, almost Doc and Sneezy short; all are older than sixty with the statures of ten-year-old boys. When one goes up on his tippy toes to pat Big Rick's shoulder, his bright red socks are revealed, and RayAnne realizes every usher is a retired jockey who worked as a waiter or bartender for Dot. Back in the days of Dorthea's, they had begun their tradition of wearing socks the color of their former silks. The spaces between dark pant cuffs and polished shoes reveal slivers of fuchsia, lime, electric blue, canary yellow.

The minister obviously did not know Dot, but then no minister would, considering her nondenominational status. Brunch was her church, and when asked where she attended, she would always reply, "Ascension of the Bloody Mary."

During the minister's mercifully brief portion of the service, he drones hollow praise and recites a few rote passages from the Bible, a book Dot didn't think much of—her review was that it was rather an outdated thriller and about as factual. His words are bereft of personal flair. Dull as rice, Gran would say.

When Bernadette takes the podium, orders her notecards, and adjusts her reading glasses to begin, her voice is melodic with meaning and clear, perfectly pacing Ky's eloquent eulogy.

RayAnne leaks tears but is able to not blubber because she's intent on not missing a word, wants to remember everything, no matter how hard. The sound system sends Bernadette's voice high into the rafters. Ky had settled on a "what is a grandmother" theme—after years as a sportswriter, he is rather good at sound bites; his portion is sweet and the perfect length, one page.

Bernadette follows with her own contribution, a sad poem about a field of barley bending by the sea. This has people blotting their eyes. She pauses and gives a moment for all to blow noses before she winds it up, reading the short tribute RayAnne has written.

"My daughter's words, Dot's granddaughter—her only granddaughter." Bernadette nods at her in the front pew. "RayAnne."

"Dot loved simple things: cotton eyelet, Italian light on a steep lane, a glass of good wine. She loved the ocean and finding a piece of beach glass and looking at handsome men. She loved a ripe peach, having her toenails painted, and meeting people. She loved her little dog, Trinket, and her three-wheeled bike.

"Dot loved a dirty joke and sad movies and Saturday mornings at the farmers' market. She loved to cook and she loved to feed people. More than anything, she loved the people she fed. There wasn't much Dorthea Dahl did not like, although she did not like good-byes, and she did not like to write things down. She didn't leave us a note." Bernadette scans faces, settling lastly on RayAnne's. "She didn't tell us she was going. In leaving us, Gran acted as she did in life, simply . . ." Her voice rasps across the next line. "Not wanting to cause a fuss or make any grand exit. She just left."

Bernadette requires a huge intake of breath to propel RayAnne's last words into space. "Good-bye, Gran."

With that, she walks to the altar and places a white rose in front of Dot's framed portrait, a hand-colored studio portrait taken in Italy, in which she's wearing an off-the-shoulder dress, looking absolutely beautiful. Next to the portrait is the urn. As Bernadette makes her way to the pew, the echoey silence peculiar to churches descends: rustlings punctuated by soft coughs, soles scuffing marble, sniffs and discreet honkings into handkerchiefs.

Without warning, the organist leans in hard with a note that sounds like the shift whistle at some old-time factory. It goes on long enough that people begin looking at each other, fearing the keys might be stuck, but then the organist sets off on a familiar if odd choice—a happy tune played on the instrument of dirges. When RayAnne recognizes the song, she snorts loudly.

Of course it's meant for her; who but Gran would make such

a request for a funeral? RayAnne clearly remembers the first time she heard Gran trilling "You Are My Sunshine." She'd been about thirteen, racked with puberty and bitterly complaining about some petty thing. Gran had pulled her up from her chair and spun RayAnne into a sort of goofy waltz while singing the song in a falsetto trill: *"You'll never know, dear, how much I love yooooou.* Now stop acting like a twit!"

From then on, whenever RayAnne was acting twittish, she was Gran's *sunshine.* Which she didn't mind, since it was also the name of Little Big Man's Cheyenne wife, his one true love. When the organ reaches the siren pitch at *You make me happyyyy,* a second bark of laughter escapes her and she looks quickly to Ingrid, who smiles and shrugs as if to say, "You guys!"

RayAnne could not meet Ky's eye even if she wanted to, because he is bent forward, elbows on knees, shaking with either silent laughter or tears, his hands forming blinders at each temple. Over his bowed back, she sees Big Rick is quietly sobbing.

The sight stills her. Having never seen her father cry, she watches a moment before leaning toward him, but she is separated by Ky, which is the way it has always been, either him shielding her or her shielding him, taking turns being the buffer against Big Rick. But right now their father is sobbing—a shoulder-jostling sob that threatens to work up to some great spew, like bad weather.

Something shifts sideways in RayAnne's chest, as if the bulk of her grief has budged over a nanometer to make room for another's. She slips off the pew into a crouch and duckwalks around Ky in her glittery, squealing Keds. She hips her brother aside a few inches and wedges in. By the time the song ends, she is holding Big Rick's hand, which makes him bawl even louder.

The minister returns to the altar, bestows a blessing over the urn, and carries it over to the family, unaware it holds only oatmeal. Right now Dot's body is probably being refrigerated at some medical school, soon to be under the knives of medical students, whom hopefully Dot will teach a thing or two. RayAnne lets go of Big Rick's hand so he might accept the urn. Trinket sniffs at it once, then growls.

The minister stands at the door, patting each mourner on their way out as if counting them. The entourage piles back into the limos and carts. The journey back is serrated by sniffles from the twins and whimpers from Trinket. Michael and Wilt are behaving for once without a bribe. Seeing their mother distraught makes them cry, and seeing them cry just makes Ingrid cry harder. She sits across from RayAnne, blotting the boys' tears and her own with one hankie, trying to avoid snot.

After mourners are dropped at the gates to Dune Cottage Village, they walk back toward Dot's cottage following the golf carts that ferry the oldest and frailest. The sun is already low, early evening tinged mauve. In contrast, Dot's deck and a wide portion of the boardwalk are covered with a jumbo striped awning that is lit by swaying strings of lights, like a small carnival.

A trio of aging men with mustaches serenades the incoming mourners. They wear red, white, and green sashes and dip with each note of their fiddles. The accordionist scowls while playing jovial Sicilian tunes. Their eyes dart around under bushy eyebrows, triggering a memory of Dot describing musicians who were old coots retired from the Mob. Indeed, they look like they might know where a few missing bodies are.

Under the awning, an impossibly long table has been set with white linen, gleaming cutlery, and bone china, each place with its own family of crystal water glass, white wine glass, orbed goblet for reds, and champagne flute, all reflecting the light of a hundred candles. Considering the stemware, RayAnne can assume there will be alcohol. Lots. Just as she's wondering where her father is, he emerges from the cottage with a cup of coffee.

The patio has been transformed into an Italian terrace, the sort of atmosphere Dot always aspired to in her restaurants but could never achieve, pointing out, "Well, we're not in Italy, are we?"

But in a pinch the Florida coast is a reasonable second to Naples. The weather is cooperating, clouds parting to reveal a rising moon, a warm evening with a mild breeze. There are menu cards at intervals along the table, even a placard listing entertainment, beginning with the trio, Tre Guidos, and concluding with sparklers and a bonfire on the beach slated for midnight.

The reception line is more serpentine than straight. RayAnne and Ky slink to the receiving end, where Bernadette is somehow able to stand next to Big Rick without hitting him—very gracious of her, RayAnne thinks. If the tables were turned, her father might be all-avenging.

Mr. D is in the line as the emissary of Dot's neighbors and her present life. From her past, Mr. Rondo, the reigning ambassador of Dot's restaurant days, hunches forward from his walker to greet mourners. He'd been Dot's maître d' for thirty years at four different restaurants. He is someone RayAnne would like to sit down with—if anyone has stories to tell about Dot, Mr. Rondo would.

She elbows Ky. "Did you know about all this?"

"A little. Dad showed me the orders for rentals and the booze. She planned a real *partay*-party. All those guys?" Ky nods at a few of the former jockey-waiters who had ushered at the funeral. In jockey fashion they'd beaten the motorcade back to the cottage and had traded their dark suit coats for snowy white waiters' jackets and bow ties. "They're all here at Gran's request."

RayAnne frowns. "She must've been planning for months. Do you suppose she told them she was about to kill herself? And, *Oh by the way, will you come wait tables at my funeral?*"

"Maybe. Maybe something like that." As Ky lowers his voice, his eyes fill. "Listen. I think it's pretty apparent that she wanted us to enjoy this, or at least appreciate her effort. I mean she did all this fucking planning, right? So let's do that."

"Have a good time when she's—"

"Yes." Ky cut her off, whispering, "She'll still be dead after the party. Let's just pretend she's here for now, because she is. Look at it all." He squeezes her hand. "Just do as close to happy as you can—it's only one night."

Through the sliding glass doors, RayAnne can see the steamy kitchen is bustling with a uniformed staff.

The first mourners in the reception line reach them, sympathy oozing from sad smiles and moist eyes. RayAnne and Ky endure an onslaught of comments they would normally argue with, such as Dot being in a better place or in the Lord's hands now, having gone to meet her maker, smiling down on them.

Actually, she's dead.

RayAnne holds her tongue and returns polite hugs and pats. The receiving line ends near the bar. She could use a glass of something. Ky's cheeks are stippled by faint lip marks in old-lady shades of pink, coral, and poppy.

Since the church service, RayAnne's curiosity has been piqued by the presence of a pair of cadets in full dress uniform. How might they factor in Gran's life? They introduce themselves. Gerard and Benjamin. Both *adored* Dot. And both watch *Fishing* every Sunday and love it. Love. It. Gerard touches the fabric of RayAnne's sleeve and correctly guesses the vintage of the suit. Benjamin tears up upon learning Dot was married in it. They had a running date each Sunday afternoon with Dot for GTG— Gin and Tonic and Gossip.

Gerard has a trumpet case tucked under an arm.

"Are you going to play something?" RayAnne asks. "Did Dot, um, book you?"

Benjamin steps up. "I talked him into bringing it, wondering if maybe you'd like him to play 'Taps' for Dorthea." He leans in and whispers, "I know it's not on the program, but Gerard is amazing."

RayAnne smiles. "I'm sure Dot would like that."

Ky motions for the other musicians to lower their instruments and Gerard raises his trumpet, polished to a glare.

By the third note everyone has gone still. The clear brass strains rise into the sky. A few of the older fellows—veterans— hold a salute for the duration. Gerard's eyes remain closed while he plays, bending notes liquidly, not adhering to the military standard, but adding a soulful flair of jazz. The purity of it. Mr. Zagate is shaking his head.

At the finish, every eye needs dabbing.

The first drinks are knocked back like anesthesia. From a distance, RayAnne watches Bernadette gulp a chardonnay in two goes. The waiters scurry to refill glasses with bottles that look vintage and expensive. Dot always said serve the best wine first, when guests are still in possession of their taste buds; save the lesser stuff for the drunken half of the evening. Peering in the crates behind the bar, RayAnne sees there is no cheap stuff— tonight it's all top-shelf.

Her father, she notes with some relief, seems nearly oblivious to the imbibing. It's as if he cannot drink enough coffee. Milling mourners are steered to seats at the long table, their faces softened with spirits and candlelight. She finds the placard with her own name and plops down between Mr. D and Dr. Phillips. Both reach for covered baskets of crusty warm French bread, conducting with their butter knives.

A perfectly chilled Chablis is poured, and an appetizer of seared scallops in a ginger-lemongrass reduction is served. Mr. Rondo kick-starts the evening with a toast and a few instructions. After each course, guests are to change seats and sit with someone different. This is pure Dot—the tradition at her dinner parties. After scallops, RayAnne shifts down the table to sit with two women who are volunteers from the homeless shelter where

Dot cooked. They spear at their arugula, pear, and glazed-walnut salads, declaring them "Almost too pretty to eat!" They entertain RayAnne with Dot-isms. The Guidos play lively tunes accompanied by the clinking of cutlery and stemware. Deborah has come, resplendent in a Jamaican print with matching turban. She attracts a smattering of applause when she dances the length of the table on her way to use the bathroom, slowing just long enough to twirl both of the twins. There are a surprising number of younger people present, from the women in Dot's book club (all under fifty) to her farmers' market friends—an organic citrus grower, the manager of the nonprofit Ethical Tomato, a young orchardist just getting established, and the flower farmer who had decorated the table so simply and elegantly, all ivory petals and pale greenery, nothing remotely funereal.

Dot's water aerobics classmates are easy to pick out; they've all worn swim goggles around their wrists like bracelets. They make a production of presenting RayAnne with Dot's goggles, which they have decorated with tiny shells and rhinestones. She is able to not cry only because looping the goggles around her own wrist makes her inexplicably happy.

During the course of Italian wedding soup, a pair of sisters barely in their twenties tell RayAnne how Dot mentored them with her many suggestions and encouragement when they had launched their Cuban food truck.

The musical chairs take on a slower pace, a humorous shuffle of people reluctant to leave their seatmates and newfound friends. RayAnne finds herself joking with the same elderly bakers who had made the cake for Dot's birthday party only months before. Afterward, she shifts between two new tablemates. They are awed by all the fuss, relative newcomers to Dune Cottage Village who had only met Dot a few times and had been invited here by Dot herself.

"Are all the funerals here like this?"

RayAnne laughs.

Those who knew Dot well are not at all surprised at what she has accomplished here. And whether they know Dot intimately or merely in passing, all have lovely things to say to RayAnne about her grandmother.

A very tiny woman named Alice with a white beehive muses over how Dot was always able to convince whomever she was speaking to that they were the most important person in the room. "Oh, yes, wasn't that just Dot! Your grandmother was like that—just like Bill Clinton, of course not so much with the she-nanigans." Alice rises on her toes and winks. "At least as far as we know." When she throws her head back to laugh, Alice tips off balance stiffly, like a bowling pin trying to decide. She slips from RayAnne's reach like something greased, but fortunately Ky happens to be passing and handily catches her, which everyone finds hilarious.

The jockeys parry and retreat with their wine bottles and serv-ing trays, spiriting away dirty china and dealing in clean replace-ments. The main course is an autumn vegetable ratatouille with tenderloin medallions and sage gnocchi. A neighbor stands up to toast and tells how Dot brought her suppers every night for a week after her hip surgery but insisted on serving them outside, each time setting the table a few feet farther down the boardwalk, giving her no choice but to walk for her suppers. She laughs. "Dot's version of physical therapy—dangling a ginger-glazed carrot."

By the time the cheese and fruit course is wheeled out, most everyone has made some toast or tribute; even the waiters have, at some juncture in the meal, stopped in midserve or midpour to offer their own few words, making many versions of the same joke: *I'll keep this short.* Most tributes begin with a smile and end on a sniffle.

They are celebrating a life and everyone is feeling very good. Most ignore the proffered coffee and hold out their glasses for the carafes of liqueurs and brandies.

Ky has given up trying to keep the twins from under the table, though no one seems to mind. It will be discovered too late that they've been taking cell phones from purses and jackets hung on chairs, then snapping pictures with them under the table— blurred shots of men's shiny ankles and women's stocking toes with shoes or sandals pried off their bunioned feet, dim snapshots of hiked skirts and legs not quite prim, thighs puffing out of girdles as if from sausage casings. One catches a man's hand caught on a thigh not his own, the blur of a slap.

After investigating the flashes going off under the tablecloth, Ky pulls the boys out by their ankles, and they return the phones to pockets and purses, though not necessarily the right ones.

Big Rick stands, clears his throat, and pulls a folded scrap from the breast pocket of his suit jacket. "This is Dot's toast. Many of you have been wondering if she'd written something. She did." He scans the table while putting on his reading glasses. "It's short." He looks and sounds sober as a judge.

"Beautiful people. Thank you for indulging me. I know some of you are shocked by the way I've chosen to go. For those of you who are angry, please forgive, so that you can stop being sad and disappointed. Be kind to my family." Big Rick raises his champagne flute of Diet Coke, reading on. "I have loved you all. Please enjoy your meal, and don't forget to take doggie bags of leftovers the boys will pack for you."

This gets a few mild chuckles.

Big Rick makes a sweeping gesture as he reads the final line, "Eat, drink, and be merry."

RayAnne waits for the end, but Big Rick is shoving the paper in his breast pocket.

No *for tomorrow we shall die.* There is a silence, then glasses begin clinking. Crystal and smiles reflect candlelight.

RayAnne readies to get everyone's attention to thank them for coming and to remind them that the fireworks on the beach will commence shortly. Surrounding her are wise and lovely old people who will follow Gran to their own endings, and plenty of younger people who will only take more time to catch up to the end. It's going to be rough with no Gran in her future; surely RayAnne is in for more heavy grief. Someday the memories will uplift rather than squeeze—the day may come when the taste of celery and raisins will not make her cry.

For now, she adores every person in her sight, loves them all for loving Dot. The meaning of what Gran had said with such conviction—despite being weak and ill—comes clear. *All we have is who we have.* She's about to tap her glass with her knife so she might quote and toast Gran herself, but just as she's taking a breath, something damp snuffles into the space between her shins. She yelps and, expecting one of the twins, yanks up the tablecloth, but it is a dog's snout poking from underneath, a dog too large to be Trinket. Her instinct is to knee it away, just as the dog's head tilts into the light. She does a double take, crying, "Rory?"

It can't be. How? But it is, and he's out from under the table, his tail thwacking at speed. She squeals, "Hey! This is my dog!" RayAnne holds his paws up as if dancing with a short man and twirls. "It's Rory!"

She spins to the empty space behind, looking around, scanning faces for Cassi, one of the few people on the planet clever enough to beam a dog from Minnesota to Florida. Ky sidles up and points down the length of the table.

"Ray, I think you have company."

20

.

.

.

.

Most waiters have stopped serving and are plunked down. Some are slamming shots, others are engaged in a napkin-folding contest; having cleared a middle section of the table, they work their mastery, creating intricately folded bishop hats, rockets, and a horse's head to appreciative murmurs. To a cheer and a round of applause, one flourishes a surprisingly anatomically accurate penis, erect. Dot would have loved it.

Guests RayAnne thought would surely have nodded off or wheeled themselves home by now seem to have gotten a second wind. The latecomer is being badgered with greetings, everyone wanting to know who . . . another of Dot's posthumous surprises?

Rory clings to RayAnne like a toddler, having jumped into her arms, sniffing as if to confirm it's really her, his barky little complaints translating to "Where have you been?" His tail sweeps a champagne flute clear off the table to shatter against one of the awning poles. Fifty heads turn.

RayAnne shrugs. "It's not a real party until a glass gets broken. That's what Dot always said." People laugh as she shifts Rory's warm weight in her arms. Something that isn't anything seems to have descended over the celebration, over her. Not Rory's impossible arrival nor the presence of everyone gathered, but everyone and everything at once—the surroundings, the sea air and torchlight. All pulls into full Technicolor surround-sound focus. Talk and laughter and the sounds of surf swell. The present—for lack of a better word—and all it entails has suddenly become more. There's no expressing the feeling, but maybe it's what poets are always trying to get at.

In the commotion, she has slipped into stillness herself. The nightmarish clutter of the last week, the knots of emotion, wringing as they are, fit somehow, at least in the scheme of things, and she understands it is her duty, painful or not, to know this.

He's standing at the end of the table, looking down the bowling-alley length of linen, now stained with wine, dribbled with candle wax, littered with cherry stems, cheese rinds, crumbs, and cigar ash. She's not at all surprised to see him. Making his way along the table, Hal politely stops to answer questions and explain his presence, canting his head repeatedly toward RayAnne.

Even at this distance, she sees the days of stubble carving a shadow across his jaw. He moves a bit stiffly, rolling his shoulders as if they ache. He's driven, of course. From Minnesota to Florida to bring Rory to her.

When he's closer, she can see he's wrecked. Her first words are laced with concern. "Oh. You look so tired."

"And you look lovely."

She begins to balk but then lets the compliment wash over her.

He stops and grins, the dimples in play, unsure. "Timing, huh?"

RayAnne shakes her head and gently sets Rory down. She straightens to face Hal, and unblinking, she steps forward. "Your timing isn't so bad."

A
C
K
N
O
W
L
E
D
G
M
E
N
T
S

Thanks to the amazing crew at the University of Minnesota Press: Erik Anderson, Doug Armato, Louisa Castner, Emily Hamilton, Rachel Moeller, Dan Ochsner, Heather Skinner, Laura Westlund, and the rest of the publishing jedi at the Press. Kudos to Dawn Frederick and Stacey Graham of Red Sofa Literary. Fabulous niece Mickey Smith spawned the idea of a talk show in a boat and inspired a character who possesses none of the fashion savvy she does.

Thanks to the people of Minnesota who voted for the Legacy Amendment, which protects and funds the two essential resources that make our state sparkle: clean water and the arts.

Utmost gratitude to Jon, the most patient and handsome man on Earth. And to Betsy, for sectioning my hours into manageable units, dog rest your soul.

And finally: thanks, Dad, for teaching me how to fish.

Novelist and screenwriter **Sarah Stonich** is a Minnesota native. She is the author of *These Granite Islands*, *Vacationland*, and *Laurentian Divide* (winner of a Minnesota Book Award and a Northeastern Minnesota Book Award), as well as a memoir, *Shelter: Off the Grid in the Mostly Magnetic North*, all published by the University of Minnesota Press. She lives on the Mississippi River in a repurposed flour mill with her husband, Jon.